RETURN

TO YOUR

SKIN

ALSO BY LUZ GABÁS

Palm Trees in the Snow

RETURN TO YOUR SKIN

LUZ GABÁS

TRANSLATED BY NOEL HUGHES

amazon crossing

This is a work of fiction. Names, characters, organizations, places, events, and incidents are either products of the author's imagination or are used fictitiously. Any resemblance to actual persons, living or dead, or actual events is purely coincidental.

Text copyright © 2014 Luz Gabás
Translation copyright © 2017 Noel Hughes
All rights reserved.

No part of this book may be reproduced, or stored in a retrieval system, or transmitted in any form or by any means, electronic, mechanical, photocopying, recording, or otherwise, without express written permission of the publisher.

Previously published as *Regreso a tu piel* by Planeta in Spain in 2014. Translated from Spanish by Noel Hughes. First published in English by AmazonCrossing in 2017.

Published by AmazonCrossing, Seattle

www.apub.com

Amazon, the Amazon logo, and AmazonCrossing are trademarks of Amazon.com, Inc., or its affiliates.

ISBN-13: 9781477823187
ISBN-10: 1477823182

Cover design by Shasti O'Leary Soudant

Printed in the United States of America

RETURN

TO YOUR

SKIN

*To José Español Fauquié,
with whom I have spent years sharing centuries.
A breath.
A brief moment in time.*

Once again.

The water and the gusting wind furiously lash her body.

Or is it mine?

A woman runs. Her boots sink into the mud. She has long dark hair. Clumps stick to her face and shoulders.

They weigh me down.

She's panting. In shock. Desperate.

Now she clambers over a stone wall and jumps down onto a path, nearly tripping on the uneven pebbles.

I can't breathe . . .

Thorny branches hit her face, rip her clothes, and prick her flesh, but she presses on. Red leaves from the trees rot on the ground. Suddenly, the path ends.

She looks up and spots a narrow aqueduct over a gully.

I know she knows—because she's been here before, when she wanted to be alone—that the aqueduct carries water down the hills to the meadows.

A brief moment of relief. She flings herself to the ground and begins to crawl, trying to straddle the narrow waterway. Her hands slip against the viscous dampness of centuries-old moss.

It is soft and delicate, a little sticky.

It feels unpleasant.

Raindrops trickle down the orange rocks like tears, pausing for an instant before falling into the chasm and crashing on the rocks below.

I see them fall, one and thousands at the same time—infinite, terrifying.

Plink, plink, plink, plink . . .

I am afraid. This noise frightens me. The position of the woman frightens me . . .

Who are you?

Watch out!

She is sitting on the aqueduct now, her legs dangling over the void!

She clings to the stone on either side of her thighs to prevent herself from being knocked over by the roaring wind. She looks down, and the vertigo seems to jolt something to the surface.

Her chin drops to her chest and her body convulses in violent sobs.

I feel a deep grief strangling me.

What's wrong with you?

What's wrong with me?

It is that feeling again. It is as if . . . I don't know.

She just wants to disappear.

The drops fall and fall.

The drumbeat of hooves. A whinny. An enormous black animal gallops up and rears at the edge of the gully. A body falls and smashes against the rock.

I think she recognizes the horse.

The body under the bridge isn't moving. It is facedown, very close to the water. The horse stamps nervously.

You have to help! Get down from there!

Somehow, as if by magic, she manages to climb down the sharp rocks. She leans over the body, pulls back the cape that's fallen over his face, and rests a hand on each shoulder to turn the body around. His face is covered in blood.

"You!" she exclaims, relieved.

I think I've seen him before too. But where?

Those eyes burning through me, whose are they?

And here they come again, the shouts filled with hate and fear.

And that monotonous voice repeating, over and over, the words I cannot understand.

"Omnia . . . mecum . . ."

1.

2012

"I'm here," she heard someone saying softly. "It's over."

Brianda slowly opened her eyes. It was over for now, but she knew the nightmares would return, as they had with increasing frequency over the past few months. What was happening to her? She blinked a couple of times in the light. Her heart pounded against her ribs, and her body was sticky with sweat.

"Esteban." Her voice was hoarse. She wanted to add something else but didn't know what. No one could help her, not even him, because she didn't know what was wrong.

"Relax, darling." Esteban waited until her eyes focused and she returned to the present. Then he sat up, leaned against the headboard, and pulled her into his chest. "Feeling better?"

Brianda nodded, smiling slightly to appease Esteban, but she felt troubled. He was so patient with her, maybe too patient. In all this time, he hadn't shown even the slightest reproach. She wondered if she would be so calm if things were the other way around, if Esteban woke her up at all hours in a state.

She sat up. Her head hurt. Headaches were becoming a permanent fixture in her life.

"I don't know what's happening to me," she whispered. She raised a hand to her aching throat.

"It must be because of today's meeting." Esteban patted her hand. "In a couple of hours, it'll be all over." He looked at the alarm clock. It was seven. "I'd better get up. I have a busy day too."

As he walked toward the bathroom, Brianda snuggled back into the blankets. The Latin words still echoed in her head: *Omnia . . . mecum . . .* She closed her eyes and saw disconnected images and sensations: a woman, a horse, water, something sticky between her fingers. All the same as before. She knew dreams didn't usually recur so often. Maybe her mind was warning her about something, but she couldn't think of anything beyond her job, which was being affected by the lack of sleep. Everything else was fine.

She heard the water in the shower and voices on the radio. It wasn't long before Esteban appeared with his brown hair tousled and beads of water on his naked body. He opened the closet and chose a pair of gray trousers and a white shirt. Brianda watched as he got dressed.

"How about this jacket?"

Esteban put it on and posed.

"Perfect for a forty-year-old lawyer," she said.

"Hey! I'm not forty yet!" he said, feigning offense. "Anyway, you're only a few years behind me." He sat at the foot of the bed to put on his shoes. "All ready for your big day?"

Brianda nodded without much enthusiasm. After weeks of hard work, she would be presenting a new project to the hospital's management committee. There was a lot of money at stake. If she succeeded, her company would earn a juicy contract, and she might get a promotion. However, despite her experience, she was horribly nervous. She hadn't told Esteban about last week's slip up—she'd been afraid to—but another mistake like that and her reputation in the company would be ruined.

Esteban gazed at her for a moment, and, in his eyes, Brianda saw what he had told her so many times—that he loved her morning fog. It was easy for him to jump out of bed, but for her, each morning was a battle against sleep. Her heavy eyelids, her rosy cheeks, and her messy dark hair gave her an air of charming untidiness. She wondered if he could see the veil of worry over her dark eyes.

"I'm sure everything will go great." Esteban leaned down to kiss her. He then stroked her cheek and got up. "Call me when you finish, please."

"I will."

"And don't fall back asleep!" he said teasingly before he left.

Brianda lay in bed for a couple more minutes until she saw dawn breaking. Then she got up and went to the window. Bit by bit, the bustle of daytime Madrid was gaining ground on the night: delivery vans, a young woman hurriedly pushing a bleary-eyed child in a stroller, a man with a newspaper under his arm stopping for a coffee, some foreign women entering the apartment buildings where they worked as housekeepers, the first car horns from impatient drivers. No different from any other autumn day on the street where she and Esteban had bought and renovated their old apartment. Brianda knew how much she had to be grateful for: a stable partner, a managerial job, a beautiful home.

I shouldn't get so stressed about it, she thought. She was good at public speaking: dealing with smart alecks in tense meetings, keeping an audience's attention despite dry topics, meeting her goals. There was no reason today should be any different. What happened last week wouldn't happen again; besides, Tatiana had saved the situation.

Ugh, Tatiana. She was an efficient, intelligent, charming woman who Brianda couldn't stand. She didn't trust her new colleague's extreme friendliness. Had the nightmares begun when Tatiana arrived? Did they have anything to do with the young assistant gaining ground on Brianda, the veteran? The bridge, the running, the water . . . Maybe it all represented her fear of losing control.

Brianda shook her head. She needed a shower. She turned up the radio and let news of the troubled world distract her while warm water fell over her body like a balm. After getting dressed, she made some hot tea with honey to soothe her throat and took some ibuprofen for her head. A steaming mug in one hand and a laptop in the other, she crossed the bright, spacious living room. She settled into a cushy armchair beside the large window to the terrace, admonishing herself to relax and enjoy the expansive view of the skyline. But after just a few sips of her drink, she couldn't wait any longer. She switched on the laptop.

She knew she should rehearse the presentation, but she couldn't get the dream out of her head. What did it all mean? A man with an unknown face, a horse, and then there were those Latin words. An online dictionary of dream symbols left her unsatisfied. A horse meant a happy and prosperous future life, or a love affair if it was being ridden. But she wasn't riding in the dream. Also, if the animal was dark, it could mean misfortune. A foreign language meant a subconscious message trying to be heard. And, finally, the heavy rain forecasted a stormy period.

She turned off the device and drained the last drop of tea. She heard her phone chime: a cheerful text from Tatiana about being nervous. *So fake*, Brianda thought. She left her mug in the sink, gathered up her work folders, put on a raincoat, grabbed her bag, and headed out.

Not until the elevator doors closed did she realize her hands were cold and damp as moss.

"You look great!" Tatiana exclaimed. "Trying to impress the committee?"

"You're not looking so bad yourself," Brianda replied.

Both women wore suits, but Tatiana had on a pair of very high heels and her long brown hair hung loose. Brianda, always one for comfort, had chosen a pair of flats and pulled her hair back in a bun.

A hospital receptionist had escorted her to the meeting room, where Tatiana had already laid out presentation folders in front of each chair at the large mahogany table. The first slide of their presentation glowed on the screen. Brianda took her place and suggested they do a quick run-through. This presentation was extremely important. The country was in crisis, the markets had hit rock bottom, and jobs were hanging by a thread, so every contract signed was cause for relief and celebration. Besides, she was grateful to have an exciting job that she loved—a job she hoped to keep for a long time to come. She absentmindedly tapped her pen against the folder.

"Are you all right?" Tatiana asked.

"Yes, of course," Brianda snapped, blushing. "Why do you ask?"

"You seem different. You're fiddling with your pen." She paused for a moment and then shot her arrow: "Are you nervous? Don't worry. If what happened the other day happens again, I'll give you a hand."

"The other day I had a fever," Brianda said. It was a lie, but she had to say something. "I'm perfectly fine now, thank you very much."

Just then, the door opened, and the committee entered. They chatted among themselves as they sat down. Brianda used the moment to take a deep breath. She put on a smile, straightened her back, crossed her hands on the table, and tried to feign interest in Tatiana's introduction. She had five minutes before it was her turn to speak.

Suddenly, Brianda was overcome by a strange feeling of unreality. She heard Tatiana's voice but could not make out her words. The room faded, and her heart began to race. She shifted in her chair and slid her right hand as casually as she could to the back of her neck, which felt hard as a rock.

"Now I'd like to introduce my colleague Brianda," said Tatiana, tapping the key that brought up a slide with the word "Cogeneration" on it.

Brianda didn't move.

Tatiana came over to her, smiling anxiously, and put a hand on her shoulder.

"Whenever you're ready, Brianda."

Brianda struggled to her feet. Her head was spinning. She'd never fainted before but imagined it would feel something like this. She looked at the screen, and a torrent of words filled her mind. She had to get ahold of herself. Once she began to speak, the words surely would flow by themselves.

"Cogeneration is the joint production of usable electricity and thermal energy," she began, "by the users themselves—" She coughed and raised a hand to her throat. She couldn't even hear herself. She tried to raise her voice. "This simultaneous generation of heat—"

She coughed again and met Tatiana's eyes.

Brianda had no explanation for the anguish that flooded her body. A rational voice in her head pointed out that, if she were ill, she couldn't be in a better place, surrounded by doctors and nurses. The fog eased for a moment, and she could see that the only way out was to ask Tatiana for help.

"My sincerest apologies," she whispered, "but I've been hoarse for a few days, and I'm afraid I'm not fully recovered." She fixed her gaze on an elderly man and smiled apologetically. "I'm sure Tatiana will be kind enough to . . ."

She leaned a trembling hand on the table and with immense relief accepted the refuge of the leather chair. Tatiana didn't waste a second in taking over. Brianda only partially understood what her colleague was saying.

"The big advantage is its greater energy efficiency . . . its use in hospitals for heating, refrigeration, and preparation of hot water . . ."

Why was she still so warm? she wondered.

"By avoiding transportation and tension changes that represent a significant loss in energy . . ."

A loss in energy. If Brianda had been run over by a truck she wouldn't have felt this flattened.

"The surplus energy can be sold to the electric grid . . ."

Being surrounded by all these people only made the feelings more terrifying. *Please, let it be over soon*, she thought. *Let them not ask questions.*

"Could you tell us, Tatiana . . . to what point could political policy affect . . ."

Brianda had really screwed up. If they somehow got the contract, Tatiana would obviously take all the credit. After Brianda's years of experience, her engineering degree and specialization in environmental management, her parents' pride, her salary . . .

She had to get some air. She stumbled out of the conference room and looked for a bathroom where she could hide. There, she took off her jacket, undid the top buttons of her blouse, turned on the tap, and splashed water on her face and neck. The mirror reflected a pale, puffy-eyed stranger.

Her phone rang and, pulling it from her bag, she saw that it was the office. She didn't answer. Seconds later, a text message came in: *How did it go?*

And then a message from Esteban: *Any news?*

Why were they asking already? She looked at her watch and her heart skipped a beat. More than a half hour had gone by without her noticing.

She closed her eyes and focused on her breath.

She needed more help than a dream dictionary could provide.

"And when I got back to the office, the manager said I should use my vacation time and take a couple weeks to rest." A knot in Brianda's stomach prevented her from eating dinner. "He didn't even look me in the eyes, the asshole. I almost told him to take his rest and shove it."

Return to Your Skin

"It's probably not a bad idea to take a little time," Esteban said.

Brianda looked up in surprise. Esteban had listened without asking any questions, and she'd been so grateful for his silent support, the way he'd held her hand while she tearfully let it all out.

"But we always take our vacation together! What am I going to do here at home alone?"

Esteban shrugged. "Rest, like he said. What happened to you today must have been exhaustion. You've been working way too hard recently. If you're not better by Friday, we'll go to the doctor."

Brianda spent the week cleaning out closets, going over paperwork, organizing kitchen utensils, updating her address book, and reading. But instead of subsiding, her anxiety increased to the point where she started to wish she didn't have to leave the apartment ever again. Her phone was her only link to the outside world. Thanks to e-mail and text messages, she could present a picture of normalcy to her friends and colleagues. The reality, though, was that the streets below her terrace seemed like a hostile universe, and the very thought of returning to work made her chest tighten. She felt her whole self emptying out, a big hole growing inside her. Even in the peace of her own home, she was periodically rocked by vertigo as if she were peering over a cliff. When it got really bad, the only thing she wanted was to crawl into bed, but she feared her recurring dream too much to sleep.

Seeing Brianda withdraw more every day, Esteban dragged her to his family's doctor who was also a friend—too close a friend in Brianda's opinion. He'd known Esteban's father since childhood, and Esteban's mother and sisters had gone to him for years.

"I just don't see why it has to be him," she protested yet again in the waiting room, clutching her medical records from a recent physical.

"Roberto is an excellent doctor," Esteban assured her. "And if he can't help you, he'll know who to refer us to." He gave her a kiss on the cheek. "What are you so worried about?"

"I'm embarrassed! I don't want your family to find out about my problems."

"Brianda, Roberto is a professional. He's very discreet."

Was that impatience in his eyes? Brianda couldn't help feeling guilty that, in some way, she was letting down her boyfriend, the man who might be her future husband. At this point in her life, she should be healthy, successful, excited for the future they were making together. Instead, her eyes filled with tears, and she squeezed Esteban's hand hard, wanting to promise she'd be strong enough to face whatever was happening, that it was just a momentary lapse.

A few minutes later, the door opened, and a white-haired nurse showed them into an office ringed with bookshelves. A bearded man of about sixty was writing some notes at a walnut desk. He got to his feet and greeted them warmly. After some courteous small talk about Esteban's family, Roberto said, "Well, if you're ready, we'll start now."

Esteban looked at Brianda. "Do you want me to stay?" he asked.

Brianda didn't know what to say. Esteban had been witness to many of her symptoms, but he didn't know everything. If she said no, she was afraid that he would take it as a sign of mistrust. Roberto came to her rescue.

"If you wouldn't mind, Esteban, I'd like to talk to Brianda alone. Please wait outside."

Roberto began by asking general questions about her life and her work. Then he reviewed the results from her physical and concluded that everything was as it should be. Brianda let herself relax and be guided by his friendly and firm questions, trying to be as precise as possible in her answers. She told him about her nightmares, the sensation of unreality, the tingling in her arms, the shivers and racing heart and tightness in her chest. And in the end, she shared the thing she'd been most ashamed to admit.

"I'm afraid to leave the house. I've never been easily frightened, but now it's like I'm scared of everything. Worst of all is that I feel . . ."—she fiddled with her hands nervously—"a terrible and deep fear of dying."

She had finally said it.

And Roberto hadn't batted an eye.

She felt a wave of relief. "I'm fine one minute and then the next I get dizzy and feel like I'm going to faint, or die. And I get really scared. I don't know how to explain it exactly. At first the fear paralyzes me, but then I need to escape." She dropped her head into her hands and began sobbing. "What's happening to me? A few months ago I was ready to take on the world, and now . . . everything is a struggle . . . it's like I can't . . . like I don't have the strength . . ."

Roberto moved closer and held out a box of tissues.

"Brianda, what's happening to you is not unusual."

She stopped wiping away her tears and looked up at him.

"Everything seems to indicate that you are suffering from anxiety attacks."

"Anxiety attacks? But I've always been a really easygoing person."

Roberto smiled. "You'd be surprised how many people suffer from anxiety."

"But I don't have any health problems. You see that in my medical records. And no money or family problems."

"The causes of anxiety disorder are many and varied. It can be hereditary, or caused by personal loss, by unexpected changes, substance abuse . . ." To each of the items on the list, Brianda answered by shaking her head. "A traumatic episode can also produce panic attacks."

Brianda racked her brain, going over her childhood and teenage years, her time in college, her first boyfriend, first job, her habits and daily routine. She had lived a completely uneventful life, and, until a few weeks ago, she had felt confident about reaching every goal she set for herself. There was just no reasonable explanation.

"Are you worried about anything?" the doctor asked. "This fear you describe is like a warning about something you feel as a threat."

She shook her head again.

"And everything is OK with Esteban?" Roberto pressed. "Life as a couple, the loss of freedom, and aging can prove stressful for many people."

Brianda felt herself getting annoyed. Of course Esteban wasn't the problem. This was supposed to be a medical exam, not a psych evaluation! She wasn't some tragic movie character with secret childhood trauma. All her friends and family were in perfect health, physically and mentally. And so was she.

She had to get out of this office immediately.

"Hmm," Brianda lied. "Maybe you're right about stress. I've had a lot to do at work over the last year, and they keep expecting more and more, you know, because of the economy. Maybe it's been getting to me . . ."

Roberto nodded and smiled knowingly, clearly pleased with his diagnosis. He encouraged her to read about the causes and symptoms of anxiety and prescribed a low-dose sedative in case of another attack.

Brianda took the prescription, forcing herself to smile in thanks. The paper burned in her hand. She couldn't bear the idea of having to take pills and wondered if it might have something to do with her age after all, the fact that she was approaching thirty-seven. Just recently, she'd been a happy, ambitious young woman, and now, without warning, she was being told she had to drug herself to leave the house.

As she walked home with Esteban, the sadness didn't loosen its grip. The doctor had said what was happening to her was common. She looked around and wondered how many of the people they passed might be on medication for anxiety. If she could just talk to one of them, she would ask what to do. She wanted to know if people talked about it openly, if she should tell her family and friends, if they would understand or if they'd just pity her.

A toddler collided with her knees, plopped on his bottom, and looked up at Brianda with a confused expression, as if deciding whether or not to cry. His mother took him in her arms, and he began to howl, clinging to her neck like he'd just survived a great tragedy.

Brianda envied the look of surrender on the child's face. Hopefully, she would always have a safe place to hide, a pillar to hold her up, a clear path through uncertainty.

Esteban laughed. "Did you see that? If his mother hadn't picked him up, I bet he wouldn't have cried."

Brianda squeezed his hand. She hoped nothing would ever separate them, that they would stay like this forever, holding hands through the good and the bad. She remembered his words leaving the doctor's. He'd said they would get through this together. He would help her recover her joy and her courage.

He was her refuge, her support, her beacon.

2.

Brianda took a deep breath and dialed. She'd decided to tell her mother. After all, Laura was bound to notice Brianda was taking vacation time that didn't coincide with Esteban's. They talked at least once a week, usually on Fridays. And it was Friday.

She counted six rings before Laura picked up. After their usual hellos, Brianda told her mother she was having panic attacks brought on by anxiety.

There was a brief silence, and then Laura gave her high-pitched reply. "What panic attacks and what anxiety? You are a very strong woman. Who told you such nonsense?"

Brianda wasn't surprised. She knew her mother was cautious about raising family problems with outsiders, but it irritated her when her mother initially resisted facing up to them even in private.

"I went to see Esteban's family doctor."

Silence. Brianda used the pause to briefly catch her mother up on what had been happening.

"Why didn't you tell me sooner?"

"I don't know exactly. I was ashamed."

Another silence.

"I'll call you back, Brianda."

This abrupt good-bye could only mean one thing. Brianda pictured her tall, dark-haired, elegant mother relaying everything to her father, Daniel. First she'd be distressed and ask herself why this was happening to her daughter; then she'd scan her memory and recall some similar case among her acquaintances; then she would talk through every possible way of helping her daughter. In the end, she would apply her favorite maxim that desperate times call for desperate measures. Neither Brianda nor her older brother, Andres, had inherited their mother's frenetic energy.

Brianda smiled thinking about her brother, who lived in Burgos. They were only two years apart, and they got along well and called each other often, but since his twins were born three years ago, he'd only come to Madrid for Christmas and their parents' birthdays. Maybe she should have called him before their mother, but he had enough to deal with right now. She realized, with amazement, how well her brother had adapted to his new life. Andres, who used to be game for every trip, activity, and party, had become a serious and responsible adult who divided his life between work and family and didn't have time for anything else. Maybe the source of her anxiety lay in the fear that the same might happen to her.

The phone rang. It was her mother.

"I talked to Aunt Isolina and she'd be delighted to have you in Tiles for a bit. I think a change of scenery is just what you need." Laura's upbeat tone turned serious, indicating there was one problem to resolve for the marvelous idea to be perfect. "If Esteban thinks it's all right, of course . . ." The brightness returned. "Oh, I'm sure he will; he's a darling."

Brianda was in a daze after she hung up. She'd said she would think about visiting her aunt, which to her mother meant a definite yes. For a moment Brianda felt like a child, and she was annoyed with herself for letting her mother run her life. She could imagine her parents deciding that she just needed some country air, as if she were a feeble nineteenth-century damsel with bad nerves. And by sending her away, her mother guaranteed that Brianda's illness would stay a secret. She hadn't even asked if Brianda wanted to go away. And to Tiles, of all places—just thinking about her mother's childhood village gave her the creeps.

Esteban's smiling face appeared on her cell phone screen.

He was calling to invite her out to dinner with their best friends, who had left their five-year-old son with his grandmother. His voice sounded tempting and kind when he said he didn't want to pressure her, and he assured her they could go to a restaurant near home and leave whenever she wished. Brianda decided to make an effort for him.

While she got ready, her mind kept traveling to a distant valley in northeastern Spain. Her earliest memories of visiting Tiles, when her grandparents were still alive, were happy ones. She remembered the smell of recently harvested wheat under the hot sun, the earthen feel of an old pot, the cows and sheep on the paths, the quiet, everyone's tanned skin. She and Andres used to look forward to summers in Tiles because they meant freedom. There were no rules, no schedules or responsibilities. They'd sleep in, have a late breakfast while being doted on by Aunt Isolina, play in the fields, feed animals on the neighboring farms, dance at the festivals where trays of sweets covered the tables, and listen to the old folks' stories before passing out on wooden benches in front of the fire.

But something changed.

It was after their grandparents died and Aunt Isolina married Uncle Colau. The trips became sporadic and then ended completely. Aunt Isolina occasionally would come to Madrid on her own or they'd meet her at the beach, and there were frequent phone calls. Brianda tried to remember why she didn't get upset when the trips stopped. She recalled fragments of her parents' conversations about Uncle Colau, about Isolina's mistake, about run-down, old Anels House.

As Brianda headed out to meet Esteban and their friends, unsettling memories bubbled up with stark clarity. She hadn't thought about her mother's village for ages, but now she was inundated by scenes from the last time she'd been in the house, how she'd left hoping her parents would never make her go back. She must have been around eleven or twelve. The cooing of the pigeons on the roof had become oppressive, the howl of the storms unbearable, the creaking of the wood threatening, the presence of Colau . . .

She remembered a tall, strong man, with an unfriendly face and a bitter character. Always wary. Always alert. With the curiosity typical of a child, she had gone into his office one afternoon looking for treasures. She remembered the overstuffed shelves, the dark paintings on the walls, the dim light from the thick-shaded lamps, the upholstered armchairs, the mess on the table, and that precious little red velvet box with a brass ball catch. A box like that just had to hold something wonderful, and she was eager to look inside. But Colau had appeared out of nowhere, snatching it from her. She remembered the rage in his voice, the fury in his eyes, the violence of his hands.

That was twenty-five years ago. If her mother hadn't suggested that she go to Tiles, the images would probably have remained buried in her mind.

Esteban came over as soon as he saw her. He kissed her on the lips, whispered a compliment about her dress, and led her by the hand to the table. The candles in a heavy silver candelabra lent the scene a soft warmth.

Brianda greeted her friends, sat down, and promised herself she'd try to enjoy the evening. Memories belonged to the past. But a new thought refused to loosen its grip: her childhood fears rested in a certain man. Her current fears had no form.

◆ ◆ ◆

Silvia and Ricardo made a strange couple. He was a serious, polite forensic scientist, and she was petite, blonde, and lighthearted. Silvia never stopped laughing and talking, especially about her interior design business. The men had known each other since school, and luckily for everyone, Brianda got along well with Silvia. In fact, she regarded her as her best friend, which was saying something, given that Brianda wasn't the most open or sociable person.

When they finished eating, they relocated to the restaurant's bar for a drink. It was filled with comfortable armchairs, low lighting, and piano music. At the back, there was a small dance floor and a pool table. When Esteban and Ricardo realized no one was playing, they shot their partners a pleading look, then ran to the table like teenagers.

Brianda and Silvia made themselves comfortable. Brianda's first thought was to have a gin and tonic, but she remembered the pills she was taking.

"Just tonic?" said Silvia. "You're not pregnant, are you?"

"God, no. It's just that I had a fair amount of wine with dinner, so I'd better slow down." In fact, she'd barely drunk anything, but she figured her friend hadn't noticed. She didn't want to mention the pills.

"Maybe the next round," said Silvia. She paused before adding, "Esteban mentioned you weren't feeling great."

"It's nothing. Just tired, I'm sure."

"Hmm. I've noticed too. It's OK; there are times in life when stress just gets to you, y'know? I haven't been feeling so good either lately. The business is going from bad to worse. I had to fire a shop assistant who's been with me almost since I opened."

"I'm so sorry. That sounds awful."

"It was. And Ricardo and I had been thinking about . . . well . . . expanding our family . . . but now I have so much more work that I just don't know anymore."

"At least Ricardo's job is safe, right?"

"Yeah, but his salary's been cut. No one's escaped the recession. Besides, I don't want to be financially dependent on Ricardo or anybody else."

Brianda frowned. She'd never thought of her situation in such clear terms. On one occasion, when she had joked with Esteban about how many children they would have, he had mentioned the possibility that she might have to give up her job, but Brianda hadn't taken him seriously. She'd worked so hard to finish her engineering degree and find a good job—a goal that had been drilled into her from an early age—and be economically independent. It had never crossed her mind to devote herself exclusively to raising a family. A tightness began to grip her chest. That was how it began. Soon the palpitations would start, the cold sweat. She fought to concentrate on the music, on her surroundings, on the clothes people were wearing—anything that would distract her and help head off the attack.

As she looked around the room, a shiver ran down her spine. It was like someone was watching her. At that moment, the waiter arrived with their drinks.

"Are you OK?" Silvia asked, passing her the tonic water. "I bet they could still add a splash of gin if you need it."

"No, it's just that I was only this minute thinking about what you said. This thing that's happening to me is affecting my work. It's so hard to concentrate. I have to beat this."

"You know you can tell me anything."

Brianda thought for a few seconds, sighed, and finally told her friend about the recurring nightmares, about her anxiety and melancholy, about the devastating fear that was making it impossible to live a normal life.

"The doctor asked if anything's been worrying me and all that. But as far as I know, my life is, well, *was* perfect."

"Give yourself some time," said Silvia. "I bet it'll all sort itself out. Maybe this is just something you need to go through right now. I don't think anything happens without a reason."

"It's kinda scary when you put it like that," Brianda tried to joke. She looked around the bar and again felt eyes on her. Then she spotted the woman. At a small table near the terrace, partially hidden by some fluttering, gauzy curtains, she was moving something between her hands while watching Brianda with an insolent smile. She was slightly stocky, her wavy hair streaked with gray. A tarot card reader.

As if reading her mind, Silvia said, "How weird that they'd have that kind of woman in a fancy place like this. Bars can't figure out how to keep people amused anymore. Well? Want to see what she tells us?"

"It's just nonsense to get money out of people," Brianda said.

"Sure, but maybe it'll be fun! You're not scared, are you?"

"Not exactly. I just don't want to do it."

But Silvia kept pushing and, eventually, Brianda gave in. As they approached, she thought she saw a triumphant smile on the woman's round face. Her heart beat faster.

"Separately."

The woman's voice was very deep.

"What do you mean?" Silvia asked.

"If you want me to tell your future, it has to be first one and then the other. Not together."

"You go first," Brianda suggested. "I've got to go to the bathroom."

"Chicken!" whispered Silvia.

When Brianda returned ten minutes later, Silvia was beaming. She handed the woman some money and motioned her friend to take her seat while the woman delicately gathered the cards.

"Before we start," Brianda said, "I want you to know I don't believe in this stuff. It was my friend's idea."

The woman ignored her. She began to shuffle. Her long, slender fingers didn't match the rest of her body. Brianda noticed that she wore no jewelry. She'd pictured a tarot card reader as a bejeweled witch, dressed in colorful clothes, and wearing a silk headscarf and a chain of coins over thick, wavy hair. A cliché.

"Do you have anything to ask me?" the woman inquired.

Brianda narrowed her eyes. "If I ask a question, you'll be able to guess what I'm worried about and just riff on that."

"So, something is troubling you."

Brianda gave a victorious smile. "See what I mean?"

The woman held out the deck of cards.

"Here. You don't have to say a word. I will be the only one to speak, and I will be brief and concise. We will use the Major Arcana cards. Choose ten cards and place them one by one, faceup, where I show you. OK?" The woman's look softened. "You don't even have to take your eyes off the cards. That way, I won't be able to see your expression."

This last condition finally convinced Brianda. It might be a waste of time, but she was curious. She thought of Silvia's happy expression. The typical thing was for a fortune-teller to make reassuring promises: a shining future in love, family, work, and health.

"Fine." She accepted the deck. "Ten cards." She spread the cards facedown on the table and picked out ten. "There."

"Very good. Place the first one here."

Brianda did so.

"The Fool inverted. You find yourself in a state of abandonment, indecision, apathy. You are going through a difficult time. Emotional confusion." She pointed to the second spot, indicating the second card should partially cover the first. "The Lovers inverted. You have made the wrong choice. Your family and social world are dragging you down. They are an obstacle for you."

Brianda frowned. Her mother could be a bit of a pain, but her family wasn't in her way. She'd been independent for a long time.

She uncovered the third card and followed the fortune-teller's finger to place the card above the second one.

"The Chariot in the upright position. It reveals your possible future. You are going on a journey. You will encounter many impediments, but you must find the way."

Brianda shifted nervously in her chair. She hadn't decided yet whether or not to go to Tiles.

The fourth card, below the second.

"The Moon in the upright position. In your distant past, you were a sensitive, intuitive dreamer. You followed a difficult and dark path. You suffered. Terribly."

The fifth card, left of the second.

"The Empress inverted. This is the reason you have lost control. You are suffering a crisis you cannot explain."

The sixth card, laid to the right of the second, completed what, to Brianda, looked like a cross. As soon as she turned it over, she jumped. A skeleton with a scythe.

"Death in the upright position. It means a profound and radical change. End and beginning. You will die and be reborn."

Brianda did not want to hear any more, but she felt trapped in a dreamlike state by the dance of words, finger, card, words.

The finger pointed to the spot for the seventh card, to her lower right, close to her chest.

"Justice in the upright position. Underneath it all, you want this change. You want to awaken. You must."

The eighth card, above the seventh.

"The Wheel of Fortune inverted. You will encounter difficulties all around you, but the transformation will occur regardless. Everything comes, sooner or later."

The ninth card. A horrible figure, like a billy goat with enormous horns. Brianda felt her mouth go dry.

"The Devil in the upright position. I don't understand this very well."

Without meaning to, Brianda looked up and saw that the woman's eyes were half-closed as if she were trying to make out distant voices.

"It refers to your fears, your subconscious. I see a confused mental state. An uncontrolled carnal passion. Please, place the last one."

The tenth card. A human figure holding a lion.

"Strength in the upright position. Yes—" The fortune-teller's voice broke. "In the end, the spirit will dominate matter."

Brianda closed her eyes for a second, trying to process what she'd heard.

The spirit will dominate matter.

She felt around in her purse, took out some money, and placed it on the table. The seer's hand brushed hers as she motioned her refusal.

"No, please. I was carrying out a mission."

Brianda's eyes widened in surprise. The woman's face portrayed intense pain. The arrogance was gone.

"I can't take money for this. I'm sorry, but I have to leave."

Before Brianda could react, the woman gathered her things, got up, and began to walk away, but then she stopped, retraced her steps, and looked at the young woman in such a way that Brianda suddenly felt intensely close to her.

"Be strong," she advised. "And don't be afraid."

Something touched her shoulder, and Brianda yelped.

Instinctively, she jumped up, spun around, and brought a hand to her chest. Esteban laughed.

"So, this is how you entertain yourselves when we leave you alone! What did the old witch say? You look like you had a real shock."

"To tell you the truth, I'm not really sure."

She didn't dare tell him how deeply the predictions had upset her, or about her strange connection with the woman. She certainly couldn't mention the part about uncontrolled carnal passion.

"Didn't she foretell a wonderful future with a charming man and two or three children running around?"

The gleam in Esteban's lovely gray eyes made Brianda smile despite herself.

"Is that what she said to Silvia?"

"More or less."

Brianda looked around, but there was no sign of the woman. She slid an arm around Esteban's waist as they followed the others to the dance floor for a slow song. Esteban pulled her to him and began to sway. She threw her arms around his neck and held on with all her strength.

When they left the bar, Brianda couldn't stop clinging to Esteban. She needed to feel him close to her on the street, in the hall, in the elevator, in the apartment. She only let go for a few seconds to take off her clothes and get in bed. Feeling him on top of her, beside her, under her, made it easier to convince herself that everything was fine. Esteban was not an obstacle. She did not need to get away from him. She loved him with all her might. She hadn't suffered terribly. She didn't need any change or great journey. Her life was everything she could hope for.

But each time Esteban entered her, she felt a stab of pain in her chest. He could not be any closer. And yet, in the middle of their pleasure, a voice inside her kept chanting that something was not right, that it was not his body that should be over her, but another's, that she had to get out of here.

She had to stop.

Suddenly, she couldn't stand his touch, his smell.

She felt her skin burning wherever Esteban's fingers touched.

The man's moans intensified. Brianda twisted under him and realized he would misinterpret her writhing for excitement. She wanted to tell him to stop, but his weight on her chest made it hard for her to breathe. She held on to the headboard and struggled to raise herself a bit. Esteban was just about to climax, and she had to stop him. Her head was about to explode. All her initial desire had turned to terror. The palpitations, the accelerated breathing, the cold sweat, the feeling of drowning, the need to escape . . .

Stop! she screamed inside, but the words wouldn't come out.

Esteban was smiling. He thrust harder and came inside her. Sweat covered his face. He moaned one last time and collapsed on top of her.

Brianda concentrated all her efforts on holding back sobs.

What was happening to her?

Out of all her recent feelings, this was the worst: the incomprehensible sense of loss.

Without her knowing why, the person she loved most was turning into a stranger.

He was melting. Dissolving.

She had never before loathed Esteban's touch. How could she look into his eyes and pretend this hadn't happened? It was impossible to say the words, the ones that meant the relationship had come to an end.

Tears began to flow down her cheeks.

Now she had to leave.

At least for a while.

3.

Two days later, early in the morning, Brianda said good-bye to Esteban with her heart clenched. She picked up her suitcase full of cold-weather clothes, climbed behind the wheel of her car, and began her journey to the northeast. Since that night with Esteban, she'd burned with an urgent need to leave Madrid and everything familiar. Just the thought of what had happened in bed was so upsetting that she'd upped her dose of tranquilizers. Esteban didn't deserve this drastic change in her feelings toward him. She needed distance so she could think. She wasn't sure her destination was ideal, but she had no other options.

An exhausting five hours later, she stopped the car at an unmarked crossroads in the middle of nowhere, well past the last village. The GPS was no help.

She unfolded a paper map, but Tiles lay between two squiggly yellow lines.

Brianda opted for the road to the right. If she was wrong, she could always double back. She drank some water, ate a few nuts, and continued driving, scrutinizing the countryside for something she remembered from her childhood.

The narrow road began to climb through desperately barren terrain. To her left rose small gray hills with deep grooves of loam. The land looked haggard, mistreated by the inclement weather. To her right water trickled through a rocky riverbed running parallel to the road. As she climbed, the hills turned to pure rock on which the odd bush tried to survive, the river turned into a chasm, and the bends got sharper.

Coming around one very tight bend, she had to slam on the brakes.

In front of her, a woman stood next to a stopped car. Brianda was tempted to speed by, afraid it might be a trap, but she told herself it was broad daylight and, besides, the poor woman was jumping up and down trying to keep warm. She was tall and wore a green-and-brown dress down to her ankles, cowboy boots, and a crumpled scarf. Brianda rolled down the window.

"Can you give me a lift? I'm going to Tiles." The woman had reddish hair and a cheerful voice.

"Of course," said Brianda, although she was annoyed by the unexpected interruption. "What happened?"

"Give me just a sec, and I'll explain."

The woman quickly took out more than a dozen bags from the trunk of her dilapidated jeep and waited until Brianda reluctantly opened her own trunk.

"I'm Neli, and, as you can see, today was shopping day. But the car gave out on me. I'm lucky you came this way. I've been waiting for ages. A little longer and I would have frozen."

"Nice to meet you, Neli. I'm Brianda."

She liked Neli's openness, her determined attitude. Everything about the woman inspired confidence. Her initial annoyance began to fade.

"Excuse me for asking, Brianda, but what brings you here? It's not a place many people come."

"Oh, I've got family up here in the mountains."

"In Tiles?" Neli said in surprise. "I thought I knew everyone and their relatives, even if only by name."

"Give me just a sec, and I'll explain," Brianda said, and they both laughed.

Brianda felt at ease. A stranger had made her laugh. This journey was supposed to be about hiding from the world, not meeting new people, but her curiosity was piqued. Her urban image of the lost valley of her childhood hadn't included somebody like Neli.

"What about the jeep? Did you call a tow truck?"

"There's no signal here. I'll call from home. Or my husband will come out and fix it."

She said it as if it were the most normal thing in the world. Brianda braked, took out her phone, and saw that Neli was right. There still were places in the world with no cell coverage.

"Good thing I didn't notice before," she said. "I would have been worried. Is there service in the village?"

"Depends on the day," Neli said. Then, in case Brianda was one of those people addicted to their phones, she added, "I mean, it normally works. It's just sometimes, if it's really windy or right after a storm, the signal doesn't reach so well."

"Well, I sure hope the weather is clear." As she said the words, Brianda realized it might not be so bad to be off the grid for a while. She concentrated on the next turn, even tighter than the last. The road was dreadful.

"Nearly there," Neli announced encouragingly. "This place can seem like the end of the world, huh?"

"The truth is, I'm eager to see Tiles," Brianda admitted.

"Wait, I thought you knew it?"

"Yes and no. My aunt and uncle live there, and when I was little I came for some summers, but I don't remember it very well."

"Who are your aunt and uncle?"

"Isolina and Colau. Do you know them?"

Neli hesitated for a moment before answering. From the corner of her eye, Brianda noticed her forced smile.

"Yes, of course, from Anels House. I know Isolina better."

"She's my mother's older sister. Are you from Tiles?"

"No, but my husband's family is. Jonas and I decided to move here about ten years ago. We wanted our children to grow up in the country."

Brianda remembered an article she'd read. It talked about people who, faced with unemployment, pollution, stress, and bureaucracy, had gone in search of an idealized rural life, of the harmony and solidarity of small villages, of a physical and spiritual connection between man and nature. She also remembered thinking they were lunatics. She couldn't understand how anyone could give up the comforts of city life for ramshackle, frigid houses, or who preferred to grow their own vegetables when modern grocery stores existed. She'd forwarded the article to her mother and, after reading it, Laura had declared that the only people who could really make it in the country were those who already knew how tough it was. She wondered if Neli regretted her decision.

"So you're—what do the media call it? Neo-rurals?"

Neli laughed happily.

"Ah, labels! Neo-rural, hippie, beatnik, alternative, neo-artisan, neo-peasant, bohemian. I don't identify with any labels." Her voice took on a mysterious tone. "Well, at least not any of those." She pointed ahead. "We're nearly there!"

Brianda guided the car around three more tight turns, veering between the rock face on the right and the deep chasm on the left and, suddenly, a vast plain opened before her, rolling all the way to the base of Beles Peak, which rose like a mountain in a child's drawing: gigantic, solitary, regal.

"Take the road to the right," said Neli. "It goes to the lower part of Tiles, where I live. The other goes to the high part, where you're going."

They passed plowed fields and meadows dotted with cows, sheep, and brownish-gray stone buildings with slate or tile roofs. Bit by bit, the density increased until, past a small gas station with a sign for a hotel and restaurant, houses lined both sides of a narrow street. The street led to a square with a Romanesque church, its tower crowned by a four-sided, pointed roof.

Brianda parked and got out of the car. An unexpected gust of cold air hit her like a slap on the face. She quickly pulled on a jacket and rubbed her arms vigorously. She had a momentary sensation of regressing to an undefined past, but the idyllic images of her childhood clashed with the run-down buildings and the intense smell of livestock and mud. What she saw was pretty, but it was too solitary and oppressively dull.

Neli pointed to the church. "The portico is dilapidated, I know, and the apse is in awful shape, but we're working on restoring it! Look, here's my house."

Neli unloaded the shopping bags and left them on the stairs leading to a whitewashed house. Her steps sent a muffled echo through the deserted square. Then she returned to the car and, to Brianda's surprise, reached out to touch her hair.

"Sorry, you've got a little something."

"Huh?" Brianda felt a small tug and pulled away instinctively.

"Are you staying long?" Neli asked quickly.

"A couple of weeks. Maybe more."

"Then I'm sure I'll see you again!"

They said good-bye, and Brianda retraced her route back to the fork in the road.

When she took the high road going to Anels House, the countryside changed completely. The fields filled with holm oaks and gall oaks, and the earth livened up thanks to the bright leaves and evergreens. But Beles Peak loomed larger and larger. She was glad it was still the middle of the day. She could imagine the afternoon shadow of the colossus stretching slowly across the valley at its feet, like an eagle hovering over its prey, silently announcing the inexorable coming of death. She wouldn't have wanted to walk there alone at night.

The road snaked toward the mountain, passing a graveyard on the left, a wooded path Brianda didn't remember, a fountain on the right under a huge linden, and a final climb that she did remember. She slowed down.

On the one hand, she wanted to be done with the long journey and to see Isolina; on the other, she was nervous about seeing Colau again. She took a deep breath. That was absurd. She was a grown woman. She might be afraid of many things, but her aunt's husband should not be one of them.

She sped up and soon parked on a flat area where she expected to see a square-shaped, two-storied, stone manor house. However, a sparse forest now hid Anels House from sight, as if the dried-out branches and the wizened leaves wanted to isolate it from the rest of the valley and drag it toward the mountain. She walked a few steps along a gravel path until she could make out the high walls that enclosed the front yard through the trunks of the ashes and willows. She pictured herself with pigtails and her arms outstretched to keep her balance on those walls as she followed her brother, then a little boy in shorts. It was a fleeting image, but a sensation of well-being filled her, and Brianda clung to it with all her might. It was stupid, but in some way she felt like she was coming home. Maybe her parents were right. Maybe a stay in the country would help her find some peace.

But when she reached the low gate that led to the main door, her heart skipped a beat.

The grass grew out of control between the irregular paving stones. The shed roofs had loose slates, and one of the walls of the big house bulged dangerously, as if it might explode at any moment. The piles of logs, the remains of summer flowers in improvised beds, and the clothes hanging on a line did little to change the impression that the whole place looked completely abandoned.

The silence was so complete that Brianda could hear her own breathing. She wondered if Anels House had always been like that and her childhood eyes had not noticed the decrepitude or, if with the passing of time, places, like people, were affected by the slow abandonment of vigor and joy.

When they greeted her, Brianda realized her last thought applied to Colau but not Isolina. Brianda found her aunt as beautiful as ever. Her thick, short hair was streaked with gray, which gave her a special, natural air. Her beige outfit was offset by a bright scarf and some simple jewelry, and she wore pale pink lipstick.

"What a thrill to have you here!" Isolina said as she hugged her niece. "I can't believe I haven't seen you for ten months, since last Christmas. Does the house look familiar? You must be starving! I made something special." She turned to Colau. "Could you take her bags up to the blue bedroom?"

Colau walked over, and Brianda hesitated. She definitely was not going to hug him. A feint of a kiss on the cheek would be enough. He still had those hard features, bushy eyebrows, and large build, but he had hunched a bit. Behind his tortoiseshell glasses, puffy folds made his eyes look smaller.

"Good trip?" he asked in greeting.

"Yes, thanks." She was surprised at the tremor in her voice. After so many years, the man still intimidated her.

"We're going to have a wonderful time!" said Isolina. "After lunch, I'll show you everything: the house, the vegetable patch, the garden. I have hens, rabbits, geese, and a pair of donkeys to keep the grass down." She laughed. "Do you remember how you always used to say you wanted to be a farmer when you grew up?"

Brianda smiled—her aunt's joy was contagious. If she ever had said such a thing, she had forgotten. Out of the corner of her eye, she saw Colau disappear with her luggage through the sun-bleached door.

"My mother would not have approved!"

"Ha. Laura never liked the country. It's hard to believe she was born here. Can you even picture her without makeup, going to collect eggs with a basket? You can't, can you? Well, when she was a child, she had no choice."

Some deep, hoarse barks announced the arrival of an enormous black dog that pounced on Brianda, baring his teeth. She let out a shriek.

"Where were you, you rascal?" Isolina grabbed him by the collar. "Quiet. Brianda is family. That's it, smell her." She patted his back, raising a cloud of dust. "This is Luzer. I can't remember if you like dogs or not."

"I do like them. But this one's so big."

"Don't be afraid. He won't hurt you. Colau found him abandoned, took him in, and since then, they've been inseparable."

A sharp whistle came from the house. Luzer shot Brianda a look, then bolted through the same door Colau had used.

"Is he allowed inside?" she asked, terrified.

"If you want, I'll ask Colau to keep him outside more while you're here, at least until you get used to each other."

Isolina showed her into the house. Three rough stone steps separated the entrance from a large dark hall. Black double doors leading to the foyer were at the end of the hall. To the right were the kitchen and the dining room, whose mosaic tile floor Brianda remembered well. On the left was the sitting room with the blackened fireplace at one end and, on either side of it, some high-backed wooden benches. In front, the knotty steps of the cracked wooden stairs led to the second floor. Beneath them was the long, narrow passage to Colau's office.

"Make yourself at home, Brianda," Isolina told her. "Just don't go into Colau's office without permission. He usually keeps it locked, so I can't even be tempted to tidy up the mess."

After her childhood fright, there was no way Brianda was going in there alone. She did wonder, however, if the little red velvet box was still there.

"Uncle Colau must have plenty of time for his research now," she said, heading up the stairs toward the bedrooms. She knew that her uncle had just retired from teaching at the Aiscle Secondary School, and that he'd always been passionate about the history of the valley.

"He does nothing else. Sometimes I think it's more an obsession than a hobby. I've told him he should write a book, but he says you need to know everything for that and he doesn't yet." Isolina sighed. "It's horrible getting old! I don't know why, but for the last three or four months, he's been nervous. He's always kept to himself, but now . . ."

Isolina opened the last door in the hall and they entered a room with chipped blue paint. Brianda recognized it immediately. It was the room she'd slept in as a child. It hadn't changed a bit. There was the wrought-iron bed, the walnut wardrobe, the chest of drawers, and, as in the rest of the house, the dark and twisted beams that supported the ceiling. She'd imagined that, after so many years, the house would have been redecorated. But while she had grown up, life here had stood still.

"I love this room. It's the brightest in the house and has the best view." Isolina flung open the balcony shutters. "Down below, you can see the village of Tiles. The manor houses are all over this way. The one to the east is Cuyls House. Colau was born there, you know, but now it's in ruins. Then our house, Anels, and to the west is Lubich Manor, though you can't see it from here."

Although she knew these details from her childhood, Brianda listened attentively, grateful her aunt didn't ask any questions about why she'd come. Laura had probably filled her in.

That night, she went to bed convinced she'd have no trouble falling asleep after such a long day. But she just lay there, listening to the deep silence of that helpless house, the creaking of the floorboards, the scratching of Luzer's nails in the hall, and the gnawing of woodworm in the heavy furniture. She knew that on the other side of the bedroom walls were empty rooms with white sheets covering the furniture and mirrors, and that the closest neighbor was the gray silhouette of a lonely mountain.

And, try as she might, she couldn't stop thinking about Esteban, whom she missed with all her heart.

4.

The day dawned calm and bright. Brianda stepped out on the balcony and confirmed, to her annoyance, that the temperature wasn't far above freezing. She opened the bedroom door, peeked her head out to make sure Luzer wasn't there, and scurried across the hall to the bathroom. After an unpleasantly tepid shower, she put on a pair of jeans, a long-sleeved blouse, and a thick sweater, and she went downstairs. A delicious scent of coffee came from the kitchen.

Isolina greeted her with a smile and fresh-baked sponge cake. Over breakfast, she invited Brianda to accompany her to the cemetery. It was two days before All Saints' Day, and she wanted to tidy up the family graves before the villagers' visits.

Brianda helped her aunt prepare bouquets on a stone bench in the yard. It wasn't flower season, so Isolina had ordered some roses, and now she wanted to add sprigs of ivy and boxwood. Bouquets complete, they followed the path that led to the fountain under the linden. To Brianda, both Anels House and the surroundings seemed just as gloomy as they had the previous afternoon. The morning light only managed to accentuate the decrepitude.

"Where does this lead?" she asked, pointing to the wooded path she'd spotted the day before.

"It goes up to the mountain forests. It's the old livestock trail, and it goes all the way to France."

"Sounds beautiful. We should take a walk there sometime."

Isolina wrinkled her nose. "I don't know if that's such a good idea."

"Is it dangerous?" laughed Brianda. "Full of wild animals?"

"Not exactly."

"Then what?"

"I don't know how to explain. There's a kind of sinister legend about that place. They say it's inhabited by a strange presence and anyone who goes there is never the same again."

"I didn't know you were superstitious!" Brianda exclaimed. "Don't tell me there's also a spooky castle where the local children disappear to."

"Something like that."

"Seriously?" Brianda had been joking, but now she shuddered. "Wait a second. I just remembered—you never let us go there. You said there was a cliff or something."

"Actually, there's a sort of mansion, burnt and in ruins—the old Lubich Manor I mentioned yesterday. I've been near there a few times, collecting firewood with Colau, but it gives me the creeps."

"Does it belong to anyone?"

"Another mystery. Everyone thought it was abandoned, but about four months ago, a man turned up at town hall with the deed, saying he wanted to restore it."

Brianda felt a shiver run down her spine.

"What do you know about him?"

"Not much. I heard he hired builders from down in Aiscle and a couple from here—they practically live on site. They say he's a foreigner and not very friendly, but he pays well."

"And apparently not bothered by strange presences," Brianda added.

As they continued their walk, Brianda thought about what Isolina had said. The stuff about a ghostly presence was stupid, but the mysterious stranger intrigued her. She wondered how a foreigner could have ended up in a place like this. Maybe he was running away from something too, or maybe he was a rich playboy looking to set up his private paradise. Then again, Tiles sure didn't seem like much of a paradise. The landscape could be described as beautiful, but it was indisputably harsh and inhospitable. Not to mention, even though her aunt swore this was a mild autumn, Brianda couldn't get warm and could not imagine how anyone survived winter here. The stranger must have chosen this remote place in order to hide from the world.

The sharp squeak of a rusty gate made her jump and, all of a sudden, Brianda thought she was entering another world.

Like an oasis in the desert, a copse of tall pines gave shelter to a small plot surrounded by dark stone walls covered in moss. The graves and vaults were neatly laid out, the former on the ground and the latter against the walls. Weaving through stone crosses with engraved inscriptions, or iron ones with white-enameled plaques bordered in black, Brianda followed Isolina to the family crypt, a small building with a double sloping roof and five niches that looked like worn marble windows. On the upper part was the inscription "Property of House of Anels."

While Isolina removed the old flowers and washed out the vases, preparing them for the fresh bouquets, Brianda busied herself reading the inscriptions on the crypt. She spotted the names of her grandparents and an uncle who'd died as a child, but she was ashamed that she didn't even know her great-grandparents' names. *Human memory is so short,* she thought. Its scope did not span more than a century.

When Isolina finished, she stood in front of the graves, blessed herself, smiled at her niece, and asked, "Shall we pray?"

"Yes, of course." But Brianda was at a loss. She could not remember the last time she'd prayed.

She imitated her aunt's pose and concentrated on following the woman as well as she could, adopting a murmur to the rhythm of the Our Father and only pronouncing clearly those words that finished sentences: "heaven . . . name . . . come . . . earth . . . heaven . . . day . . . bread . . . trespasses . . . those . . . us . . . temptation . . . evil . . . amen."

Isolina's prayers included a Hail Mary, a Glory Be, and a Salve, the last of which Brianda had problems mouthing along to. With the prayers finally finished, they cleaned up the remains of the dead flowers and piled them by the gate. Just then they saw Neli, flowers in her arms as well. Isolina didn't seem surprised, and Brianda wondered if the task of tending the graves fell upon the women of each house, whether they were from the village or not.

Neli greeted them with a smile.

"Brianda, hi! How was your first night in Anels House?"

"Good, thanks."

How odd, Brianda thought. Neli didn't want to know about her first night in Tiles but her night in that house.

Neli turned to Isolina.

"Your niece rescued me yesterday."

"Yes, she told me!" said Isolina. She pointed to Neli's flowers. "It's that time of year, huh? If you want, we'll wait for you."

"If you'd like. I'm not afraid to be alone in a graveyard, but I appreciate the offer."

She went through the gate and returned a few minutes later. Brianda squinted with confusion when she saw that Neli still carried some fresh flowers.

"I like to visit another place as well," Neli explained. "It's around back. Would you like to come with me?"

Brianda saw Isolina's hesitation. Was her aunt in a hurry, or did she not like the place? Curious, Brianda decided to follow Neli, and Isolina was left with no choice but to follow.

The path led to a series of steps worn into the rock. Brianda had to support herself against the graveyard wall. When she turned the corner, the first thing she noticed was a huge pile of stones, most of them black: the remains of a building. A few steps away were more than a dozen solid flagstones, some with stone crosses, either standing or partially buried.

"Why are these back here?" Brianda asked.

"Nobody knows," Isolina answered. "The original site included the graveyard where we were and a church, but as you can see, it burned down." She pointed to the graves. "These have always been here. Colau says that, for some reason, they couldn't be buried in holy ground. Maybe they committed suicide. It's strange, though. If they didn't want to bury them in holy ground, why would they put up crosses?"

Out of the blue, Brianda began to feel odd. She started shivering and felt a slight pressure on her chest. She walked between some of the old gray graves partially covered by a fine film of dark green mold. On several of them, she made out engravings of a number or letter.

"It makes me sad that no one remembers them," said Neli as she placed a handful of flowers beside each stone.

Brianda nodded in silence. It really was a beautiful gesture.

Then she noticed one grave set apart from the others. Drawn to it, she knelt down and brushed her right hand over the inscription, feeling a little buzz of energy in her fingertips. Using her nails, she began to scrape the moss from the letters like plaster from an old wall. She didn't know if it was curiosity or something else that compelled her, but now she used both hands.

Slowly, three words came into view.

Brianda moaned.

It was the phrase from her dreams, now complete.

Omnia mecum porto.

She read the words, then she fainted.

◆ ◆ ◆

When she came to, the first thing she saw was her aunt's anguished face.

"Brianda, darling." Isolina stroked her cheeks. "What happened? You fainted just like that, no warning. How do you feel?"

Brianda's mouth felt dry. She did a mental checklist of her body and noticed nothing out of the ordinary. She sat up slowly, supporting her back against a hard surface. She turned and found herself leaning on the cross above the stone where the inscription was written. She was sitting right on it. Her hands remembered the shape of the letters. She closed her eyes and took a deep breath.

Had her dreams been some sort of premonition? Or could it maybe just have been a memory? She might have come here as a child, even if she didn't remember.

"Are you feeling better?" Neli asked.

Brianda nodded and opened her eyes. Neli was looking at her in a curious, tender, and oddly understanding way.

"I saw you touch something and fall. Perhaps I shouldn't have brought you here. Some people get bad vibes."

"Must have been low blood sugar," Brianda lied, remembering a phrase she'd heard once from a work colleague. She had never fainted in her life, and she was frightened, but she didn't want to try to explain.

"Did you feel anything unusual?" asked Neli.

"No. What do you mean?"

"In some places, the graves warn you if something is going to happen."

"Don't say those things, Neli!" Isolina reproached her, shivering. She took her niece's elbow. "Can you stand up?"

With the help of both women, Brianda stood. She stared at her feet, which covered the Latin words. For an instant, it seemed as if the soles of her shoes were burning. A gust of wind hit her face. She raised her eyes and saw black clouds darkening the horizon.

"That doesn't look good," said Isolina. "We'd better get home. Neli, did you bring your car?"

"No, I walked. It didn't look like there'd be a storm."

"Well then, you'd better come to my house. It's closer."

Brianda allowed herself to be guided down the rocky descent to the dirt path that began at the graveyard gates, marking the way for the inhabitants of Tiles, from their houses to their final resting place.

Thunder sounded in the distance and again seconds later. The clouds closed in at a dizzying speed.

The women quickened their pace. Just before the fork to Lubich, they heard horse's hooves. They stopped short, and a magnificent black animal ridden by a man in dark clothes galloped past in a flash.

"Watch out!" exclaimed Isolina, pulling Brianda back to protect her. "Did you see that?" She turned to Neli. "Do you know who that was?"

"It looked like the new owner of Lubich. I've seen him a couple of times in the bar. He sometimes comes down on horseback. Actually, my husband says he goes everywhere on horseback."

"Well, he's as rude as they say!" complained Isolina. "A little closer and he would have knocked us all down!"

Brianda kept her eyes fixed on the dark figure now disappearing down the overgrown trail. It was her dream exactly. First the inscription, now the horse . . . She fought back tears. Was she taking a walk with her aunt or still under the covers back home in Madrid?

She felt some drops wetting her cheeks, first softly and then harder until the wind suddenly stopped and the heavens discharged their ire in the form of a downpour so hard they couldn't see past the ends of their outstretched arms.

When the trio finally reached Anels House, they were soaked. Their hair was matted in dripping clumps, and their clothes hung heavily from their bodies. On their way to dry off, a deafening drumming of raindrops on the roof told them that the storm was getting even worse.

But just a little while later, as unexpectedly as it had begun, the rain ceased.

"In all the years I've lived here, I've never seen anything like that before," said Neli, wearing a dry white blouse and simple skirt borrowed from Isolina.

After hot showers, they were now sipping tea in front of the fire. Neli and Brianda sat on a bench facing Isolina. After lurking for a while in the sitting room, Luzer at his heels, Colau finally had come in to sit with his wife, which surprised Brianda. They had told him about her fainting, and he'd suggested going to see the doctor in Aiscle, but Brianda insisted she felt perfectly fine. Besides, she suspected Colau was just saying it to apologize to Isolina for his initial rudeness to Brianda. Now he seemed annoyed by Neli's unexpected visit.

From the large windows, located on either side of the fireplace, they looked out on a panoramic view of the sunny evening in the valley, which now shone clean and innocent after the unexpected bath.

"I've lived in Tiles my whole life, and even I don't understand what happened today," said Isolina. "And there was no warning on the TV either. This place is famous for its storms, but nothing predicted this one. Not even the rheumatism in my knee, which gets it right more often than the weatherman."

Neli smiled at Brianda. "Maybe you fainted because of the drop in air pressure. Just before a big storm, the animals can feel it and they go quiet."

Brianda laughed. "I didn't imagine I was so sensitive."

"Plus, there is something unnerving about that old part of the graveyard," said Isolina. "Neli must be one of the few people who isn't afraid to go there."

"I don't know," Brianda replied. "I don't usually scare so easily." But was that even true anymore? She thought of her panic attacks and the visit to Roberto, her embarrassing confession that she was consumed by a fear of dying.

"It's the living we should be scared of," declared Neli, "not the dead."

Brianda noticed her uncle eyeing the young woman skeptically. Colau opened his mouth to say something, but seemed to change his mind. Finally, rubbing his chin with one of his enormous hands, he said, "So you were touching one of the graves."

"I was trying to read the inscription," explained Brianda, grateful for the opportunity to ask the question whose answer she longed for. "You know Latin, don't you?"

Her uncle raised an eyebrow.

"It said *omnia mecum porto*." Brianda would never forget those three words.

Colau's face darkened as if he'd heard some terrible news. His right hand flinched on the arm of his chair. Lying at his feet, Luzer raised his head, alert.

"What, something you actually don't know?" Isolina teased.

Colau lit a cigarette. After two drags that seemed to take forever, he answered, his eyes fixed on the ground.

"More or less it means, 'I take all with me.'"

Brianda wondered if Neli had noticed Colau's reaction. He seemed almost angry, but in his eyes she saw worry and something like pain, as if the translation had come not from his brain but from his gut.

After a long silence, Isolina said, "What a beautiful epitaph. And very true."

Brianda wondered who was buried there and why anyone would choose that phrase. Most of all, she was desperate to know how much that "all" might include.

The sound of a car horn made them all jump. Luzer barked.

"It must be Jonas," said Neli.

"Why don't you ask him to come in for coffee?" Isolina suggested.

"It's late, Isolina," grumbled Colau.

"Perhaps another day," said Neli, getting to her feet. "The kids are waiting for me. Thanks again for the clothes. I'll get them back to you soon."

Brianda walked her to the car and met Jonas, a man of around forty, with very short hair and a face that was handsome despite the many wrinkles that outlined his expressive eyes.

The women said their good-byes with a kiss on the cheek. They had only met twice, but after what had happened, Brianda felt a closeness bordering on kinship. In Neli's insightful eyes, she saw the exact thing she needed: understanding.

"Come over to my house whenever you want," Neli suggested. "I spend a lot of the day in the church. If you want, you can see my work there. Then, I'm free from five until the children get home."

Yes, thought Brianda.

Perhaps one day she would open her heart to Neli.

5.

Hunched under her thick coat, Brianda wandered through the lonely streets of Aiscle, waiting for her aunt to finish her shopping. The streets were barely lit by the dying sunlight of the last day of October; the cold seemed to dampen all noises and to paralyze her senses. She imagined the scarce autumn birds refusing to sing, the disoriented flies searching for a crack to sneak into a house, and the lifeless leaves of the trees falling in silence onto the damp earth and dreary grass.

She reached a small square surrounded by low buildings built over a long porch of consecutive arches. A spotted cat lazily stretched in one home's vaulted doorway; two old men chatted with their hands resting on the crook of their walking sticks; a young woman helped a child push his own stroller. Brianda watched them all as if from far away, as though they were in a silent film. The cat did not mew. The men did not laugh. The stroller wheels did not squeak.

She sat on a faded wooden bench and watched.

But not even these quiet scenes of village life brought her any peace. If anything, the trip was making her anxiety worse. If it weren't for Isolina and her new friend, Neli, Brianda felt like she'd be falling apart as badly as Anels House.

She decided to call Esteban, having only sent him short text messages the last few days. She missed him terribly but knew how busy his weeks were. Besides, she hadn't had much to say. She had considered telling him about the inscription in Latin, how her dream had been a premonition, but ultimately she decided against it. And hearing about her fainting would only make him worry. The purpose of this trip was to unplug and rest, not complicate things. Besides, she didn't know how to explain her strange sense that something here was against her. It wasn't just her uncle's grave disposition, which had gotten even worse since the day of the storm, or Luzer's low growls whenever she got too close. An amorphous, dismal foreboding was unfolding inside her. Who could possibly understand that?

Despite her reticence, she couldn't stop thinking about Esteban all the time . . . and about that man on a magnificent black horse in the rain.

She had not been able to see his face. She wondered whether he was old or young, tall or short, dark or fair. He must be strong to handle an animal like that . . . she knew that much.

A text message from Esteban brought her attention back where it belonged. He said he was in a long meeting and couldn't take her call. He'd be out that night, but they would talk tomorrow, and he missed her.

Brianda sighed, not so much from disappointment as from the feeling that it didn't matter whether or not they talked.

This profound apathy startled her. Esteban was the man she had decided to spend her life with. Since moving in together, they'd only ever been apart for short work trips, and the joy of reunion had always led to a long session in the bedroom. She thought about their last time together, and her eyes filled with tears. Why had he felt like a stranger? And why was she so unhappy, whether at home in Madrid or out in this godforsaken corner of the country? What could she do to fix it?

A car horn broke the oppressive quiet, and she heard her aunt's voice calling. She couldn't remember how she'd gotten to the square, so she had to follow the echo of her own name through the narrow streets until she reached the spot where they'd parked. Isolina was piling shopping bags into the trunk.

"Expecting visitors?" Brianda laughed. "That looks like enough to feed an army."

"I still have to get the marzipan Saint's Bones for tomorrow." Isolina pointed in front of her. "This is a marvelous pastry shop."

Brianda smiled as they walked toward the old shop. Her mother and her aunt were very different, but they agreed on one thing: they celebrated all the feast days with their traditional sweets and pastries, not to mention a few new ones invented by the big stores. So, in her family, after nougat and marzipan at Christmas, a year began with a ring-shaped Three Kings cake and was followed by San Valero cake, Saint Agatha's breast-shaped sweets, Saint Valentine's chocolates, buns and biscuits for Saint Joseph, Palm Sunday sweets, fritters and chocolate figurines at Easter, Mother's Day cake, pastries for Corpus Christi, Saint Daniel, Saint Robert, and the Assumption in August, finally finishing off with pumpkin and squash pies and the marzipan Saint's Bones. Add to this the family's birthday and anniversary celebrations and someone could say Brianda's life had been sugar coated.

Recalling her mother's and Isolina's continuous efforts to please their families, Brianda felt a twinge of nostalgia. She didn't know why exactly. She hadn't lost anything yet. Her stay here was temporary. Soon she'd return to her normal life. Back to work. Back with Esteban. She would enjoy the things that used to make her happy. She would again desire Esteban's hands on her body. Maybe someday they would plan an unforgettable wedding and undertake the adventure of being parents. They would raise beautiful children whom they would spoil and with whom they'd celebrate all the feast days. They would relive their own childhoods, from their first birthday cakes when they applauded with chubby fingers and were asked to blow out the candles over and over again.

She felt dizzy. The damn symptoms had snuck up on her out of nowhere. The feeling of insecurity . . . the trembling in her hands . . . the buzzing in her ears . . . the feeling of being about to faint.

"Why the face?" Isolina asked, frowning. "You're so pale."

Isolina guided her to a nearby bench. She took her hand and spoke to her in a gentle but firm voice: "Relax and take a deep breath in. Now hold your breath and count to four. One, two, three, four. Now let the air out slowly through the mouth, very slowly. Good. And again. Breathe in, hold, let it out slow." She waited until Brianda opened her eyes. "Better?"

Brianda nodded in surprise. She actually was.

"Who taught you that?"

"I learned it years ago in yoga."

Brianda squeezed her aunt's hand in gratitude.

"It's not your blood sugar again, is it?" Isolina's eyes were full of tender assuredness. "Could you be pregnant by any chance?"

Brianda shook her head as her eyes filled with tears. If only. Then, at least, there'd be a logical explanation.

"I don't know what's wrong with me. A few months ago, for no reason, I just started having anxiety attacks. I'm fine one minute, and the next it's like I'm dying. They gave me pills, but maybe the dosage isn't high enough."

Isolina patted her hand.

"I've known many people in your situation. I myself—" She stopped herself, but too late.

"You?! Why?"

"Nothing I can say will give you comfort. Whatever it is, you'll have to sort it out yourself."

"But what were you anxious about?"

Isolina sighed.

"I had a hard time deciding whether to stay in Tiles or follow your mother to the city. Then Colau of Cuyls appeared . . ." Her look darkened. "Then children didn't come . . ." She crossed her hands in her lap. "Anyway, everyone has their story. Don't worry about it. You look like you're feeling better now. Are you?"

Brianda nodded. She felt completely normal, if normal meant this shadow version of herself. She thought about her aunt's confession, her regret over not having a baby. She'd always assumed it was by choice, especially since her parents had mentioned that Colau didn't like children. Selfishly, she was a little bit jealous; at least Isolina had a tangible reason for her sadness.

Her aunt stood up, a determined look on her face.

"And now we'll buy that marzipan. Did you know that in the old days they baked Saint's Bones to make the long night of the dead easier? Everyone used to stand vigil all night while the church bells tolled, and they needed the extra calories."

Brianda shivered, imagining the funereal peal of the bells echoing through the frozen streets.

She followed her aunt into the warm bakery and spontaneously bought some pastries for Neli.

Brianda parked her car beside the church, smiling briefly at a group of curious women. Neli's house was easy to pick out because it was the only one whose façade was white rather than bare stone. She went up the steps and raised the long, clunky knocker. No answer.

A woman with short straw-colored hair and wearing a printed housecoat, shouted kindly, "She must be in the church! If you want, we'll get her for you."

"Don't worry about it, thanks," said Brianda, not wanting to have a conversation about who she was.

Several long seconds passed. Brianda was sure the women were analyzing her gestures, her dress, and the package she carried, hoarding judgments for later. She was about to retreat to Anels House when the door opened and the expression on Neli's face changed from distraction to joy.

"Did I catch you at a bad time?" Brianda asked as she handed Neli the box of pastries.

"I was doing some things upstairs," answered Neli, accepting the gift. "Nothing that can't wait. What's this?"

"Just a little thank-you for your help in the graveyard."

"You shouldn't have!" Hearing her own words, she burst out laughing. "It's a cliché, but I mean it. I was happy to help. Would you like to come in for tea?" She laughed again. "You can tell we don't get many visitors. All my small talk seems to come from movies. Please, don't tell me I have a beautiful house."

"But it's true!" Brianda laughed. "You have a very nice house."

Neli and her husband clearly liked antiques. Brianda saw two wooden chests, a copper cauldron filled with dry flowers, and old farm tools decorating the walls. Down the hall was a wooden table covered with little decorative touches and baskets of dried flowers floating above a sea of mail. A plasterwork arch led to a welcoming sitting room.

"Ugh. It's impossible to keep this place clean with the children around. They got home from school a little while ago, messed everything up, and ran off to a friend's birthday party. And when they get back, they'll still have more than enough energy to wear out their father and me!"

Brianda liked the fact that Neli didn't waste her time collecting the Legos, books, game controllers, and pencil cases strewn all over the place. Of course, Brianda would have tidied it up, but the clutter made her feel welcome, as if Neli were opening her world to Brianda without fear of judgment, like they'd been sharing this space for centuries.

"I love sitting here in the evening and having a quiet cup of tea. What kind would you like? I have lots of flavors. Or would you prefer coffee?"

"Tea is fine." Brianda was a coffee addict, but she was eager to be agreeable.

"Red berries? I make the mix myself."

"Great."

Neli headed for the kitchen and Brianda looked out the big window. There was a paved patio with flowerpots, a wooden swing, and a wrought-iron table. A small gate connected it to the fields beyond and, to the right, there was an enormous walnut tree and the back wall of the church.

"So, this was your husband's family's house . . . ," she said when Neli returned with a tray.

Neli nodded.

"His grandparents left Tiles soon after the Civil War. Jonas's dad used to come up occasionally, but now he mostly stays in the lowlands. When we decided to change our lives, we bought out his cousins' share of the house and plunged ourselves into renovating it."

"And what do you do for a living?"

"I'm a restorer, specializing in old paintings, and Jonas has a small construction company. He works for private individuals and the local towns. What about you?"

"I'm an engineer." Brianda couldn't think of anything else to say about her job. She envied Neli's passion. If only she had half the woman's vitality. "And neither of you has ever regretted the decision to move out here?"

"No. We miss some things from the city, but I think we found the place we want to see our children grow up. Why do you ask? Are you thinking about doing the same?" She tilted her head. "It's hard to imagine you living in Anels House forever."

"Are you saying that because of me or the house? The day we met, you were surprised when I told you who my aunt and uncle were. And the next day, you asked me how I had slept there."

Neli was surprised by Brianda's insight and candor. She was silent for a few moments, unsure how to proceed. She had always liked to observe people and her intuition was rarely wrong. Brianda seemed intelligent and charming, but Neli sensed negative vibrations. If she could take a Kirlian photo of her, her aura colors would certainly show blue, violet, and maybe some gold. Behind the pleasant façade, Neli saw a disoriented woman in search of spiritual relief. She wondered if she would find it in Anels House.

"Your aunt Isolina is lovely," she said at last. "And I don't like gossip. But if you are going to be here a while, you should know that Colau is not well liked."

"Do you know why?"

"I only know what people say, and I don't feel comfortable talking about it. It's your family. Also, Colau has always been polite to me, and Isolina seems happy with him. That says enough, don't you think? We all have our peculiarities."

"For that very reason, you should tell me what they say. It can't be that bad."

Neli hurriedly poured some more tea. Brianda kept quiet, staring at the woman's flushed face until she finally gave in.

"It seems that, until this generation, Anels House was pleasant and well looked after. The villagers remember your aunt and your mother as two very happy girls. But everything changed when Colau appeared. Your grandparents considered it a punishment that the last descendent of the House of Cuyls won one of their daughters, but they died before changing their will in favor of your mother. They saw him as lazy, reclusive, and more interested in his books than the house and the land. The house he was born in lies in ruins, and he doesn't care about keeping

Anels alive either. There's supposed to be a curse. The old people say that wherever a Cuyls goes, life ends."

Brianda frowned.

"See what I mean?" said Neli. "I shouldn't have said anything."

"I'm not angry. I'm amazed. You talk about houses like living things that are born, grow up, and die in tandem with their inhabitants. The houses are so powerful, it's like they replace last names. Here, I'm Brianda of Anels and you're Neli of—"

"Nabara." Neli smiled. "Houses here have nice names. By the way, Neli is short for a weird old name that's common in my family. How does House of Nelida sound?" She made a face. "Better than Lubich, at least, which means something like wolf."

Brianda was quiet, mulling over what Neli had told her about Colau's house.

"That thing about the curse . . . It's so ridiculous. I'm surprised my grandparents believed in such things."

Neli shrugged.

"People's beliefs are a mystery. More tea?"

"No, thanks." Brianda smiled. "In fact, I need to use the bathroom."

"Oh! Um, of course. The one down here is broken, but you can use the one in my bedroom." She led her to the foot of the stairs and pointed. "It's at the end."

Brianda noticed that Neli was blushing. Maybe she was uncomfortable having a near stranger in her bedroom, or embarrassed about not having cleaned in there either. Brianda hesitated, but she really did need to go, so she headed up, trying not to look around.

Entering the bedroom, she spotted a door that was, indeed, the bathroom. She saw the light switch outside the door and turned it on.

On her way out, Brianda felt around for the switch to turn off the light but turned on another by mistake. Light came from a pretty little lamp on a shelf that was covered in muslin. Her eyes could not help settling on the varied collection of objects. There were strange ornaments, statues, candles, small glass jars, a bowl of water, a bowl of what might have been salt, little stones, an incense burner, a carved boxwood cane, a five-pointed star in a circle on a leather-bound book, a knife, and a goblet that made her think of the word "chalice."

So, this was why Neli had blushed.

Brianda examined the knife. It was a double-edged dagger with a black handle decorated with astrological symbols and runes.

"It's an *athame*."

Brianda jumped when she heard Neli's voice. In a flash, she set the knife back where she'd found it. Her cheeks burned.

"I'm so sorry. I didn't mean to snoop!"

But Neli didn't look angry.

"Do you know what this is?" Neli asked tentatively.

Brianda shook her head.

"It's an altar," explained Neli.

"That's what I thought, but I don't see any images of the Virgin or saints, no rosary beads." Her voice sounded too cheerful, forced. She hoped she hadn't upset her new friend.

"That's because it's a Wiccan altar," Neli said, picking up the dagger.

"The *athame* is used to trace the circle of power and direct the energy. It represents the masculine." She took the chalice. "And this is the smaller version of a cauldron." She looked for a sign of recognition on Brianda's part that did not come, so she continued, "It represents the feminine. Together they evoke the act of procreation as a universal symbol of creation."

Brianda listened in puzzlement. On one hand, it all sounded vaguely familiar, maybe from a movie she'd seen or a book she'd read. On the other, she was taken aback to discover that Neli had such weird interests. She wondered whether she would have felt the same if they had been images of Catholic saints. A part of her wanted to end the conversation and leave, but an inner voice urged her to learn more.

Neli set the objects back in their places and pointed to the symbol on the book.

"This is a pentacle. Our symbol of faith." Her finger stopped at the top right point. "Water: symbol of the cycle of life. The liquid of the maternal womb and the tears of death, emotion." She pointed to the bottom right. "Fire: passion, impetus, the part of our being that reason wants to overthrow." She continued to the bottom left. "Earth: the mother, the food that makes us grow." She moved up to the top left. "Air: thought, mind, reason." And she finished at the top center point. "The spirit: the ethereal, the eternal. Spiritual love. Our souls."

A long silence followed, a magical pause that ended when Brianda realized that Neli was staring at her, waiting for a signal of whether or not to continue. She sighed.

"All this sounds like . . . I don't know. Ghost stories, magic. I'm not sure which words to use. It sounds to me like"—she feigned a shiver of terror—"like witchcraft, like—" *Nonsense*, she was about to say.

"Wicca. And that's because I am a Wiccan," Neli said.

"What does that mean?"

"I don't know if you're ready to hear that . . . yet."

Neli's direct gaze and frank smile showed that she was being serious. Brianda was speechless. First the curse on her uncle's house and now this. She needed to get away. Her impression of Neli had changed completely. They'd had such a pleasant conversation downstairs, but now it seemed like the woman was not right in the head. And to think that she had considered opening up her heart to her!

Voices from downstairs revealed that Neli's family had arrived—perfect cover for Brianda's exit.

They went down to the hall to greet Jonas, his overalls covered in white dust, as well as the two boys. They had unruly brown hair, dark eyes, and their mother's fine features. About eight and ten years old, they were loud and lively, telling their mother all about the birthday party while asking Brianda a thousand questions.

Neli took advantage of the commotion to fetch Brianda's purse from the sitting room and slip a small white pouch into it. Then she accompanied her to the door to say good-bye.

"On Saturdays and holidays, some of us get together in the bar by the gas station," she said. "Sometimes Isolina comes along . . ."

Brianda understood that, with the invitation, Neli was trying to get back to where they'd been before her discovery. But she wasn't sure how to feel. She quickly said her good-byes and headed to the car.

Neli leaned against the closed door for a few minutes. The previous night, to the light of a sky-blue candle, she had filled the little pouch that Brianda now carried with a pinch of sea salt, a sprig of rosemary, a touch of cinnamon, and a red rose petal. Then she added the hair she'd pulled off Brianda's head when they first met. It was a good-luck charm to protect her body and soul. She had prayed to all the gods of goodness that they would not abandon Brianda and that evil would not torment her.

Because, unless every one of her faculties had deserted her, Neli was sure the young woman from Anels House had a long and tortuous path ahead.

6.

It was a few moments before Brianda's eyes adjusted to the darkness of the damp church. She heard the monotonous murmur of the parishioners, who were waiting for the priest to leave the sacristy and start six o'clock mass. In front of her, Isolina was looking around for a pew. There was some space in the one closest to the door. The congregation fell silent as they sat down. A woman nearest to Colau furtively slid down to the far end of the bench.

Brianda shifted uncomfortably. People turned their heads to stare at her and then whispered to one another. She regretted having come. She wasn't religious but hadn't wanted to be rude by staying home on the feast of All Saints, when mass would surely be a social occasion in a place like Tiles. She'd heard Isolina telling Colau that not even he could miss mass today or on Christmas. But now Brianda wanted to flee. She scanned the crowd for Neli's red hair, but didn't see her.

She looked at her watch. Still fifteen minutes to go before the start of the ceremony. She didn't understand why they had to be there so early. A woman went up to the altar and began reciting the rosary. The voices came in a soft, intermittent hum that acquired a special resonance as it echoed off the vaulted central nave and the side chapels filled with the images of saints, their gazes lost toward the heavens. The woman prayed and the congregation responded, but instead of relaxing her, the repetition of "ora pro nobis" pounded painfully in Brianda's chest.

She slid her gaze to a small chapel to her right and an object caught her eye. On the cold stone of a narrow altar stood a beautiful Virgin, delicately carved in wood, holding a curly-haired child who was missing an arm. She could make out the perfect folds in the Virgin's clothes and the blank expression on her face. From a thin leather string around her neck hung a pretty, tiny, ancient-looking key.

Isolina leaned close to her niece. "You should have seen the state she was in a few years ago," she whispered. "If it weren't for Neli, she'd be dust by now, what with the woodworm."

"It's gorgeous," said Brianda, admiring Neli's work. "Has it always been here?"

"Jonas found it when he was looking for old bits among the ruins of the old church, the one you saw behind the graveyard. The stones had formed a dome around her, as if protecting her. Don't tell me that's not a miracle. We don't know when the church burned down; it must have been before they built this one at the beginning of the seventeenth century. Anyway, the poor thing was just lying there with her little key around her neck."

"Can they tell what century it's from?"

"Around the sixteenth, I heard."

Brianda marveled at the great changes that had occurred, the history that had passed before the Virgin's empty gaze. She bowed her head to hide the tears that filled her eyes. Again. She loathed being so sensitive now. There was no place left where she could just relax and be at peace.

"A while ago, some people wanted to take her to a museum," added Isolina, "and we were just up in arms. Now I don't think anyone would dare deprive Tiles of our Virgin. We're a very strong-willed people—which, by the way, is hereditary."

Someone shushed them.

Brianda took her aunt's hint. She smiled gratefully and set herself a goal to try with all her might to get out of this emotional pit. She would learn to master her fear. She would take up yoga, tai chi, meditation, or whatever it took to get off the pills. She would push herself to get out more, make new friends—

Just then, the women sitting in the front rows announced the beginning of mass by screeching the opening hymn: "I also want to be reborn; be happy, for all eternity; and live, with those I loved so much, a never-ending peace . . ."

The priest, a tall man of around forty with a South American accent, gave a sermon about how All Saints was such an important day because it celebrated the perpetual glory the saints enjoyed in heaven and made people want to join them and share in it. He urged the faithful to ask in their prayers for all the saints to defend them, protect them, and intercede for them.

Brianda concentrated on the priest's impeccable rhetoric. His description of eternal Eden—illustrated by a quote from Saint Augustine, who confessed that he would swap all the riches and delights of a million years for one hour in that paradise without pain or suffering—was so vivid that she hoped such a place truly existed.

"To get there," he said, "we must fight like the saints; we must resist our desires and temptations, withstand our trials with faith, patience, resignation, and love. Pain is momentary; the happiness that follows will never end."

Brianda liked that idea. She wanted her pain to disappear with the same speed it had come. She wanted to be content, the way she'd always been, and she wanted to share it with Esteban.

In a loud and clear voice, the priest asked, "When we are at death's door, what will our feelings be? Will we have been slack, weak, and negligent? Or will we deserve heaven, deserve to enjoy paradise for all eternity?" He paused so that those present could examine their souls. "Will we be satisfied or will we wish we had lived in a different way?"

Brianda frowned. She wondered if she would like to live in a different way. Looking around, she wondered how many others were pondering the same. The old people, did they feel satisfied or regretful now that their final hour was approaching? Were Isolina and Colau happy?

She continued with her reflections while the ceremony proceeded with the celebration of the Eucharist. When the priest took the chalice in his hands, Brianda could not help but recall the peculiar altar in Neli's bedroom, and she wondered what she would be doing at that moment.

Communion was beginning. The faithful approached the altar to receive the bread and wine while the women in front sang another high-pitched hymn: "I want to be, my beloved Lord, like clay in the potter's hands. Take my life, make it new. I want to be a new vessel . . ."

Brianda recalled the words of the fortune-teller in the bar. She had said Brianda would undertake a journey and that her life needed to change. How had she known? She closed her eyes and let the words of the hymn resonate in her heart. Start from zero. A new vessel. A new life.

Just then, she was taken over by a strange feeling of unreality. The altar, the walls, the people, and the priest began to blur, as if someone were rubbing them with a cloth doused in turpentine. She heard voices, but couldn't make out words. She couldn't understand why it felt like she was outside her body, or how she knew that Brianda was that emaciated, young, oddly dressed woman with very long hair who someone was pointing to and shouting at from the altar.

She did not know why she was being shouted at.

She had done nothing wrong.

Dozens of blank yet hostile faces turned toward her. She clenched her fists, trying not to break out crying in front of them all. She felt a deep fear, a certainty that she was going to die at that very instant. She had to escape, run, flee . . .

But she had done nothing wrong!

Someone grabbed her and every muscle tensed up.

"Brianda, darling." She heard Isolina's voice.

Brianda was stunned. People were returning to their seats after receiving communion and nobody was looking at her. It must have been a vision, or maybe a hallucination. She wondered if that could be a side effect of her pills. Instinctively, she raised her hand to check that her hair was not a long mane reaching her waist. How absurd.

Brianda needed some air to try and recover from the strange experience. Smiling weakly at her aunt, she got up and hurried outside.

Without knowing what to do or where to go, she circled the perimeter of the church. The mist that had covered Beles Peak all day began to dissolve with the coming of night, extending itself first like spilled liquid and then becoming smoke before disappearing. The stillness, the silence, and the cold remained, however, as if recognizing the day's dedication to the dead. The land oozed dampness.

A soft voice reached her. It was coming from the back patio of the house beside the church.

Neli's house.

Brianda was not at all sure she wanted to see Neli again, but the voice she heard was too strange to ignore. It was a uniform, insistent, hypnotic chanting. She crept closer and positioned herself behind an enormous walnut tree, hoping that it and the twilight would hide her. An intense smell of pine and vanilla incense wafted over to her. She peeked out and saw Neli, wrapped in a dark shawl, her long hair loose, tracing a circle on the ground around a small table with the black-handled knife she had called an *athame*. She was so close that Brianda was afraid her nervous breathing would betray her.

The small table covered with a dark cloth reminded her of the bedroom altar. She saw apples, pomegranates, nuts, and chrysanthemums.

Smoke from a violet candle danced over a small bowl where a weak fire burned. Neli sat in front of it in a meditation pose. She stayed there with her eyes closed for a few minutes. The weak light of the candles and the fire produced a phantasmagorical effect on her face. Then, she took some papers and burned them in the bowl while murmuring some phrases Brianda couldn't understand. After another silence, she took a small wooden wand, raised her hands and her eyes to the sky, and said in a clear voice, "On this Samhain, I celebrate the memory of my ancestors and those that have preceded me on this path. Lord of the forests, I honor your memory and await your return from the womb of the Goddess. Lady of the Waning Moon, guide my steps in the darkness, protect me, and show me that, just as from the night Light is born, so the eternal cycle is reborn, forever, eternal."

Brianda's jaw dropped. Unless she was very much mistaken, she was witnessing some sort of magic ritual. It was impossible that that word, Wiccan, could refer to anything else. Neli was a witch! She couldn't even get her head around it. She knew there were weird people in the world, but Neli had seemed so friendly and normal. More unsettling still, while Brianda's feelings toward the occult had always been negative, this simple ritual was suggestive and magnetic. She couldn't take her eyes off Neli's serene expression.

Neli cut a slice of apple and taking some pomegranate seeds said, "I offer this food in honor of my ancestors. Their memory endures and their teachings live in me. Blessed were they in their existence and blessed are they in the Land of Eternal Summer. They left this plane for a better one. The physical is not our only reality, and the soul does not perish."

Suddenly, Neli raised a hand to her bosom and shrank back as if she had been stabbed. Her breathing became labored, and she cried out as if in pain. Brianda wanted to rush over and help her but didn't dare. Neli began to shake her head from one side to the other, as though a malignant spirit wanted to take over her body. Then she stopped, opened her eyes, looked around with a confused expression, and finally focused her attention on the walnut tree.

Brianda had no time to hide. She stood dead still, not breathing, with Neli's deep and piercing gaze directly on her. The leaves on the tree stopped moving. Time stopped.

Neli showed no shock, anger, or shame. On the contrary, there was power and certainty in her eyes. She smiled, closed her eyes, made a slight gesture of assent, and crossing her hands over her belly, returned to a calm position of repose.

Brianda ran as fast as she could, unnerved by what she had seen, ashamed to have been caught spying, and upset by the woman's reaction. She had felt the intensity of Neli's gaze running through her, her mind and her heart; thinking about it, recalling that sensation even if only for a second, made her terribly afraid.

She turned the corner of the church and leaned against the damp gray wall to catch her breath.

"Are you all right?" asked a dry voice.

Colau was so close that she jumped back, intimidated by the annoyance written on his big, stolid features.

"Your aunt sent me to look for you," said Colau. "She was worried that you were feeling unwell again."

She thought she noted a twinge of sarcasm in that "again."

"I'm fine. I just needed some air."

Colau scrutinized her face and frowned, but he said nothing. He turned around and headed toward the church with his heavy gait.

Brianda followed him while an insistent little voice began to repeat over and over in her head the catchy verse of the opening hymn.

She also wanted to be happy, said the voice, so familiar that it could be her own. For all eternity.

◆ ◆ ◆

Most of the parishioners had already left, so at least Brianda didn't have to make small talk standing in the cold and dark outside the church.

"There you are." Isolina welcomed her with a relieved smile.

Brianda repeated the excuse she'd given Colau.

A woman with short straw-colored hair, whom Brianda recognized from the square, came over and invited them to come to the bar. Isolina looked at her husband, who was waiting a few paces away.

"I'm not sure Colau is feeling up to it," she murmured.

"We could drop him at home and come back," Brianda suggested.

She wanted to free herself of everything that was suffocating her even if just for a short while. There was still plenty of time before dinner. She knew she would find the evening in the house long, Colau's silence uncomfortable, and Luzer's growls maddening.

Isolina gave her a puzzled look, but she agreed.

After taking Colau home, they drove to the bar in Brianda's car.

"Lots of noise and people make Colau tired," said Isolina.

"Is there anything that doesn't make him tired?" Brianda replied without thinking. After several days at Anels House, she understood that the man was a true loner, but hearing her aunt defend and excuse him irritated her. Still, she regretted her lack of tact. "I'm sorry. I know he's a solitary person; it's just—"

"You don't understand why I put up with him." Isolina finished the sentence for her. She let her eyes wander over the dark fields. Then, she fixed her hair nervously and turned toward her niece. "He wasn't always like this. And it wasn't his fault he was born in a place everybody hated."

"Do you mean Cuyls House?" Brianda didn't want to reveal what she had heard from Neli. "Why?"

"I don't know, and I don't care to. Villages are like that. Something must have happened in the past that marked his family forever. I suppose every new heir to the manor houses was warned to be wary of the Cuylses."

"Didn't your parents tell you anything?"

Isolina shook her head. "They just rejected him. But they were wrong. He has always been good to me."

Brianda raised an eyebrow. She was unconvinced.

"They warned me that the same as had happened to previous generations of the House of Cuyls, according to the oldest villagers, would happen to me," continued Isolina. "Each generation had several children, but only the first male survived. The same happened to Colau's family, but as you see, nothing like that has happened to us. They rejected him due to stupid yarns like that one."

"You said that Colau wasn't always like this. What was he like?"

Out of the corner of her eye, she saw Isolina smile sadly.

"As a child, he was clever and charming. He used to chase me through these fields. I remember how he'd catch up and tickle me, and we'd laugh and laugh. Then, when he was ten, his older sister died. A couple of years later, the twins. His mother got pregnant again and had a fifth child, a boy, but he died after just a few months. With each death, Colau grew sadder. He began to hate the house; he told me it felt like an enormous stone coffin. He studied so he wouldn't have to work on the land, and the only reason he didn't leave the village was because I asked him not to. After we got married, he sometimes got a glimmer of his old self back. Until this summer—" She shook her head. "Why am I going on like this? Look, we're here."

Brianda parked in a small lot beside the gas station. Her aunt's explanation did shed light on Colau's gloominess, but she suspected there was something more. Even if he had suffered a lot and didn't get along with people, Brianda was part of the family! And yet he treated her like the enemy—coldly, even with hostility, as if he didn't trust her. Isolina didn't seem to notice how closely he watched Brianda, how he muttered under his breath when she was near. Or was it just her imagination?

◆ ◆ ◆

The only bar in Tiles was a cold place, devoid of charm, and it clearly hadn't been redone in decades. Brianda couldn't remember ever seeing a floor so ugly: yellowed marble slabs interspersed with cement in dire need of a polish. There was a long wooden bar with decorative tiles and a dozen square tables with ratty wicker chairs. The music competed with the tinkling of a pinball machine, a loud television, and the voices of the card players.

Stepping inside, Brianda again felt the unpleasant sensation that unknown faces were scrutinizing her. She wondered whether it had been a good idea to come. And what if she ran into Neli? But a quick glance around confirmed that the redhead wasn't there.

From a table in back, the short-haired woman who had invited them waved Isolina over. Isolina introduced her as Petra. She wore a turtleneck sweater and several gold chains and medallions that she constantly fidgeted with.

Berta, a thin, unkempt woman who owned the bar with her husband, Alberto, came over; Brianda and Isolina ordered tonic waters. Brianda tried to relax and take it all in. The layout of the bar looked simple. The men played cards while the women chatted. After a few minutes, Berta joined them.

"The only person we're missing is Neli," said Berta.

"She won't be long," Petra assured them. "She had her in-laws visiting today to look after the children." She looked up and smiled. "What did I tell you? Here she is."

Brianda shrank in her chair. She wondered how she'd be able to act normal after what she'd seen. To her consternation, Neli sat down right next to her.

"Evening, all," she said. "How are you, Brianda?"

"Fine, thanks," she murmured.

Neli easily joined in the conversation, but Brianda was in turmoil. She had always considered herself an open-minded person, but now she wasn't so sure. It didn't seem fair to reject Neli based on something she didn't even understand. Brianda was worried about people judging her, but here she was rushing to judge Neli.

When the other women were distracted giving advice about life in Tiles to a young Romanian woman named Mihaela, Neli discreetly turned to Brianda.

"This afternoon, did you come to see me about something?"

"I was at mass with my aunt and uncle," she replied nervously. "Then I felt like taking a walk around the church."

"You must have been surprised at what you saw."

"You could say that."

"Yesterday I told you I was a Wiccan and—"

"Yes, and you told me that you didn't know if I was ready for you to explain. Am I ready now?"

"I would have preferred for you to find out differently, but I suppose you've already worked out that I am a witch."

Brianda blinked in confusion. In the twenty-first century, in the postmodern era, in the age of social media, this woman thought of herself as a witch. It was one thing to see costumed clairvoyants on television, or occultists who pretended they could contact the next world, or old-fashioned fortune-tellers like the woman in the bar trying to earn some cash by telling stories about the future. It was quite another, however, for an apparently ordinary woman like Neli, with her work, her husband, and children, to devote herself to casting spells. Brianda remembered the ritual she had witnessed, and shivered. She wondered if Neli would teach her children this doctrine or whatever it was. First the curse on her uncle's house, and now this. She had to get out of this madhouse.

"In another age, they would have burned you for saying that," Brianda joked, not knowing what else to say.

"I know. Thank goodness it's not like that anymore."

"Didn't you tell me you worked in the church? How can you go inside?" Brianda's tone turned cruel. "Whatever, witches don't exist."

"Old women with warts and hooked noses that fly on broomsticks? No, they don't. But witches do. We exist. There are thousands in the world. And I am one."

"So, you tell the future and that sort of thing?"

Neli laughed, but immediately her expression turned solemn.

"I don't. This is much more serious. I practice a neo-pagan religion that is officially recognized in some places. Look, I understand how strange it must sound. In fact, very few people know, so people don't go around telling people." She leaned forward, opened her eyes wide, and put on a silly, guttural voice. "Perhaps I shall initiate you into a coven in the moonlight—"

Loud voices from the card table interrupted them.

"Fuck, Bernardo! Didn't you see I signaled with the jack?" protested a leathery-faced blond-haired young man. "Well, then bring out the ace, man! The game was ours!"

"And where was I supposed to get an ace when all I had was garbage, Zacarias?" the other retorted.

Brianda was afraid for a second there'd be a fight, but the laughter of Neli, Isolina, and Petra, Bernardo's wife, convinced her there was no need to worry.

Once things had settled down, Berta whispered, "Did you see who just came in?"

Amid the commotion, nobody had noticed when the man stationed at the counter had entered the bar.

Several of the women turned their heads so boldly that Brianda thought it patently rude.

The whispers spread to the whole table.

"He hasn't been in for weeks," Berta commented.

"Guess there's a lot of work to do at the mansion," said Petra.

Brianda gave a start. The mansion! Now she could barely resist spinning around to stare.

"Is this man from Tiles?" asked Mihaela in her heavy accent.

"No," Petra replied. "He only arrived a few months ago, though it looks like he's here to stay. He's Italian. My husband told me he's not much for talking. He comes in, asks for what he needs, and that's it. He pays well, however."

"Bernardo is a carpenter," Isolina explained to her niece. "An artist in wood."

Petra smiled contentedly. "In this case, he needs to be an artist—our new neighbor asks for very special things."

"Like what?" Neli wanted to know.

"Things you'd like. Replicas of antiques or restorations of old doors. I can't believe what he's spending on that place!"

Brianda looked over furtively, but several men blocked her view.

"No way could I live there," said Berta, "in the woods out at Lubich."

"Me neither," Isolina admitted. "I don't know what it is about that place." She turned to Brianda. "I don't know if your mother ever told you how, when we were young, the older people lowered their voices when they talked about Lubich. My mother, your grandmother, said that it had something to do with damned Beles Peak and the stories about it."

"What stories?" Brianda asked. "I don't remember her saying anything."

Berta leaned forward. "In my house, they said Beles Peak was a favorite meeting place for witches."

Brianda glanced at Neli, who blushed.

"In mine, they said the same," said Petra, "but it's nonsense. Old wives' tales."

"Well," Isolina began, "I remember my grandmother telling me that sometimes when she went up to forage for herbs in the fields to the west of Beles, she found clothes on the rocks—"

"My great-grandmother foraged for herbs?" Brianda asked. "I had no idea."

"She knew all about them," Isolina said. "She mainly used gentian for blood pressure. To thin the blood, she used to say."

"And who did she say the clothes belonged to?" Mihaela asked.

"Witches and friends of the devil. She was extremely religious, and she said she used to put a cross on top of the clothes and go off looking for her herbs. She said that whenever she returned, the cross was still there but the clothes had disappeared."

Loud voices signaled that another intense card game had just ended. No longer trying for subtlety, Brianda finally turned around to see the mysterious man.

He had his back to her, with one arm resting on the bar. He looked young, younger than she had imagined. Tall. Strong. She glanced up from his thick-soled boots to his faded jeans to his broad back, which was covered by a red-checked, lumberjack-style shirt. His hair was dark—more than dark, it was completely black and shiny. The hair partially covered his neck and a stray lock hid his profile.

Someone tapped Brianda on the arm, but she couldn't take her eyes off the man. She desperately wanted him to turn around so she could see his face.

"Brianda, who are you staring at?"

Damn it, she thought, as she turned back to the table.

"Oh, just thinking about your witch stories," she improvised. "They're really wild. Did you know about all this, Neli?" She instantly regretted her words. How could she have asked Neli that in front of everyone? "I mean . . ."

But Neli handled it with grace. "No, the truth is I didn't, but this makes Tiles an even more fascinating place!"

"Anyone need another drink?" Brianda asked, getting to her feet. She needed an excuse to go over to the bar and see the man's face.

"Leave it, I'll go," said Berta, also making a movement to get up.

"No need." Brianda stopped her. "I have to go to the restroom anyway."

Neli agreed to a beer. Brianda went straight to the ladies' room, turned on the tap, and wet her wrists. Suddenly, she felt nervous and excited, like a teenager about to talk to the boy of her dreams. It was very different from the lead-up to her anxiety attacks; this time, she wanted everything that was about to happen. She took a deep breath.

She went to stand at the bar next to the man. She ordered a beer and a tonic water. Out of the corner of her eye she noticed a slight movement, his hand brushing the lock of hair behind his ear. Now he would turn and so would she. She would offer the typical polite smile of someone waiting for the bartender to serve the drinks. As simple as that. She calculated the seconds. The man began to turn . . .

Now!

But the smile would not come.

Her brain couldn't process his features, being too busy with disconnected images from a dream where a man lay facedown by a river, images from a nightmare with a confusing sound track.

I know you. I've seen you before.

Those eyes looking at me and burning me . . .

7.

Brianda felt a stab of pain in her chest. She grabbed the drinks and hurried back to the table. Her cheeks were burning, her heart was racing faster than ever, and her hands were trembling. First the inscription in Latin, then the vision in the church, and now this man who she'd nearly called by name.

Corso.

She would bet her life that his name was Corso.

The unusual name had sprung from somewhere deep in her mind, as if it had always been there and was now claiming its rightful place. But she'd never met this man; she was certain of that. She would never have forgotten a face like that.

"Are you tired?" Isolina asked. "Shall we go?"

Brianda shrugged. On one hand, she wanted to run away as fast as she could. On the other, she felt inexplicably compelled to stay right where she was.

"Don't you want to stay?" asked Neli. "We could have dinner here."

"Don't worry about me," Isolina said. "Stay! Spend time with someone your own age! Petra and Bernardo can give me a ride home."

Brianda nodded. She'd stay.

The older folks drifted out, and Jonas and Zacarias joined their table. Every few minutes, Brianda couldn't resist turning slightly and throwing furtive looks toward the bar. The man was still there. Sometimes he was chatting with the owner, sometimes with one of the locals. But most of the time he was sipping his drink and glancing over at Brianda's table. She knew he was watching her just like she was watching him. She was tempted to go start a conversation, but decided against it. She had no idea what to say. And she didn't want him to think she was a flirt.

"I wonder if I should ask him to join us," said Jonas.

Brianda tensed up. It was obvious who Jonas meant.

"Whenever he comes in, it's always the same," said Berta. "He loiters near the door, has one drink, chats a little with my husband, and leaves."

"My father is overseeing all his building work," Zacarias added. "He says he's a great employer and a great worker but a bad talker." He turned to Jonas. "You work for him too, right? What do you think?"

"I've had no problems with him," said Jonas. "He's just a loner is all."

"And he's Italian?" Brianda ventured.

"But he seems to speak good Spanish," Zacarias replied. "My father says he's shy because he's embarrassed about his face. Have you seen it up close?"

Brianda shivered. She'd seen it at the bar. She closed her eyes and imagined running her fingers along the deep scar from the man's right eye to his chin, as if a lava flow of tears had opened a furrow in his flesh.

"It's pretty intense," Neli admitted. "And on top of that, he's new here. Jonas and I were talking about how maybe we should be friendlier to him."

"I don't know," said Jonas. "When all is said and done, he's my boss. Maybe once the house is finished—"

"Well, it'll have to be another day," Zacarias announced, "because he just left."

Brianda spun around. *Damn it*, she thought. She wondered if she would see him again. Tiles wasn't very big, but time was against her. She'd come to the country for a few days of rest, and a week had already gone by. Soon she'd have to return to Madrid. The longest she could stretch her stay would be to the following weekend, and she'd just have to hope that he came to the bar again. A feeling of dread gripped her chest. What if he didn't come? If he didn't leave his mysterious house?

She scarcely recognized herself. Why was she so anxious to see him again? She wiped her brow with a clammy hand. She must be sicker that she'd thought. Strange things kept happening to her, both inside and out. Maybe she should never have come to Tiles.

She was getting worse and worse.

Something in her brain was not right.

Brianda headed back to Anels House. As soon as she pulled away from the bar, she regretted not having returned earlier with Isolina. Complete darkness reigned; it was only broken by her headlights. Beyond them, there was nothing.

When she took the turnoff toward the high part of the valley, she stepped on the gas, eager to reach the safety of the house as quickly as possible. But the car did not accelerate. Instead, it jolted. The engine choked and then gave out.

Brianda cursed, banging the steering wheel with both hands. She tried repeatedly to restart the car, but to no avail. Not a single light on the dashboard came on. She pulled the hand brake and began crying in fury. She couldn't believe it. Stranded in the middle of the night. On a deserted road. Too close to the graveyard.

Stopping to catch her breath, she realized it wasn't that serious. She'd just call her aunt. She rummaged in her purse, but couldn't find her phone. She emptied the contents onto the seat beside her and, among tissues, lipsticks, a compact, pens, keys, and other miscellaneous objects, there was a little white pouch she didn't recognize. How had it gotten there? Then she spotted her phone. Brianda typed in the code to unlock it, then stared at the screen for several long seconds as she recalled her first encounter with Neli.

In this backward and godforsaken place, there was no signal.

She wiped the condensation off the window and looked out; her heart beat as if afraid someone or something was about to pounce on the car, and she hit the automatic lock button. She estimated that Anels House was about fifteen minutes away by foot. She kept a flashlight in the trunk, though she wasn't sure the batteries were charged. All she had to do was open the door, get out of the car, open the trunk, grab the flashlight, pray that it would work, and run. She repeated the sequence out loud to give herself confidence, and then she threw open the door.

With her senses on high alert, Brianda faced the outside world. The dampness of the earth filled her lungs. Luckily, the flashlight worked. She locked the car and began walking, trembling and hunched, a thin scarf her only protection against the cold and the fear. She concentrated on the luminous circle projected on the ground from her flashlight and began to recite comforting words to shield herself from the imposing silence. However, no matter how she repeated these positive messages—a technique she'd gotten from a book on how to control fear—menacing thoughts persistently flashed through her mind. She'd never make it home, they said. An animal would attack her. Or a murderer. Or a ghost. Maybe a witch? She couldn't do anything about it. Death was close. The pain. Her blood on the earth. The end. The grief of her loved ones . . .

Suddenly, she heard something and her heart jumped. It was a dull, repetitive sound. She turned back and raced for the car. The noise was getting loud. It seemed to rise from the road itself. A freezing sweat covered her body.

Still short of her refuge in the car, she recognized the sound: a horse's hooves. Brianda stopped dead, accepting defeat. The fear made her tremble uncontrollably, and she could only breathe by gasping. She heard the gallop ease to a trot and then a walk. A whinny revealed that the horse was very close, too close.

"Hello," said a raspy voice. "Car trouble?" He had a slight accent.

Brianda pointed her flashlight toward the looming figure, first on to the black horse and then its rider, whom she immediately recognized by his lumberjack shirt under a leather jacket. She cautiously took a few steps toward him.

"The engine died."

The rider dismounted. Brianda couldn't see his face clearly, but it was imprinted in her mind. The scar. The black eyes. The straight nose, slightly narrow. His creased brow. The serious expression on his lips. Despite the darkness, she noticed his surprise when he realized who she was. She wondered whether he too had her face etched in his mind. They remained in silence for a few moments.

"Maybe I could try?"

"If you want, but I don't think it'll start. It's completely dead."

"If you hold my horse, I'll take a look."

"Hold the horse?"

Brianda shone her flashlight at the enormous animal. It had a long and wavy mane, thick hair partially covering its hooves, and a tail that nearly reached the ground. It was a magnificent and elegant specimen but intimidating. She kept her distance from it.

She felt tempted to run the light over the man as well but stopped herself. He came a little closer and handed her the reins.

"Don't move and neither will he. May I have the keys?"

Stunned by the proximity of the horse and its owner, Brianda handed over the keys and waited. He tried to start the car without success. He then lifted the hood, looked at the engine, and closed it again.

"Too sophisticated," he said. "You'll have to take it to a mechanic."

Brianda wasn't surprised, though for a moment she had harbored the hope that he might magically fix the car so she could go home. She would never have imagined wanting to get to Anels House so badly. At least the fear of being out here alone had let up, pushed aside by the tension between her and the strange rider, as well as the concentration required to hold that impressive horse.

The man crossed in front of her and took the animal by the bridle.

"See? He stayed quiet. Because you did."

"I've never been so close to a horse before." She didn't know what else to say. "Is it a Friesian?" She spoke the word without thinking.

"You've never been close to a horse," he replied in amazement, "but you recognize the breed?"

Brianda blushed in confusion. She must have read it somewhere and gotten it right by chance, but she wasn't going to admit that.

"Well, I should go."

"Alone? You're brave."

Brave? She could barely contain a laugh. If he only knew!

"I'll go with you," he proposed. "Where do you live?"

"A little past the turnoff to Lubich."

"Very good. Let me help you up on the horse."

"Oh, no."

"No?" He shrugged. "We could walk, but it'll take longer." He gently rubbed the Friesian's jaw, and his voice got husky again. "There's nothing like riding a horse at night. It is a unique feeling. The perspective is different. A mixture of peace and absolute freedom."

The horse responded to the caress by stretching its neck, half closing its eyes, and twitching its nose. Brianda found the gentle, masculine scene oddly relaxing. For a moment, she was compelled to take part in this intimate connection. She ran her hand along the magnificent animal's back. The man studied her, and she quickly pulled her hand back.

"If you're afraid to touch," he said with a hint of disappointment in his voice, "I won't push you to ride."

She wanted to explain that it was one thing to touch but quite another to get up on that colossus. She wanted to explain that he'd seemed annoyed when she touched the horse, but that sounded absurd. His presence was disorienting; the words didn't want to come. She took a deep breath and forced herself to tell the truth.

"I'd really like to try riding, but I have to admit I'm terrified."

"Then we'll go slow."

He took the flashlight and put it in his pocket. Then, he held the stirrup and motioned for her to place her left foot in it. He took her left hand in his—big, strong, weathered—and guided her to the withers. Brianda felt a shiver that increased in intensity when he applied light pressure on her waist with both hands.

"Push yourself up," she heard him say.

Brianda concentrated. She was agile, but the horse was very tall. She counted to three, bending her knee with each number, then pushed. The pressure on her waist increased until she was seated properly on the saddle. Unsteady, she gripped the front saddlebow with both hands.

"Very good," he said, placing himself a handsbreadth away from the animal's nostrils. "Now just hold on tight and enjoy."

Brianda sat bolt upright, totally alert to the new sensations she was discovering: simultaneous fear and pleasure. She was afraid that the horse would buck and rear or bolt out of control. She was afraid of falling and breaking her neck. Once more, twisted thoughts tried to edge out the pleasant ones, but she fought them back. She enjoyed the gentle rocking, the rhythmic clopping of the hooves, the power of the animal's muscles between her thighs. She found she now enjoyed the silence and even the shadows just outside the space occupied by the three of them.

"Are you OK?" he asked after a while.

"Better than I expected," she answered. "But at this pace it'll take us as long as if we walked."

"In a hurry?"

"Huh? No. I mean that I don't think it's right for you to have to walk."

"Do you want to get down?"

"It's not that." Brianda wasn't sure if he was being kind, testing her, or making fun of her.

"Ah, you want me to join you."

She bristled at the hint of laughter in his voice, but she said nothing. She certainly didn't want to get back down and walk in the dark.

He took her silence for assent. He guided the horse to an outcropping of rocks and climbed up. Then he motioned for her to take her feet out of the stirrups.

"Could you move back a bit?"

Brianda scooted back onto the hindquarters. He leapt from the rocks down into the saddle.

"And now, hold on to me very tightly."

He took the reins with one hand and rested the other on Brianda's clasped hands wrapped around his waist. He squeezed his legs against the horse's flanks, and it began to move, slowly at first and then a little faster. The walk became a trot.

Brianda held on for dear life. She couldn't believe this was reality. In the middle of the night, she was riding a black steed and clutching a stranger, her cheek and chest against his back, her arms around his waist. She could smell his sweat, and something elemental, like fire, earth, storm, and maybe a subtle hint of tobacco.

She prayed the little bumps that brought her body closer and closer to his would never end. It had been ages since she had felt so relaxed, so safe, so complete. Now she wished Anels House were miles away so that this unexpected journey could continue into an infinite dawn.

"Are those the lights from your house?" he asked.

Her rider turned around, and a lock of his long dark hair brushed her face.

Brianda opened her eyes reluctantly. With a gentle pull on the reins, the horse returned to a leisurely walk and stopped in front of the gate. Luzer's hoarse barking could be heard in the distance. Corso swung his leg over the horse's head, slid to the ground, and then helped Brianda dismount.

The weak light of the lamps on the façade of Anels House gave Brianda a few final seconds to enjoy his features, especially the intense gaze that successfully diverted attention from the scar.

"Thank you so much," she finally managed to say. "I'm so lucky you passed by."

"It was a pleasure," he whispered. "I hope we meet again."

He mounted the horse again and began to walk into the night, but then doubled back.

"By the way, what's your name?"

"Brianda, and yours?"

"Corso. It's Italian."

8.

Four days later, when Brianda returned to Anels House after picking up her car in Aiscle, she was amazed to see Esteban's car parked out front. She rushed across the yard. He must have gone to great lengths to get free from work midweek; he must not have been able to stand being away from her. She suddenly yearned to return to Madrid with him, to get her daily routine back, to flee this strange valley where her worries had only increased.

Then she felt a twinge in her chest and froze.

Leaving Tiles would mean leaving Corso.

She hadn't seen him since that night, and yet whenever she closed her eyes, there was his face, his dark, penetrating, tormented gaze. She would give anything to ride again on his horse, arms around his waist, his back protecting her from the night's cold. She wanted to know everything about him: why he'd come here, how he had gotten his scar, what his horse's name was, where he was from, if he had family. She'd been tempted to ask when they said their good-byes at the gate of Anels House but hadn't wanted to seem nosy. And, after the magic of their nocturnal ride, part of her had been afraid that general, even banal, questions and answers could have broken the spell. The abrupt good-bye had preserved the mystery.

For the past four days, the walk from Anels House to the turnoff to Lubich became her sacred ritual, morning and afternoon. She crossed the graveled yard where Luzer now looked at her with indifference, passed the linden beside the fountain, walked down a hill framed by walls of rock and thyme, rosemary, and lavender plants, dormant with the coming of winter; then she took the fork to Lubich, leaving the gloomy environs of the graveyard, its old pines and its hidden, ruined church. Then she walked a short way, straining her ears for the sound of hooves. She continued a little farther to where the undergrowth became thicker, where the aromatic plants gave way to familiar bushes—juniper, blackthorn, holly, and boxwood, and then to trees—birches, ashes, walnut, maple . . . And when she reached the spot where the forest began in earnest, she stopped, the warning from her childhood ringing in her ears: beyond that point there was only danger. After a few minutes of indecision, she hurried back home, kicking herself all the way. It was absurd and illogical to fear the woods, of course, but she had recently learned that fear and anxiety were powerful forces.

And it was such a terrible lesson. Brianda had always been an intensely rational person, an engineer, interested in the laws of movement, the behavior of fluids, the transformation of energy, and other phenomena of the physical world. She'd never had time for anything that wasn't of the tangible, structured, controlled, and controllable world. Now, however, she felt an inexplicable attraction to a mysterious man who lived on the far side of a haunted forest.

She entered the house, convinced that seeing Esteban would free her of this crazy obsession with Corso and that he would ease her crippling anxiety.

Esteban was waiting for her in the hall, and he looked extremely well. He'd gotten his hair cut in unruly layers and had let his stubble grow a little, which made him look younger. He wore a thick light-brown sweater and a pair of worn jeans.

When he saw her, he took her in his arms and kissed her on the lips.

"I missed you," he whispered.

Brianda smiled and moved closer to him.

"I missed you too."

"Isolina told me that you were down in Aiscle picking up the car from a mechanic."

"It broke down on me last Saturday," Brianda explained without mentioning her nocturnal adventure. She had told her aunt and uncle that she had walked back from the bar. "No big deal."

Isolina let them know that lunch was on the table. They went into the dining room and saw Colau trying to open a bottle of wine. The corkscrew looked tiny in his big hands. Esteban offered to help, but Colau refused. Then came a crack of the glass breaking, and a cry of pain followed by a loud string of expletives.

As the blood spurting from Colau's hand rained onto the immaculate tablecloth, Isolina sprang into action. Without hesitation or disgust, she grabbed the napkins, went to her husband, pulled a large shard of glass from his palm, wrapped his hand gingerly, and led him to the bathroom to check for more glass and decide whether they needed to go see a doctor.

Brianda couldn't take her eyes off the red stain spreading across the tablecloth. A curtain of black dots clouded her eyes. She wobbled and had to support herself on the back of a chair. Esteban came over, worried, and helped her sit down. Brianda closed her eyes, and the curtain of dots parted like in an old theater to display dizzying and disjointed images. She saw fragments of bodies and open wounds, tense faces silently shouting and grotesque grimaces . . . and it all caused a painful stabbing sensation in her chest.

"I'll be right back," she managed to babble.

She darted upstairs to the bathroom, knelt in front of the toilet, and vomited. Even when her stomach was empty, the retching continued, as if her body were trying to expel some unwanted presence. When the heaves finally subsided, she took slow, deep breaths like her aunt had taught her.

"Brianda?" Esteban called through the door. "Are you all right?"

She did not want him to see her like that. She mustered her strength, got up, flushed the toilet, turned on the faucet, and called, "I'll be out in just a minute!"

Esteban opened the door halfway.

"Was it the blood?" he asked. "I didn't know you were so squeamish."

"I'm usually not. It's just that there was so much."

"Yes, it was pretty gruesome." He observed her puffy-eyed reflection in the mirror. "Want me to stay here?"

"There's no need. I'll just change my shirt and be right down."

She went into her bedroom, sat on the bed, and cried as quietly as she could. She needed the tears to wash away those intense glimmers of evil. They had shown her misery and suffering. She wanted to believe it was just her imagination, but she felt the pain in those visions as her own.

After lunch, Esteban suggested they take a walk, just the two of them. Wanting to steer clear of Lubich, Brianda guided him toward the gullies that bordered the neighboring town of Besalduch, to the east. For the first time, Luzer followed her. When they shouted at him to go home, the baleful chaperone disobeyed, although he did hang back.

The late-afternoon sun was too weak to warm their backs, but it spread a golden aura over the unplowed fields to the left of the path and the pastures encircled by rows of poplars to the right.

"Tiles is duller than I imagined," said Esteban. "Seems like a good place to rest, but is there even anything to do here besides sleep and eat? You must be looking forward to coming back to Madrid."

Brianda hesitated. She didn't know which was worse, the frenzy of Madrid or the boredom of Tiles. For the moment, though, she wanted to appear cheerful.

"Yes, with you. And I'm sure going back to the office will do me good."

Esteban didn't reply.

"What's wrong?" Brianda asked.

He took a letter out of his back pocket.

"This arrived the day before yesterday. I didn't want to tell you over the phone. I hope you don't mind, but I opened it."

Brianda recognized her company letterhead and knew immediately. A letter of dismissal. Her eyes filled with tears. She'd just been convincing herself that it was time to go back to Madrid, to her work, her routines, her responsibilities, and suddenly, that was no longer possible. The letter hurt more than she would have thought possible. They regretted to inform her that they were restructuring the workforce. They assured her it had nothing to do with her worth. They explained that orders had decreased, that it was not a good time for new technology projects, that potential clients were not taking risks. They bade her farewell repeating their regret and wishing her well. Wishing her well . . . On top of everything that was happening to her—her anxiety, her apathy, her fear—now she had to try and find a new job?

"Don't worry," said Esteban cheerfully. "We'll get through this. I thought that maybe now we could . . ." He coughed. "What I mean is, wouldn't you like to have a baby?"

Brianda closed her eyes and fought back laughter. She could barely manage her own life, never mind creating another. She remembered what Silvia had said about the danger of financial dependence. That had been just before the fortune-teller proclaimed that she was going through a period of emotional confusion, that her family and social world were weakening her, that she would undertake a journey of radical transformation.

She would live and be reborn, the woman had told her. The transformation would not be denied. Spirit would dominate matter.

She realized that she wanted all that, wanted transformation and rebirth! But right now, she just felt further away from the day when this terrible anxiety would leave her.

A sarcastic thought rose in her mind: what a shame Neli wasn't the kind of witch who read tarot cards. Brianda could have confirmed the predictions with her.

"I can see you don't think it's a good idea," she heard Esteban say sadly.

"It's not that." Tears slid down her cheek. "But before I can think about something like that, I need to get better."

Esteban rubbed her back.

"I'm so sorry about everything that's happening. I know how important your work is to you. But I'm with you, no matter what." He drew her toward him.

Brianda nodded weakly. She wiped her tears and hid in Esteban's embrace.

Then the sound of galloping hooves set all her senses on high alert.

Luzer began to bark threateningly and shot off like a bullet.

Moments later, the enormous Friesian towered over them. The horse kept its ears pinned back and its eyes wide, unnerved by the persistent growls coming from Luzer, who prowled at its feet, teeth bared.

"Is that your dog?" demanded Corso. "I don't think it likes me."

Brianda adjusted the collar of her thick jacket to mask the full-body shiver set off by Corso's gaze, and at the same time to distract from the heat that burned her cheeks. Esteban took her hand.

"Actually, no, he's my uncle's."

Corso looked at their intertwined hands, and Brianda noticed a hint of irritation on his face.

"What a magnificent horse," said Esteban.

Corso gave a slight nod. He fired a final glance at Brianda, kicked his heels into the horse's flanks, and took off at a gallop, raising a cloud of dust as he left, pursued by Luzer.

"Who was that charmer?" Esteban asked. "I never saw such a horrible scar."

Brianda remained silent. The meeting could not have been stranger. Corso had seemed annoyed about having to stop and talk to them, like he had someplace important to be. He'd been nervous, impatient—more than that, even.

Corso had been hostile.

"So. In this rural Eden, the guy on the black horse is the devil," joked Esteban.

"Corso? Not at all!" Brianda blushed again, realizing she'd answered too fervently.

"Corso? What a name! Strange, dark. It suits him." Esteban paused before asking in a neutral tone, "You know him, then?"

Brianda shrugged. "Not really. I've seen him a couple of times."

"But you must have met, if you know his name."

"My aunt probably told me. We've just exchanged a few pleasantries," she lied. "As you saw, he's very awkward."

Brianda wasn't happy with the way this conversation was going. For the first time since she'd met Esteban, they weren't being open with each other, and they both knew it.

The advancing night enshrouded the fields and blurred the trees, bushes, and scrubland into evocative shadows. A few lights shone here and there from the houses, announcing the phantasmagoria the valley would soon become.

Brianda felt another shiver and rubbed her forearms.

Esteban, ever attentive, put his arm around her shoulders and pulled her closer. Brianda showed her thanks with a half smile that he did not return. She didn't know whether he was tired from the long journey, disappointed, annoyed, or a combination of all three. Maybe it was her fault, she thought. She had been cool and withdrawn with him, and yet, that fleeting moment with Corso had been enough to ignite a little flame of controlled euphoria inside her.

She prayed that Esteban hadn't noticed how her eyes and her heart had lit up when she saw the other man.

9.

Several times that evening, Brianda caught herself thinking about Corso. While she and Esteban were drying the dishes, in her imagination she was riding with the foreigner toward Lubich, which she pictured as the mansion in some etching where a few impromptu broken lines evoked, with their contrasts of light and shadow, a stormy sky, trees vanquished by the wind, a mossy spring, and walls hidden behind thick, undefined foliage.

Esteban wrapped his arms around her waist and nuzzled her neck with his nose.

"I'm looking forward to having you in my arms tonight," he whispered to her.

Brianda freed herself from his embrace.

"You're tickling me."

"You love my tickles."

He seized her again and again she moved away. She knew that roguish gleam in Esteban's half-closed eyes. Before her illness, or whatever this was, any time used to be a good time to enjoy Esteban's caresses. Now, even thinking about sex increased her apathy.

A loud noise made her jump. Someone was insistently banging the knocker of the main door.

"I'll get it!" Brianda quickly shouted to her aunt and uncle, so they would hear her from the sitting room. Whoever was at the door had saved Brianda from another uncomfortable situation with Esteban.

She went out to the hall and opened the main door a few inches to peek and see who was there. Neli's haggard face appeared in front of her, outlined by the black background of the night.

"Can I come in?"

A gust of wind hit the door, slamming it into Brianda's shoulder. Neli looked like she'd thrown on her coat and scarf in a terrible rush. Small bits of dried leaves adorned her long, messy hair.

"Something happened to me." Neli looked around. "Could I speak with Colau?"

"What a surprise!" Isolina appeared in the hallway. "Is something wrong, Neli?"

"She wants to talk to Colau."

Isolina raised an eyebrow. "Now? He just told me he wanted to go to bed."

Neli, nervous, opened her bag and pulled out a thick wad of papers that rustled in her hand.

"This afternoon, I was restoring the last drawer of an enormous walnut chest in the sacristy and I could tell it had a false bottom. I took it apart and found these. They're original documents written in old Aragonese, Catalan, and Castilian."

Now Brianda understood. Neli wanted to share the discovery with someone who could appreciate its historical importance. And history was not Brianda's strong suit.

"So, does it say anything interesting?" she asked, just to have something to say.

"They're from the Council of Tiles, something like the town hall of old. There's a lot of information about the daily goings-on of the council for over half a century, from the middle of the sixteenth century until the beginning of the seventeenth—"

"Let's go to the sitting room, Neli," Isolina interrupted, gesturing for her to follow. "I'm sure Colau would like to hear all this."

Trailing behind them, Brianda yawned. She didn't understand why Neli was so worked up about some old papers.

"Colau?" Isolina called from the door of the sitting room.

Colau was standing with his bandaged hand resting against the mantelpiece, contemplating the burning logs. He didn't answer, but Luzer raised his head. When his eyes fixed on Neli, he let out a low growl, jumped up, and raced toward her barking and baring his teeth. Isolina quickly got between them, shouting at Luzer to stop, but he ignored her.

"That's enough, Luzer," she shouted again. "As if you didn't know Neli! Colau! Make him stop this instant!"

Colau whistled loudly and Luzer turned to him with a confused expression.

"Come here!" Colau ordered. The animal returned to his feet and lay back down in front of the fire. Colau patted the dog and murmured, "You don't like unexpected visitors either."

While Isolina apologized to Neli and began to explain to her husband the reason for Neli's visit, Brianda decided to run upstairs for a heavier sweater. A strange cold sweat had taken over her body, making her tremble. On the way to the stairs, she bumped into Esteban.

"What's going on?" he asked.

"Luzer went crazy when he saw Neli. It scared the hell out of me. I'll be glad never to see that beast again."

"Wait, who's Neli?"

Brianda briefly explained that she was a neighbor and wanted to show Colau some documents she'd found in the church. Esteban leaned toward her.

"And do we have to be with them or—?"

Brianda ran her gaze over his handsome face and raised a hand to caress his rebellious auburn hair. Another man might have reproached her for hiding out here in the country instead of facing up to her problems, but not him. He respected her independence. What more could she ask for? What was stopping her from leaping into his arms as she always had?

"I think it'd be rude to disappear without saying a word," she said. "Go on. I'll be down in a second."

A few minutes later, Brianda returned. Colau and Neli sat on the wooden benches by the fireplace, so deep in conversation and wrapped in such a dense cloud of cigarette smoke that they appeared to be in their own world. In the darkest corner of the sitting room, sitting in two low armchairs, Isolina and Esteban listened in silence, as if they'd been banished there so they wouldn't be a nuisance.

Isolina motioned to her to listen, but Brianda couldn't understand what Neli was saying to Colau, who bent over the yellowed papers. At great speed, she listed dates and events. Several times, Colau took off his glasses and rubbed his eyes. On his face, Brianda read more worry than excitement. She understood that Colau and Neli were both passionate about history, but they were acting as if something incredible had happened.

She sat on the arm of Esteban's chair and he whispered, "There's a list of twenty-four executions from fifteen hundred and something."

"Executions? Were they prisoners of war or something?"

"They were women from right here in the valley, Aiscle to Besalduch," said Isolina. "Supposing that there were around three hundred inhabitants and thirty-three houses back then, that means one woman from every house—or every second house at the very least."

"Does it say what happened?" asked Brianda.

Neli turned around, and her gaze was caught for a moment on Esteban, whose arm was wrapped around Brianda's waist. "Very clearly. The list of houses is short but terrifying. Almost all of them still exist today." She ran her finger down a page. "Between February 19 and April 2 of 1592, these women were beaten and held prisoner for being witches. They were killed between March 4 and April 29 of that same year."

Neli shuddered as she spoke. Now it all made sense. If there was anybody who'd be especially moved by a witch hunt, it was Neli.

"Does it list their names?" Brianda asked softly.

"Yes. Some are repeated." In a respectful tone, Neli began the tragic litany: "Antonia, Maria, Margalida, Gisabel, Juana, Cecilia, Isabel, Aldonsa, Acna, Catalina, Esperenza, Leonor, Barbara . . ."—she paused before adding—"and Brianda of Anels."

"What?" Brianda rushed over to see for herself. "There was a Brianda of Anels? Did you know about this, Colau? In your genealogy work, have you found Briandas? I've never met any others, but maybe it was a common name here?"

Colau shook his head. "I've only made it as far back as the middle of the seventeenth century, and I haven't found any."

Brianda frowned. Colau seemed suspiciously preoccupied. And his answer wasn't very convincing. She turned to Isolina.

"Do you know why my parents named me Brianda?"

"I always figured Laura had read it in a book. Once, jokingly, she told me she'd dreamt it."

Dreamt it. Brianda was so affected by her recurring dreams that she was shocked to hear her mother might have gone through something similar and never mentioned it.

Esteban intervened. "The name is pure coincidence. The important thing is that such an important case of executions for witchcraft has come to light! I'd love to read the Spanish Inquisition trial records. Sounds like we have a new Salem on our hands, eh, Colau?"

But Colau did not answer. His eyes were glued to the ground.

Isolina went over to him, rested a hand on his arm, and asked gently, "Do you have any information on Inquisition trials?"

Colau shook his head. "It wasn't the Inquisition," he whispered.

"I don't understand." Isolina leaned toward him.

"I need more time," he pleaded through clenched teeth. "Just a little more."

A somber silence followed, broken by Neli.

"In the treasurer's register, the extra costs of the bell-ringer, hangman, and tavern on the days of execution are recorded. And it says that the executions took place here in Tiles, but not where exactly. I think that's everything"—she partially closed her eyes—"oh, except that all the entries related to the executions are signed by the same man, whose name was—"

She started searching among the yellowed pages, but Colau placed his huge hands over them possessively.

"That's enough for today."

"Why?" Neli objected loudly. "I believe you know something about this, Colau. If there's anyone who knows the secrets of this valley, the way houses were lost or gained, their division or enlargement, if they sank or triumphed, it's you."

"I didn't know about these executions!" Colau snarled.

"I don't understand!" Neli insisted in frustration. "What are you trying to hide?"

"Neli!" Isolina snapped.

But Neli wasn't going to give up so easily.

"Fine, then. I'll retrace your steps, Colau. I'll start in the Besalduch monastery archive."

"A waste of time," said Colau between gritted teeth. "There's nothing there."

"We'll see," responded Neli. "I'll call Petra early tomorrow morning. Her niece is in charge of the place. I'll let you know when I head over in case you'd like to come help me."

Colau shook his head obstinately.

"And what about the papers?" Esteban interjected. "I suppose you'd better hand them over to the authorities right away."

Colau glared at him. "After being hidden for four hundred years, I think they can wait a few more days, Mr. Lawyer. If Neli doesn't mind, I'll keep them here until I've studied them in depth."

"Of course she doesn't mind," Isolina said soothingly. "You'll have time to scan them for your collection. Isn't that right, Neli?"

Brianda appreciated her aunt's mediation. She was used to Colau's bad manners, but tonight he was more disagreeable and evasive than ever. He obviously wanted the unexpected meeting to be over as soon as possible. Maybe he wanted to savor this missive from the past alone. Or maybe there was something else.

Colau had interrupted Neli just when she was about to say someone's name. Who cared about a name from the sixteenth century? Brianda wondered. But she had to admit that a bolt of lightning had gone through her when she heard about poor Brianda of Anels, hanged for being a witch. She wondered if Brianda was young or old, single or married, if she'd had children. She wondered what it would have been like to live through those terrible times in the valley.

Brianda shook her head. Maybe everything was much simpler. Maybe the valuable research Colau kept locked away in his office was the reason for his sour moods. How sad that he hadn't had children to pass his great knowledge on to.

"Until tomorrow then," Neli said as she stood.

Brianda walked her to the front door, where Neli stopped for a second, her hand resting on the handle. After a long moment, she said, "When I first started reading the papers, I was very disappointed, because they were very repetitive. I was searching for something special. A little voice told me that discovering them at just this time of year had to mean something." She lowered her voice. "Remember when you saw me the other day?"

Brianda frowned. "Mm hm."

"The ritual I performed was in remembrance of our ancestors. In this time of Samhain, the laws of time and space are suspended temporarily, and the barrier between worlds disappears. It's the perfect time to communicate with the dead. I felt like it wasn't by accident that I found the documents, but that I'd somehow been chosen, as if the gods wanted to warn me of something."

"Well, they sure did, didn't they?" said Brianda, immediately regretting her sarcastic tone. Neli had trusted her, confided in her. And a few minutes earlier, she herself had understood the woman's pain over the executions. Then again, it was a completely different thing to believe that some "gods" had handpicked this self-proclaimed witch to find out about the deaths of others.

Neli stared at her coolly. Outside, the wind howled.

"I know that finding it now means something, Brianda. Samhain is the Wiccan new year, the end of the cycle of life, when everything dies and begins again. I can't stop wondering what it is that's about to begin again, but I guess we'll find out."

Neli turned, opened the door, and disappeared into the darkness. Brianda heard the sound of her car engine and returned to the sitting room. Esteban had already gone to bed. She said good night and headed up the stairs slowly. Neli's visit had interrupted Esteban's amorous plans, but she was sure he hadn't forgotten about them.

She went into the dark bedroom. In silence, she got undressed and slipped into bed. Immediately, Esteban began to caress her. Brianda felt guilty for not being able to respond as he wished; she didn't want to reject him. She climbed on top of him and began to kiss the length of his body.

Esteban understood and let her continue. And Brianda satisfied him without allowing him to enter her.

10.

Brianda and Esteban left the land of Beles Peak and headed down a narrow road through woods of beech, oak, pine, and elm trees. Shortly afterward, it led into a narrow gorge that traced the undulating boundary between Tiles and Besalduch, the next town to the east, where the monastery was. Neli had called early that morning to tell them she would be at the archive around ten. Since Brianda was curious and had nothing better to do, she'd agreed to go. At the last minute, Esteban had also decided to come, even though he'd have to catch up on work later.

As they drove, Brianda noticed that the walls of the canyon acted as a guide for the river that could barely be seen below. The limestone rock face had been eroded by water, molded into a grotesque sculpture accustomed to the absence of sunlight. A little farther on, a sign told them they had to leave the car and continue on foot, so they parked in a small clearing where Neli, her nose and cheeks red, was waiting for them beside her dilapidated 4x4. When they joined her, Neli blew on her knuckles while complaining about how the weather had turned so fast. There was no wind that morning, but frost stuck to the hard earth.

Neli led them single file down a damp, untended path toward the river. After a while, the path grew wider, ending at a steep stone bridge.

Brianda was awestruck. In an area no bigger than a couple of acres, there were two beautiful buildings and a third in ruins. It seemed like time had stopped, like she'd walked into a scene from a movie about the Middle Ages. The only thing missing was a line of peaceful monks huddled at the foot of the high, misty mountains.

"I must admit I wasn't expecting this," Esteban said. "It's magnificent."

Brianda nodded but couldn't really agree. The place was stunning, but she found its beauty cold and soulless.

They crossed to the other side of the bridge and Neli quickly showed them around the buildings. To the south, there was a small twelfth-century hermitage, partially hidden by the bare trees. To the north, the ruins of the old abbot's palace and, in the center, their destination: the main church, a small basilica with a high central nave and two small lateral ones ending in curved apses decorated with lattice friezes. Between the arched windows, several small blind arches formed niches in the walls.

They went into the church and toward a table in the corner that served as an information booth. A tall young woman with brown hair greeted them. Neli introduced her as Elsa, Petra's niece. Elsa had been kind enough to open the monastery just for them; it was usually closed between October and April since no tourists visited during the winter.

"But today we're open just for you, and later some friends of my mother's," she said with a smile. "I don't know what you're looking for, Neli, but there's not much here."

Elsa signaled them to follow her through a door. As soon as she went in, Neli sighed in disappointment. The archive was nothing more than a small room with four or five shelves, a few boxes perfectly ordered by date, and a pine table in the center.

"The important stuff was moved to the diocesan archive years ago for security reasons," Elsa explained. "There's nothing left here but birth and marriage certificates, wills, and funerals up to the beginning of the twentieth century."

"Any records of trials?" asked Neli.

Elsa shook her head. "Not as far as I know." She spoke to someone behind them. "Good morning! You've been here lots of times. You can confirm what I'm saying."

The three turned in unison.

"Colau!" Brianda said in surprise. He seemed to have aged overnight. More stooped than ever and with his forehead furrowed with lines, he leaned against the doorjamb as if steadying himself. She wondered if he'd come out of curiosity or to spy on their advances.

"I told you already, but you didn't want to believe me," said Colau in a hoarse voice.

"Of course, it depends what you're interested in," Elsa added. "I remember the last time you were here and found that will from Anels House. It was from the end of the sixteenth century, if memory serves. A lucky find! Papers from before the seventeenth century aren't supposed to be in this archive."

A shadow crossed Colau's face.

"A will from Anels House? Whose was it?" Brianda asked.

"No one important," he replied laconically.

"But, like I said, that was a fluke," continued Elsa. "What kind of trials are you wondering about, Neli?"

Neli hesitated. Brianda figured she must agree with Colau about keeping quiet about the documents from the sacristy.

"I am interested in finding out if, like in other mountain places, there have been any trials here . . . for witchcraft."

Elsa raised her eyes to the heavens.

"If you'd said that when you called, I would have been able to save you the trip! A while ago, a doctoral student came looking for information on the subject and found nothing. Besides, as far as I know, the archives of the Inquisition have been closely studied and there's no record of any witchcraft trials in this area." She giggled. "Either nothing survived or in this valley we were all sweetness and light."

"I'd still like to take a look," Neli insisted.

"As you wish." Elsa opened her arms. "If you need anything, I'll be outside."

When she had gone, Neli went over to the boxes, chose the oldest ones, and placed them on the table.

"Want to give me a hand?"

"Of course," Brianda answered, sitting down beside her.

Esteban joined in and the three set about poring over the old documents under the attentive gaze of Colau, who was still leaning against the door.

An hour later, Neli slammed shut her last file.

"I give up," she declared. "There's nothing here. Just like Elsa said, baptisms and marriages. Have you got much left?"

Brianda shook her head. She finished reading a final page, piled it on top of the others, and rubbed her eyes.

"At least we tried. Did you find anything, Esteban?"

"What year were the executions again?" he asked pensively.

"In 1592," answered Neli, rapidly approaching him. "Why?"

"It's probably nothing, but . . ."

Brianda noticed Colau straightening up.

"Here's part of a request by a man to have the body of his wife exhumed." He brought the paper closer to his eyes. "I think the date is April 1592."

"And the name?" asked Neli impatiently, standing behind him.

"It says Master of Anels," Esteban answered, pointing with his finger. "That's all. I wonder what he wanted the body for." He pouted. "This historical research is fun, but it's so frustrating!"

"I suppose you know nothing about this either, Colau," said Neli drily, snapping a photo of the document with her phone.

Colau did not answer. Brianda looked at him. His face showed astonishment, as if trying to take in that piece of information.

They returned the boxes to the shelves and filed out.

"Anything?" Elsa asked them. She glanced at her watch. "If you'd like, I can show you the church and the exhibition. We are taking it down next week."

They followed her as she put on a tour-guide voice and began to explain in monotone that the construction of the church followed the musical harmonies, the proportional architectural system popular in the Middle Ages.

"The numbers three and seven are repeated throughout the church. There are three naves in seven sections, three windows in the central apse and seven in the three other apses. Three is the most sacred of the numbers. It is associated with the Supreme Being in its three personalities—material, spiritual, and intellectual—and with its three attributes—infinite, eternal, and all-powerful. It is also the number of the Holy Trinity, as it represents God in His complete expression."

"It's also the number of the nocturnal planets: Moon, Diana, and Hecate," commented Neli under her breath. "And the symbol of Earth, whose fertility is provided by three elements: water, air, and fire. And the perfect harmony among all things, which have a beginning, a middle, and an end; or a present, past, and future; or body, spirit, and soul."

To each of Elsa's lessons, Neli countered quietly. If Elsa explained that seven corresponded to the days of the creation of the world, to the words that Jesus Christ spoke on the cross, to the sacraments, mortal sins, theological virtues, the gifts of the Holy Spirit, and the seals in the Book of Revelation, Neli retorted in a low voice, explaining that there were also seven musical notes, arts, colors of the rainbow, celestial bodies that gave their names to the days of the week, and chakras in the human body.

Esteban leaned down and whispered in Brianda's ear. "Neli's pretty weird, huh?"

"What makes you say that? Is anything she's said a lie?" The protective impulse surprised Brianda.

"No, but—" He shrugged. At that moment, his cell phone rang. "It's work. I'll be right back."

Elsa briefly pointed out the objects in the exhibition, which was dedicated to the district's religious history. Brianda tried to listen attentively, but she was unable to shake a vague sense of déjà vu. Elsa pointed to the final piece. It was the remains of a rudimentary wooden closet on a small rectangular pedestal, separated from the visitors by a burgundy-colored cord.

"The confessional," Brianda stammered.

"That's right," Elsa confirmed. "It is one of the few valuable pieces of religious furniture that have been preserved in the area. Unfortunately, it suffered the devastating effects of a fire. As you can see, on the lower part of the door, there is a lattice with a decorative vegetable fan motif. It is from the middle of the seventeenth century."

"No," corrected Brianda. "It was made at the end of the sixteenth century."

"The carved decorative motifs on the sides show—"

Brianda interrupted her again, ignoring the odd looks that the others were giving her.

"In a corner of the back panel, there are garlands and open flower buds carved in miniature." She could see the hands that hit the chisel with the hammer, the scattered shavings, hewn from the wood. The images surged before her eyes. "Underneath them is a sprig of boxwood and another of gorse in bloom."

Colau stalked over to her.

"And how do you know that?" His voice trembled and there was mistrust in his eyes.

Brianda did not answer. Stunned, she bowed her head.

Colau spoke urgently to the guide. "Is it true?"

Elsa shrugged. "I don't know."

"Could we check?" Neli asked anxiously. "We only have to move it a tiny bit."

Before Elsa could answer, Colau said, "Pieces as old as this must not be touched. It's too fragile."

Neli came over to Brianda. "What's wrong? Are you—?"

Brianda was incapable of defining what state she was in. She once again saw isolated images, but unlike the horrible visions provoked by the sight of the blood from her uncle's wound, these were cheerful: a man dressed in dark colors with a look of restrained happiness giving directions, a young girl drawing flowers, a man carving, another young girl—or was it the same one?—kneeling down in front of the confessional door. She closed her eyes.

"The confessional was in Tiles, in a small church," she said firmly. "It was the first one made." She took a deep breath. "I need air. The rest of you go ahead."

She went outside and leaned against the wall of the building. Esteban came over with a frown, tucking his phone into the pocket of his fleece jacket.

"I'm fine," Brianda lied. "I just got tired of so much information."

Esteban took her hand and squeezed tight.

"I thought you were getting better," he said with affection and concern. "Last night—"

"All I had for breakfast was coffee," she assured him. If she couldn't make sense of these strange visions herself, she didn't know how to share them. Not even with him. "I'm sure it's just low blood sugar."

A few minutes later, Neli and Elsa came out. They thanked Elsa for everything and she offered to walk with them to the bridge to wait for her mother's friends.

"What about Colau?" Esteban asked.

"He wanted to take some pictures of the confessional," said Neli. "And we don't need to wait; he came in his own car."

They had just begun walking when Brianda said, "I'll be right back."

Intrigued by her uncle's interest in the old confessional, she crept stealthily into the church. What she saw paralyzed her. Colau had moved the confessional away from the wall and was squatting behind it. He was too absorbed in examining the wood to notice her presence. From time to time, he repeated some words that echoed off the stones and reached her with complete clarity: "Why have you come? What are you looking for exactly?"

A moment later, he let out a gasp of surprise.

"The boxwood and the gorse," he exclaimed, caressing the carving with trembling fingers. "How did you know? It can't be. Have you been going through my things again?"

Brianda fled the incomprehensible scene. Her shaking knees slowed her down and made her trip over stones. At the top of the bridge, she stopped and knelt on the freezing ground, refusing to look back. She closed her eyes and began to sob. Her visions had turned out to be true. And what was Colau talking about? She didn't understand anything.

A hand rested on her arm.

"Let's go, Brianda," Neli said gently.

Feeling as if she had no strength left to control her body, Brianda accepted Neli's help getting to her feet.

"You know why I came here, Neli, don't you?" she groaned. "I started having anxiety attacks and my mother thought I'd get better in the country, but it isn't working; I just feel weaker and weaker. And everything here is so strange! And my uncle isn't right in the head! And you're a—" She stopped. "Why are you looking at me like that?"

"I've been watching you closely, Brianda. I need more proof, but I think I have a fair idea what's happening to you."

"Can you help me?"

"I'm scared too, and I'm worried you'll think I'm crazy if I tell you too much. But I'm sure of one thing: if my suspicions are correct, you will have to endure great suffering before this is over. Are you willing to suffer in order to regain peace?"

Brianda took a step back and stared at her. She'd do anything to feel like herself again, but she didn't understand what someone like Neli could do for her.

Just then, she realized that Colau was beginning to climb the stony slope of the bridge.

"I'll think about it," she said, and made her way back to the car.

11.

Brianda barely said a word for the rest of the day. The headache she'd had since returning from the monastery forced her to keep her eyes half-closed and her head down. She'd thought that at least it would allow her to avoid Colau's sinister look, but there he was now, sitting across from her, waiting for Isolina to serve dinner. His mere presence was increasingly unbearable, and it irritated her that neither her aunt nor Esteban seemed to notice how he scrutinized her every movement. While it was terribly unsettling that one of her visions had turned out to be true, it was even more upsetting that, as he examined the confessional, Colau had spoken aloud as if talking to her, had accused her of snooping in his office, even though she hadn't set foot in there. She couldn't imagine what secret related to the carvings he could possibly be hiding, and there was no way she was going to ask. And then there was Neli and her bizarre belief that she could help Brianda get well.

The house phone rang, and Isolina answered it. By the rhythm of the conversation, Brianda knew immediately that it was her mother. After a few minutes, Isolina brought the phone to Brianda, who went to the hall for privacy. She really wasn't in the mood to talk to Laura. She would have no choice but to tell her the truth: that she wasn't feeling better and now, on top of it, she had lost her job.

"How are you?" asked her mother cheerfully.

"Fine."

"Isolina told me that Esteban is there to see you. I suppose you'll come back with him in the next couple of days. I guess it's back to work; your vacation is over!"

"Not exactly. Look. There is something I should tell you." She took a deep breath. "I got laid off. Cutbacks."

Laura was quiet a moment, then said, "Even more reason to return. You'll have to get your unemployment papers in order and start looking for another job immediately so you don't miss the boat."

"Boat? What boat?" Brianda muttered under her breath.

She closed her eyes and rubbed her temples while her mother kept on talking. She had no clue what to do with her life. At the moment, she didn't feel capable of getting on any boat or restarting a life that felt distant in a place like Madrid, which had also begun to seem very far away. Madrid meant Esteban, but how was she supposed to sleep every night with a man her body rejected? She could probably stay in Tiles for a while, but between Colau's attitude and Neli's mysteries, it hardly seemed like the place where she'd find peace and quiet. She had always thought of herself as sensible; she had always done what people considered the right thing, but now she was disoriented.

At the first opportunity, she passed the phone back to her aunt. When Isolina hung up, she said in a very low voice, "We heard you. I didn't know, love, I'm sorry. You know you can stay here as long as you want."

Brianda gave her a grateful hug. She poured herself a glass of water and took some ibuprofen.

"Do you mind if I go to bed early, Esteban?"

"Not at all," he responded. "I'll stay here and read for a bit. I have a couple of cases to prepare for Monday, and it's already Friday."

Brianda climbed up the creaking stairs to her room.

Her last thought before sleep overtook her was that she would be sad to leave that place without seeing Lubich. It was obvious she hadn't mastered her fear. She still hadn't dared cross that line in the forest into the unknown.

When she woke up the following morning, Esteban was working at the desk near the balcony. The sunlight beaming into the room was so intense she could barely open her eyes.

"Good morning, sleepyhead." Esteban came over, sat on the bed, and leaned over to kiss her. "It's already eleven, and it's an incredibly beautiful day. Are you feeling better?"

Brianda nodded.

She got up, took a quick shower, and put on a pair of jeans, a warm blouse, and a white sweater topped off with a colorful scarf. She was in a surprisingly good mood. Sleeping in had done her good.

"Would you like to go for a walk?" she asked.

Esteban pointed to the papers. "I'm pressed for time. I'm sure Isolina will go with you."

Brianda went down to the kitchen, had some coffee with milk, and went out looking for Isolina, who she spotted at the back of the house cleaning the remains of dead flowers and plants from some anemic beds. She watched her for a moment and wondered why she'd work so hard at something that even in twenty lifetimes would never look like a real garden. But there Isolina was, year after year, continuing her challenge. Brianda was about to call out, but she remembered her thought from the previous night and stopped. It was time.

She walked around to the front and resolutely took the path toward the fountain. As if he had been waiting for her, Luzer got up and began to follow. Under a shriveled ash tree, Brianda found a thick stick in case she had to get rid of him. If there was anyone or anything she would not miss when she left Tiles, it was that animal and his owner. With the beast at her heels, she walked to the path toward Lubich, just before the graveyard, and stopped. Her heart began to pound.

She thought of all the times she had taken this path of lush undergrowth just to where the climbing plants overtook the landscape, and decided to try one more time. It might be a long time before she got another chance. She wondered if she could finally make herself cross the woods to Lubich.

Everything was in her favor. It was a beautiful, sunny day without a cloud in the sky. Luzer, although still looking at her suspiciously, made a good guard dog, alert to everything, his bark frightening off every other animal.

The walk warmed her up, so she took off her sweater and tied it around her waist. Luzer left the path to sniff among the trees, but came back rapidly, as if realizing he should not leave her alone. But Brianda was surprised by the peace she felt for the first time in months. She was calm, serene, and even happy. She thought it must be the result of her overcoming a specific fear: on her own, she had managed to enter the unsettlingly dense forest from which she had fled so many times before, trailed by an animal more wolf than dog. And nothing had happened. There were no monsters, no ghosts, just a riotous display of nature on a living canvas of green, yellow, ochre, gray, and blue.

At last, she, the path, and the woods came to a halt before a stone wall whose only opening was a forged iron gate about ten feet high. Calm gave way to wonder. This was the forbidden place, the gloomy castle where the valley's children could vanish. She wondered where the dangerous precipice was—if it even existed.

The open gate tempted Brianda to enter that corner where time had stood still for centuries. She took several steps, and Luzer began to growl as ferociously as he had that night with Neli, but this time he kept his distance. The hair on the back of Brianda's neck stood on end. She had the absurd impression that Luzer wanted to stop her—not because of any imminent danger but out of frustration, as he himself didn't dare to enter. But having come so far, she had no intention of stopping now.

With her heart thumping, Brianda crept along the graveled path that curled slowly toward a terrace with some building materials stacked up beside a centuries-old stone mansion. The imposing sight of the somber building of unpolished masonry made her forget Luzer's now-distant growls.

Loud noises and voices led her to a colossal stone gate; from its hinges hung a gigantic wooden door, decorated with iron rivets as big as eggs on top of diamond-shaped metal strips. She peeked past the gate to an interior patio. She tilted her head back to appreciate the elaborate wooden latticework that covered the entrance passage, and felt dizzy, both from the movement itself and from the magnificence of the work. Then she entered the patio, which was as big as the main square of many small villages, and she was awestruck. A tall tower was a solemn junction between the first building she had passed through and a more elegant one covered in ivy. This second building was probably the main residence, and it had windows framed with stone blocks, some with carved wooden ledges, and a pair of beautiful windows with three arches each. The other attached buildings were simpler—she thought they must have been the old stables and hay barns—but the eaves with their corbels, carved and decorated with spirals and wreathed motifs, conferred a unity to the whole site.

Lubich was magnificent and sumptuous, but there was something in that stone-filled world that made her shudder. She understood better why Corso was so occupied with the house, but couldn't imagine why a single man had decided to undertake a project of such enormous proportions in this out-of-the-way spot.

In the farthest part of the patio, where there was still scaffolding up, a group of workers continued their tasks, oblivious to her presence. Brianda recognized Bernardo, Petra's husband, and wondered whether to go over to him.

"What a surprise!" exclaimed Jonas. His smile made the small wrinkles around his eyes stand out. "What are you doing here?"

"I was out for a walk and got curious. I hope that the owner won't mind me just dropping by." She hoped Jonas couldn't tell that she was fishing to find out if Corso was there.

Just then, a dump truck roared up at great speed despite being loaded with rubble.

"Nah, I don't think he'll mind," said Jonas. "There he is."

The vehicle stopped and Corso, bare-chested, jumped down. He quickly untied a shirt from around his waist and pulled it on. He instinctively smoothed down his rebellious hair and brushed his pants, clearly trying to look respectable for the unexpected visitor.

Brianda froze. In a few seconds, she would have to greet him. She was afraid she wouldn't be able to utter a word.

She looked up, and her eyes met Corso's. The mansion, the patio, the tower all faded into the background. If it weren't for the clarity of his imposing figure, shirt loose over his jeans, his unruly dark hair, his deep eyes, she would have thought she was going to faint. She noticed her racing pulse, the tightness in her chest, the strain in her neck. She had to say something, but no words came. How well did they know each other? Did thinking and dreaming about him count?

Corso leaned down to kiss her politely on the cheeks and Brianda saw each frame of the scene in slow motion: Corso's hand on her forearm, Corso's face nearing hers, the brush of his rough skin against her cheek, the closeness of his lips and breath on their way to the other cheek, and his eyes, open and captivated, as they separated.

That gesture of greeting affected her very being. In this historic mansion, unaltered for centuries, her internal clock lost its rhythm. It halted in an eternal present of simultaneous events that might or might not have already happened. The distant appeared close; the close, disconcerting; the disconcerting, a loop where time bent over itself and returned to the past.

A question rescued her from the vertigo.

"Would you like to see the house?"

"I'd love to but perhaps another time," she managed to say. "I don't want to interrupt your work."

Brianda went red at her own lie. There was nothing she would have liked more than to tour Lubich with Corso, but she didn't want to seem too eager.

"The good thing about being the owner is that I can stop whenever I want." He pointed to the dumper. "Jonas, it's all yours."

Jonas said good-bye and went back to work.

They stood in silence for a few moments. She wondered if he was just as overwhelmed as she.

"OK, then," Corso finally said. "Let's start at the beginning."

He led her to the door of the most elegant building, over which there was a lintel with some words inscribed.

"Johan of Lubich, 1322," read Brianda. It sent shivers through her to think of its age.

"We found this stone in a pile of rubble. I thought this was a good place to relocate it. Almost everything you see was nothing more than a shell a few months ago."

"I must say, I'm really impressed." Brianda glanced over the buildings to avoid looking at him directly. "I didn't see it before you started the restoration, of course, but the result is magnificent. How did you know what to do?"

Corso smiled at her compliment.

"I had a few sketches from an ancestor that I used as a guide."

"Your family lived here?"

"Not exactly. For centuries, Lubich was just a neglected part of the estate of my family in Siena. From the oldest wills, each new owner had to sign a compulsory clause to become sole heir, to take charge of a piece of property in the old Spanish county of Orrun. The clause didn't specify what 'take charge of' meant, so for centuries my family just paid the taxes in order to retain ownership. When my father died, my brothers and I divided up the inheritance and this part fell to me."

"So, you'd never seen it before?" Brianda asked in astonishment.

"No one in my family has been here except for one relative in the nineteenth century. He crossed the Pyrenees to see the valley of Tiles. He made an illustrated travel notebook with quill drawings of the remains of what must have been the original Lubich Manor. I based the restoration work on those sketches at first and later . . . I don't know how to explain it, but a sixth sense showed me how to continue. Has something like that ever happened to you?"

"Knowing something without knowing why?" Brianda smiled sadly. "Yes, as a matter of fact it has."

In response, Corso gave her a look so riveting that she began to tremble all over again. She sought refuge in the old hall, as massive and grandiose as the rest of the building, dominated by the most beautiful staircase she had ever seen. The stone steps and bannister led to a landing presided over by a religious painting. There, the stairs forked in two diverging arms with ironwork bannisters, then swooped around and converged on a door.

"That door leads to the bedrooms, but let's begin downstairs." Corso pointed to some antique doors under the stairs.

Brianda thought she'd use up her repertoire of adjectives and expressions of amazement during her tour of the main floor. She opted for politely nodding at Corso's explanations. Even though she found the decoration as excessive as the construction, he kept telling her how many things still needed to be unpacked and or to arrive from Italy to make the house warm and welcoming. Brianda didn't know what world Corso came from exactly, but it had to be very different from the world of other mortals. He talked about the furniture without any affectation, as if the grand pieces were family. On his lips, a word like "cornucopia" to describe the gold mirror he was now showing her didn't sound extravagant; instead, it simply expressed an object with a history, an anecdote on how he had come by it. His words transformed the house from a cold, static museum to a vibrant gallery full of life.

"And this is the last room on this floor." Corso led her into a small room where most of the objects were still wrapped in padding. "It leads to the front patio."

Brianda's gaze fell on a small walnut chest with traveling handles at either end. The chest sat on a narrow, bowlegged table. She didn't know much about antiques, but the piece seemed special.

"What is this?" she asked.

Corso approached and opened the lid, revealing a series of drawers inside.

"It's a writing desk or cabinet." He pulled the ring of one of the little drawers. "It was used for storing important documents, valuable objects, or money. The lid was used for writing on. I inherited it with the house."

Brianda was puzzled by how this piece was with the house. Corso must have noticed she was curious and explained, "I don't know why, but this particular object is attached to the house. Generations of my family members have been very clear about that in their wills."

Brianda ran her hand along the surface to appreciate the smoothness of the polished wood and the tiny pieces of bone and boxwood that formed decorative motifs that looked Moorish. There were so many magnificent objects in the house, but if she had to choose one, it would undoubtedly be this. In the center was a charming little door decorated with a simple lintel and closed with a minute lock.

"I suppose the most important things were kept here," she observed.

Corso took out a minuscule key from a drawer and opened the compartment.

"Yes, as you can see, a real treasure chest," he joked.

Brianda stroked the interior, in which there were small pieces of wood in each corner like columns. All four had been polished, but one of them had a slot, invisible to the eye but not to the touch. Suddenly, her heart jumped, and she was filled with emptiness. She brought her hand to her brow and found it cold and damp. She had to lean on the table to prevent herself from fainting.

"What's the matter?" asked Corso in alarm. "You've gone pale." He looked at his watch and realized the tour had lasted almost two hours. "It's my fault, exhausting you with so many explanations. Would you like a drink?"

Brianda shook her head. The dizziness had already passed. Perhaps it was just a reaction to so much overwhelming art—a touch of Stendhal syndrome.

"I'm fine, thanks." She gave him a reassuring smile. "Maybe just some fresh air."

Corso led her back to the entrance hall, then hesitated.

"We could go out to the garden, but the workers are out there. Are you sure you don't want something to eat? Or would you prefer to see the tower? The views are stunning."

Brianda looked at her watch.

"Oh, is it getting late?"

It was, but she didn't know when she'd have another chance to be alone with Corso. She was desperate for any excuse to stay in his company.

"Just let me know. I have all the time in the world," he said.

"Then I pick the tower."

So, there's the infamous precipice, Brianda thought, carefully peeking through one of the openings on the second story of the tower.

Behind Lubich Manor, the land fell off into a deep ravine. From up here, she could see that the buildings were resting on solid rock. She struggled to imagine the complicated scaffolding that had been needed to build the walls of the tower and the back part of the house. A marvelous landscape unfolded above the chasm: vast, fertile lands that extended from the edge of the Lubich forest on the right and Beles Peak on the left to the foothills of even higher summits in the distance, their peaks already covered with snow. Brianda now understood that Lubich Manor had been a fortress. She wondered who the original owners had been so afraid of. The ravine must certainly have received many bodies in its depths. She wished she knew more about the history of the valley.

"What do you think?" whispered Corso. "Was it worth the climb?"

Brianda nodded without taking her eyes from the horizon. She felt Corso so close, but didn't dare turn around and meet his eyes. A sudden breeze brushed her cheeks, offering some relief to the heat running through her body.

"I've spent many hours up here," he admitted. "When I arrived and saw the amount of work that was needed, I had serious doubts. The first thing I rebuilt was the tower, maybe because from here I could see everything. Later, the more often I came up, the happier I felt about the progress I was making. Now I feel like this is my place; that I finally found it." He let out a little laugh. "It sounds nice: my place."

"And why wasn't your place in Siena? This is so far away from your home and your family."

Corso shrugged.

"I don't know. But the day came when I knew I needed a change."

His words only heightened Brianda's curiosity. It was as if she wanted to hear from Corso's lips the answers to the questions she was continually asking herself.

"But what made you change?"

Corso was quiet for a few long moments. Brianda regretted being so bold, but she resisted apologizing.

"Soon after my father's death, I was in an accident. My best friend, Santo, died." Now Brianda did turn to look at him, and Corso was grimacing with the pain of it. "It wasn't my fault exactly, but I was driving." Instinctively, he raised his hand to his scar. "It took me a long time to get over it. I don't know if I have, really. I named my horse after him to keep his memory with me always. Then, when I received this inheritance, I took it on as penitence and as a challenge. I needed something different, far away, and something that demanded so much effort that it would force me to keep going—"

He stopped abruptly, as if embarrassed at being so open with a near stranger. He bent down toward her and asked, "And you, Brianda, are you just here for vacation? Will you be staying in Tiles for long?"

Brianda blinked. For the first time in weeks, she knew something with certainty. Next to Corso, in this soaring tower, her heart screamed that all she wanted was to stay here forever.

She dropped her gaze, ashamed of her own desires. Incapable of answering the simple question, she thought of what Corso had said. His life changed because people close to him died. But she had nothing like that to point to, no excuses. She had not found peace in Tiles, and she was afraid she wouldn't find it by going back to Madrid either.

She looked at Corso's face. If only she had a physical mark to make her suffering seem real, obvious proof of a wound—and of healing. She wanted to run her fingers along the long, deep scar . . .

And then she did.

She gently stroked the man's cheek, from his right eye to his chin. She noticed the contrast between the soft burnt skin, and the roughness of his unshaven face.

She hoped he would not pull away, and he did not. Corso closed his eyes and seemed to enjoy her caress, lightly pressing his face against her fingers. He put his large, leathery hand on top of hers and guided it toward the other cheek and then to his lips. He kissed her fingers with exquisite tenderness before continuing the journey to his chest, where he kept her hand wrapped in his for a few eternal seconds, as if checking for a signal to release her, which she never gave him.

Then, Corso circled her waist with his arms and brought her toward him. He leaned down in search of her lips, and she offered them up in a tentative kiss, shy and contained at first, then increasingly steamy and hungry. He leaned back against the wall beside a pair of windows open to the void to make her more comfortable in his arms. Brianda could feel every inch of his body pressed to hers, and she felt a sensation of abandonment and need, of urgency and intimacy that she hoped would never end.

Brianda momentarily opened her eyes and found herself staring into the vast landscape beyond the tower. Her head spun, but this time, the vertigo felt good. She leaned into the intoxicating feeling of the oscillation of the stones, the fields, the trees, the peaks, and Corso's body. For the first time in months, she welcomed the symptoms that had been causing such grief. She wished that her racing heart, her trembling and weak legs, and even her fear would force her to seek permanent refuge in the strong arms of this man.

For an indefinite spell, each kiss, each caress, each touch of her fingers marked a territory that she yearned to return to immediately after leaving. She felt as if, at any moment, their intimacy might transform into a physical and temporal abyss. Before falling into it, she had to hurry to share with him the urgency to get undressed, recognize each other, examine each other, attach to each other, feel the tension of each muscle and the dampness of the skin, sway with each other, and share knowing whispers and sighs.

Brianda felt she had to love him before there was no more tower to protect them, before the vertigo of her guilt and confusion returned. Her sudden love felt as old as the graveyards, the monasteries, the manor houses, the churches, the stone blocks of the walls, and the antique desks on which others like them had leaned, with their own hopes and fears, worries, desires, and frustrations, long before she ever rode with Corso on the back of his black Friesian.

She had to love him because, without knowing why, she knew she needed to make up for lost time.

12.

The insistent beeping of a car horn broke the spell. Then they heard a high-pitched, cheerful voice. Corso brusquely separated from Brianda. She instantly missed the heat of his skin on her body. Corso peeked out through one of the arches overlooking the patio and swore. He began to get dressed as fast as he could.

"What's the matter?" asked Brianda, sitting up to collect her clothes.

"My wife—"

Brianda heard nothing more. Feeling like she'd been struck, she threw her clothes on while he ran down the stairs. When a cry of joy came from below, she cautiously peered out and saw a beautiful black-haired woman throwing herself around the same neck Brianda's arms had just embraced. Anguish flooded her chest.

Corso took some luggage from the trunk of the car, threw a quick glance upward, and disappeared into the house with the woman. Brianda tottered down the stairs, feeling like instead of flagstones there was something viscous under her feet. Elsa's words at the monastery about the significance of the number three beat in her mind like a diabolic drum. Material, spiritual, intellectual. She had fully felt that man, she had absorbed his breath, she had wanted to cling to him and ask him to help her free herself of worry and suffering. Infinite, eternal, all-powerful. She barely knew Corso, but she had felt a powerful force attracting her to him, as if he'd emerged from the depths of time, before death and beyond it. But three was the sum of two plus one.

And at that moment, the one too many was her.

Checking that no one would see her, she ran across the patio, her eyes blind with tears.

She found Luzer in the exact spot she had left him, at the gate that separated Lubich from the woods. In spite of the urgency that gripped her, Brianda hesitated. She was afraid that as soon as she crossed the threshold, he would attack her for having disobeyed. Then again, maybe she deserved punishment.

What had she done?

A van stopped beside her.

"Hop in, I'll give you a lift," said Jonas. "I didn't realize you were leaving."

Brianda didn't want to talk to anybody, but she was already going to be late for lunch, there was no phone signal, and Luzer's eyes were terrifying.

She got in.

"Wow, time just flew by!"

"Are you surprised?" Jonas laughed. "Look, I've worked in many places, but this is different. In this house, you know when you start but never when you'll finish."

Brianda's head was spinning. Surprise seemed an insufficient word for what had happened. After the confusion and disappointment caused by the arrival of Corso's wife, Brianda was crashing back to earth. How was she supposed to face Esteban? She was grateful for a fast ride to Anels House, where Isolina and Esteban must be worried, but she wished she had more time to collect herself. Her back and knees were sore; the taste of Corso was on her lips, his fingerprints on her skin.

She needed more time to practice the casual voice she'd have to fake to explain her delay.

"It's an incredible place, for sure," she said. "A bit big, maybe."

Overwhelming. Impressive.

Like its owner.

Why hadn't he said he was married? She felt betrayed. But that was stupid, she reflected. She hadn't said anything about Esteban either, though he had seen them together.

"You need to be very rich or very crazy to do what Corso is doing," continued Jonas. "Or both."

Or maybe just brave, thought Brianda, *brave enough to take risks and change your life*. She envied his courage, the same courage she now needed to control her nerves. She couldn't understand how she had given herself to him like that just a few days after meeting him. And even worse? It had been the most amazing encounter of her life. And there was something more disconcerting still: her current agitation wasn't just guilt or shame at being unfaithful to Esteban, but the realization that she would do it again in a heartbeat. Even if Corso was married. She doubted anyone else in the world would understand her. On the contrary: anyone else would think her stupid, irresponsible, and unfaithful. And rightly so.

As the van neared Anels House, Brianda cringed. There was no way she could look Esteban in the eye. He'd be able to tell that she had willingly thrown herself into the arms of a stranger.

Jonas parked in the yard of Anels House. The door opened and Isolina appeared.

"That was a very long walk, dear!"

"You wouldn't believe where I've been," said Brianda, forcing herself to act normal. "Thanks for the lift, Jonas."

She rushed into the house, locked herself in the bathroom, and took the quickest shower of her life, scrubbing herself clean. As she changed her clothes, she had to make a tremendous effort to recognize herself in that woman who had enjoyed Corso in the tower. She had acted like a hormonal teenager instead of an adult in a committed relationship. It was not as if sex was strange and new. She'd had physical relationships with other men before Esteban, and with him, sex had evolved from the initial passion to the measured, customary enthusiasm of recent times. Except for the current bad patch, she'd never had any complaints in the bedroom. But if she was truly satisfied, why had her encounter with Corso been so powerful, so desperate, and so painful, even afflicted?

She felt a throbbing in her chest. Something dormant inside her had awoken.

Why, damn it? she thought. Why now? Wasn't she confused enough?

When she came back downstairs, everyone was already at the table. Isolina had decided to celebrate Esteban's last day in Tiles with a special lunch: roast beef and several elaborate vegetable dishes.

"We thought we'd have to start without you," said an irritated Esteban. "Where have you been?"

"I'm sorry," apologized Brianda. "I didn't mean to take so long."

With feigned cheer, Brianda began to tell them about her walk along the path to Lubich, her surprise at finding the mansion, and her natural curiosity to look around the place. She had run into Jonas and Corso, and the two of them, she lied, had shown her around.

Out of the corner of her eye, she noticed Colau lift his head when he heard the Italian's name.

"It was excessively ornate for my taste," she lied again. "There are so many antiques you'd think you were in the past, or maybe at a museum."

She was lying so well that it just made her feel worse about herself. Here she was betraying two of the people she loved most, telling them one lie after another. Right after betraying Esteban with her body. And with her soul?

"And what was the owner like?" Isolina asked. "Imagine living all alone in such a huge house!"

Brianda took a sip of wine. The owner was the best thing that had happened to her in a long time. Yes, she had also betrayed Esteban with her soul. She felt her cheeks beginning to burn.

"He's actually pretty friendly, maybe a little long-winded about his things. I didn't know how to stop him politely so I could get out of there—"

She was about to add something about his wife but caught herself. In fact, she had not met her . . . fortunately. She drank more wine to have a good excuse for her red cheeks. Torrid images of her body intertwined with Corso's flashed through her mind. She felt sick. Esteban didn't deserve this.

"He must have enjoyed himself, showing off his antiques to you," Esteban said acidly.

"He wasn't showing off!" Brianda retorted, instantly regretting her defensive tone.

"Ah, no?"

Brianda avoided Esteban's look.

"He was just describing them is all." She managed to sound casual, even with her heart beating wildly. The more she talked, the greater her sense of guilt grew. "Since I don't know much about those things—"

"And did he tell you why he's here, this Corso?" Colau suddenly asked. His tongue seemed to reject the name.

"He inherited the house," Brianda answered.

"Inherited it? Who from?"

"Apparently, it's been in his family for centuries," Brianda explained, "but since they lived far away, nobody had taken charge of it."

Colau frowned. "Do you know if he has any old documents?"

"I didn't ask him, actually."

"Colau, what's with the interrogation?" a surprised Isolina wanted to know. "You've never been so interested in Lubich. Does it have something to do with the witch trials? I don't remember Neli mentioning any women from the mansion."

"I have my reasons," replied Colau.

Isolina threw him a reproachful look. "You never kept it to yourself before when you found something interesting. I just don't know what's gotten into you recently."

An uncomfortable silence followed. Brianda stared out the window at Beles Peak, the unmoved witness to everything that happened in this place. The sun had lost its morning intensity, but the rocky mass still shone. She observed how different the mountain was depending on where you were looking from. From here, it seemed like a triangle of straight lines, overbearing in its solitude. From Lubich Manor, the slope spilled down from the summit, deformed into threatening angles, one on top of the other, until fusing with the fields. She wondered which part was the most beautiful or the most real, the front or the hidden part, the part everybody knew or the one nobody knew, the present or the possible.

She thought of her forebearers being whipped and executed for witchcraft and shivered. Centuries ago, another Brianda had looked at this same mountain. Did she wonder about its shape, its lines, its colors? What was she like? What were her worries?

In the past, another Brianda had existed in Tiles, but that radiant morning, she was the Brianda who climbed the tower of Lubich, absorbed the landscape, and crowned the summit of Beles with her soul. For a few hours, she had fully belonged to that place. But the moment had passed. The sky was growing overcast. The wind began to rustle the leaves on the trees.

Now she was in Anels House, with her aunt and her Esteban. This was her life. There was no room for anything else. No room for Corso. As with the mountain, she was the front part, the part everybody knew, the present. She might feel disoriented, even lost, but she could not be a different person.

She bowed her head and sighed deeply. Esteban stroked her hand. "Are you all right?" he asked.

Brianda nodded, although his touch confused her even more. Other hands had enjoyed her body that day. With vigor, with devotion. She struggled to hold back the tears as her regret grew and grew.

"I don't like to see you so sad," he whispered in her ear.

Brianda wondered if a person could die of guilt. Esteban's tenderness reminded her of the years they'd spent together, of the many more ahead, and of all the difficulties they would overcome. She had to leave Tiles—the sooner the better. The rational part of her personality had finally regained control. She thought about how she had achieved her goals in life with effort and perseverance, with interest and good judgment, and suddenly, she was afraid of losing it all. Perhaps the trigger to that realization had been her meeting with Corso. She had dived into the well of recklessness as a last resort, but instead of drowning in its depths, she had returned to the surface gasping for safe and familiar air. It was high time to face reality and her own life.

The words of the fortune-teller echoed in her ears, and she repeated to herself the parts the woman had gotten right: Brianda needed to make a journey and she had made it; she would experience carnal passion and so she had; she would undergo a much-needed change and that was taking place. Now it was time to go home. Far away from Corso. With Esteban.

She offered her boyfriend a loving smile, but inside she ached. She vowed never to reveal the betrayal, knowing it would weigh on her forever.

"I'm ready to go home," she said. "With you."

At dusk, a fine rain began to cover the fields, blurring the landscape beyond the windows of Anels House. Brianda spent the rest of the day in the sitting room, contemplating the flames of the fire and frustrated by the slow passing of time. She had a book in her lap but found it impossible to read a single word. She felt as if her spirit were fading and darkening with the same resignation as the surrounding fields, giving in to the coming of night at the foot of Beles Peak, dark because of the absence of stars around its summit, rigid in the cold November dampness.

After dinner, Petra came to pick up Isolina to go have a drink at the bar. Brianda begged off, saying she and Esteban had to be on the road early. What if Corso was there? It seemed unlikely with his wife in town, but she couldn't risk it.

"Don't you want to say good-bye to Neli?" asked Isolina.

"I'll be back someday. Anyway, I don't like good-byes."

The truth was, she couldn't bear to speak that word to Corso.

Once in bed, Esteban fell asleep immediately, but she lay awake. The rain beating against the roof, the gurgling of the drainpipes, and the frightening thunder made her tremble, but the real reason for her insomnia was something else. She could neither get her unexpected adventure with Corso out of her head nor the guilt out of her heart.

Around midnight, she was startled by a noise outside. She got up and looked out the window.

A shadow moved like an indecisive ghost under the tenuous light of the lone lamp. She knew immediately who it was. Astride Santo, Corso paced back and forth across the yard. After a while, the horse whinnied loudly in protest.

A flash of lightning announced the thunderclap rising from some dark corner of the valley, and Brianda's heart began to race. She rested her hand on the cold windowpane. The murmur of thunder gained momentum and then paused for an instant before bursting over the mountain in a deafening roar. The glass shook, and the outside light went out. The rain fell in torrents over Corso, turning his powerful silhouette into a pitiful smudge.

Brianda wanted to open the window and shout his name. She had to talk to him once more before she left. She wanted to call to him to wait for her, to tell him she'd race downstairs as fast as she could, that she would run to him and calm Santo by stroking his nose, that she would calm Corso by caressing his face.

"Brianda?" asked Esteban.

Brianda tensed up, wishing she were invisible. She had to get away from the window or Esteban would see Corso, but her body refused to obey. Her eyes peered desperately into the darkness, praying for more lightning.

Esteban used his phone as a flashlight. He came over to her, circled her waist with his arms, and rested his head on her shoulder with his eyes closed.

"What a storm," he said hoarsely.

Like a whip being lashed, another flash of lightning lit up the yard. Brianda saw Corso looking up. She thought she could make out a tense and aggressive look on his wounded face. Then, Corso loosened his painful grip on the reins and furiously spurred Santo to jump the railing. At a gallop, he dissolved into the night.

The piercing anguish made Brianda grit her teeth. She couldn't remember the last time she had felt such stress in her jaw, in her hands, in her neck. Esteban's silence indicated that he'd not seen anything, but that was not the cause of her anxiety. Earlier that day Corso had been completely hers, and now he had disappeared, gone back to his wife, while she still had his movements, his scent, his voice, and his taste imprinted on her body. This was the end. *Good-bye.*

The affair was over almost before it had begun.

13.

Brianda packed up the last few things with the light on. The previous night's rain had not abated, and the room that had been hers for nearly two weeks seemed gloomier than ever.

She carried her bag downstairs, surprised when Luzer failed to give her his customary growl from the door of Colau's office. She stuck her head into the kitchen and the sitting room. Nobody.

She noticed a strong smell of tobacco coming from her uncle's study. Funny, the door was ajar. She tiptoed over and listened. Not a sound. She pushed the door, which opened with an indolent squeak, and peeked inside. The study was exactly as she remembered it. It was a large, dark room stuffed with books and papers. There was a big worktable, shelves, cabinets with thick hinges, a pair of armchairs, and several small side tables. She found it difficult to make out the color of the walls as they were covered with walnut-stained wooden or golden frames that were filled with fragments of old documents, religious etchings, or portraits.

She wondered where Colau kept the mysterious little red velvet box. She felt compelled to go in and look for it, but the fear of being discovered and inciting his fury like when she was a child paralyzed her.

She closed her eyes and took a deep breath. The same inner voice that had impelled her to go to Lubich now insisted that she could not leave Tiles without searching Colau's office. *Just for a minute,* it said. *A quick look. Another fear overcome.*

She hoped this gesture of bravery wouldn't bring as much guilt as the last.

She crept toward the table and something caught her eye. Hidden under a stack of papers, the tip of a wine-colored object was visible. She quickly moved the papers, but it was just an old hardbound notebook. She smiled at her own disappointment. That would have been too easy. Then she closed her eyes and concentrated on the image of the child with the box in her hand. Where had she found it? She saw herself going through the room, opening all the drawers before stopping at the walnut desk beside the worktable and stroking the surface of the first drawer with her small hands.

Excited, Brianda hurried to the desk. She opened the drawer and stuck her hands deep inside, identifying and discarding various objects with her fingertips. An intense heat ran through her body, the fear of being caught, but she had gotten this far and had no intention of stopping now.

Her heart skipped a beat. There it was. She grabbed the little box and pulled it out. This time, she did not hesitate in rapidly pressing the small brass button. A worn leather pouch appeared. She undid the knot and emptied the contents onto the desk. A folded piece of paper fell to the floor, but she didn't pay attention to it because what was hidden in the box was far more beautiful than she could ever have imagined.

It was an antique ring, gold with a shimmering emerald. When she picked it up to look closer, her hands shook. Inside, there were words engraved. The letters were so small that it was difficult to make them out. She tried again and had to sit down to avoid fainting.

Omnia mecum porto, read the inscription.

I take all with me.

She froze. They were the same Latin words she'd seen on the grave. Why hadn't Colau said anything when he had translated them? She wondered what other secrets he was hiding in his office.

On an impulse, she tried the ring on the fourth finger of her right hand, and, although it was big on her, she had the feeling that it had been designed for her skin. She raised her hand and marveled that she had never seen such a beautiful ring. It must be very valuable.

Suddenly, she heard footsteps and was stricken by panic. In a split second, she calculated that she wouldn't have enough time to put the ring back, so she slammed the drawer shut and ran to the door.

"There you are!" said Isolina.

"I came to say good-bye to Colau, but I can't find him," Brianda explained with her fist so tightly clenched that her nails dug into her palm.

"We're waiting for you. Esteban is in a hurry."

On her way out, Brianda slipped the ring into her pants pocket. She regretted taking it, but didn't see how she could sort it out without admitting she had violated Colau's rule.

They said their good-byes in the front hall because of the rain. Esteban was already in his car. After thanking Isolina for everything with a big hug and giving two cold kisses to Colau, in whose face she read relief, Brianda ran to the car and started the engine. With the ring burning in her pocket, she was more anxious than ever to get out of there. She then saw Colau raising a hand.

"Wait!" he shouted.

Brianda's stomach dropped. There was no way he could know.

Colau held the umbrella so Isolina could come over to the car. Brianda rolled down the window.

"I almost forgot!" said Isolina, handing her a thick envelope. Tears shone in her eyes. "Neli gave me this for you last night. She was sorry she couldn't say good-bye."

Colau took Isolina's hand and led her away from the car. It seemed to Brianda that he was holding her too tightly, as if he did not want to be separated from her, as if away from her he would lose his balance.

Brianda left the envelope on the seat and followed Esteban's car. Luzer's howls faded into the distance. She was glad to be in her own car so she could say a silent good-bye to Tiles. She wondered if there was anything she would miss, but given the blackness of the nights, the isolation and dilapidation of Anels House, Colau's hostility, Neli's strange beliefs, the awful weather, and the menacing specter of Luzer, the only thing she could think of was Isolina . . .

And Corso.

She passed the clearing with the linden and fountain. The rain poured down, tearing off the last dead leaves and forming them into a damp, dense blanket on either side of the road. At the fork to Lubich, she slowed for a moment. It seemed as if centuries had passed since she'd ventured down that path yesterday. Beyond the curtain of water, she pictured Corso first in Lubich and later under the torrential rain. No matter how much distance or time between them, she would never forget him. She was afraid she'd always feel a stab in her chest when she recalled what had happened between them, when she wondered what might have been.

She shook her head, took a final glance at Beles Peak in her rearview, and sped to catch up with Esteban.

It would be best to forget it. The sooner she convinced herself that Corso had been a mistake, the sooner she could put her life in order. It had been a terrible mistake, she repeated every time she recalled his name, his face, or his body on the road from Aiscle to the highway and from there to Zaragoza and then to Madrid. She had to forget about him.

But Corso stayed with her all through the welcome-back dinner at her parents' place. And he stayed with her the following days, as she got her unemployment papers in order, while she had coffee with former colleagues or dined with Silvia and Ricardo, as she worked on her resume, as she waited each night for Esteban to get home from the office, as she caressed the emerald ring.

She thought about Corso at all hours, as if he were the "all" on the ring's inscription, as if he had always been hers, as if the fleeting hours she had shared with him had been years.

The obsession with Corso caused her such anxiety that, weeks after returning to Madrid, she increased the dosage of her medication. She should really ask a doctor, but seeing Roberto again—or worse, a real psychiatrist—was more than she could handle. All her good intentions and resolutions about taking control of her life had come to naught. And convincing her family nothing was wrong left her exhausted. As soon Esteban went to work in the morning, she went back to bed, but at night she had to fabricate a list of things she had done. She didn't need a shrink to confirm that her symptoms were leading to deep depression. Her only solace was when she climbed into bed, closed her eyes, and imagined scenes from Tiles with Corso and herself as the main characters. When she was lucky, she managed to relax to the point where the scenes crossed into full-fledged dreams.

Brianda wondered what role the pills played in this dissociation. She knew she was falling into a complicated vortex she wouldn't be able to escape by herself, and she tried to resist succumbing to total abandonment. As the late fall faltered under winter's first attacks, her mood was erratic. And as hard as she tried to hide her apathy, to play at being the old Brianda, she knew that, for Esteban, she was becoming a stranger. She was fading away before his eyes.

One afternoon, shortly before Christmas, Brianda came upon the envelope Isolina had given her when she left Tiles. She had thrown it in the closet while unpacking and forgotten about it completely.

She carried it into the sitting room, got comfortable on the sofa, broke the seal, and took out several pieces of paper, including some photocopies. A lavender-colored pouch fell out, and she recalled the white one she'd found the night her car broke down. On the first handwritten page, she found the explanation. Neli had placed the pouch in her bag for good luck during her stay in Tiles and then done the same for her return to Madrid.

Brianda snorted. She certainly didn't feel lucky.

In the letter, Neli recommended some books to read, and included excerpts to entice her. She wrote,

> *We have not known each other for long and you have no reason to trust me. But I am convinced that one day you will understand.*

Brianda looked over the reading list. The titles were revealing. The most repeated words were soul, life, journey, and time.

The letter included contact information for a doctor and Neli closed with,

> *If you have recurring nightmares or visions, or feel your heart suddenly taken over by nostalgia and melancholy when remembering something, or thinking about someone who is far away, call me.*

Brianda felt a chill. Neli might not have power to tell the future, but the woman was extraordinarily perceptive.

She picked up her laptop and spent a long time researching the books Neli had recommended. What she read seemed so incredible, implausible, and irrational, even bordering on science fiction, that she felt unwilling to accept it. However, a curious skepticism drove her to keep reading.

By that night, she already had a fair idea of what Neli was trying to tell her, and within a few days, her skepticism had become reasonable doubt. The fact that the books had been published by major presses, and that some of them were even written by respected psychiatrists, gave them a degree of credibility. Each time she came to an idea she struggled to assimilate, her brain asked: "And why not?" The books talked about people who suffered the same symptoms as she did and who had gotten better thanks to these therapies. What did she have to lose?

Some detractors accused the books of pseudo-science, of fraud, and of taking advantage of people's capacity for self-suggestion. A few months ago, she would have agreed, but now she was too desperate to write anything off.

Finally, one day in January, she picked up the telephone. She made an appointment for the following Monday. Immediately after hanging up, she regretted it. She felt tempted to call back, but she did not. There was a week to go. She had plenty of time to change her mind.

The office was located on the fifth floor of an innocuous building on a well-known and central street. It was near her house, but not close enough to walk there, so she took the Metro. A young woman with a South American accent opened the door and showed her to the waiting room, decorated simply in warm tones and framed philosophical quotes. Brianda read one of them several times over:

> *I did not begin when I was born, nor when I was conceived. I have been growing, developing, through incalculable myriads of millenniums. All my previous selves have their voices, echoes, promptings in me. Oh, incalculable times again shall I be born.*

The quote came from *The Star Rover* by Jack London, which surprised her because she associated the author with adventure novels. Although on reflection, she said to herself ironically, there could be no better adventure than crossing the barriers of space and time and becoming a star rover.

The young woman reappeared and showed her into a fairly large office with a desk covered in books and a big sofa. It looked just like she had imagined it would. What did surprise her was the therapist himself: a slim man, of uncertain age, elegant in an exquisite blue suit and graceful in his movements. He introduced himself as Angel and invited her to sit in a comfortable armchair near the sofa.

Brianda sensed that Angel was watching her closely, which increased her nervousness. She felt ridiculous, unable to prevent her hands from sweating and her voice trembling.

Amiably, professionally, and with a deep, persuasive voice, Angel questioned her about her family, work, and health. When Brianda detailed her physical symptoms, he frowned a couple of times, but made no comment. He just took notes in a black book until it seemed he decided he had enough information, and then he closed the notebook and looked directly at her.

"If you've gotten this far," he finally said, "I presume you have done your research. Why do you want me to treat you?"

"Isn't everything I've told you enough?" Brianda thought over all the promises written on the webpage she'd read on the subject. "I want to be cured."

"Yes, but there are more mainstream approaches. This is something very specific and special. Let's say that, normally, people try other therapies before coming here."

Brianda felt uncomfortable. Since her one visit to Roberto, she had relied on the pills to keep going, but they weren't enough, and she couldn't keep recklessly upping her dosage. And he was right, she hadn't done anything else; her stay in the country certainly couldn't be counted as therapeutic. If not for Neli, she wouldn't even be here. She chose to keep quiet.

"Have you had any strange experiences?" Angel prompted.

Brianda thought of the dreams, her visions of the angry mob in the church in Tiles, fainting in the graveyard, the decorations on the confessional in the monastery, and her inexplicable attraction to Corso—whose name she had somehow known without being told. She considered telling Angel everything, but was suddenly assailed by the same mistrust she had felt with the tarot reader: she didn't want to give too many clues that could guide him.

"Apart from the nightmares, nothing at all," she said.

Angel smiled strangely, as if acknowledging and accepting her lie, and she lowered her eyes, a little embarrassed.

"Fine," he said, getting to his feet and asking her to move to the couch. "We'll start the first session now. Do you have any questions?"

"Actually, I do. Will I get back to the way I was?"

"Brianda, you must be sure of one thing: we are always changing, every day of our lives. It's impossible to be who you were." He rested a hand on her shoulder. "Now lie down, close your eyes, and relax."

Brianda heard Angel drawing the thick curtains and switching off the light. Then he adjusted a pillow for her to lie on, brought the armchair over to the sofa, and sat down beside her.

From that moment, the man's voice became even deeper, even slightly stern. He began giving firm and methodical instructions for her to control her breathing, with perfectly measured pauses that reminded her of Isolina's instructions that day in Aiscle. With studied slowness, Angel guided her thoughts around her whole body, from her little toe to her scalp. Finally, he asked her to visualize an intense white light at the top of her head, inside, and to make that light travel again over her whole body, through all the muscles and nerves under her skin.

Brianda felt her breathing relax and the tension leave her. Her body felt as light as a feather.

Nestled on the sofa, she began to lose perception of her surroundings. An intense light invaded her body, occupying all the physical spaces of her being and bringing a sensation of peace and well-being only interrupted by a voice she felt incapable of disobeying.

"I'm going to count backwards," he told her, "from ten to one. When I get to one, you will be in a state of deep relaxation. Then you will remember nothing. You will live again." A long pause. "Ten . . . nine . . . eight . . . seven . . . six . . . five . . . four . . . three . . . two . . . one . . ."

14.

1585

Brianda crossed the paved patio, intending to take a stroll in the fields. She had heard that Nunilo was coming back that morning and she was impatient. When Nunilo or her father went to France, they always brought her something nice. She raised a hand to her neck and stroked the necklace that Johan, her father, had given her last spring as a present for her sixteenth birthday: a delicate glass-and-silver locket with beveled edges, filled with some dried edelweiss that looked like velvety stars. Johan had picked them for her in the mountains and gotten them immortalized at a jeweler's in Toulouse.

 She stopped for a second beside the improvised pen that prevented the cattle from straying into the main patio, and watched an enormous bull playfully butt several hens before plodding back toward the stables. After the freedom they had enjoyed that summer in the mountain pastures, the animals would soon have to make do with hay in their pens, although in comparison to other places, at least they could not complain of hunger. She looked around at the buildings that surrounded her house, the biggest in the valley, enclosed by a wall, protected by the natural moat of the precipice behind it, and guarded by a tower.

It had been a magnificent year for Lubich Manor.

At this point in September, not another wisp could fit in the hay sheds, the amount of wheat guaranteed an abundance of flour until the following harvest, the pigs had begun to waddle with difficulty, milk leaked from the cows' udders, and the mares had given birth to many mules. Even the doves spent their days lounging lazily on the stone windowsills, too full to coo.

Brianda took a deep breath and followed the path that led first to the fields and then to the forests. Some servants were taking the oxen to plow the land not set aside for winter grains; two shepherds and several dogs minded hundreds of sheep; and, the harvest finished at last, the day laborers contracted from Tiles had begun pruning and collecting wood.

The only person with nothing to do was her. As the sole heir to Lubich Manor, her main task consisted of observing and learning. One day she would be the mistress of this old, solid, unshakable place; she would wear with honor the emerald ring of the first master, a ring presently on her father's little finger; and all her forebearers would be proud of her, from the first Johan—whose name had been carved in the lintel of the door in 1322—to her own father. No feeling could be as intense as that of belonging to that place, that house, that family, that bloodline. For almost three centuries, in the hands of good masters, Lubich had gloriously resisted the passing of time. Brianda's only wish was that, when her turn came, she would preserve it for the generations to come.

Absorbed in her thoughts, she walked to the top edge of the biggest field to the north of Lubich and entered the woods she knew so well. She could continue for half a league along the shaded path before it became one with the trees. At some point beyond that, the climb to the mountains and the pass to French territory began. Maybe one day her father would take her there. Johan never spoke openly about the trading business that supplemented their finances, but she had known about it for a while. Every so often, Nunilo and Johan took turns crossing into France with good horses and came back with young mules they later sold in the fairs in the lowlands, where they bought new horses. Once, she'd secretly listened in on their conversation and learned why they kept so quiet about it. The Inquisition did not hesitate when it came to persecuting horse smugglers. Any contact with France and its Protestant Huguenots, who stalked the mountains to sneak into Spain, was the same as dealing with the devil himself; thus, dealing in horses was regarded as a religious offense. She remembered how her father had trembled when recalling the interrogations Nunilo and he had undergone before she was born. If it had not been for the intervention of the king, both likely would have been hung. Now times had changed, Nunilo had said. They doubted whether the king would defend them again. And this comment had puzzled Brianda. Why would the king no longer defend his nobles?

She heard the horses' hooves and smiled. It must be Nunilo and his servants. In the middle of the path, she waited to see the gray hair and beard of the Master of Anels. That tall, well-built man with a sharp nose was like a second father to her, even though he looked much older than Johan, despite being the same age. *What a pity he had no children,* she thought. He would have been a kind father.

Suddenly, she found herself surrounded by a half dozen riders she did not recognize. Her first reaction was one of puzzlement. Strangers never came that way; otherwise, her father would have forbidden her to walk alone. The county was overrun with bandits, but they never dared come to the highlands of Tiles, and even less to enter the woods belonging to Lubich. For a moment, she feared they were Inquisition spies waiting to trap Nunilo. Then she studied them more closely. The men had a disagreeable look to them. Their faces were sweaty and their clothes dirty and worn. A wave of fear made them all look the same.

"You are the daughter of Johan of Lubich," one of them said, bringing the nostrils of his mount to Brianda's face. "How is it that you are allowed alone in the wood? Perhaps you don't know of its dangers?"

"The wolves don't come out during the day," she said, trying to sound resolute.

"Some do," said a man with very blond hair as he dismounted his horse and came over to her with a repulsive leer on his face. He spoke to the others, "We couldn't have wished for better booty."

Brianda looked around. She could slip under the belly of one of the horses and run, but she wouldn't get very far. Her heart began to beat faster. No one in their right mind would dare touch the daughter of Johan of Lubich!

"Leave her," said another. "We have clear orders from Medardo. For the moment, some pillaging and nothing else."

"Exactly." The blond took her by the arm and pulled her toward him, resting his other hand on her waist and running his eyes over her body. "Since we can't enter Lubich . . ."

Brianda's fear turned to disgust. The men exchanged sly looks, and she realized no one would come to her aid. She shouted in rage and, with a push, managed to get free for a second, but with a cackle, the man grabbed her tighter. She twisted around using her free arm and her legs to hit and kick him, but this only made him laugh more, and then a smack knocked her to the ground.

"Hold the horse," he ordered another man. "I'll open the way for you in this ambush . . ."

He took her by the wrist and dragged her toward the woods as if she were a hunting trophy about to be butchered. The rocks and dried branches on the ground tore at her flesh. The broken sky filtered through the treetops. Her eyes filled with tears. She knew what would happen next, and there was nothing or nobody to prevent it. Images of Lubich came to her mind, as if bidding her farewell. After this, she would only want to die, assuming these animals did not kill her first.

She felt the man let go of her wrist and saw how he undid the cord that held up his breeches.

Brianda began to scream with a rage until then unknown to her while crawling away, desperately trying to get to her feet and run. But the man already had hold of her ankle. She crawled along the ground until her fingers bled, but it was not enough.

"If that's how you want it," the man grunted. He grabbed her long hair, wrapped it around one hand like a rein, and forced her head back while he raised her dress.

Brianda shouted again, her voice her only weapon.

Her sight blurred and her mind went black. Then, through the darkness, she thought she made out the sound of more hooves, whinnies, shouts, and footsteps. The pressure on her body eased, a steel blade whistled through the air, someone gasped, and hot red liquid fell over her. A moment later, someone was cradling her in his arms.

"Tell me I'm not too late, Brianda," she heard a familiar voice say.

Brianda opened her eyes and recognized Nunilo. She hugged him tightly and broke out sobbing.

Nunilo helped her up and led her to the path, where his men had finished disarming the two bandits who had not managed to escape.

"Take his body!" he shouted, signaling to the woods where her slain attacker lay. "And display it in Aiscle as a warning!"

He and one of his men helped Brianda onto his horse, and he climbed up behind her. He covered her with his long cloak and, galloping, headed for Lubich. Minutes later, they burst onto the patio, calling loudly for the master, frightening the animals and the servants, all of whom came running.

Johan of Lubich, a tall, strong man with a beard and long dark hair, came out of the house followed by a thin woman with fair skin and a haughty bearing. He crossed to Nunilo and took the reins of his horse.

"I was about to go looking for you," he said. Brianda, hidden under Nunilo's cloak, trembled when she heard her father's voice. "Was there any problem?"

"Our friend Captain Agut came to the agreed place," Nunilo said. "But something else has happened." He opened the cloak and showed Brianda, huddled and covered in blood.

"Brianda!" Johan threw open his arms and lifted her down from the horse. The girl ran to her mother sobbing. "What happened?"

Nunilo got off his horse and described the scene his men had come upon.

"Brianda has told me that he didn't . . . you know."

Johan's face lit up in rage.

"It was them!" he bellowed. "Last week they tried to attack Bringuer of Besalduch's house. At first he thought it was ordinary bandits, but we are convinced they were rebels incited by—" In four strides, he was beside his wife and daughter. "Did you recognize them? Did you hear any names?"

"I don't know who they were," responded Brianda, trembling in her mother's arms, "but they named a certain Medardo."

Johan roared.

"That's him! Medardo has more supporters every day and our count has fewer. What is the king waiting for?" He ground his teeth, then began to give orders to the dozens of people around him. "You," he said to some servants, "take extra care to secure Lubich while I'm away." He pointed to a handful of men and said, "You get ready to come with me. And you"—he looked at the servants surrounding his wife, Elvira—"have my luggage and Brianda's prepared within the hour."

"What do you intend to do?" Elvira asked coldly.

"The king is holding parliament in Monzon. Pere of Aiscle went down a few days ago to accompany Count Fernando until the king deals with his complaints. For months, the rebels have undermined Pere's role as justice of the county of Orrun and refused to carry out his orders as the count's representative. As long as Aiscle continues to be the rebels' camp, there will never be peace here. And I'm not prepared to wait any longer!"

Elvira stepped in front of him. "You're not thinking of bringing Brianda with you? After what's happened, I won't tolerate you putting her through such a long and tiring journey."

"Whoever attacks my heir attacks Lubich," he replied in a tone that allowed no argument. He looked at his daughter and his expression softened. "You have to come with me and respond to the attack, child. The king will listen to your testimony. Go, wash yourself and change your clothes. And chin up. The people of Lubich are not easily humiliated."

Nunilo came over. "One of my men is on the way to Besalduch to warn Bringuer. I'm going to Anels House now to tell Leonor. We'll meet past the mill in Tiles."

"You've only just returned," Johan objected.

"I can't ride as well as I used to," his friend replied, "but I have no intention of letting you go alone. I also refuse to believe that someone like Medardo would have the nerve to claim in Monzon that he is acting in the king's name. It's high time they heard from the lords of the mountains."

An hour later, Brianda, nervous and excited, said good-bye to Lubich and her mother. While they were waiting for the others at the boundary between Tiles and Aiscle, she gazed over the scattered country houses at the foot of Beles Peak. Each chimney represented a family that struggled every year to survive on a bit of land, with a half dozen cows, a bullock or two, a pig, some hens and rabbits and a pair of mules. This was unlike in Lubich, where no one wanted for anything. In the same way that Johan paid his taxes to the count, year after year, the peasants paid rent to Johan with hens, wheat, wine, and oil. Compared to many other nobles who oversaw miserable mountain villages and found themselves on the verge of ruin, the masters of Lubich and Anels enjoyed a good income. For the first time in her life, Brianda wondered how many peasants from Tiles could be tempted by the promises of that Medardo to switch loyalties. The fear she had felt barely two hours ago made her see things differently. Tiles was no longer a quiet, peaceful, happy place. She did not understand exactly what men like her father were up against, but she had never seen him or thought of him like this before.

Johan paced on his horse. Not even when she was small and had to tilt her head back to look at him had her father seemed so big and terrible. He had put on a dark doublet, wide breeches, and a pair of high boots he only wore for important journeys. In the incipient wind, his black hair got tangled in his short chain cloak. Since leaving the house, he had barely looked at her, and his brow remained creased in a gesture of worry and contained aggression. When he saw the men from Nunilo's house on the horizon, he set off at a gallop that the others matched. Brianda was grateful Johan had taught her to ride like a man. At this pace, she would need to make full use of her ability.

They took a long detour to avoid going through Aiscle and risking attack from Medardo's men, and continued without respite for four hours. They then rested briefly beside the river and, at dusk, finally halted at the dam in the small village of Fonz, at the foot of some south-facing crags. Brianda, red-faced and exhausted from riding ten leagues, went to the river to refresh herself. She scooped water in her hands and poured it over her long black hair, which she had gathered in a tight braid. Her scalp was sore from the incident in the woods. Discreetly, she loosened her jerkin. Even though it was nearly autumn, it was so hot her blouse stuck to her body.

She heard hooves and, then, voices of greeting. She turned and recognized Bringuer of Besalduch, a thickset man of medium stature with small and lively, if baggy, eyes, and his son Marquo, whom she found as handsome as ever.

"Hurry up," Johan said to them. "There are still two hours to ride."

"We should spend the night here," suggested Nunilo. "We can do nothing in Monzon until tomorrow morning."

Johan reluctantly acceded. He ordered the servants to dole out bread, cheese, and bacon, and then to lay out blankets on the ground around a fire. Brianda ate greedily. Without any doubt, the day had been the longest and hardest of her life. She closed her eyes and remembered in anguish what she had suffered in the forest, but the change of scenery and the exhaustion made it feel very distant in time, as if it had not happened that very morning. Perhaps her father's energy and his capacity to overcome all adversity were also in her blood. She had left her tears in her mother's lap.

Marquo sat down beside her. Brianda had met him on several occasions at the highlands fairs and when the nobles gathered at Lubich. He was slightly older than she, enough for her to feel embarrassed in his presence, and she thought him very handsome, perhaps the most handsome man in the valley of Tiles, but arrogant. He had brown curly hair, big expressive eyes, and an elegant and determined manner. The way he spoke made him sound more like an heir than a second-born son, which he was.

Just that week, Brianda had heard her father telling her mother that Bringuer complained his sons had been born in the wrong order. Marquo would have been a better master than his older brother, yet his future was uncertain—unless he married well. Brianda remembered the silence that had followed.

"Is this your first time out of the valley?" Marquo asked, looking at her directly.

"Yes," answered Brianda, not knowing what else to say.

"It's not mine," he bragged. "I've been to the Catalan valleys. And a while ago my father took me to France." He paused, then added, "You ride very well. It's rare in a woman."

"My father taught me," she answered proudly. "As he has no other children, he's taught me to do everything. I can also read."

Marquo, slightly surprised, tilted his head. "And embroider as well?"

Brianda detected a note of mockery in his tone. She blushed but was undaunted.

"My mother saw to that, but I don't like it. I prefer riding a horse."

Marquo guffawed, openly and with satisfaction, which pleased the girl. More than once, her mother had insisted that she should curb her masculine impulses or she would never find a good husband. These impulses included her habit of walking alone in the woods, hunting with her father, collecting taxes, and visiting the fairs, where instead of looking at the merchants' brocades, she preferred to admire the qualities of a good mare. Brianda had told her mother, insolently, that as the only heir to Lubich, she would not have to try very hard to get suitors. A shiver went down her spine. If that disgusting blond man had carried out his intentions, things might now be very different.

"I heard what happened today," Marquo said in a serious voice, looking at her intently. "I would have liked to have killed him myself."

"Thank you," she responded, wrapping herself up in her blanket.

Marquo nodded and got up to go speak with the men. Brianda looked at him one last time and settled down to sleep. Despite the unfortunate reasons for it, this journey had just become much more promising.

As soon as dawn broke, Johan woke everyone and urged them to be on their way. He led the way through the vast, flat, vine-populated landscape, so different from the mountains and forests of Orrun, with its bad roads and sparse population. They passed by muleteers and mule trains laden with firewood, farmworkers carrying tools to the fertile fields, and merchants and artisans leading their carts, arriving at last in the town of Monzon, fortified at the base of a hill on which stood an enormous castle.

They passed a huge monastery outside the walls, and then, when they reached a big building with a sign announcing it was a hospital, Johan, without slowing, led the company over a bridged stream toward one of the entrances to the town. The merchants, artisans, courtesans, and bystanders that filled the narrow streets were forced to move aside to avoid being knocked down by the riders whose long cloaks flapped in the wind.

Brianda noted the confusion on the faces of the townspeople. With the passing of her party, the festive atmosphere on the streets disappeared. With them came the fury of the mountains, the anxiety of uncertainty, the fear of paid assassins, and the constant threat to the townspeople's families.

They went to the main square, where the Royal Palace was located. It was empty. Johan looked toward the arched galleries, also empty, and realized that the royal party was already in the place where parliament was being held. He raised his hand to signal his group to follow him up a steep lane of tightly packed houses until a crowd blocked their path.

"Johan!" shouted Nunilo. "We have to stop! The guards will arrest us!"

But Johan spurred his horse forward, shouting at the people to get out of the way. Brianda had never seen him like this. Her father was a well-mannered man. Now, the fury burning in his eyes said no one would prevent him from getting to the king. The people stood aside to let the angry group through and they reached the square where the Moorish tower rose over the sober church of Saint Mary's. Johan did not stop until he got to the first of the building's wide steps. Then he jumped triumphantly from his horse, tossing the reins to one of his servants. A deep silence descended on the square, while, a few steps higher up, some soldiers crossed their lances to deny him entry.

"I am Johan of Lubich, master from the highlands of Orrun, as are these who come with me, and I must see the king!" he declared, resting his right hand menacingly on the hilt of his sword.

Without waiting for an answer, he gestured for Brianda to come beside him and began to ascend the steps confidently before hundreds of attentive eyes.

"Women cannot enter parliament!" one of the soldiers shouted.

"The heir to Lubich can!" Johan replied sternly.

The soldiers exchanged nervous looks and finally moved aside.

Brianda made an effort to stand tall beside her father. Although the galloping had ceased, the muscles in her body remained tense, preventing her from collapsing. They entered through a high wooden door, followed by the others in their party. The sound of their boots on the flagstones echoed off the church's stone columns before rebounding against the vaults of the high ceiling. A murmur of surprise and indignation accompanied them up the wide aisle, along whose sides long benches were occupied by royal officials and men from the different kingdoms. They were arranged according to their rank in the ecclesiastic, noble, or military branches or membership of city and town corporation. At last, they arrived at the sumptuously decorated high altar. On a large platform, built for the occasion and decorated with rich and beautiful tapestries, was the canopy and, below it, the seat occupied by the king.

Brianda took a deep breath while the sweaty and tired men around her knelt down, without forfeiting an ounce of the pride and dignity that characterized the lords of the mountains.

15.

The bow seemed eternal to her. At last, when a movement from Johan signaled she could stand, Brianda got a good look at King Philip II of Spain, who was the very same man as King Philip I of Aragon. The man was dressed in black from head to toe; fatigue and tedium showed clearly on his face. He scowled at the rough men who had interrupted parliament with their loose clothes, long hair and beards, and weather-beaten skin. The king's own skin was pallid, almost sickly, Brianda thought, and his short gray hair, long face, wide forehead, pointed chin, and grave, composed expression all combined to chilling effect. Her knees began to shake, and she wished she could hide behind her father.

Beside her, Johan kept his shoulders straight and his bearing calm, even when one of the king's secretaries, a balding man with a goatee and mustache—the ends curled to his fat cheeks—demanded, "Who do you think you are to appear like this?"

"I am Johan of Lubich, from the lands of Tiles, in the north of the county of Orrun. I am accompanied by Nunilo of Anels and Bringuer of Besalduch with his son Marquo. I am here to set forth to His Majesty the reality in which we live. Criminal representatives of the commoners have taken over the government, justice, and rents of the county. Over time they have organized to such a degree that they have their own squads and lackeys. Nothing is done there without their say-so, to the extreme of committing vile attacks such as the one my daughter had to suffer yesterday and that she herself will relate."

Resting his hand on his daughter's back, Johan motioned for her to step forward. Brianda felt the eyes of all the court boring into her back, but she was determined neither to be intimidated nor to offer a pitiful image of herself that would shame her father. She took a deep breath and concentrated on setting out the facts in a clear and concise manner. When she finished, a slight pressure on her arm let her know that Johan was congratulating her for doing so well.

"His Majesty has rather more important things to listen to in this parliament than the upsets of your daughter," smirked the secretary.

"Your Majesty!" Nunilo exclaimed. "These rebels are nothing more than bandits who defend their actions by claiming royal privilege. They are prepared to use arms in support of it!"

The king straightened in his seat while the secretary shouted, "Measure your words! Do you dare accuse the king of connivance?"

"Ask Count Fernando!" Bringuer shot back.

The secretary looked at the king, who nodded his agreement. A murmur extended throughout the church as everyone waited for Count Fernando of Orrun to approach the altar.

Brianda had seen Count Fernando in Lubich when she was small. She remembered him as thin, with a big nose and thick lips. He had said something to her then that now took on a new meaning, *"You are Johan's daughter? If it were not for the blood of people like him . . . I hope you never have to regret being born in Lubich."*

The count walked up the main aisle and greeted the men from the mountains warmly but also with the distance expected from someone in his position. Though he was gracious, the difference between them was illustrated by the contrast of his rich and elegant clothes to their traveling garb. He wore a quilted velvet jerkin with a high collar and a small ruff and a belt adorned with garnets. Like the majority of those present, he wore his hair short and his mustache trimmed. He was accompanied by his representative, Pere of Aiscle, a tall, thin, blond-haired man, who looked serious and tired.

Pere came over to Johan and whispered in slight recrimination, "You've been bold, Johan. The count has been waiting days to be received."

"He should be thankful, then." Johan's expression darkened. "If someone had tried to defile his daughter, he would also have brought forward his reception."

"Who is secretary to the king?" Nunilo asked, also in a whisper.

"Diego Fernandez de Cabrera, Count of Chinchon," said Pere.

"Not good," Johan said.

Nunilo groaned at Johan's comment.

Brianda would have liked to ask her father what he meant, but the Count of Chinchon interrupted.

"If you all have finished with your little reunion," he said bitingly, "His Majesty would like to hear what the Count of Orrun has to say. But first, Johan of Lubich, be so good as to remove your daughter from here."

Johan moved forward, putting one foot on the altar steps. Two soldiers hurried over.

"My daughter stays with me," he said firmly. "One day she will be defending the interests of Lubich."

Pere grabbed him by the arm. "The king is being extremely patient with you, Johan. I will tell one of my servants to escort her to the house where I am staying."

"If she goes, we all go," said Nunilo. "Maybe the count would prefer to continue speaking alone?"

The king sidestepped the matter by greeting Count Fernando informally and fondly invoking his friendship with the count's father when, as prince, he had accompanied him on his travels to England, France,

Italy, and Flanders. He also reminded everyone that, for his merits and feats in war and other services, the count's father had received various compensations. Finally, gesturing with his hand, the king invited Count Fernando to speak.

"Concerning the county of Orrun," Count Fernando began, "there is a dispute between Your Majesty and my person. More than twenty years ago, my father, then count, was dispossessed of the county, and it was incorporated into the Crown with its fortresses, jurisdiction, and rents, based on the allegation that the original fiefdom had expired."

"His Majesty knows those facts, Count Fernando," interrupted the Count of Chinchon. "I would counsel brevity."

A new murmur rolled through the crowd, and the secretary called for silence. Count Fernando took a deep breath and continued.

"My father appealed and, as you know, the court of justice found in his favor. Since then, this dispute has kept the land in constant turmoil. When my father died four years ago and I inherited the title, I asked the Viceroy of Aragon to grant me the investiture and possession of the county, admitting all homages of a feudal prince. I only got excuses. I came to you again three years ago—"

"Excuses, you say?" the king boomed. "Did I not ask my ministers to go to this land and gather information?"

"Your Majesty, the reality is exactly as Johan of Lubich has described," Count Fernando said. "Your royal ministers do not dare go to Orrun for fear of attack. This dispute does nothing but encourage those lawless criminals who want no master."

The Count of Chinchon counterattacked. "And what do you say about your own attitude? Are you unaware of the accusation that your lords exploit the towns with abusive taxes? And what do you do? Nothing! When the petitions of the people are not heard, will they not resort to arms?"

"We commit no abuses!" Nunilo retorted. "It is they who violate the rights of our land by preventing the General Council from meeting.

Why do you now want to end our rights? Have we not always served Count Fernando and His Majesty?"

"His Majesty respects your rights and privileges!" roared the Count of Chinchon. "But he must also be mindful of the will of his subjects. How do you expect him to ignore the wishes of commoners to emancipate themselves from petty masters? We do not recognize the perpetuity of fiefdoms or manors. What interest can the inhabitants of Orrun have in following you when they can serve their king directly?"

Another murmur, this time louder. The secretary called for silence several times, but the crowd paid him no heed. At last, a man dressed in a purple habit and seated on the first bench of the ecclesiastical estate with the prelates and ecclesiastics of the Kingdoms of Aragon and Valencia, shouted, "Your Majesty, stop this nonsense immediately! First they enter without being summoned and then they force us to accept the presence of a woman! How many are like her, heirs to their houses? Must we then let them all in? Unless you remove her, we shall leave!"

Thunderous applause. The Count of Chinchon, the king, and other secretaries exchanged indecisive looks, but before they could decide how to resolve the issue, a group of men approached the altar in a threatening manner. Brianda clutched her father's arm.

Bringuer turned to his son. "Take her to the street and wait for us there!"

Marquo looked at Johan, who nodded. Marquo led Brianda to the side of the church, the aisle packed with men who had risen from their benches to block their way.

Brianda was roughly separated from Marquo. Dozens of men's arms buffeted her, pushing her body as if she were a filthy sack they wished to be rid of. The shouts and insults stunned her. The heat and the stench were overwhelming. A final shove pushed her out of the church. She fell onto the steps she had so proudly climbed on her father's arm. The doors slammed with an insulting bang. Some laughter came from the square, and she realized people were enjoying the show.

She looked around, not knowing what to do or where to go, and her eyes filled with tears. One day, she would have to take charge of the lands and income of Lubich and defend her rights as if she were a man, so why should she not be permitted to learn about the affairs of the county that affected her so directly? She thought of her father's words and got to her feet, beating the dust from her clothes. The people of Lubich were not easily humiliated.

Three ragged young boys slipped under the guards' lances and approached her. Brianda noticed that one of them did not take his eyes off the jewel around her neck; she covered it with her hand, but that did not stop them from accosting her with dirty hands and a string of dirty words. They had black scabs around their mouths, stinking breath, and spots across their skin. The boldest extended a hand toward her neck and tried to snatch her pendant. Brianda slapped him and ran down the steps; the hateful laughter of the people increased. It seemed to her that even the guards were smiling. She tried to escape through the crowd, but was dogged by the beggars at every step. She just wanted everyone to shut up and keep their hands off her.

Suddenly, she bumped against something hard and metallic, and her knees went weak. Strong hands supported her. She looked up and saw a military uniform and then a broad, weather-beaten face with a light brown goatee and mustache. She did not know this man, but could have sworn his features looked familiar. She pressed against him for refuge, certain that a soldier must defend a young woman of noble birth.

Then a shadow appeared and confronted her pursuers. The shadow said nothing; he simply stood before them with a hand resting on his sword, his figure dark and daunting. The beggars stopped, looking annoyed that the fun had ended. They let fly a few curses and then melted into the mob. The laughing in the square stopped too. The shadow turned, and as he approached Brianda, she saw a tall, strong man with long black hair, also dressed as a soldier. He walked with a slight stoop, as if unaccustomed to raising his eyes from the ground.

"My poor Italian friend!" the first soldier teased. "Just can't wait to try out the new sword given to you by His Majesty yesterday, can you? Next time."

Several passersby started to whisper that this man had been champion of the important foot-and-horseback race held during the festival of Saint Matthew. Brianda studied his face and felt such an intense shiver that she crossed her arms to stop her body from trembling. No powder from tree, plant, insect, mollusk, or stone could achieve the black, rabid, stormy color of the man's eyes. No sculptor could ever faithfully carve the proportioned tension over his brow, his jaw, and his lips. No painter could capture that uncertain, opaque expression, in which she thought she read a small glint of expectation.

Though his features, build, and movements corresponded to those of a young, strong, attractive, and healthy man, there was a sinister sense of unease in him.

The first soldier asked, "Could you explain to us who you are and how you got into this mess?"

Brianda told him what had happened. Out of pride, she tried not to shed a single tear, but ended the tale sobbing in rage.

"And they threw me on the street as if I were garbage—"

The man burst out laughing and, turning to the other, said, "Haven't I told you, Corso, how beautiful are the women from my mountains? But don't trust their tears. If she has inherited even a drop of Johan of Lubich's character—"

Brianda did not let him finish the sentence.

"Your mountains? Do you know my father?"

"I'd bet anything that today he is with the master of Aiscle."

"Do you also know Pere?"

"You could say that. He is my brother."

Brianda's jaw dropped. So, that was why the face looked so familiar! She had heard incredible stories of this spy, bandit, and assassin wanted by the court of justice. She was talking to the very devil of the mountains, hero to some and villain to others. She did not know why he had disappeared for so long, just that something had happened between him and his brother.

"But then—you are—"

"Now I'm Surano, got it?"

She nodded with certain mistrust. If he had changed his name, it was because he was hiding something.

"Are you going to meet Pere?"

"He doesn't know I'm here yet," Surano said, then deliberately changed the subject. "Why don't you tell me what they were talking about inside?"

Brianda related the discussion.

Frowning, Surano said, "It sounds as if there may be war, depending on whether Count Fernando and his lords get satisfaction." He turned to his dark friend. "We shall be much occupied."

"What do you mean?" Brianda asked in alarm. Until now, she had lived in peace, protected by her parents in a fortified home. But from the little she knew about history, she was aware that mightier men had fallen when people took up arms in open war. Could mighty Lubich and her family truly be in danger?

Surano did not answer. Something had caught his eye, and he pressed himself against the wall as if to avoid being seen. Brianda turned and saw two men headed up the steps to the church. The first was young and good-looking despite his hawkish nose. The second, a little taller and with a head of abundant brown hair, chewed a small branch from which some small white flowers hung. An angry, mocking smile was affixed to his face.

"From the gorse flower, I deduce they're county men from the opposing side," observed Brianda. "Do you know them?"

Since the county had split into two factions, those in favor of the king often wore a sprig of flowering gorse and those of Count Fernando a sprig of boxwood.

"You don't?" replied Surano, surprised. "The one with the curved nose is Medardo of Aiscle—"

"Medardo!" she exclaimed, finally able to put a face to the leader of the rebels, the one responsible for her nearly being dishonored the previous day. She had imagined him as a horrible being, and yet, despite his nose, his appearance was pleasant.

"And the other is Jayme of Cuyls—" Surano was about to add something, but stopped himself and eyed Brianda uncertainly. He gestured for her to remain quiet. Then he turned to Corso. "Follow those two inside. See if you can hear who they talk to and what they say. If you take too long, I'll wait for you at the back."

Corso immediately obeyed. And Brianda, who had felt the Italian's presence as though she were being crushed by his weight, even though he hadn't even touched her, sighed with relief.

16.

Stationed behind a column inside the church, Corso tried to follow the count's final arguments without losing sight of the men he was spying on, but his mind was distracted by the enraged girl he had left outside with Surano. Her vivacious eyes and expressive lips had captured his attention from the first moment. For someone like himself with no scruples—accustomed from an early age to screaming and blood, to following orders to sack or kill—the unexpected sense of calm that had overpowered him when he saw the girl had caught him unawares. For the first time in a long while, his thoughts had slowed and his reflexes had relaxed.

Perhaps he just needed a woman, Corso thought. Surano had decided that it was safest not to stop in any brothel until they reached Orrun, and the journey had been very long. The less suspicion raised by the two deserters, the better. Things would change, Surano had told him, when they got closer to the mountains. There, they would go back to doing as they pleased. And indeed, as they had gotten closer to Monzon, his friend had become more daring, almost forgetting the fear of being captured. But then he'd spotted the two men Corso now watched.

The pair had found seats in one of the back benches on the left of the church. Medardo ran his eyes over the faces of the nobles at the other side of the altar and, every now and then, saluted one with an imperceptible nod. Jayme of Cuyls, with a crafty smile, did not miss a word the count said—speaking far too cautiously, in Corso's opinion, for someone defending what was his by right, according to what he had understood from young Brianda's explanations. He focused on Jayme and, for a moment, it seemed as if the man was not smirking at the count but at one of the men with him, a tall man whom Brianda resembled.

A profound silence filled the room when the count finished speaking, and the monarch sat up straight in his chair. He meditated for a few minutes that Corso found too long until, at last, he spoke. "What an inconvenience it would be for the safety of the lands and lives of people like yourself, Fernando, Count of Orrun, who has always been loyal to the Crown, if we were to reward men for disobedience. Therefore, we are approving an ordinance that we name *De rebellion vasallorum*, in which we order that vassals who rebel against their lords *ipso facto* incur the penalty of death. Furthermore, we establish that all those vassals who do not defend and serve their lords will be treated as rebels and traitors. Tomorrow afternoon, you will have my resolution in writing." King Philip gestured to his secretary. "The Count of Chinchon will write it up."

While a murmur of approval spread along the benches, Count Fernando and his followers, visibly stunned by how quickly the monarch had closed the matter, allowed themselves to be ushered toward the exit.

Corso noticed that the king's secretary discreetly signaled to Medardo and Jayme to follow him to a small chapel. Corso snuck over as close as he could.

"I will prepare an offer," he heard the Count of Chinchon say. "When things become more difficult, Fernando will sell the county."

"You've said that before," responded Medardo. "Your only concern is to acquire the territory in a way that is not too onerous to the king's purse. But what about us? Our men are tired, and they worry that you won't keep your promises."

"All will come in due course, and when it does, His Majesty will not forget your services."

"He must remember them now. If I don't get something today—"

"Don't you have more power now than ever?" the Count of Chinchon asked Medardo.

"An uncertain power. We get more in booty from the skirmishes than from your commission, which is poisoned. The count's followers are many and they don't surrender. If in the end they won, what guarantee do we have that the king would protect us? I'll remain here until you give me some proof that you support our rebellion. Otherwise, I make no guarantees."

"You're looking at it all wrong," replied the secretary. "You enjoy the favor of the people. They are tired of this Count Fernando, who spends more time in his distant lands than in Orrun."

"Do you know what some of the people think?" Jayme of Cuyls spoke up at last. "That the king doesn't live in Orrun either. They fear simply exchanging one absent master for another."

After a few moments of silence, the Count of Chinchon said reluctantly, "Come back this afternoon. I'll see what I can do."

Corso hurried outside. He saw the group of men from the mountains walking off with Brianda beside the tall man Jayme had stared at. At the other end of the square, some footmen brought a horse for Count Fernando, who rode in another direction. Just as they had agreed, Corso went around the back of the church, where he found Surano and repeated everything he had heard.

"My brother would like to know this," murmured Surano.

"The men from Orrun have already gone off toward the east. I don't think it will be difficult to learn where they are staying. They stand out a bit."

Surano felt the urge to go looking for Pere but restrained himself. His brother had always helped him, and now he had the opportunity to return the favor. However, it meant he would have to explain the reason for his premature return, which he had planned to do in Aiscle, calmly, just the two of them. He had not reckoned on a chance meeting here in Monzon.

His mind went to that night, four years ago, when he'd fled after being unjustly accused of two murders. The king and the Inquisition had put a price on his head. If not for Pere, who'd advised him to seek refuge in France while he negotiated with the monarch to have Surano spy on the Huguenots, he would be dead now. In gratitude for his services, the king had commuted Surano's death sentence but forced him to enroll in the *Tercios Imperiales* and serve in Sicily as an infantry captain. Without a doubt, Pere would need time to understand his brother's desertion, his breaking of this contract. Who knew what false conclusions he would arrive at when that girl, Brianda, told him of their meeting.

"You say, Corso, that they'll have the king's resolution in hand tomorrow. So, we'll wait until tomorrow." Surano gave a roguish smile. "Both you and I could do with a night of fun before things get complicated."

Pere stopped before a three-story adobe house, simple but large, located on a narrow street in the upper part of the town.

"I hope the owner doesn't dare object," he told them. "The rascal has asked me for three hundred *reales* in rent for a month for a house that is worth forty *reales* per year. With the General Parliament held here, the city has gone crazy." He wiped the sweat that had beaded on his forehead. "This blasted heat. There are already some cases of typhus. All we need now is an epidemic." He let out a sigh. "How I miss the fresh air of home! Is it true that it snowed at the end of August? From here, the mountains looked white, to everyone's wonderment."

Johan put a hand on his shoulder.

"We're all tired, Pere."

"It's not tiredness, Johan. It's mistrust. The king appears to have come down on the side of our count, but I don't trust it."

He called brusquely into the house. A young dark-skinned boy called Azmet appeared and took charge of accommodating them. Johan and Brianda had a sitting room and two separate bedrooms on the top floor, near the rooms given to Bringuer and Marquo. From her window, which looked out on a courtyard, Brianda saw that Pere and Nunilo were lodged on the middle floor, near the common room where they would all eat together. On the ground floor, the servants and soldiers shared a large single room.

Brianda couldn't remember when she'd been so exhausted. Helped by an orphan gypsy girl named Cecilia, she had a bath and spent the rest of the day in the house. Azmet and Cecilia, who were the same age as she, pestered her with questions about life in the mountains: the bears, the wolves. They could not understand how a girl could live in the middle of the woods and yet possess the elegance and manners of the nobility. Marquo was not amused to see her waste time with this olive-skinned pair: Azmet with his suspiciously Jewish features and the orphan gypsy with her strange habits and language. Brianda enjoyed their company, delighted to find them so different from the mountain people she'd known her whole life. What most attracted her was their spontaneous laughter and carefree attitude.

"Do you know that the king was very ill with a fever and gout?" Cecilia asked her. "Several of his party, very close to him, died. They now call Monzon the tomb of his faithful servants. People brought saints' relics from all over to help cure him, but the only thing that worked was oil from the monastery of Saint Salvador in Fraga."

Brianda was pensive. Her family would need many relics to protect them if the king did not keep his word. Perhaps the king's signed and sealed document would satisfy the count and prevent a war.

Before retiring for the night, Brianda entered her father's bedroom. She needed to ask some questions that had been running through her mind all day.

"Father, why does Chinchon hate the count so much?"

"A few years ago, Count Fernando's brother, who was married to a relation of Chinchon's, murdered his wife when he suspected her of infidelity. Fernando's brother then fled to Italy, to the states of Ferrara, but he was captured. They hanged him and burnt his servants as accomplices. But it seems this wasn't enough for Chinchon. He takes every opportunity to slander the Count of Orrun. I fear he won't stop until our county belongs to the king."

Brianda thought about this for a moment. It seemed absurd that anyone would put so many lives at stake for personal revenge.

"And who is Jayme of Cuyls?"

"Why do you ask?" Johan raised an eyebrow.

Brianda explained that she had seen him enter parliament with Medardo when she was waiting with Pere's brother, Surano.

"Surano?" Johan gaped. "Why didn't you tell us sooner?"

Brianda shrugged.

"It seemed he didn't want it known that he was here, but later he asked a man with him to spy on Medardo and Jayme." She wondered how Surano and Corso had met. Corso had seemed so attentive to Surano's movements, protective. "Surano found it strange that I didn't know this Jayme of Cuyls. Who is he? Why should I know him?"

Johan was slow in replying. He would have liked to protect his daughter from this, but knew that arrogant and jealous Jayme would never stop in his efforts to usurp Johan and take over Lubich. Once, years before, Jayme had made an attempt on his life, but the judges believed it was an accident. Johan thought sadly of how they had played together as children and teenagers, when Jayme looked up to him like an older brother. Then, one day, everything had changed.

"He's my cousin. We do not get along, and for that reason we don't even mention his name in the house." He tenderly placed his hands on his daughter's cheeks to ensure that she looked straight at him. "Until yesterday, child, you were too young to understand hate, but now I'm asking you to remember one thing: you must watch out for that man."

The following morning, the men of Orrun decided to make the wait for the king's written decree more bearable by going to the markets. The fact that Johan had not objected to Marquo's request to entertain Brianda led her to believe her father also planned to close some horse deals. Chaperoned by Azmet and Cecilia, they walked through the packed streets of the city. Brianda enjoyed the rich clothes of those called to parliament, the abundance of products in the stalls, the magnificent horses of the Royal Guard, the shining weapons of the soldiers, and city life in motion. Before lunch, Marquo suggested riding to the old castle that presided over the city and she agreed. Accompanied by two servants, they went to the stables, then up the unpaved path.

"I wonder if those who lived here were at liberty to visit the city streets," said Brianda as they rode through the entrance arch of the abandoned grounds, their horses' hooves echoing on the paving stones. "If not, they must have felt very lonely up here."

"Royalty is never alone," responded Marquo. "Have you not seen the retinue that follows His Majesty? They all want to gain his favor. This is like Lubich, only much bigger. Is it possible to feel completely alone in Lubich?"

Brianda thought about the people who continuously filed through her house. Apart from the servants, stable boys, shepherds, laborers, and knights, the majority were peasants who came to pay her father dues. Sometimes the bailiff and the justice appeared to resolve conflicts between neighbors. But except for visits from Nunilo and Bringuer, when her father brought out the best wine and the house filled with laughter, Brianda could hardly picture any scenes where Johan did not wear a frown. Her mother frequently criticized him for it in a tone halfway between resignation and contained contempt.

"Yes, it is possible."

Marquo looked at her out of the side of his eye and was puzzled to see the face of the girl darken. He hoped that Brianda's sadness was fleeting. His father had warned him that the greatest misfortune for a man and his estate was a woman afflicted by melancholy. So, if the woman was young, healthy, pretty, and from a good house, like Brianda, what could await him but a pleasant life? He immediately decided to put a smile back on the girl's face, as soon as he could shake the bothersome servants.

They followed the steep ramp through successive entrance gates and looked over the sober, thick-walled, and narrow-windowed buildings before arriving at the upper part of the castle grounds, an extensive yard with several turrets and a stunning view over the city. Marquo asked the servants to hold the horses so that he and Brianda could explore. To his satisfaction, the door of a high tower gave way easily and they entered a square room. A mysterious set of stone steps led up into blackness.

"Shall we?" he asked, offering his hand to Brianda.

Without hesitation, she took Marquo's hand and followed him up the dark passage until they reached a small, unprotected terrace. The earth ceased to exist for a few seconds, swallowed up by the sky.

"It's like we're flying!" Brianda exclaimed, stretching her arms. "And our mountains, how far away they seem!"

"You miss them already?" Marquo asked.

"Of course! You don't?"

"I hope I never have to leave them."

"Why would you?"

Brianda looked into his eyes and then dropped her head, ashamed at her stupid question. As the second son of Bringuer, he could not inherit the house. His options were limited: the church, the king's army, work for his brother, or marry an heiress.

"Would it make you sad if I left?" asked Marquo.

Brianda turned her back on him and concentrated on the caress of the gentle breeze on her face. Suddenly, her heart began beating faster. She had never been alone so long with a boy. With a man. With the handsomest man in all the highlands of the county of Orrun. He was strong, brave, hardworking, and from a good family. And her parents liked him. She wondered if she should begin to hope.

She did not know what to do next. They should go back with the servants, who would be impatient. On the other hand, what better opportunity to know if Marquo was the right choice? The girls in Tiles smiled like fools when they saw the valley boys, and more so when they were about to get married. Although, later, they changed; some stopped smiling. Her own mother hardly ever smiled. She did not want that; she wanted to always feel as she had since childhood: as light as a sparrow, happy as a nightingale, alert as a hawk, strong as an eagle, and quiet as an owl. That was her ambition. Marquo seemed brave and cheerful. It was not hard for her to imagine sharing her life and her bed with him.

She felt Marquo step closer. She thought about his curly brown hair, his inquiring eyes, and the tautness of his body, always alert to sounds, movements, and dangers. She wondered what it would be like to have his arms around her waist and his mouth upon hers.

"You haven't answered my question," she heard him whisper.

"Nor you mine," she said, turning to look straight into his eyes. "Why would you have to leave?"

Marquo understood and came closer until his face was just a breath from hers.

"Have you been kissed before?" he asked.

She shook her head.

"May I kiss you?"

Brianda nodded and he placed his lips tenderly against hers for a few seconds. Then he backed away, looked at the girl's face, and liked what he saw. Her flushed cheeks. Her closed eyes. Her calm and expectant expression. He waited for her to open her eyes and invite him with her eyes to continue. He then moved his body closer to hers, rested his hands on her hips, and kissed her again, this time parting his lips enough to dampen hers without forcing her.

Brianda responded by caressing Marquo's neck, ears, and temples as delicately as she would stroke the fur of a newborn pup.

She contemplated the moment calmly, conscious that she would never forget it, even if the happiness between them someday ended. She allowed the kiss to go deeper and Marquo's hand to audaciously run over her body. And when they finally separated to catch their breath, she responded to his satisfied smile with her own.

"And now?" she asked.

"When you say so, I'll talk with our fathers."

"Not here. Everyone is tense. We'll wait until we get back to Tiles. Meanwhile, we can use the time to get to know each other better."

"Good idea," Marquo said with a mischievous smile. "I would love to discover your mysteries."

They descended from the tower, casually describing the marvelous view so as not to make the servants suspicious.

As he helped her onto her horse, Brianda whispered, "Just one thing, Marquo. Whoever marries me also marries Lubich."

"I know," he said.

"Good. Because that commitment lasts forever."

17.

Quite some time before Count Fernando was expected with the king's document, Pere of Aiscle went out to wait for him. Impatient, he looked up and down the long, narrow street, deserted in the intense afternoon heat. A few minutes later, two figures appeared in the distance. Pere was startled to recognize his brother, even though Johan had told him the man was wandering around town under the name Surano.

Pere was moved to see him after three years, but his instinct told him his brother must be in trouble again. He shook his hand firmly.

"What are you doing here? Do you need more money? I hope it's just that, although it will mean a drain on my estate."

Surano looked at his brother affectionately. He found him changed—thinner and older. It was unsurprising, as there were fourteen years between them, which was evident not only in their physical aspect but also in their characters. Pere had always been more like a father to him than a brother, interceding prudently on every occasion—and there had been many—that Surano had gotten into trouble.

"No more money, I promise." The costs of a company of soldiers were paid for by its captain, so Surano had had to rely on his brother's generosity to keep afloat. "That's over now."

"Over?" Pere asked. "What do you mean?"

"I got royal permission to go to Rome and ask for forgiveness from the Pope, who granted it. One of my soldiers came with me." He pointed to Corso. "I then asked to be transferred to Flanders, expecting a promotion that never came, and remained there a while. We headed back to Spain, but a storm dragged us to the Azores, and we were forced to wait there until a Spanish fleet coming from the Americas picked us up. On the way to Portugal, another storm wrecked the captain's ship. We attempted a rescue, but could do nothing for them, so we pressed on to Lisbon. When we reported what had happened, the ship was accused of not offering aid, and the crew was sentenced to three months in prison and a fine. It was unjust." He paused a moment. "So I fled. I left the militia." He pointed to Corso again. "Him too. He declared in my favor. I had saved his life and he later saved mine. So now we are deserters."

Pere remained in thought for a long while. He knew Surano well enough to know that he was telling the truth. His brother had never been an obedient man, rather the opposite, but it was bad luck that had gotten in his way once again. Perhaps he should not have been so impulsive. If he had served his brief sentence, he could have kept his post in the army. That is what Pere would have done, but now there was no way to change it.

"And what will you do now?" Pere finally asked. "What shall we do?"

Grateful that his brother was not going to give him a sermon, Surano hurriedly replied, "Set myself up in the mountains? Raise livestock? Marry and settle down?" The memory of a woman came to him and he felt a pang. Would Lida have waited like they had promised each other? Of course, then, neither of them knew it would take him so long to return. "With a little bit of luck, Lida will still be waiting for me—"

Pere shook his head.

"I'm afraid you're too late. And I'm puzzled that you ask. Someone like you—" He did not finish the sentence. In the end, who was he to judge his brother's heart?

Surano clenched his jaw. It took him some time to ask the next question.

"Whom did she marry?"

"Medardo."

"That traitor!"

"Her brother didn't stop pressuring her until he got his way," said Pere. "Jayme has always wanted to be in with the most influential people."

"Jayme of Cuyls," Surano spat. "That jealous, wretched bastard!" He remembered the conversation Corso had overheard between the three men and rage consumed him. "Now I understand why he was conspiring with Medardo and the king's secretary!"

"Johan's daughter said you'd seen them together. I am eager to hear what was said." Pere pointed toward the house. "It won't be long before Count Fernando arrives with the written answer from His Majesty. Wait with us. Afterward, we shall all confer and decide."

Surano took a deep breath and grunted. During his absence, the rebel Medardo had not only gained ground but had married the woman he loved. He smoothed his hair and tried to regain his composure. He then turned to stone-faced Corso and muttered, "Corso, my friend, you should know that the people of the mountains resemble their land. They are hardy and hardworking, prone to worry and unease, but implacable in rage and revenge. If you are going to accompany me on this journey, don't ever forget this."

Corso was unmoved. He had seen too much blood spilled to fear petty squabbles between locals in a small, godforsaken place.

In the room, and at her father's bidding, Brianda stood silently by the door leading to the patio in order to follow the conversation when the count came and to make sure that no one from the house came close to pry.

The door opened and Pere entered, followed by Surano and Corso. Pere motioned to his brother to sit down at the table and Corso to stand watch.

Corso obeyed and joined Brianda at the door. She had on a pumpkin-colored petticoat and a dark skirt in the same brocatelle as the jerkin hugging her bosom and highlighting her hips. Her hair hung loose, framing her pretty face. She was far more attractive than any of the women he had been with. The previous night's woman had not been bad, but there was no comparison to Brianda, whom he had been unable to get out of his head even after several jugs of wine.

Corso stood so close to Brianda that she stepped away. She could not help it: the man caused an inexplicable sensation of alarm in her and, right now, he also needed a bath. His stare compelled her to look away, something that had never happened to her with any man, not even Marquo. She was afraid that if she had to talk to him, she would stutter; if she had to listen to him, she would be mesmerized by the movement of his lips; if she had to touch him, she would shake; if she had to kiss him, would it be like kissing Marquo?

She immediately put an end to these ridiculous thoughts. What the devil was happening to her? The future of her land depended on the imminent meeting, and there she was, unable to stop thinking about a murky stranger.

Just then, the Count of Orrun entered the room, his face and gestures betraying his bad mood. Without any preamble or greetings, he took his seat, grabbed a goblet of wine, and emptied it in one gulp. He took out a rolled-up piece of paper, unfurled it, and began reading in an irate tone. "'That the Count of Orrun is to be put in possession of the county and those of the county understand it is the wish of His Majesty that the count be obeyed and paid his dues and that he be their lord until such time as justice declares the right of His Majesty over said county . . .'"

He paused and asked that his goblet be refilled.

"Given the circumstances, my lord, it's the best you could have hoped for," said Pere. "At least you gain time and, up to now, justice has always been on your side. We should trust in it."

"Not so fast, Pere, my friend," said the count. "Now comes the worst part." He returned his gaze to the document and continued. "'That the Count of Orrun treat his vassals well with no memory of past deeds, and that the execution of sentences and condemnations be suspended against those given—'"

"Pardon the rebels!" shouted Marquo, scandalized. "But, what is this? Don't tell me he intends to leave Medardo free!"

The count passed the document to Nunilo, who read it in sober silence before summarizing it aloud. "'His Majesty will give possession of the county of Orrun to the count in a short time, but in exchange demands the pardon of Medardo and his accomplices, and the Royal Treasury has the right to continue its action for possession of Orrun.'"

"Pardon Medardo!" repeated Pere. "Surano, tell us what your friend heard yesterday."

Surano relayed how the Count of Chinchon had asked Medardo and Jayme to be patient.

"He said that the troubles would continue until Count Fernando got tired and was willing to sell the county at a good price."

A long silence descended upon them. Brianda wondered if everyone else thought the same as she did: Was Count Fernando capable of selling? Would he deem it easier to take the money than to fight?

"The very presence of Medardo at parliament is provocation enough," muttered Bringuer. "How can we trust the word of the king if he favors the rebels and his ministers honor criminals?"

"They are not all proven criminals," Johan pointed out. "Jayme is of noble blood. And as for Medardo's followers, if one noble sides with him, so will others."

"Johan is right," Nunilo said. "They will try to bribe us. All of us."

The count looked at them one by one, searching his old friends' faces for confirmation of their loyalty to his cause.

"According to the document," Surano asked, "when will Count Fernando be put in charge of what is yours again?"

Looking over the scroll, Nunilo replied, "It says the count will receive credentials from the king addressed to the General Council of Orrun when it convenes in January."

"Very well, then. We will wait until January." Surano glanced at his brother. "I see now that my services are needed here." He addressed the count: "In my friend Corso and in me, you have two valiant soldiers. If my instincts are right, this has just begun. I don't believe the king will ever give up these lands. This matter of continuing the suit is only a ruse to gain time and wear you down. You must prepare yourself for a fight."

Brianda was terrified to hear that war was inevitable. The General Council of Orrun had already rejected the count's aspirations once; why would January be different? However, if Surano came to live in her mountains, the fierce and intractable Corso would too.

The count got to his feet and paced the room. His house had always been loyal to the king, so why was the monarch set on taking what was his? There were strategic justifications, perhaps. With Orrun, the king would control the mountain road to France and increase the extension of his kingdom. A sale would free Fernando of years of bitterness and gain the king's favor for his family for generations. But the blood of his ancestors boiled in the count's veins. And how could he desert the men standing by him today? In other baronies as well, the king was using these same tactics to usurp the rural nobles. What would become of them if he renounced his past? They would be relegated to their big houses and subject to the whims of people like Medardo.

The Count of Orrun stopped pacing and rested his hands on the back of his chair. "We shall do as Surano says," he said at last. "Go back to your homes and await my instructions. We'll travel to Aiscle in January. If the council sees reason, well and good. If they don't, we'll use arms. I'll remain here a few more days. Next week, Prince Philip III will be sworn in and all and sundry will be in attendance. I'll seek more allies among the nobles of Aragon."

The men nodded. Count Fernando thanked them all and left.

There was a brief silence, then Johan sighed. "I hope it's not too late. So many years of mismanagement cannot be erased overnight."

Just then, Azmet burst in and shouted to Brianda, "Mistress! It's Cecilia! They're going to kill her!"

Brianda raced from the room without waiting for the men's reaction. Corso followed.

Azmet guided them to a small square ringed by some run-down buildings. Brianda followed as Azmet pushed his way through the crowd, who responded with shouts and insults.

When they reached the front, Brianda nearly screamed. Two soldiers were holding Cecilia by the arms and getting ready to tie her to a post while a third was training his whip against the ground. The crack of the whip was violent and cutting. Three such cracks would surely be enough to kill the girl. Cecilia screamed and writhed, to the amusement of her torturers.

Brianda shouted with all her might, "Release her!"

But her words were drowned out by the mob. Some laughed, while others openly cheered on the captors. The majority, with anxious eyes, waited for the entertainment to begin in earnest.

"What has she done to deserve this?" Brianda shouted again. "Azmet, do you know what she has done?"

Azmet shrugged. Tears rolled down his cheeks.

A woman carrying a baby said, "She is a gypsy! I hope they eradicate this plague."

The man with the whip stopped practicing and ordered the multitude to be quiet. Then, he extended a paper and read: "His Majesty orders that male gypsies aged eighteen or over that are found in the kingdom using gypsy habits, speech, or customs shall be sentenced to the galleys; those under eighteen and over fourteen and women shall be whipped and banished from all the kingdom in perpetuity." He rolled up the document. "This gypsy has been caught stealing in the market and will now receive her punishment."

Brianda's head spun. She looked around but did not see her father or the men of Orrun. Then she spotted Corso, standing a full head above the crowd two rows behind. She made her way over.

"Please!" she pleaded. "You have to help her! I know her! She is a good girl!"

Corso shook his head. "It's none of my business," he said simply.

Brianda felt rage rising from her stomach. "I beg you! I'm ordering you!"

Corso stared at her, puzzled that she would react like this over a simple gypsy, then shook his head again. "I don't want problems."

Brianda let out a howl and punched him in the chest with all her might before pushing her way to the first row again. They had already tied Cecilia to the post. Brianda thought of the conversation they had had they previous day, during Brianda's bath. Cecilia only had one dream: to wear a dress as pretty as Brianda's and get a boy to fall in love with her. But Cecilia wanted to know who would love a girl with dark skin. Brianda had told her that, given her beauty, more than one boy would love her in the mountains, where the peasants' skin was deeply tanned in summer and beaten by the snow and wind in winter.

Now no one was going to do anything to save her. Not even that animal Corso!

The man with the whip tensed his arm, and just as he was about to let it fly, Brianda roared toward the post.

"Stop! There has been a mistake! This girl is my servant!"

The soldier sized her up coldly, and Brianda's heart skipped a beat. There was no going back now.

"I don't know what happened. They must have confused her with someone else. This girl has lived with me since she was born!"

What luck that Cecilia was wearing the blouse and skirt Brianda had given her the night before. In her normal rags, the argument would have lacked any credibility.

Corso cursed Brianda's foolishness. If she thought that the protestations of a girl, no matter how nicely dressed, could divert a soldier from his task, she was very wrong. Then the soldier pushed Brianda to the ground and, in four bounds, Corso was there, lifting her up.

He turned toward the soldier, who had been joined by two more when they sensed trouble, and put his hand on the hilt of his new sword so they could see its quality. Corso introduced himself in a stern tone, using the name of an infantry company he knew but had never belonged to, and telling them he was second-in-command to a captain who had come to present some delicate issues to His Majesty.

"And this," he said, pointing to Brianda, "is the daughter of one of the noble benefactors of my company. The girl you intend to whip is her servant. I don't doubt your good intentions, but believe me when I say that it is not in your interest for the king to receive complaints. They say he is already in a disagreeable mood, what with the pretensions of that embittered lot from Orrun."

While the three soldiers conferred among themselves, Brianda saw Johan, Marquo, and Surano entering the square. She gestured firmly for them to stop and wait for her. She rushed over to them and, after explaining the situation, asked that they not intervene unless things got more difficult.

"Your actions are laudable, but I have no intention of letting you go back there," her father said.

"Forgive me, Father, but I have given Cecilia a reason for hope, and I cannot abandon her now. It would be crueler than having done nothing at all."

Surano came over and put a hand on Johan's shoulder. "With Corso here, there is no reason to be afraid. Three soldiers are nothing to him. And if necessary, we will intervene." Brianda took the chance to slip away and did not hear his last words: "I don't know how your daughter convinced Corso to help her. That man only listens to me and the devil."

Marquo felt a stab of worry. During the meeting with the count, he had noticed how the dark-haired man had looked at his newly betrothed, gazing at her body from top to bottom. Marquo knew men like him. If he was such good friends with Surano, it must be that they were cut from the same cloth: both quarrelsome, loose-living, and contemptible. Fortunately, he and Brianda would soon return home. *The sooner, the better*, he thought. And the sooner the wedding could be arranged, the sooner Marquo could solidify his hold on Brianda and on the extensive properties of Lubich.

After much deliberation, the soldiers decided to free the girl rather than risk the displeasure of the king. Cecilia ran over and threw her arms around Brianda. Her sobs shook them both.

"Come, come," Brianda said to her. "Head up and walk with dignity. We have to get out of here as fast as possible, and you must behave like one of my servants."

"How do I do that?"

"Make your back so straight that it hurts, raise your chin, turn your head slightly toward them, and glare at them out of the side of your eye. Then maintain that posture, a step behind me, until we leave the square. Can you do that?"

Cecilia nodded and took the role so seriously that Brianda could barely keep from laughing. Johan, Marquo, and Surano were waiting for them at the edge of the square, along with Azmet, who was bursting with joy. The crowd began to disperse sluggishly, irritated that their fun had been spoiled.

On the walk back to the house, Brianda turned in search of Corso, who trailed them with his head down.

"So, you can talk when you want to!" she crowed. "What was it? Ah, yes!" She imitated his deep voice: "'The pretensions of that embittered lot from Orrun.'"

"I only speak when necessary."

"Well, today you saved a life."

If you knew how many I've taken, he thought, *your voice would not sound so light.*

"And you got me out of a serious mess." Brianda laughed. "Well, two. Yesterday and today! The two times we have met!"

"Surano warned me that mountain people are restless and rowdy. I've now seen it myself. I'll keep my distance."

"But aren't you going to live there now?"

Brianda regretted her impulsive question. It revealed her interest in the man's future.

Corso shrugged.

"Well, in case we don't meet again," she rushed to add, "thank you for your help."

Corso did not answer. He quickened his step and came level with Surano.

"The soldiers accepted my story," he whispered, "but if they just investigate a little bit, they'll discover the lie. We should go."

Surano agreed.

Corso turned and took a last look at Brianda, who was happily laughing with the gypsy.

Suddenly, he felt an overwhelming need to distance himself from her.

What strange substance was that woman's soul made of? Although there were hundreds of people in the square, only she had risked her neck to save an insignificant girl no one would miss. If she had done that for a gypsy, what would she do to defend what was hers?

18.

Surano and Corso left town immediately, agreeing with Pere that they would wait for the others on the outskirts of Fonz. Now that the count's decision was known, there was nothing keeping the company in Monzon, and it seemed prudent to leave at dusk, taking advantage of the return of the farmers to their homes, the departure of merchants, and the line of mules going to collect firewood. The lords of Orrun ordered their servants and men to gather together the horses they had bought and they began their return journey to the highlands. But when they tried to leave through the same gate in the city wall they had galloped through on their arrival, two soldiers stopped them and asked for their papers.

Johan handed over the documents that showed the sale of animals and the resulting payment of the corresponding taxes, but the soldiers did not seem convinced.

"We will have to count the heads," said the youngest one.

Brianda saw Johan and Nunilo exchange a meaningful look, and she understood that the figures on the papers were not the real ones. She thought of the Inquisition's punishment for the trafficking of horses and became frightened. She turned to Cecilia, but since it was the girl's first time on a horse, all her attention was focused on trying not to lose her balance. Then Brianda realized that Bringuer, Marquo, and their men had their hands on their swords.

Pere motioned to them to remain calm.

"They would catch us before we got a league," he whispered. "Leave it to me."

He went over to the soldiers and said, "They're waiting for us at Saint Thomas Hospital." He pointed to the other side of the river. "We're late."

"Who is waiting for you?" asked the soldier, eyes narrowed.

"The nephew of the recently deceased Bishop of Barbastro. You can come with us to verify if you'd like."

The soldier raised an eyebrow and, after looking at his companion, nodded his head. The change of guard was about to take place, and it would be simpler just to let them pass. He returned the papers to Johan and waved them on their way.

"Is that true?" Brianda asked her father once they had crossed the bridge.

"Yes," was all he said.

They stopped in front of the big building Brianda had noticed the morning of their arrival in Monzon. Azmet had told her there were other hospitals in the city, but this one exclusively treated servants of the king who'd come for the parliament meeting.

"Take the others onward without me," Johan said to Pere as a servant tied his horse to a ring in the wall. "I won't be here long."

"May I come in with you?" Brianda asked, seized by curiosity.

"It's not a place for a young woman."

"Then Marquo and Cecilia will wait with me."

Marquo was annoyed she had not consulted him, but he obeyed. Johan entered the hospital, and the rest of the group left. Brianda dismounted and tied her horse and Cecilia's to other rings on the wall. The little gypsy slid off the back of her horse to the ground. Her face, still damp from the tears she had shed when saying good-bye to Azmet, reflected a mixture of sadness and nervous excitement about her new home. Brianda smiled, watching Cecilia peek through the slits in the building's closed shutters. She'd been overjoyed when Johan agreed to bring the girl with them to the mountains, where she could live a safe and peaceful life. She had always regretted not having a sister to amuse herself with during the long winter evenings, and she suspected she had found a loving and loyal companion in Cecilia. She would teach her how to ride and many other things, such as read, embroider, set traps, tell a bird by its trill, rear pups, arrange flowers . . .

The minutes went by and Johan did not return. Brianda began to grow impatient and she went over to the door.

"You heard what your father said, Brianda," Marquo warned her. "Don't even think about going inside."

"And if something has happened to him?"

"What could happen?" he snapped, revealing his irritation.

He was still shocked at Brianda's behavior the previous afternoon. Defending a gypsy in public was not an act befitting a young noblewoman. And truly, she had warned him that her father had educated her in a peculiar manner. Seeing her ride like a man, dominating her large horse with mastery, was terribly attractive, as was her enjoyment of his kisses, and her desire to find out what men talked about. However, a small doubt clouded his feelings. On no account did he think of renouncing the opportunity to marry her, but his ideal woman was rather more docile, obedient, and disciplined, like his own mother. And possibly someone slightly thinner than Brianda, who, compared to the exquisite, stylized, and fair-skinned ladies of the court of King Philip, sometimes looked to him more like a pretty house servant. He let out a frustrated sigh. If Johan had not been so free with his daughter, it would not be up to Marquo now to repair the damage.

Cecilia came over to Brianda.

"I only know that people who go into places like this never come out," Cecilia said in a low voice.

"Don't be silly," said Marquo. "Those people are the sick ones."

"There are illnesses that appear in seconds," said Cecilia with conviction. "You're fine and the next minute you're dead. I once saw a man with maggots in his guts who didn't know it, because normally they are peaceful guests until something upsets them and then they begin to multiply and run around inside the stomach. This man was talking and, suddenly, he fell to the floor and began twisting in pain, as if he was possessed by a demon or under a spell. Soon afterwards, the worms began to spill out of his mouth and he died."

"You're just making that up!" Marquo shouted at her. "Look at Brianda! You've frightened her!"

"No, I saw it," Cecilia insisted, looking intently at Brianda. "And he died. I swear." She moved her head haughtily from side to side just as her new mistress had taught her, and said to Marquo, "And I never lie."

"How do I know you haven't cast the evil eye on me, gypsy!" snarled Marquo.

Brianda shivered. As far as she knew, intestinal worms were not life threatening, but she could not tell if Cecilia's story was true or false. In any event, the way she had told it had been upsetting. Just the thought of never seeing her father again frightened her terribly.

She turned around and marched into the building before the others had time to stop her.

The first room, small and square, was empty and bereft of furniture. A penetrating and disagreeable smell stopped her for a few seconds. Brianda took out a handkerchief and held it to her nose, then decided to continue through the only door that she could see, which led to another, bigger room that seemed to lead to many others like a foyer. Several figures crossed in different directions without noticing her presence, concentrating on their overloaded trays full of jugs and cloths. The smell here was even more repulsive: it reminded her of the butcher's in

Tiles on a hot day. She almost retched and wanted to run away, but the desire to find Johan drove her forward.

She peeked into the first room, and what she saw paralyzed her.

She had seen beggars, people in rags, starving men, deformed bodies, and one or two dying people in her life, but always one at a time. They had not caused the same chilling effect on her spirit as the sight in front of her now, which her eyes felt incapable of absorbing.

Scattered on the floor on straw mattresses were weak and wizened figures, tormented and moaning in pain. Some moved their fingers as if looking for a hand to hold; others opened and shut their mouths when they heard the scrawny monk doling out water from a bucket. The most unfortunate ones had not even the strength to shoo away the flies sticking to their wounds.

Brianda backed out quickly, tears in her eyes. Then she heard her father's voice at the far end of the long room. She felt a sharp pang of relief, wanting to throw herself into his arms, but caution held her back—she had again disobeyed him.

And this time she was really sorry! Her father had wanted to spare her the horrible sights inside the hospital and the possibility of catching something from that foul air. If this was a hospital for servants of the king, she did not dare imagine what one for the poor, the abandoned, and the lepers would be like!

Beside her in the foyer was a tall, carved cupboard, and Brianda leaned against its side, where she could listen without being seen.

"Finish your task, Father," she heard Johan say. "I can wait. Everyone needs a good death."

"I won't be long," said the priest. "If you wish, you may accompany me."

They entered a room opposite her. Brianda waited a few moments and began walking quickly toward the exit, but the sound of a strong and perfectly modulated voice reached her from the room that Johan and the priest, who carried a bundle of books, had gone into. "Illness is a sacred path that leads us to heaven to enjoy the Divine Essence. We should not deny or lament it but instead welcome it with virtuous acceptance. Dying has its good side; it is not something to fear."

After what she had just seen, it was difficult for Brianda to believe those words.

The priest continued. "You should know that those who are about to die, when the last moment comes, have greater temptations and incitements from the devil than ever before. They are tempted to renounce God even though faith is the foundation of all salvation, to despair because of the rigors of divine justice, to be arrogant and look out for only themselves, to express impatience and disaffection with God because of the severity of their pain, and to be greedy due to their excessive attachment to family and estate."

Then he began to read the Passion and Death of Jesus Christ. Brianda had never heard anyone read with such perfect diction, clarity, and rhythm. She crept to the door and peeked in.

A gaunt man with greenish-yellow skin lay on the floor. To his right, a crying woman dressed in rich clothes stroked his hand. To his left, a man with a tonsure and wearing a habit, whom she could only see from the side, held up a book. Johan, his head bowed to his chest and his hands clasped, stood a few steps away. The weak light of dusk, creeping in from a patio, cast a straw-colored light over the scene.

"The power of Divine Mercy to forgive is infinitely greater," continued the priest, "than man's power to sin." He leaned toward the dying man. "Do you believe that Jesus Christ, Our Lord, died for you?"

"I do," the man murmured.

"Do you give thanks for this with all your heart?"

"I do."

"Do you believe that you cannot be saved except through your death?"

"I do."

"Then give thanks while your soul is in your body. And put in this death all your solace and strength." He paused. "Shroud everything in this death." Another pause. "Now, be of good heart and good faith and give thanks to Our Lord God because you are in a state of grace. And firmly believe and say and confess that He alone is all your succor, all your defense, all your remedy, refuge, repair, redemption, remission, reconciliation, and all your salvation. And only in the Holy Cross and in the death of the Son of God be your heart, affection, and faith. Repeat with me: *In manus tuas, Domine, commendo spiritum meum.*"

With a faltering voice, the woman helped her husband repeat the act of deliverance: "Into your hands—O Lord—I commend—my spirit—"

The priest then said to her, "If he has answered with true faith, you may have complete certainty of his salvation. Ensure that you comply with his final wishes over his spiritual remains for burial, masses, and donations. In the meantime, pray to the Holy Trinity, to God the Father, to God the Son, to the Virgin, to the guardian angels, and to the saints to whom your husband professed his devotion."

Brianda sensed that the ritual had reached its end and went outside before they saw her. The priest's elaborate words echoed in her head. It was the first time she had heard a man of God take such time and care in seeing off a dying man.

Outside, Cecilia threw her arms around her.

"Why did you take so long? Is your father all right? And are you? What did you see?"

Marquo, sitting on a rock, was sharpening a stick with the blade of his dagger. Without looking up, he said angrily, "You shouldn't get so close to her. Who knows what plague she's caught."

Brianda was going to answer in kind, but she heard Johan coming out, accompanied by the priest and his bundle of books. She went over to Marquo and whispered, "If you say anything to my father, I won't kiss you for a year."

"Good. That way you can't infect me with anything."

"I warn you that I mean it."

Johan apologized for taking so long and introduced the monk as Father Guillem, the new parish priest of Tiles, whom they would escort on his first trip to the mountains. He was a young man of little more than twenty years, not very tall but good-looking, of timid and modest appearance but with a subtle look of severity. In Brianda's opinion, the voice she had heard fitted him perfectly. He was dressed in a linen tunic and a short cloak with a hood. From his waist hung a large rosary.

They mounted their horses and began distancing themselves from Monzon. After riding in silence for some time, Johan said to Father Guillem, "Pere of Aiscle has told me about your excellent preparation, unusual for someone as young as yourself."

"That is thanks to my uncle, the previous bishop."

"I hope you won't think it wasted in the mountain villages."

Father Guillem gave him a puzzled look, as if trying to decide whether Johan was being ironic.

"Do you know what my uncle said when he decided to send me to Aiscle? Knowing my wish to go off and follow in the steps of illustrious Dominicans like Bartolomé de las Casas and Francisco de Vitoria, he said to me, *I'm not sending you off to colonize and evangelize, as here in this very place there is a land that needs order and discipline.* I suppose you know better than I the meaning of his words."

Johan nodded slightly. Since the building of the cathedral and the founding of the bishopric of Barbastro fourteen years ago, territorial disputes had arisen between the new diocese and the monastery of Besalduch. The bishop had gone behind the abbot's back and visited Aiscle, Tiles, and other villages in western Orrun to show them the documents that accredited the new boundaries, using as arguments the principles and canon law established by the Council of Trent. Abbot Bartholomeu of Besalduch and his monks responded fiercely to the attack on their ancient rights—not to mention their tithes—refusing to carry out their duties and even threatening those same villagers with excommunication. He refused to accept that the donations of the faithful would be taken by another. Just like the count's lawsuit with the king over the county, the religious conflict continued. And the lords of Orrun defended the count and the abbot. Nevertheless, Johan preferred to act with caution.

"The lords of the mountains," Johan said, "continue to pay dues for the benefit of our souls."

"That is good, Johan, as the salvation of your souls is the one mission with which God and my earthly superiors have entrusted me."

Brianda, who had followed the conversation with interest, suddenly felt a shiver run through her body.

19.

When they all met that night to pitch camp beside the dam at Fonz, Corso sensed that something was wrong with Brianda. The impetuous young woman's eyes had dimmed, and she did not say a word before going to sleep or when the journey continued early the next morning. He deduced that there had been a disagreement with Marquo, who did not even deign to look at her, which was something he had done constantly in Monzon, with a glint of possessiveness in his eyes. Corso knew that if Brianda belonged to him nothing would prevent him from looking at her at all hours, and, instead of glinting, his eyes would gleam. But he knew a girl like her would never notice someone like him, a man brutalized by war with no profession other than killing for a living. Other soldiers fought convinced they were serving a land, a king, a god. He did not. He had never had anything personal to fight for because he had never had anything. When Surano had saved his life in a skirmish, it was the first time someone had helped him without demanding something in return, and that was reason enough to owe him loyalty. No matter what Surano did, Corso would accompany him, support him, and defend him.

They left behind the golden fields, and the air became fresher. By midafternoon, they began to climb a damp, rocky outcrop overgrown with ferns. The path was so narrow and steep that they had to ride single file and considerably spread out from one another. Without ever taking his eyes off Brianda, Corso made sure that Surano and he rode behind the lords and women and in front of the rest of the troop. He'd heard a servant say that many past travelers had fallen into the deep precipice on the left, and the little gypsy refused to ride at all, trusting her own feet over the bouncing horses.

Corso saw Brianda's shoulders sink more and more, as if she struggled to remain upright. Her rocking on the horse became pronounced, a swaying he'd seen in wounded men about to faint. Without a second thought, he rode up next to Brianda and placed his horse between hers and the edge of the cliff moments before Brianda fell over. Corso held her by the waist with one hand and with the other grabbed the reins to stop her horse. Then, he lifted her in the air and put her in front of him on his horse, still unconscious in his arms. Surano came to his aid and took charge of Brianda's horse.

"You have saved this woman's life," he said. "She and her family are much in debt to you."

Corso used those moments of proximity to Brianda's body to observe her closely. He ran his gaze over her face, her fine eyebrows, the line of her nose, the faint purple of her slightly opened lips. He remembered the forceful way she had pleaded with him to intercede for the gypsy and how she had punched him in the chest. He much preferred her awake, but he couldn't help hoping she'd take her time waking up because he knew he'd never again hold her so close. He took advantage of the moment and caressed her forehead, noticing it was too hot, and he dared to run his fingers through her soft dark hair until a slight flutter of her eyelids told him the beautiful moment had passed.

◆ ◆ ◆

Brianda slowly opened her eyes and discovered the sky above her. For a few seconds, she felt a pleasant tranquility and a comforting surrender to the rocking, the repetitive sound of the hooves against the stones, the fresh air on her cheeks, and the soft support under her neck. She turned her head slightly and met a man's deep and penetrating stare. Then she began to remember. The exhaustion. The ache all over her body. The increasing pain in her head. The nausea. The distress at what she had seen in the hospital. The shivers.

"How did I get here, Corso?" she asked.

"You fainted on your horse when we were going along the precipice," he answered, pleased that her first reaction had not been to pull away from him.

"And you got there in time to catch me."

"Yes. I'm used to having to react quickly."

"Thank you." She sighed deeply. "I don't feel well."

"I think you have a fever."

"Yes."

Brianda closed her eyes and remained that way for a while, then grimaced.

"Do you need to change position?" Corso asked.

"I don't know. Everything is sore."

Gently, Corso helped her sit up. She rested her head against his chest, and his heart fluttered. He would have done anything to keep her there forever. But he also felt the excessive heat and weakness of her body, and it worried him.

"How far are we from Aiscle?" she asked after a while.

"I don't know."

"Oh, of course. You've never been there. We must be nearly at the top. Soon you'll see the mountains in the background and the valley at your feet, with all the autumn colors decanted over the forests. Let me know."

Brianda fell asleep. For a second, Corso panicked, thinking now that he had just gotten to know her, that he had just saved her, she might be seriously ill or she might die. Brianda had spoken to him as if he were a man and not an animal. She had not shouted at him, and she had not been frightened. She had not shown displeasure at his appearance or the fact that he had her in his arms. The fever may have clouded her reactions a bit but not to the level of delirium. She had asked him to tell her when he saw the valley and the mountains, and he would, because from now on he would do anything she asked. It would not be much, unfortunately, as their paths would part at the end of the journey.

The ascent finally ended, but the lords riding far in front did not stop. Corso deduced that they were afraid of letting night fall on them during the descent, so they were attempting to reach the valley as quickly as possible. There they would discover Brianda's illness and take steps to help her. Meanwhile, he could hold her in his arms a little longer.

He whispered her name several times until she answered.

"We are starting to descend, Brianda. I will have to hold on to you tighter as the slope is steep."

"Tell me what you see."

"On the horizon, high mountains."

"And is there snow on the summits?"

"Yes, some. And closer, a huge solitary mountain."

"Beles Peak, which reigns over Tiles. Did you know I live in a place called Lubich? It's very beautiful. You must come see it."

"Maybe one day." He would have to find a good excuse, he thought, and the sooner the better. "On the sunny slopes of the mountains, I can see small groups of houses among the woods and, at their feet, meadows, plowed fields, herds, and flocks."

"They are now preparing to take the livestock to the lowlands. It's sad."

"Sad? Why?"

"The good-byes. The men won't return until spring. The women are left alone. One of the servants in my house, Gisabel, got married two years ago, and most of the time her husband is gone. Thank goodness that won't happen to me."

"Ah, really? Why not?"

"Because I won't marry a peasant."

Corso remained silent. *Or a soldier*, he thought bitterly. After a few seconds, he said sarcastically, "Some women must be happy to see the backs of their men."

"I hadn't thought of that." Brianda laughed, but the laugh made her cough so much that she was exhausted and fell back asleep.

Just before the end of the descent, she suddenly woke and said, "By the entrance to the church, one of the ragged boys came so close I could smell his terrible breath. He had black scabs around his mouth and spots on his skin. I might have caught the plague."

"That's not plague. If it were, the gates of the city would have been closed and the king would have left."

"Well typhus, spotted fever, or whatever else that kills."

"You're not going to die."

"In the hospital, I saw horrible things. The people were all dying in terrible pain."

"And what were you doing in the hospital?"

"I went to look for my father because he was taking a long time. When was that? Yesterday. I got infected there. But you can't tell my father. He told me not to go in, and I disobeyed him."

"Illness like that doesn't appear overnight," Corso assured her. "What you have is a simple cold. Your father doesn't have to find out about yesterday."

"Have you seen people die, Corso?"

Many, he thought, *and killed more.*

"Why do you want to know?"

"Because I can't stop thinking about what I saw. I'm too young to die. I haven't even married, and I need to have children who can inherit Lubich."

"You're young and strong. Get those thoughts out of your head."

"I can't. Father Guillem told a dying man that it's good because he was closer to God, but those poor people didn't look happy. I wish there was something to make me forget their faces."

He would probably regret what he was about to do, but Corso followed his instinct rather than his common sense.

"Look at me, Brianda."

When she raised her head, he leaned down and kissed her lips, ardent and parched from the fever. The kiss was not sweet or gentle or delicate. What he wanted to do was to bite her, extract her heat, wake her from her lethargy, bring her back to a life where there would only be strength, energy, taut muscles, throbbing veins. Her body was not going to die, could not die, and her soul was not going to languish, not while he was near.

Brianda did not pull away. All Marquo's kisses together did not equal the power of this one. Momentarily, she forgot her sore body, and her mind was emptied of fear.

"You shouldn't have done that," she whispered, looking into his eyes.

"I know."

"Now you'll get sick as well."

Corso laughed in delight. "If that's all you're worried about, I'm willing to risk it a thousand times."

Corso leaned down and kissed her again, this time with a tenderness that surprised even him. When they parted slightly, Brianda rested against his chest and looked as if she had surrendered to a moment of happy stupor.

"Now when you close your eyes," he whispered, "you will only see me."

Just after reaching the valley, Johan turned and saw his daughter on Corso's horse. He rode quickly toward them. He had not seen Brianda so feverish since she was a child. He gave orders to the servants to bring the large group to a halt, let the horses graze beside the river, and make up an improvised bed on which the girl could rest. Then he returned, lifted his daughter off the horse, and laid her down by the river. Cecilia, her feet destroyed by the hours of climbing the rocky path, forgot about her own pain and sat beside Brianda to dampen her face, wrists, and ankles with a cloth soaked in cold water. As Father Guillem murmured some prayers, Johan thought of the previous day's last rites and shivered. Crestfallen, he sat down on a rock a few steps away.

"I don't understand. When we left Monzon, she was like a rose. Maybe it's just fatigue."

Bringuer shook his head. "She has a high fever and we have nothing to treat her."

Father Guillem came over and said, "They are the symptoms of the parliament typhus. I have been in the hospital for weeks and seen similar cases."

"But many have had it and survived," Bringuer hurriedly added.

"If she is ill now, we are all in danger," Johan again intervened. "You most of all, Corso."

Marquo took a couple of steps back. "I told her not to go in the hospital," he said in a huff, "but she wouldn't listen to me."

Johan looked up sharply.

"She went in?"

"To look for you because you were taking so long. I warned her that nothing good could come of going in a place like that."

"She told me she only peeked in the entrance," Corso said to defend her. "Besides, you can't get infected that quickly. With so many sick people in the streets, anyone could catch it."

Nunilo rubbed his beard pensively and asked, "What shall we do now? It's a short distance to Aiscle, but I don't know if anyone would shelter us, given her state."

"My house will," Pere said.

"Thank you, Pere, but even so, it's very risky," Nunilo said. "Lubich is still far away, and she is very weak. If we stay here, we are exposed to Medardo's bandits—plus, we don't even have a goddamned jar of vinegar to help get her fever down."

Father Guillem clucked his tongue in reproach, but Nunilo ignored him.

Then, Surano returned from surveying the area.

"Guess who's coming." He did not wait for an answer. "Medardo and his brother-in-law Jayme, with a dozen men."

They all jumped up in search of their weapons. Pere calculated the distance that separated them and realized they would not have enough time to flee unless they abandoned the horses. They opted to face them head-on at the foot of the slope. Together, their group tripled Medardo's in number.

Johan spoke to Marquo, "You, don't move from Brianda's side."

"I'd prefer to fight," Marquo responded, patting his arquebus.

Corso knew those words were not spoken out of bravery but from Marquo's fear of contagion. He went to Johan and said, "I'll take care of her."

"You helped her just the other day, and today you saved her life." Johan looked at him with eyes full of gratitude. He saw in the face of that rough, dirty, young soldier a certain nobility. "I hope her life is not in danger."

"Not with me," Corso asserted.

◆ ◆ ◆

One of Medardo's men, who had gone ahead to scout for any danger, had informed them that Pere and his group had stopped at the entrance to the valley. But Jayme and Medardo decided to continue on. They were convinced that, with the king's resolution in hand, the count's ever-cautious men would not risk getting blood on their hands—at least not for the moment. Nevertheless, they made sure that all their arquebuses were loaded.

Medardo cursed when he saw Surano. Where the devil had he come from? He noticed the sprig of boxwood in his jerkin and frowned in disgust. He had come to hate that bush. The lords of Orrun were arrogant even in that: they had chosen as their emblem that immortal evergreen plant, certain that it would thrive even in the frozen inferno to which he would send them.

By the hatred in Surano's eyes, Medardo knew the rascal had been informed of his wedding to Lida. Medardo wondered if they had told him how pleased she was to be the wife of the most famous man in the region. Lida valued his ambition, which was nothing but the defense of the people against the tyranny of a count who did not even live there. Bit by bit, his cause was gaining ground. He was the son of a peasant who now rubbed shoulders with the king's ministers, something unheard of. He was close to achieving his dream of being the first commoner named justice or general bailiff of the county. And if he could do it, so could others.

Surano brought the arquebus dangerously close to his face, and Medardo realized that, if one shot was fired, even by accident, nothing could prevent a bloodbath. And, being so outnumbered, his men would be the losers. He signaled to his men to lower their weapons.

He found Pere and spoke to him. "We are not here to fight. Like you, we are returning from Monzon, and we want to get home quickly after having been away for these past weeks."

"Your words cannot be trusted," replied Pere. "The last time you promised peace, the count barely made it out of Aiscle alive."

"That day he provoked the situation with his attitude." Medardo leaned on his horse's withers. "He came as lord to the place where he was least wanted. Each time he does so, he will get the same reception."

"He says he doesn't want to fight, and yet he threatens," whispered Bringuer beside Nunilo. "We won't have a better chance to be done with him than today."

Nunilo gestured for him to be quiet. It was one thing to act in self-defense, or in a pitched battle, but it would be very different to kill these men in cold blood, and would only bring terrible retribution on their houses. He trusted Pere's ability to avoid a fight, although it was also true that, with men like Medardo, you could never lower your guard. How could they know that Medardo was not preparing an ambush?

As if he had read Nunilo's mind, Pere said, "Medardo, you are only quiet when you're hiding something. Perhaps you're waiting for others and merely wish to gain time."

Then Jayme got off his horse.

"Do you also doubt my word?" he asked, looking directly at Johan. "We fight on different sides, but I am also a noble and my word is worth the same as any other's."

"The word of an opportunist cannot be trusted, no matter where he's from," Johan replied.

Jayme was tempted to ask what Johan would have done in his situation but held his tongue. His father, Johan's father's younger brother, had been born in Lubich, and had married for love the heiress of Cuyls, a house in decline. The relationship between the brothers was always friendly, and the cousins had been close until the appearance of Elvira, a temperamental girl from a good family in Besalduch. Jayme and she fell in love and made plans in secret: she would bring a good dowry, and he would work dauntlessly to increase his estate. When Elvira's parents found out about the young couple's intentions, they sent her to family in France and they warned him to forget about her. Then they arranged her marriage to Johan, heir to Lubich, a much greater property.

After that, Jayme developed a deep loathing for the cousin he had once loved. Everything Jayme desired, Johan had: the magnificent house, the lands, and woods of Lubich, and the only woman he had ever loved. He hadn't even seen Elvira since Johan had cut ties with him for wearing the royalists' sprig of gorse, a decade ago already. The more Johan was admired by the other lords of the county and by the count himself, the more Jayme detested all of them. Soon the tables would turn. The day would come when these presumptuous followers of the count would lose their power, and he would be there to occupy the privileged position to which he was entitled.

"We know you are traveling with women," he said.

Johan tensed up.

"And by your reaction, I see it's someone close to you. Your wife, perhaps?" For a moment, Jayme hoped he could see Elvira. "I wouldn't mind paying my respects after so many years."

"A pity she doesn't feel the same." Johan straightened his back, as if wanting to intimidate him with the difference in stature. "And it's not her. It's my daughter, who's ill, and her servant. If you really don't want a fight, be on your way."

"And is the illness serious?"

Johan's face went red with fury. He was sure any words of concern from that mouth carried the poison of a thousand snakes. In the case of both his death and Brianda's, the next in line to inherit Lubich was Jayme of Cuyls.

"I've told you once, and I'll tell you a thousand times: the devil shall have Lubich before you do!"

The silence that followed was so complete that everybody could hear the rustling of Father Guillem's sleeves as he blessed himself.

Medardo noticed him and said, "I do not know you, Father. I presume you are the new priest. I hope you come well trained because I'm afraid that you'll find it difficult to work out which side the demons are on here." He snorted. "If you asked me, I could save you the effort of trying to sort it out."

Father Guillem went over to him.

"Satan appears where least expected," he said in a serious voice that was loud enough for everyone to hear. "Don't question either his ability"—he raised his index finger—"or mine."

Jayme returned to his horse. "We are leaving, and we will do nothing. You decide whether to shoot us in the back."

He kicked the animal's flanks and set off at a light trot. When Medardo went to follow him, Surano blocked his way and hissed, "I hope Lida is as happy as I remember her."

Medardo pushed past and rode off, followed by his twelve men.

Pere and the others did not lower their arms until they had disappeared from sight. Leaving this place was more urgent than ever.

They returned to Brianda, whom Corso and Cecilia had wrapped up in a blanket to try to stop her trembling.

"Tell me, Nunilo, what should we do?" asked Johan nervously.

Nunilo thought for a moment. He finally answered, "We will all ride together until the fork in the mountains. There, Surano will go with Pere and stay with him. The rest of us will continue. The higher up, the less danger."

"And Brianda?"

"We will have to carry her, as Corso did, at least until we reach my house in Tiles."

Soft murmurings arose. Everyone knew that, in order to take charge of the young woman's body, one not only had to be strong but unafraid of her illness. Johan understood that no man would offer himself for such folly. Not even Marquo.

"She's my daughter. I'll do it."

"And I'll help you, Johan," said Nunilo, "but it won't be enough."

Corso came over. "I'll carry her," he said firmly. "I only need a faster and stronger horse."

Nunilo and Johan exchanged a quick glance. Nunilo pointed to the newly purchased horses being watched over by the servants and said to him, "Choose any you desire."

Corso went to look.

A few minutes later, he returned riding a magnificent black Friesian.

20.

Brianda stayed at Anels House in Tiles until the middle of November. At first, she was looked after by Cecilia and Leonor, Nunilo's wife, a woman with curly hair, a long face, and a kind heart. When the risk of infection had lessened, Johan finally returned to Lubich and sent their servant Gisabel to look after his daughter. He insisted that Elvira wait until Brianda was fully recovered before seeing her. He had learned that others in Tiles and Besalduch had caught the illness, and he wanted to protect Lubich at all costs. Bit by bit, the cloths soaked in hot vinegar that Cecilia ceaselessly applied to Brianda's body brought down the fever; the brews of mullein, thyme, pine buds, and dried elderflowers prepared by Gisabel cleared her chest; and Leonor's poultices of olive oil, wax, plantain, and marigold healed the ulcers on her lips.

During all that time, there was no word from the rival factions. As the people of Orrun apprehensively awaited the inevitable, chilling north wind, so the count's men awaited news of his visit. Meanwhile, Corso became the messenger between Pere and Nunilo, Aiscle and Tiles. His new task allowed him to ride, visit his friend Surano, and, most important, learn of the progress of Brianda, whom he had not seen since he brought her to Anels. He had never lived better. In exchange for his simple services, he was given the best food he had ever tasted and his own straw mattress in the servants' wing. His appearance had improved, not only because of the food and the rest but also thanks to the attentions of Leonor, who, since learning what he had done for Brianda, took special care of him. In fact, she had insisted he get a bath and a change of clothes every week. Corso could not remember the last time his hair had looked as bright and silky as the horse's he combed every morning. Nobody had told him to stop riding it, and he felt more the Friesian's owner each day. Nunilo could surely have gotten a lot of money for the animal, but for the moment, nobody except Corso dared master him, to the admiration of the servants and peasants, who were getting used to seeing the solitary foreigner racing across their lands each morning.

Corso was surprised that in such a cold, hard, isolated place where nothing grew for months, the men were sturdy and the women were healthy and vivacious, always with several children stuck to their skirts like pups. When he saw the peasants herding the livestock, chopping firewood, or putting away the tools from the last grain harvests, he supposed that their physical build and their bright, hardworking character had been molded by the hard climate and the intense cold. He wondered if someone not born here could become used to it, if someone not born a peasant could learn the secrets of the land, if such a person could live at the pace of mallets beating wool, at the mercy of harsh weather and uncertain harvests. He wondered if *he* could live in this place to be near Brianda.

One sunny morning, Nunilo sent a servant to Lubich to let them know that Brianda had begun to take short walks inside the house and wished to return to her home in a few days. Corso positioned himself beneath the windows of her room hoping to talk to her before she left, but Brianda did not look out. The following morning, he combed his horse in the yard, alert to any movement from the main door. It finally opened and Brianda emerged with Cecilia, Leonor, and Gisabel.

Corso could not take his eyes off her.

She was pale and baggy-eyed, thin and fragile, dressed in a simple skirt and a sky-blue bodice, wrapped up in a thick blanket and with her hair loose over her shoulders. He watched as she looked at the sky, closed her eyes in a gesture of pleasure, and took a deep breath of fresh air. She then slid her gaze around the yard, as if discovering it for the first time, and then laid eyes on a tall, tanned man with his shirt undone, standing beside the biggest and strongest Friesian she had ever seen. She recognized Corso immediately. She searched for his eyes, remembered the images from her delirium, and blushed.

"See?" Leonor said. "You're scarcely out the door, and you already look better. We'll just take a short walk to build up an appetite. We won't go too far today, and when you get tired, we'll come right back."

They crossed the patio and, so as not to warmly greet Corso, which was, in fact, what she wanted, Brianda asked him, "Are you not Surano's friend? You look different!"

Corso understood that she referred to his white hemp shirt and tight-fitting breeches held up by a brightly colored sash. The only thing remaining from his previous outfit was his leather boots.

"Mistress Leonor gave me these clothes," he said, staring into Brianda's eyes. "I have to admit that I am more comfortable without my breastplate, backplate, and pouch."

Leonor laughed. "I was keeping them in the hope that one day Nunilo would fit into them again, but it doesn't seem likely. If we had—" She halted before saying out loud that she had also kept the clothes in case they ever had a son. That would not happen now. "They look good on you."

"I'm pleased you're better, Brianda," said Corso.

Gisabel, a small girl with fair hair, frowned at this stable boy, footman, soldier, or whatever he was, talking to the heiress of Lubich with such familiarity. She gently tugged at her mistress's arm, but Brianda did not move.

"I haven't had the chance to thank you," said Brianda. "I know what you did for me. I'm happy that you didn't get sick. Not you or anybody else, from what I know. Everyone took such a great risk."

Leonor and Corso exchanged a look. Brianda had not been told that the illness had taken two of Pere's men and been especially virulent in Marquo's family.

"What's wrong?" Brianda wanted to know.

"Others have not been so fortunate, Brianda," responded Leonor.

"Who?" Brianda went weak in the knees.

"You shouldn't think about that now—" Gisabel intervened.

"I want to know!"

"Bringuer and his youngest daughter have died," Leonor told her. "Nunilo has gone to the funeral. Bringuer's wife is still ill."

Brianda's eyes filled with tears. She felt a strange mixture of relief knowing her father was well and sadness imagining the suffering in Marquo's house.

The sound of horse's hooves announced someone was coming. It was Nunilo. He wore a serious expression, but he made an effort to talk cheerfully to Brianda.

"What a good sign to see you out of the house!" he exclaimed. "You will soon see how quickly you'll be back to your old self."

"If only you could say the same about Bringuer and his daughter." Tears rolled down Brianda's cheeks. "I just found out." She worriedly asked, "And Marquo?"

"He is fine," Nunilo answered. "You'll see him tomorrow."

Corso scrutinized Brianda's face, looking for any reaction about Marquo, or about her return to Lubich, but she seemed unmoved. Perhaps the same thoughts went through her mind as his: once she returned to Lubich, they would not see each other or be close to each other. Instead, Marquo would return to her life. Would she remember when Corso had held her in his arms and kissed her? Would she put it down to delirium from the fever? If only they could be alone for a few minutes.

Nunilo looked at Leonor, and she understood that he had something to tell her, so she suggested that the others walk ahead.

Leonor rested her hand on her husband's arm.

"What news do you bring?"

"Bringuer's wife has also died." He took off his cloak and handed it to Leonor. "She didn't even survive a day. The apothecary didn't have a chance to do anything—not even apply the remedies Gisabel taught him when he attended Brianda."

Leonor blessed herself.

"How sad," she said. "The poor family."

"Bringuer's funeral was a lonely affair," her husband commented.

"People are afraid of the typhus."

"So are we, Leonor. But wouldn't we risk it for our friends? The fear of infection was not the sole reason that only Bringuer's sons, Johan, the abbot, the new priest, and I were present. By the way, you should have seen Abbot Bartholomeu defending his right to say the final words over the body instead of Father Guillem." He shook his head. "And now that Bringuer is dead, I'm afraid of losing the support of his house."

"Do you doubt the loyalty of his heir?" asked Leonor.

"It was he who organized the funeral in secret, without warning. Bringuer's eldest is not like Marquo. He doesn't want to be associated with us. He prefers to keep his distance until he sees which side is stronger. I heard how he argued with Marquo on the subject."

"And what will happen to Marquo now?"

"Johan spoke with him after the funeral. Tomorrow, Marquo will go to Lubich to talk with Elvira and Brianda about their wedding. He says that she agreed to it in Monzon. Johan and Elvira have asked me to be present. Do you know anything?"

Leonor shook her head. After a few seconds, she said, "It's not a bad idea. Marquo could be a good master for Lubich—and loyal like his father. Joining the two houses would make Marquo's brother really think about where his loyalties lie. But, is it just my impression or are you unconvinced about this marriage?"

"Well, would you like a coward for a son-in-law?" Nunilo asked her. "When Brianda fell ill, he ran from her. True bravery is not shown on the battlefield but rather when facing death. There you can see the nobility of a man." He softened his tone before concluding, "Would I abandon you if you got the worst of plagues? You know I wouldn't."

Speechless, Leonor thanked God for allowing her to share her life with such a man. The designs of the Almighty had been very confusing for her. On one hand, she had been punished with never having children, and on the other, she had been compensated with one of the few men in the world who would never reproach her for it and who avowed that he would risk his own life for her.

The whinny of a horse made them turn their heads, and they realized that Corso had been there all the time. If anyone else had overheard, Leonor would have been ashamed or afraid or both. However, she saw in Corso a young man who—for his age, stature, and disposition—could well have been the son Nunilo and she had not been able to have, the heir to the House of Anels. His hangdog appearance, still sometimes distrusting and indolent, and his habit of clenching his jaw as if growling awoke in her maternal feelings that she materialized into small daily strategies to gain his confidence. Each step in his training she considered a triumph, and each triumph a reason to continue growing fond of him.

What Leonor now saw, however, was new. It seemed that the conversation between Nunilo and her had caused neither surprise nor puzzlement, not even indifference.

In Corso's face, she saw heartbreak. And the source could not be in the loyalties of Bringuer's family, or in the devotion between the master and mistress of Anels. Rather, it must be something so impossible, unthinkable, and extravagant as the foreigner having feelings for Brianda.

The last thing Corso wanted was to hear firsthand the details of Brianda and Marquo's marriage agreement, but since he had not had the chance to speak with her alone, and since Nunilo had insisted that he accompany him as his personal guard, he had no option but to visit Lubich under very disagreeable circumstances.

The fortified house of Lubich Manor struck him with its size and the number of its servants. It seemed more like a small castle than a house. As they first rode through the woods and later along the path to Lubich, he noticed Brianda undergoing a transformation, leaving behind the illness and recovering the resolute, vivacious, and slightly arrogant spirit that he had so admired. He also noticed how she surveyed every stone, nook, and cranny of the estate, as if wanting to make sure that nothing had changed in her absence. From the greetings of the workers and servants, shouts of joy from the windows, and the frantic barking of the dogs, Corso saw that the soul of the house had just returned.

A beautiful, tall woman, dressed in elegant clothes and with her dark hair tied up, came out of the main door. Brianda, helped by Johan, got off her horse and ran to her.

"Mother! I'm back at last!"

The woman, who Corso thought seemed quite young to be Brianda's mother, received her daughter in her arms without losing her haughty bearing, although for a few seconds the severe look on her face relaxed. Then she stepped back and submitted Brianda to a visual inspection, frowning as she looked her over. Brianda was too thin, her hair did not shine, her nails were unkempt, and her clothes looked like those of a peasant. She would need time to turn her child into a lady again. She threw a reproachful stare at Johan.

Nunilo dismounted, and Corso and Cecilia did the same.

"It's been a long time, Elvira," said Nunilo. "I'm delighted to see you."

"Thank you for looking after Brianda," she replied. "I've written a letter for Leonor that I'll give to you before you leave."

"That's very good of you. You know that your daughter is well loved in our house."

Brianda took Cecilia by the arm and presented her to Elvira.

"Mother, this is Cecilia. She was my servant in Monzon, and I brought her here. She has looked after me as if we were sisters. Gisabel has used our time at Anels to teach her the customs of our house and has become fond of her." She paused to remember the arguments she had practiced to justify hiring Cecilia and that no one could verify or question. "She was born in the south, became orphaned, and the owner of the house we stayed in was going to give her position to a niece."

"Mistress." Cecilia curtsied as she had practiced dozens of times, making some of those present laugh, as they were not used to such formality.

Elvira thought that Cecilia had very dark skin and strange features, but in front of so many people she refrained from making any comment. She would discuss it with Johan later. She asked Gisabel and Cecilia to accompany Brianda to her room so she could change her clothes.

After the young women left, her husband introduced Corso.

"And this is the soldier I talked to you about, the one who carried Brianda to Tiles."

"He now works for me," Nunilo added, trying to differentiate Corso from a normal servant. "And he is an intimate friend of Pere's brother."

Elvira bent her head and mumbled a few words of thanks. She felt uncomfortable at having to thank strangers who had intervened to help her family because of a journey that she had always been against. If Brianda had not gone to Monzon, she would not have gotten ill. It was that simple.

Johan looked toward Beles Peak. From the way the sun's rays fell upon one of the gullies, he was able to tell it was close to midday.

"Let's go to the hall," he proposed. "Marquo will be here soon."

Intimidated by Elvira's cold elegance and the dimensions of the room, richly adorned with tapestries and bear and wolf skins, Corso kept himself apart beside an enormous stone fireplace while the others spoke together around the big wooden table located in the center of the room. A short time later, Brianda entered. She had tied up her hair like her mother's and put on a tight bodice. Corso did not like how it forced her to keep her back and her neck too straight.

Elvira instructed the servants to tell the kitchen that the food should be served immediately. When the first stews appeared on the table, Marquo entered dressed in an elegant outfit that hid neither his thinness nor his sad and tired appearance.

He greeted Elvira first, and then Johan and Nunilo. He ignored Corso, looking puzzled to see him there. He went over to Brianda and bowed his head to her.

"I'm pleased that you have recovered," he said. "We've all been terribly worried."

Brianda was shocked by how much older Marquo looked. His brown hair was cut short and his gray eyes had lost their shine. She paid special attention to his lips as he spoke, because those lips had kissed her several times and yet she could not remember them. When she thought of kisses, she could only feel Corso's black hair brushing against her cheeks and his strong mouth over hers. In front of Marquo and her parents, she was unable to look at Corso, standing there by the fire, taking up so much space in the main hall of her home. If she looked at him, she would become distressed. And he would realize she could not get him out of her head and the others would suspect something was awry.

"I'm very sorry to learn about your parents and your sister," she told Marquo sincerely.

Elvira signaled everyone to sit.

When Marquo saw Corso accept the invitation, he asked Brianda under his breath, "Why doesn't that one eat with the servants?"

She was quite sharp in her reply. "Because he is Pere's and Nunilo's friend and he saved my life, so now he is our friend as well. The doors of my house will always be open to him; I hope you don't mind."

Marquo did mind, but he did not want to cast a shadow on Brianda's mood on this particular day, so he said nothing more on the subject. When he was master of Lubich, he thought, his opinion would be respected and he would choose her friends.

A servant served bowls of thick pumpkin with mutton sauce, goat milk, eggs, cinnamon, and sugar. Afterward, they ate roasted leg of pork and stewed hare in a liver, garlic, and hazelnut sauce.

"Don't you like the food?" Johan asked Corso, who was picking at his plate.

"It's delicious, sir; I'm just not used to eating so much."

Actually, he'd never tasted such elaborate stews and would have loved to accept second and third helpings, but there was a knot in his stomach. He was uncomfortable having to share a table with Brianda without being able to talk to her.

The arrival of the cheese, preserved fruit, and fritters announced that the important moment was at hand. It was Marquo himself who spoke. "Brianda, you know why I've come, apart from wanting to see you?"

She nodded.

"Remember in Monzon when you asked me to wait to talk to our families? I think the time has come. I hope you haven't changed your mind."

"I haven't," she said, "and I hope my parents are pleased, and I see they are, as they have prepared this feast."

Elvira stretched out her hand and took her daughter's.

"Your father and I think that it is a good choice and the wedding can be held as soon as spring comes. This winter we'll be busy preparing."

"Yes. We have to draw up the papers detailing Marquo's contribution and my arrangements for the future," Johan said. "Marquo, I'm sorry that your father, my friend Bringuer, did not live to see this day, but I know he would agree because we had spoken about it. And I would be pleased," he said, turning to Nunilo, "if, in the absence of more family on my side, you would be witness to this engagement."

Nunilo raised his glass of mulled wine. "May it be for the best," he said flatly.

Corso got to his feet and left without saying anything.

Johan asked for paper to outline the marriage agreement, and Elvira suggested they make a provisional guest list. Brianda pretended to stifle a yawn.

"Might I be excused? I need to lie down for a bit."

"Of course," Elvira consented.

Brianda gave them a grateful smile and went out. Rather than sleep, what she really needed was air and space to think about what was happening, so she wandered around the stables before going to the back gardens. She loosened the stays of her too-tight bodice, which hardly let her breathe.

Who was she trying to fool? She was looking for Corso.

She wanted with all her heart to talk to him and the prospect excited her more than the formalizing of her engagement to Marquo.

But Corso was nowhere to be found.

Behind the main house, where the gardens ended, a narrow, rocky path that bordered the tower began. One needed to walk practically holding on to the rocks in the wall, because the other edge was a deep chasm. From a very young age, she would sit down there with her legs dangling over the abyss. She could spend hours following the shapes of the clouds and the shadows of the birds.

She sat down on the ground, took off her shoes and her outer bodice, and let her hair loose. She closed her eyes, took a deep breath, and realized how much she had missed this place, especially during the last days of her illness, when each hour seemed eternal. She gave thanks to God for making her well enough to enjoy Lubich again and she asked Him to bless her with a good marriage and strong, healthy children. She also asked that her memories of Corso not prevent her from leading a quiet and happy life.

"You are very pretty like that."

Brianda recognized Corso's deep voice. She looked up and daringly patted the ground beside her, but he stayed on his feet.

"What would your betrothed think if he saw us?" he said with irony.

"I have never come across anyone here," Brianda insisted, and he sat down. "Did you follow me?"

"I haven't been able to speak to you alone since—"

"Ah, yes, since I asked you to save Cecilia," she lied and her cheeks reddened. "I don't even remember how I got home. They told me that you brought me. I think I've already thanked you."

Corso smiled.

"Well, it's a pity the fever clouded your memory—"

"Why? Is there something I should remember?"

Brianda's heart began to pound. She could not believe her daring.

He put an arm around her waist and drew her toward him. He raised his hand and caressed her cheek, as he had done when she lay fainting in his arms, not taking his eyes off hers, as if this was the last time he would see her so close. Brianda closed her eyes, and he kissed her, trying to imitate the feverish kisses of that day on the back of his horse.

When they separated, she held his gaze and said, "I hadn't forgotten. I wanted to feel it one more time, and I didn't know how to ask. That was our last kiss."

Corso shook his head.

"You heard me." Brianda freed herself from his embrace. "I will marry Marquo in the spring."

"That is still months away." Corso came closer and tried to kiss her again. "I have all winter to convince you of your mistake."

Brianda got to her feet and leaned against the stone.

"It's not a mistake. It must be this way. I don't deny I like you, but someone of my rank can't give you anything more. Marrying well is my most important duty"—she extended her hand to the landscape that surrounded them—"for Lubich."

It was not her refusal but the firmness of her words that irritated Corso. She had warned him that she would never marry a peasant—much less a soldier and deserter. He was wasting his time. He could kill a man, or several, in a battle, and his pulse would not even rise, but against Brianda's convictions no force sufficed. Or maybe it did? A fleeting and awful impulse crossed his mind. He was used to getting what he wanted. He got to his feet and stood in front of her, imprisoning her with his body.

Brianda felt the pressure of Corso's flesh against hers and, rather than fear him, she grabbed the cords of his shirt to draw him even closer. She threw her head back and allowed him to smell her neck and her hair.

"If only things were different, Corso," she whispered. "My body responds to you as it doesn't to Marquo, but if you feel anything more for me than mere animal instinct, I'm asking you to let me go now."

"You ask for the one thing I don't want to do, damn you!"

Corso bent his knees to slide a hand under her skirts.

"I don't want to either! That's why I'm asking you!"

Corso stopped for a second, stunned. Brianda stroked his hair.

"You told me that when I closed my eyes I would only see you, remember? I listened to you. If with a few kisses it's already happening, what would it be like if you took me? Is that what you want? To torment me forever?"

"And you? Don't you think it will be torture for me knowing you are with him? I'd prefer to—"

"What?" she interrupted him. "You can't force me to want to be with you, or take me away from here, because I'd die. I could only be with you if Lubich disappeared!"

"Well then, I'll burn it down!" Corso punched the wall and blood spurted from his knuckles.

"Don't say such a thing!" Brianda took his hand and blew on the cuts before pressing her fingers against them. "How long have you known me? You'll find another woman who suits you, if what you want is a family. If not, you'll continue as you have until now, with one here, another there."

"I don't want anyone else," he murmured.

"And with time, we'll both forget," Brianda said with a faint smile.

Corso held up her wrists tightly at both sides of her face. He leaned down and kissed her voraciously, wanting to wound her, convince her, mortify her, and excite her at the same time.

He roughly pulled away and said, "Then live with this, if you're able."

He looked her in the eye one last time and left.

After a good while, Brianda sat down on the rock, swinging her legs over the drop. She knew she had done what she had to do. Under no circumstances could she think about having any sort of future with someone like Corso. Houses that flourished did so thanks to a good understanding between solid and balanced couples like her parents, or like Nunilo and Leonor, or Marquo's parents. And, as far as she knew, all those marriages had been arranged by the previous generation. Corso's intensity would surely be as ill fated for her as Medardo and his men were for the peace of the county.

Yes, she knew she had done what she had to do, but her eyes filled with tears and the knot in her chest did not loosen even after she sobbed for a long time.

21.

"This is the coldest winter I can remember!" said Gisabel, wrapping herself up in the shawl.

The strong wind that had accompanied them from the house to the church in Tiles was stirring up the thin layer of snow that had fallen the previous night, blanketing the damp fields.

"That's not true," Brianda said. "It's just that you're more sensitive because you are with child."

"I don't know." Gisabel rested a hand on her womb and again thought sadly of her husband, who would find her in an advanced state when he returned from the lowlands. "But just the thought of having to sit inside that cold church for so long makes me want to pretend to faint so I can go back to Lubich."

"And I'd happily go with you!" laughed Cecilia, blowing on her hands.

Brianda shushed them, but she could not stop herself from giggling. "If Father Guillem hears us . . . !"

The last sermon the priest had given for Christmas had been so long and repetitive that each night, before sleeping, Brianda could still hear in her mind the warnings about all imaginable sins lying in wait for any man, woman, or child. Father Guillem told them of the threats of heresies, Jewish, Islamic, Lutheran, and more specifically, the Huguenots from nearby France; of the diabolic evil of magic, spells, witchcraft, and popular superstitions; of the sins of pride, greed, and lust; of the terrible consequences of moral offenses and hostile attitudes toward the Church and the Inquisition; of blasphemies, verbal obscenities, and statements about fornication. Brianda was astonished that she had grown up among such dangers and not known it, as the only danger that she considered real was the conflict between the royalists and the count's supporters.

Following behind Johan and Elvira, the girls crossed the small graveyard, making sure to step on the flagstones over the graves to avoid getting muddy, and entered the dark church, which was already full of people. As one of the most important families in the county, they walked to the right lateral chapel, beside the altar. On her way there, Brianda scanned the crowd. From the bench in the chapel, she would only be able to see the first benches. With a slight nod, imitating her parents, she greeted several neighbors from Tiles. She also greeted Marquo and his family and other neighbors from Besalduch, among whom she noticed a puffy-eyed young woman who turned away after giving her a twisted look.

"Did you see Alodia's face?" she asked Gisabel in a whisper when they took their seats. "I don't remember doing anything that could have offended her."

"You did the worst thing: you got engaged to Marquo."

"How could I have known she was after him?"

"It wouldn't have made any difference. Alodia is the heiress of her house, but you are a better choice." She shrugged. "She'll have to look for another suitor."

Brianda felt sorry for Alodia. There were few single men like Marquo—good-looking and from a good family—in all the highlands of Orrun. Some noise caught her attention, and she saw Nunilo and

Leonor sit down in front; with them was Corso, whom she had not seen in weeks. She knew from her parents' conversations that he was still at Nunilo's house, a fact incomprehensible to Elvira, who could not understand how Leonor could have become so fond of a total stranger. Not for one second had it crossed Brianda's mind that she might see him at church.

Unless he was there for her . . .

A pleasant heat coursed through her body. Corso looked magnificent, with a new maroon velvet jerkin and his shiny hair tied back with a leather strip, so that his features, normally hidden—the straight, sharp nose, the furrowed brow, the strong jaw—could now be seen perfectly. He turned and looked straight at her as if they were the only people there, as if this were not a sacred place. And she withstood his look—penetrating, unfathomable, and somber—until Father Guillem, on his way to the altar, came between them.

Father Guillem was pleased to see so many people in church that Sunday. Little by little, the inhabitants of the valley had begun to open their homes to his visits, but victory was not his quite yet. There were still people who could not even bless themselves or say a Hail Mary properly; or who blasphemed openly or criticized the bishopric's tithe; or who, like Leonor, resisted coming to mass every Sunday with the weak argument that the sermon was too long and she had much to do on Sundays; or those, like Johan and Nunilo, who doubted the presence of Christ in the sacrament of bread and wine and questioned Mary's virginity. And what about the laudable work of the Inquisition of the Holy Office? Some had not even heard of it. Had the carpenter not said that the mission of the Supreme Being was to persecute smugglers and bandits? And Medardo of Aiscle, had he not admitted that he did not believe in the existence of paradise, purgatory, or hell? And the other young man, Marquo of Besalduch, who insisted that voluntary carnal knowledge between two single adults was not a sin?

With a few exceptions, Father Guillem found a huge difference between the pious townspeople of Aiscle, who had grown up beside a big collegiate church, and the inhabitants of these dispersed hamlets in the high valleys and mountains, rustic people who made these sacrilegious comments out of ignorance. It was not their fault that the Holy Office came, at most, once a year—and only to Aiscle, since it had the largest population. He did not suppose that there were many places in the whole kingdom with such difficult access. But he would take it upon himself not to grant marriage licenses if the future couples, like Marquo and Brianda, were not sufficiently instructed in religion; he would teach them that mere fornication was a sin, that it disrespected the holy sacrament of matrimony. He would make Gisabel understand that the tradition of making animal and plant offerings in the church made no sense, and he would repeat the prayers a thousand times until they all were able to recite in their sleep the Our Father, the Hail Mary, the Creed, the Salve Regina, and the Ten Commandments.

"Be attentive in your daily conversations," he concluded after a sermon of an hour and a half. "Words tie you and expose you."

He regarded them in silence for a few moments and then picked up a small sheaf of papers, undid the cord, and handed them to a young boy in the first bench. On the first page, there was a drawing of a tormented man writhing in a bed framed by demonic figures.

"Every Sunday, I will tell you a true story so you can understand how important my words are. Observe the terrible images of the sinner." He asked the boy to circulate the sheet. "Look at his blackened, purple, haggard, consumed body thrown on the dung heap by those he regarded as friends. He was left there to be devoured by dogs. Do you see? It is God who punishes him in this way. Divine Justice has punished the bad Christian—and I'll tell you why—"

A horse whinnied outside, making several parishioners jump. Father Guillem continued his story, but the horse did not stop stamping the ground so it disrupted the respectful silence Father Guillem needed for his words to have the desired effect. Out of the corner of his eye, he saw how the masters of the big houses exchanged worried glances, and, aware that he would not capture their attention again, he decided to wrap things up quickly.

Nunilo and Johan hurried out, followed by Corso and Marquo. The rider was Surano.

"What news?" Johan asked, holding the horse while Pere's brother dismounted.

When Surano saw the curious churchgoers behind them, he gestured for his friends to wait as he tied the reins to a tree. Once the church was empty, he led the lords of Tiles inside. Brianda tried to follow, but her mother stopped her.

"In three weeks, Count Fernando will come to Aiscle to take possession of the county," Surano told the men inside. "Pere has convened the General Council for the twenty-second of January."

Marquo uttered a satisfied exclamation.

"And what is the mood like in Aiscle?" Nunilo, more cautious, wanted to know. The possibility of war was increasing daily.

"Our men are still entrenched in their houses out of fear of Medardo." Surano snorted. "Either this livens things up a bit or I'm going back to His Majesty's army! Everybody seems to be holding their damn breath."

"Do you have any instructions for us?" Johan asked.

"If you don't hear otherwise from me, you and your men should be at the church in Aiscle at daybreak on that date. Come down together. Meanwhile, stay close to your families in case anything happens."

As the others left, Surano stopped Corso.

"You're looking well. What have you been up to?"

Corso shrugged. "As long as you are here, I have nowhere else to go."

Surano raised his eyebrows. "You can't fool me, Corso. Nunilo's hospitality is not sufficient reason to keep you here. Be careful what you dream of—dreams are the work of the devil."

"Since I started eating better, my nights are more agreeable," Corso said with an amused look. "And you taught me to not be afraid of even the devil."

Surano gave him a slap on the back.

"Unless the devil takes the form of a woman. Believe me, I know what I'm talking about. Do you remember Lida? She promised she would wait for me, but she got tired and married Medardo. You should see how she looks at me now, with eyes like a lamb to the slaughter. I'd bet you anything she wants to ensnare me to give her husband an excuse to kill me. I never thought I would see the day when I couldn't trust her. I've warned you before."

Corso thought of the day he had met Brianda outside the church in Monzon. It seemed as if centuries rather than a few months had passed. Surano had seen the look in his eyes and told him then that the women from his land were beautiful, but that their tears could not be trusted. Then he had added something about the blood of Lubich that coursed through her veins; it was the blood that prevented her from being with him. But if Corso was certain of anything, it was that he would never meet anyone so deserving of his trust as Brianda, who spoke to him frankly and renounced her feelings in order to meet her obligations. How could he not understand her when he'd spent his whole life obeying orders? Instead of doubting her, as Surano did, he would always stay close, hoping that the God Father Guillem talked about, or perhaps witchcraft—it was all the same to him—would change their destiny.

"It sounds as if your fear of dying at Medardo's hands is stronger than your faith in Lida."

Surano scratched his beard in confusion, but then immediately recovered his jovial spirits.

"Let's say I don't know if it's worth the risk. Also, it's difficult for me to desire her after he's been between her legs." Trying to establish an exemplifying comparison, he added, "I just heard that Johan's daughter is to be married to Bringuer's son. So, it seems both of us are unlucky. Well, I've been unlucky; you just aimed too high. You've heard me say it before: maybe we should leave this place. I stay because I trust the count will pay us well for our services. Pere is a generous man, but I don't like depending on him. If it comes to it, I assume you'll come with me."

Corso did not answer, but he prayed that the moment would never come when he would have to leave that land, cold but lush, rough but patient, where Brianda lived.

The lords of Tiles and Besalduch and their men trained with their swords in the yards until the heavy January snows drove them into the hay barns. The male servants tended to the animals, stables, and firewood; the women took care of laundering and sewing the clothes and of cautiously rationing the supplies. Meanwhile, Brianda was bored, and she was frustrated she was not allowed to take part in the training. How could she defend Lubich, if it came to that, if the men would not even let her practice shooting an arquebus?

On a cold but sunny morning, Johan decided to improve Brianda's mood by asking her to go with him to Tiles, to the house of the carpenter. Accompanied by Gisabel and Cecilia, they collected some mules and took the path that joined Lubich to the church before going down to the lower part of Tiles.

"Why are you bringing an unladen mule, Father?" Brianda wanted to know. "Are we collecting someone?"

Johan shook his head but did not dispel her doubts.

When they got to the workshop, they found a small, wrinkled man contemplating a section of tree trunk about an arm in length. He greeted Johan amiably.

"From this piece of walnut, I must fashion a Virgin for Father Guillem. I've never had such a difficult order."

"Not even mine?"

With a knowing smile, the carpenter named Domingo signaled them to follow him to another, slightly bigger, room. On the table, he pointed to a small chest decorated with geometric designs and with handles at the sides. He opened the lid, and they saw small compartments and little drawers inside. It was a beautiful, delicate, and costly piece of furniture.

"It's for you, Brianda," Johan announced.

Brianda jumped into his arms.

"It looks like yours but even prettier! Thank you!"

"I thought you would like it as a wedding present. Although I expect to live for many more years, you will soon have to take charge of your own records regarding Lubich and its administration. I know Marquo will help you, but you will have to explain many things to your children, as we have done with you. You cannot and must not hold a sword, but you will govern my estate."

Brianda stroked the chest again and again and pulled on the small, hazelnut-shaped knobs on each of the drawers. Meanwhile, Gisabel and Cecilia amused themselves by touching the tools and small carvings strewn all over the place until they stopped in a dark corner.

"And this strange wardrobe?" Gisabel asked.

"It's for the priest," Domingo answered. "It's a confessional."

"To keep his clothes?" Cecilia asked innocently, and the others smiled.

Domingo opened the lattice door, went in, and sat down.

"From now on, Father Guillem wants there to be a physical barrier during the sacrament of confession. He will sit here, and we will kneel in front to confess our sins."

"How uncomfortable!" Cecilia exclaimed.

"It's not finished yet," added Domingo. "It still needs to be decorated."

"How do you do that?" Brianda asked, still admiring the workmanship of her chest.

Domingo picked up a piece of charcoal and drew a small birch leaf on a piece of wood. Then, he took a small chisel and hit it with a mallet so that shavings, looking like bread soup, flew off.

"I can carve in the leaf or around it if I want it in relief," he explained. "It's not so difficult. It only takes patience. Do you want to try?"

"I do!" said Gisabel. She picked up a piece of charcoal and drew a flower. "That's dreadful! How did you learn to draw?"

Domingo shrugged. "One day I just started, and I wasn't bad at it."

Cecilia copied Gisabel, but found she could not draw either.

"You know who draws really well?" Cecilia asked. "Corso!"

"Corso?" Brianda regretted her anxious tone and tried to hide it with derision. "Who would have thought someone like him could draw."

"I stumbled upon him drawing when you were ill in Anels House. He showed me some of his drawings and made me promise not to tell anybody." Cecilia raised her hand to her mouth. "And now I have! Promise you won't tell him!"

"Of course not, Cecilia," Brianda assured her. "And what were the drawings of? I doubt they were flowers."

"Horses, forests, faces . . . A little bit of everything."

Johan grinned at Domingo. "So, if you don't know how to decorate the confessional, just appeal to Corso for help!" he joked. "Well, we're off. Can we load up Brianda's piece now?"

Domingo nodded, and Johan asked Gisabel and Cecilia to bring the blankets that were with the mule.

Then, Domingo turned his attention to Brianda and the chest. He opened the door to the biggest compartment, and asked her to put her hand inside.

"Can you feel a little notch?"

Brianda nodded, and Domingo handed her a key the size of a pin nail.

"We all should have a place to keep our secrets," he said. "There is a false bottom inside."

Brianda smiled and thanked him. She took a gold chain from around her neck, hung the small key on it, and made sure that it was well hidden under her blouse.

"Domingo's secret drawers are difficult to find," Johan said. "Where have you put the mark on Brianda's piece?"

Domingo held the lid and ran a finger along one of the hinges.

"Here, do you see it?"

Brianda leaned down and looked closely until she saw a small notch shaped like a boxwood sprig, the emblem of the count's followers.

"I hope that nearly all of your orders come from our side," Brianda commented.

Domingo picked up the charcoal, crouched down, and drew a small gorse flower and a boxwood sprig on the back of the confessional.

"I thought about putting both symbols." He gave Johan a meaningful look. "What do you think, sir?"

Johan frowned. At his age, he had learned that some changed sides with the same ease as pulling a weed. He had faith in his own loyalty and that of the count's other followers, but sensed that difficult and very distressing times lay ahead.

"You're right, Domingo," he finally answered. "We will all kneel here and only God will know our true intentions."

Gisabel and Cecilia returned with the blankets and helped Domingo to wrap up Brianda's delicate chest and tie it to the mule with ropes. When they got on the road home, it was almost time to eat.

Brianda rode in silence. Her father's comment about true intentions, which only God would know, mixed in her head with the teachings of Father Guillem. The day she had to explain herself before the

Creator, she would probably receive the most terrible of punishments. When Domingo had shown her the false bottom, she had immediately been taken with the fear that no hiding place was safe enough for her greatest secret. All her thoughts, from dawn to dusk, revolved around one person, the person with whom she maintained a running dialogue in her head through all her daily tasks. As if he could hear and understand her, she explained how she felt when the snowflakes covered the roofs and courtyards of Lubich, she told him how many stitches she still had to embroider to finish her monogram on the soft linen that would cover the bed she would soon share with another, she described the enjoyment she got from the slow expansion of Gisabel's belly, she offered him the first bites of freshly baked bread . . .

She was lying to Marquo, to her friends, to her parents, and to God because she desired Corso more than she ever thought she could desire anything. She had even imagined, in that moment before sleep, that Marquo and her parents died and Lubich disappeared and then Corso appeared and carried her far away, so desperate was her yearning.

Yes. The lie, the unfaithfulness toward Lubich and toward Marquo, and the images of carnal contact with Corso would sentence her to hell. But . . .

Could there ever be a worse sentence than having to renounce Corso?

22.

It was still dark on January 22, 1586, when Brianda, her body taut with fear, hugged Johan under the stone lintel at the entrance to Lubich Manor.

"Be very careful, Father." Her teeth chattered from the cold and the nerves. "Are you sure the king's credentials will be enough to ensure your safety?"

Johan stroked her hair, as black as the snow on the roofs was white.

"Fear is the proof of low birth, Daughter."

He placed a light kiss on his daughter's cheek, mounted his horse, and, followed by his men and servants, rode toward the mill in Tiles, where he had arranged to meet Nunilo and Marquo.

An hour later, Johan, Nunilo, and Marquo, accompanied by Corso and a dozen men, entered the town of Aiscle. The streets were deserted, feigning a sleepiness betrayed by the flickering shadows of candles behind the windows.

Instead of crossing the main street, they took an icy path to the upper part of the town where the church was located. There, horses tied to the wall of the abbey told them the count had already arrived. They knocked at the door, and it was opened by Pere, who received them with the same expression of relief as the count.

Count Fernando, looking thinner and older since they had seen him in Monzon, was seated at a large table near the altar. He greeted them warmly.

"I have sent for Medardo," he told them. "He won't be long."

"How do you know?" Nunilo asked.

"Father Guillem has offered himself as mediator to guarantee his safety," responded Pere.

"The town is too quiet, sir," Marquo said to the count. "I find it strange that both you and we were able to enter without any problem."

"I do too," said Surano, calculating that between the lords of the valleys and the count's soldiers they did not even have thirty men. "We are well armed, but we are few."

"Maybe they have realized that they can do nothing against the king's orders." Johan pointed at some papers on the table. "Are those the credentials?"

The count nodded. Then, two of their men warned them that some men were approaching. They opened the door, and Guillem, Medardo, Jayme, and a fourth man, who Medardo introduced as his brother, entered. The priest remained beside the door and the others strutted arrogantly toward the count.

Without greeting him, Medardo declared, "The local council will meet in the square in one hour to hear what you have to say."

"We had agreed to meet in the church," said the count.

"Either you come to the square or you will have wasted the journey."

Count Fernando looked dubiously at Pere and Johan.

"And what guarantees do you give that there will be peace?" Pere asked.

Medardo kept his gaze fixed on the count. "Nothing will happen if your nobles do nothing. You have my word."

"Your word is as weak as a beggar in February!" Marquo shouted.

Father Guillem stepped forward to intercede, but Medardo was unperturbed. "We will be there in an hour. If we had wanted to attack you, we would have already done so."

Medardo turned around and left, followed by his brother and Jayme.

"You are not thinking of going, are you?" Marquo asked.

The count looked at him, trying to place the young man. Pere came to his aid.

"He is the second son of Bringuer of Besalduch," Pere whispered. "He was in Monzon. The heir of his house did not wish to come, but this younger son's loyalty more than makes up for the elder's indecisiveness."

"Do you have a better idea, lad?" Count Fernando asked Marquo.

"What if we finally confront them once and for all?" interrupted Surano, resting his hand on his sword. "We are few but well trained." He pointed to Corso, who nodded in agreement. "We know who they are and we know where they live. Let's go after Medardo. Our justification is in those papers."

With his hands nervously fingering his sword, the count paced the room for a few minutes.

"It is not my wish that this land be upset anymore," he finally said. "When they hear what I have to say, they will know that I have right on my side—that the king says so. What sort of master would I be if I whipped those I ask to serve me? Let's go and get it over with."

In the square, before one of the stone arches that supported the small homes, Medardo sat at the head of a table he had ordered brought to hold the meeting. His brother and Jayme stood beside him. The townspeople, with sleepy faces, were arrayed in a wide semicircle, as if waiting to watch a play at this ungodly hour, but they had kept a passage clear in the middle so the count, Pere, and the owners of some other noble houses could approach. Father Guillem had decided to remain in the church. The rest of the count's men spread themselves in the streets that led to the square. Johan and Nunilo, to the south; Surano and Corso, to the north.

"Have you noticed?" Johan asked Nunilo. "It's all old people, women, and children. Where are the men?"

"I certainly don't believe they're all with the livestock in the lowlands," answered Nunilo. "I'm afraid this won't end well."

In a loud, clear voice, Pere addressed the townspeople: "As bailiff of Aiscle and justice of this county, I have convened you here so you can listen to what Count Fernando has to say."

Insults and shouts against the count rang out and only stopped when Medardo stood and said, "As your representative, chosen by you and not appointed by a count or king, I have a special interest in hearing the words of someone who only comes to this land when he needs our money." Many applauded. "The count claims he has a credential from the king addressed to this council." He held out his hand toward Count Fernando. "So give it to me."

The count stood up.

"I will read it, but I will not let it out of my hands," he said in a loud, even voice. "I won't risk you destroying it."

"I understand then that you doubt the validity of this council?"

More insults and indignant voices were heard, now at a higher pitch. Johan and Nunilo moved their horses forward a little. From his post with Corso, Surano waited for a signal to intervene. He was amazed that the count kept his calm before Medardo's provocations.

"It is not I who has prevented this meeting from being held for so long," said the count.

"In that, you are correct," responded Medardo. "For the sake of justice, I have prevented the holding of the council until the land is at peace—"

"It's you who's been disturbing it!" shouted Pere.

"And I will continue to do so until His Majesty responds to a dispatch I wish to present to him!"

"And who are you to communicate with the king?" inquired Count Fernando.

"I have other documents signed by him!"

Now the count did lose his temper, saying, "The only and last document that has validity is that which I am carrying! His Majesty has signed in his own hand that I be given possession of the county peaceably—"

"Where are the royal envoys to support your words?" shouted Medardo. "And the general bailiff of the kingdom, or the viceroy? I don't see anybody! If no royal representative has attended, it would be logical to conclude that the king is not willing to facilitate you taking possession. Besides, how do we know the document isn't false? Does anyone here know His Majesty's signature?"

"In the name of the king, the rebels shall be pardoned! Things past will be forgotten! The death sentences against Medardo and his accomplices are suspended!"

The crowd roared, preventing them from hearing the final words of the count.

Satisfied by this, Medardo approached the count and whispered, "Who do you think you are to pardon my life in the king's name when I'm dealing directly with him and his ministers?"

Pere, red with rage, spat, "Traitor and villain! You gave your word that the council would be held in peace!"

"And I kept it, but today it is the people who reject you—"

Pere took out his sword and raised it against Medardo. The sound of an arquebus was heard, and Pere fell at Medardo's feet. In the seconds of silence that followed, Johan and Nunilo raced to protect the count. When Nunilo saw the listless body of his friend, he raised his arquebus and aimed at Medardo, but Medardo's brother stepped between them.

Medardo had time to briefly hold his brother's inert body. Then, he raised his arquebus and shot it in the air.

"Now!" shouted Medardo.

From the streets around the square came dozens of shots and shouts of attack and terror. Over the heads of the women, old people, and children flashed the swords of the count's men, who were disconcerted because they could not clearly identify who the enemy was.

Johan spotted Jayme, who had observed the scene from a distance. He took out his sword and approached, but Jayme was quicker, grabbing the count and putting an arm around his throat. He pulled a dagger from his belt and pushed the tip against the man's neck.

"Don't struggle or you're a dead man!" he threatened Fernando while making his way through the crowd, using the count's body as a shield. "You too, Johan. Come any closer and I'll kill him!"

Johan froze, though his blood boiled with hatred toward this traitor, his cousin who had once been his friend, his companion in mischief.

"You'll pay for this, Jayme!" Johan threatened with his sword upheld. "You'll be sorry for your betrayal!"

"And I'll be waiting for you!" Jayme shouted. "Watch your back because I won't stop until I finish you!"

When Jayme thought he was far enough away, he hesitated. How tempting it was to have the count's life in his hands! He would never have another opportunity like that. He pressed the knife a little harder and felt hot blood. But there he halted. As much as the king wanted this land, he would never permit the murder of a noble. On the contrary, he would probably put a price on the killer's head to satisfy the other nobles. Jayme withdrew his knife, threw Count Fernando to the ground, and took off running, shielded by the townspeople. The count, stunned, ran back to Johan and Nunilo. One of his soldiers brought him his horse just as Surano and Corso galloped up.

"They're everywhere!" Surano shouted. "All through the upper part of town! And they've hired Catalan bandits! They took advantage of our followers looking after the count to ransack their houses! Cowardly traitors! They planned it all!"

"Surano! Corso!" shouted Nunilo, trying to lift Pere up. "Help me carry him! He's still breathing!"

"Pere!" Surano jumped down and examined his brother. He found the hole in his stomach where the blood was coming from, tore his shirt, and plugged the wound with cloth. "Who was it? I'll kill him with my bare hands!"

The count addressed Surano. "Tell me, what options do we have?"

"Frankly, sir, your nobles are more interested in saving their houses than in saving you. But those of us left have fought in worse situations." His tone turned furious. "Give the order and we'll charge against the rebels until there are none left!"

"We can't risk something happening to you, sir," Johan intervened. "We should go now."

The count called one of his men and told him, "Quietly go around and tell everybody that we are going to the Besalduch monastery."

Worried about Pere's family, Nunilo spoke to Corso. "Accompany Surano and his men to Pere's house. They will need help. Find his wife and bring her to Besalduch. I'll carry Pere there."

"I should go with you," said Corso, thinking how he'd never forgive himself if Leonor lost her beloved husband. "Surano can look after his brother's family."

"I'm not the one who needs help now," argued Nunilo firmly. "Anyway, we'll all meet at the monastery."

Corso obeyed, but decided to steer the group to the monastery as swiftly as possible. He had a feeling the day would only get worse.

The town had gone mad. In the streets where homes were burning, cries of fear mixed with those of elation from men who had filled their sacks with gold, silver, and jewels. For the first time in his life, Corso was on the other side of this situation. Used to pillaging after taking a town, he now regretted that the friends of those who had treated him so well were suffering the violence of men maddened by greed, vengeance, or mere loyalty to the opposing side. He saw the soulless men chasing terrified women and was devastated to realize he had been one of them. Now the thought of such men getting their hands on Brianda nearly drove him mad.

Pere's house was on the outskirts of town. It was a sober, simple building with a stately appearance. The main door was destroyed. In the central patio, they saw nobody. Surano, followed by the three men from the house, began to call out. From one of the sheds came the sound of a woman's sobbing. Surano found Maria, Pere's wife, curled up in a corner naked in a pool of blood. He ordered one of the men to get a blanket to cover her. Despite her age, she looked like a child, horrified by what had happened to her.

Corso noticed that she was pressing one of her hands tightly against her bosom, but would not let any of them see her wound.

"They wanted everything," she said, "and what they couldn't carry they destroyed. The wine from the barrels on the floor, the furniture chopped up with axes. They fled to the mountains. They burned the county's archives and registries that Pere kept. My clothes. They couldn't take off my ring—"

She looked to her right, and they saw an axe and a finger on the floor. One of the house servants vomited.

"It was my wedding ring." Maria's voice began to break. "My husband—do you know where he is?"

Corso whispered something in the ear of one of the servants and, when the servant left, Surano crouched down beside her.

"Maria, Pere has been wounded," he said in a quiet and confident voice, "but he is alive. Nunilo is carrying him up to the monastery in Besalduch with the count's men, and I have orders to bring you to him."

The servant returned with a smoking bucket and tongs. Surano looked at Corso and signaled him to proceed. Corso closed his eyes for an instant and took a deep breath.

"Now we must heal you, Maria," Surano continued. "I hope you will be as brave as my brother would wish you to be. He needs you now. I ask you to close your eyes and trust me."

Maria nodded and closed her eyes.

"Help Surano to hold her," Corso ordered a servant.

He took the tongs, rooted in the bucket, and picked the most suitable ember by size and color. He knelt beside Maria and, without hesitation, pressed it to the wound. The bleeding stopped and the air filled with the nauseating smell of burnt flesh.

The woman fainted, and they carried her to her bedroom to rest.

"Stay with her until I return," Surano told Corso. "I'm going to look for the servants to let them know that the danger has passed for the moment."

Corso remained beside Maria until two servant women appeared. They dressed her and prepared her for the journey to Besalduch through Tiles. Not an hour had passed since the altercation had begun, but it felt much longer.

Meanwhile, Surano took the opportunity to ride through the center of the town to see if things had calmed down. He verified that the uproar had lessened as the ransacking had satisfied the rebels' appetites. Suddenly, a woman and child appeared in front of him, and it took a rapid pull on the reins to avoid knocking them down. He recognized Lida immediately, and in the child, Medardo's curved nose and features. He made a face of disgust and went to spur the horse onward, but she raised her hand to stop him.

"They told me your brother is wounded," she said, looking at him sadly with her hazel-colored eyes.

"It was your husband's fault."

"Medardo is defending what he believes in, just like you."

"I see that sharing a bed with him has changed you. And to think that there was a time I loved you!"

He was referring not only to her defense of Medardo but also to her appearance. Lida was too thin, she looked unkempt, and she had already lost some teeth even though she was not yet thirty.

"You ran off, and I was lucky that Medardo was even willing to marry me. No one else would have accepted the lover of a bandit in his house. Your contempt is unjust. If you hadn't abandoned me—"

"It doesn't matter now! Let me pass."

Lida held the horse's bridle.

"Medardo has gone mad over his brother's death," she warned. "He has ordered his men to meet in the church. The count's departure isn't the end of this."

"Why would you tell me this?" Surano snarled. "If it is either to protect me or because you wish for the death of your husband, you are mistaken. I don't want anything to do with you."

Humiliation burned in Lida's eyes, but she said nothing. She pulled the child to one side.

Surano dug his heels into the sides of his horse. A moment of pity and regret for his cruelty quickly vanished.

He had to warn Corso.

Medardo gathered Jayme and his twelve men at the entrance to the church. He had to avenge his brother's death.

"The count has fled like a coward," he told them. "He was seen going in the direction of the highlands. I don't know where he will be lodging, but—"

"I don't believe he will go to the villages," Jayme interrupted, looking inside the church to make sure that nobody, not even Father Guillem, was around to hear. "It would be too dangerous for the families of the lords. I'll bet you anything they are going to the monastery in Besalduch."

Medardo smiled cunningly. "No doubt, Abbot Bartholomeu will gladly give him shelter. To maintain his income and not share it with the king's bishop, he is capable of offering his monks as soldiers. Well, better for us."

"Let me remind you it's not advisable to kill the count, Medardo," Jayme warned him. "Not even His Majesty will defend you if something happens to him."

"That's rich, especially after you put a dagger to his throat." Medardo guffawed. "Today, I don't care a fig about the count or the other lords of Tiles and Besalduch. Their time will come. I want Nunilo of Anels before the body of my brother goes cold. I won't stop until I see Nunilo's body swinging from a tree!"

He mounted his horse, and the others followed. They had traveled a league in silence when the lead soldier retraced his steps, signaling them to stop while pointing toward the lower path that followed the river.

Medardo and Jayme dismounted and crept over to the edge of the bank to see a group of the count's men below. To their satisfaction, they could hear the conversation clearly.

"Pere cannot make it much farther," Nunilo said. "The best thing would be to leave him here and send for the apothecary."

"We won't leave you here alone, Nunilo," said Johan.

"I'll keep three men just in case, but I'm sure that there is no danger now. A long time has passed and they haven't followed us. Also, Surano and Corso will soon be here."

Johan shook his head. "I don't like it."

"Johan!" Nunilo raised his voice. "We can't ask Count Fernando to sit around on a rock all day. He needs to write to His Majesty as soon as possible to report what has happened and you must be at his side. Marquo can go for the apothecary."

Johan went to the count and exchanged some quiet words. Moments later, the men left Nunilo leaning against a walnut tree while his three men prepared a fire and a bed of blankets for Pere.

Medardo and Jayme returned to their men and told them they would wait until the count was out of sight before attacking. They retraced their steps, looking for an easy route to get down the bank. Medardo, impatient to avenge his brother's death as soon as possible, passed his nervousness on to his horse, which stamped and shook its head. Finally, Medardo let out a shout and launched himself down the slope.

The attack barely lasted two minutes. Medardo's men killed the three guards in an instant, disarmed Nunilo, and marched him to Medardo. He took a rope from his saddle, caressed it in his hands, and made a noose while speaking to Nunilo. "You didn't hesitate to kill my brother, and now I won't hesitate in doing the same to you."

He put the noose around Nunilo's thick neck, while the man remained silent and stolid, conscious that his end was near. Sharper than ever, his senses relayed the crunching of the frozen soil under his feet, the mist from the horses' nostrils, the cold smell of midday, the sweat of his hands, and the bitter taste in his mouth. His mind was filled with Leonor: her face, her movements, her voice.

They tied his hands behind his back and, joking about his excessive weight, they lifted him onto his horse and led it to the walnut tree. One nimbly climbed the tree with one end of the rope, tied it around a branch, jumped to the ground, and pulled it taut. Then, Medardo smacked the horse hard with a stick and it ran off, leaving its master dangling.

"Don't let go of the rope," ordered Medardo when he saw the signs of death in Nunilo's face. "Tie it to the other branch so his body is clearly visible."

"And what shall we do with him?" asked Jayme, pointing to Pere.

"Eh, he won't live long. And if he finds the strength to open his eyes, he'll just see what's left of his friend." He spat on the ground. "Let's head back. That's enough for today."

From a distance, Surano and Corso made out Nunilo's body rocking in the air. They had come as fast as they could, given that they were traveling with Pere's wife and one of her servants, but they soon realized that they were too late.

While Surano cut the rope with his dagger, Corso used all his strength in holding Nunilo's body in his arms. For the first time in his life, he felt a terrible urge to cry. That man had done more for him in a few months than anyone else in the rest of his life, including Surano. And he had given him a present of the best horse in the world.

"Why did they leave you alone with three of your weakest men?" he murmured. "Why did I leave you alone?"

Surano knelt beside his brother and realized he was still breathing.

"I'm sorry about Nunilo, but Pere is still alive."

Maria ran to him and caressed his hands and his face, moaning his name between her wails. Surano pulled her away, helped her back on the horse, and ordered Corso to help him with Pere.

Corso, his face distraught, pointed to Nunilo.

"I have no intention of leaving him here."

Surano heard the determination in his voice, so between the two of them, they picked up the body and threw it over the saddle of his horse. They used the same rope he had been hanged with to secure him. Then Corso helped to seat Pere in front of Surano.

An hour later, they passed near Tiles. Corso looked up toward Beles Peak and his sadness turned into disquiet. Some place to the west of that mountain was Brianda. He wondered if she was safe, if he should leave Surano and continue to Lubich on his own. As if Surano had been reading his mind, he said, "We have a job to do. We'll get to Besalduch as quickly as we can, then you can come back."

They continued and ran into Marquo with the apothecary, but Surano refused to dismount with Pere.

"If he's made it this far, it's best if we take him to the monastery."

They rode in silence for another hour until the path entered a dense pine forest. Soon afterward, they heard the babbling of a river and crossed a steep stone bridge. The noise of hooves alerted several monks to their arrival.

"Warn the abbot and the count!" shouted Surano. "And the rest of you, help me with my brother!"

One monk started off at a run and another pointed behind the church.

"Go that way until you reach the abbot's house. We have an infirmary there."

Surano did as he was told, and the count, Johan, and Abbot Bartholomeu, a bony man with reddish hair, met him there. Johan rushed to the immobile bodies of his friends.

"Nunilo is dead," Surano announced. "And my brother is close to it."

The abbot gave orders for the monks to take charge of the bodies, and Maria and her servant went off with Pere.

Johan, crestfallen, stayed beside Nunilo, his hand resting on his friend's back, until the body was taken away. Then, Surano planted himself in front of the count.

"Look at what your soft approach has led to! You have lost two of your best allies!"

Johan stepped forward to restrain Surano, but he stopped because he agreed with him. He felt a knot in his chest. How could he tell Leonor about her husband's death? How lonely she would be! And how lonely he was! Nunilo was his dearest friend. Brianda would also be upset, he thought. Thinking of his daughter, he felt a wave of worry for her, his wife, and Lubich. He prayed that they would be safe until he returned. Even though he had left, several men guarding the house, now nothing was certain.

"If it had been up to me," continued Surano, "Medardo would have been hanged days ago and Nunilo would be alive!"

The count reddened at the deserter's insolence. Surano was a brave man and useful for his cause, but that did not give him the right to question a count.

"Do the rest of you agree?" he inquired.

Silence.

"Well?" he asked again. "Speak, Johan of Lubich!"

"Now that you have asked me, I must tell you, sir. You will write to His Majesty asking for a firm hand in the repression of the insults we have suffered today, and the answer will take long to come, if it ever does. Meanwhile, our honor remains tarnished, our families imperiled, and our friends slain."

The count clenched his teeth.

"You are asking me to go to war."

"We are asking you to impose your rights by force," Marquo said. "Your position is difficult, but so is ours. Our houses and our families are here. Either we openly confront Medardo or—" He stopped before saying that they could not swear fealty much longer, but it was clear to everyone.

Count Fernando swore.

"For that I need a lot of men and time!"

"We could wait until spring," said Johan, "so that they think we have forgotten, and attack when they least expect it. In terms of the number of men we need—"

Two horses were galloping toward them, and a woman's voice shouted, "Johan of Lubich!" He recognized Brianda and his stomach dropped. She was accompanied by one of the house's servants.

"What are you doing here? What happened at Lubich?"

Brianda threw her arms around him.

"Father! Thank God I found you!" Without letting go, she began explaining as fast as she could. "A messenger came with an important letter for you, and I sent him to Aiscle." She pointed to the servant. "He didn't enter because in Pere's house they told him what had happened. Why didn't you send word?"

She paused to catch her breath, and Johan scolded her.

"Do you know the risk you ran, coming here? Damn it! You are my daughter, not one of my men!"

"I had to come! We heard they hanged an important lord!" she exclaimed. "I looked everywhere for you!"

Johan was furious at Brianda's recklessness, although at heart he admired her bravery and was moved by her worry for him.

"Is it true?" she asked, looking around. "Who have they killed? I see Count Fernando, Marquo, Surano—" She noticed Corso, sweaty and grieving, but she did not name him. Her heart jumped for joy to see him safe. "Where are Pere and—?"

"Where is that important document?" Johan asked.

Brianda put her hand in her chemise, took out a document, and gave it to him. Johan broke the seal and read in silence. When he had finished, the lines on his forehead were even deeper.

"It is signed by three lords of the eastern valleys. The villagers who graze our livestock between Monzon and Zaragoza have been attacked by Moors, they say. A few are dead, among them our servant Gisabel's husband. They are forming parties of armed men to avenge these deaths and writing asking for our help. In exchange, they promise to help us in the future. They have arranged to meet in Monzon the day after tomorrow."

"There are the men you need!" said Surano to the count. "I'll take forty men to fight the Moors and will come back with twice that. You round up the rest of the troops."

The count looked at Johan. "Do you still have dealings with that French captain, Agut?"

Johan nodded. Agut had been the main buyer of his horses for many years now.

"Now is a bad time to cross the snowed-in passes to France, but in previous years, we have crossed as early as March."

"Very good, then," said the count. "We will have everything ready by the end of April. We will meet up here, if the abbot has no objection."

Abbot Bartholomeu shrugged and opened his hands in resignation. Count Fernando had always been his greatest benefactor.

"In the meantime," said the count, "look after Pere or pray for his soul, as the need arises. And celebrate masses for Nunilo on my account."

"For Nunilo!" exclaimed Brianda, and began to cry. One misfortune after another. Gisabel's husband would never meet his child. Kind Nunilo was dead. The men talked of weapons, fights, and revenge . . .

The time of peace had ended.

23.

In the kitchen, Surano and Corso ate the pottage of cabbage, chickpeas, and bacon offered to them by the monks. Corso was quieter than ever.

"Aren't you looking forward to the fight?" Surano asked.

All Corso wanted to do was run to Brianda. He had no desire to follow Surano into an uncertain adventure or to kill strangers, but he had no choice. He felt responsible for Nunilo's death. If he ever returned to Anels House, he was sure that all he would see in Leonor's eyes was recrimination. And that was something he could not bear. She was the closest thing to a mother he'd ever had.

And if he could not go back to Tiles, he had no other place to go. So, he would follow Surano once again, facing all types of dangers, paying no heed to fear or pain, punishing his body with cold and hunger and compensating it later with booty and prostitutes, without any yearning for the past or expectation of more than a restless night's sleep.

Maybe it was for the best. To leave and accept that his stay in Tiles and the recurring image of Brianda in his arms had only been a pleasant dream, impossible for someone like him. She would marry Marquo and forget about what had happened between them while he roved under the stars of other lands.

Corso pushed his bowl away, stood up, and went outside.

The dull gray light of afternoon guided the solitary figures of the monks from one building to another. The skeletal trees stood out against the rocky surroundings. At this time of year, not even a miserable bird broke the silence.

He walked toward the river and sat down on a rock. He noticed the ice that had formed in some spots, halting the flow of water, petrifying its freedom and muffling its sound. He thought of Father Guillem's sermon and smiled bitterly to himself.

As far as he understood, only living souls could be saved. And without Brianda's warmth, his soul was like the water trapped in an ice floe: mute, frozen, dead.

A voice took him from his thoughts.

"Corso!"

He stood up and saw Brianda walking toward him. Her eyes were red, her chin was trembling, and she nervously rubbed her cheeks with her knuckles.

"Corso," she said again. "My father told me everything. It's terrible. I—I don't know what Leonor will do without him, all alone in Anels House. It's not fair. Why him?"

Corso kept his eyes down. "He didn't want me to go with him. If I had been with him, he would still be alive."

"Or you would also be dead!"

Corso shrugged. "And who would care?"

Brianda forced him to look at her. "I would. You know that as well as I do."

"Right, of course, that's why you rejected me."

"I can't and won't discuss that again."

Corso, irritated, clicked his tongue. "Tomorrow I leave for the lowlands with Surano."

"I heard that Surano was going, not that you were—" There was fear in Brianda's voice. The parties of armed men meant danger and death. And more so in Surano's company. The last time he got into trouble, it took him years to return. What would she do without Corso?

"Wherever Surano goes, I go. Unless you ask me not to."

"Well, I'm asking you now. Don't go!"

How unfair, Brianda thought. How could she ask the man she loved not to go when she would soon enter a marriage of convenience with another?

"It's not enough."

"I can't give you any more."

Corso leaned over her, slid his gaze from her eyes to her lips before encircling her waist and drawing her toward him. He perceived the heat of her cheeks on his chest, the beating of her heart through the palms of his hands on her back, and the heat of her skin seeping through the thick clothes. He savored those moments of stillness as if they were the last flickering of an ember before going out, took a deep breath, moved away, and made to leave.

"Wait!" Brianda cried. "I'll think of something. I promise I will."

But Corso did not turn back. Brianda felt sick. She couldn't stop thinking about how brief, sad, and unfair life was. That very morning, Leonor had embraced to Nunilo, and now she never would again. A few hours ago, Nunilo was championing his cause, and now he was a motionless bundle that would rot in the ground. And for what? This time it was for the count's war, but if people did not die in war, they died from illness, like Bringuer, his wife, and his daughter; or from unexpected violence, like Gisabel's husband; or from hunger when the harvests were bad. So why should she renounce what she most wanted if either of the two of them could die at any time?

There was only one way to convince Corso of her true feelings.

"I'll refuse to marry Marquo!" she shouted.

Corso stopped. "You will?"

"Yes." With a sob, Brianda threw herself into his arms. "Oh, but now there's more reason than ever for you to leave. Otherwise, they would realize you are the cause of their dishonor and would pursue you. They would see it in the way we look at each other. Now I'm not asking you to stay, I'm begging you to return!"

Corso caressed her hair slowly. Minutes ago, he thought, he had doubted his own soul. Now he felt it beat with the strength of a bird that takes flight again after falling dazed by a blow. For her, he would fly quickly and return before the fields sprouted their shoots of wheat and rye; before the swallows, sparrows, and pigeons chose the place to weave their nests; and long before the bees buzzed over the spring flowers.

"I will," he promised, "because you are my Lubich."

Weeks passed with little change in the mountains of Orrun. At the beginning of March, neither the men Johan had sent to France nor the soldiers promised by Surano had arrived or communicated.

Pere recovered in the monastery, as it was not safe to return to Aiscle until it was clear who ruled. Marquo and Johan tried to lead as normal a life as possible, hoping no one would suspect an impending attack.

By the end of March, the count had managed to gather a hundred men, who came to Besalduch in small, discrete groups, and he was confident that another fifty were on their way. Johan's man finally returned and reported that Agut was delayed by snow along the mountain border, but in a couple of days the French captain and thirty more men would arrive with artillery.

Everything was coming together, except for Surano and Corso, who hadn't been heard from since their departure at the end of January. Brianda, still grieving for Nunilo, was beside herself. Tearful, she wandered the paths of Lubich and Tiles, not even noticing the effects of early spring on the landscape. At least the preparations for war had delayed her marriage to Marquo until the summer. Sooner or later, she would have to tell her parents that she renounced the engagement, but as time went by without word from Corso, she was assaulted by doubts.

What if he never came back? Or if he'd changed his mind? She repeated to herself that the only thing that could prevent his return was death. Then her anxiety turned to anguish and desperation, because if he were dead, should she not marry Marquo?

One day in April, a few days after the arrival of Agut, Pere and Marquo arrived at Lubich bearing a letter.

From Pere's downcast eyes, Johan understood that it was bad news. He leaned against the enormous fireplace in front of which Elvira and Brianda were seated and unfolded the thick paper. After a while, he sighed and said, "I can't tell you how sorry I am, my friend. It's a great loss, for you and for all of us."

"What has happened, Father?" whispered Brianda, pale with worry.

"What was meant to be a rapid intervention to avenge the death of the herders got complicated. First, our men launched several isolated attacks against the Moors. But the Moors gathered together between Monzon and Zaragoza. Surano and his men attacked with fire and steel. Hundreds died, among them Surano. It says here that beside him died the one who was always with him. I suppose that refers to Corso."

Brianda felt the world around her cease to exist. The words she had heard were not real. The fire did not crackle. Her lungs did not inhale air.

"How—do you know—it's true?" she managed to ask.

"The survivors came home two weeks ago," Pere answered. "The same ones who asked us for help told us about what had happened and apologized that they don't have any men for our cause after all." He hit the arm of the chair with his fist. "It's out of control, damn it! Surano never knew when to stop."

Elvira sighed loudly. "Poor Leonor. First Nunilo and now Corso. Such a large estate and no heir."

Pere and Marquo exchanged glances.

"Excuse me, but I don't understand," said Marquo.

"In his will, Nunilo left his estate to Leonor, and his wish was that, on her death, it would pass to Corso," explained Johan.

"That can't be," exclaimed Marquo and Brianda, one out of envy, the other out of pain for Leonor, the bitterness of her own loss, and for the misfortune of Corso, who, if he had known his new situation, would never have left Tiles.

Brianda swallowed a sob. To think that she herself had told him to go! She would never forgive herself.

"We must inform the count immediately," said Pere. "If we cannot expect any more soldiers, it makes no sense to wait any longer to attack Aiscle."

A week later, at three in the morning, the silence in the monastery in Besalduch was broken by the hooves of two hundred horses stampeding over the stone bridge. They were led by Count Fernando and the lords of Orrun. It was still night when they descended on a sleepy Aiscle, attacking the houses of Medardo and his followers. The count and his men were right: they were not expected. The rebels had been overconfident after Pere's long absence and the count's flight in January. The expert artillerymen of Captain Agut, a thin man with a wrinkled face and a short beard, aimed their copper cannons at the doors of the rebels' houses and left them in splinters. They entered house after house, demanding Medardo's whereabouts.

After a half hour offensive, the group led by Marquo found the house where they believed Medardo lodged. The soldiers broke down the door and searched all the rooms, but found them empty. They heard arquebus fire coming from outside and ran to the street.

Outside, they saw it was Medardo firing from the roof. Marquo sent a soldier to go and look for the count.

"We have taken the town!" he shouted. "Give yourself up!"

"And who is ordering me?" yelled Medardo.

"Marquo of Besaduch, future lord of Lubich!" He felt great pleasure in shouting out these words.

Medardo fired at him and only just missed him.

The count, Johan, and Pere arrived.

"He doesn't want to come down," Marquo informed them. "And anyone who nears him from the inside is an easy target. He has picked off four of our men already."

"Medardo!" shouted the count. "If you come down, you have my word that you will suffer no harm!"

A guffaw was heard, followed by another shot.

"Burn the house," suggested Marquo. "We'll see how long the weasel takes to come out."

Several soldiers approached with torches.

"Medardo!" repeated the count. "We are going to burn the house!"

After a few moments of silence, Medardo peeked around the chimney, then hid again. No way could he get out of that situation alive. Nobody could come to his aid, and even if they did, they could do nothing against the count's men. How naïve he had been to think that they would not take reprisals after the last confrontation and the hanging of Nunilo of Tiles! At first, his men watched the roads day and night, but for the last month, they had let down their guard, believing that the count must be off relating his problems to the justice and the king. Medardo saw that he had no option but to surrender. He fingered a fine leather bag inside his breeches and breathed in relief. The count's weak character would spare Medardo, and afterward, the king's minister would get him out of this bind. The papers he always carried would save him. It had been a good idea to get them in Monzon.

"Wait!" he shouted. "If I can trust your word, I will surrender!"

"Come down; nothing will happen to you!" Count Fernando assured him.

A few moments later, Medardo quietly came out the front door. They dragged him to the same square where the council had been disrupted in January and exhibited him as proof that the ringleader had been captured and the uprising was over.

"Do you see that despicable smile?" Marquo asked the others in a whisper. "He still believes he will be saved."

Pere gritted his teeth. As much as he wished to support the count, it was difficult for him not to shoot Medardo down. Images of what he and his men had done to his wife, Maria, and his friend Nunilo flashed through his mind. It was also Medardo's fault that Surano had been sent for reinforcements and died. Pere knew Medardo would try to use his contacts in court to save himself and restart the rebellion. As long as that traitor was alive, there would be no peace. An idea came to his mind. He wondered whether to share it with Johan and Marquo, but feared they might talk him out of it. So, he called one of his men over and whispered in his ear, "Go over and stick a dagger in him. I'll reward you better than you could ever imagine."

The man nodded. He approached Medardo from behind and stuck the blade into his kidney. Medardo let out a cry and fell, and when they realized what had happened, several of Nunilo's soldiers joined in, plunging their daggers into Medardo repeatedly.

The count gawked at the lords of Orrun.

"I gave my word!" he exclaimed.

"And how many times did he break his?" said Pere.

"You—"

The count did not finish his sentence. What good was it now to confront his own followers?

Before the terrified stares of the townspeople, the soldiers tore off Medardo's clothes and dragged his corpse through the square until they tired of it. Then, one of them took out his sword and sliced off Medardo's head with one blow. The head rolled, spitting blood, while being kicked from boot to boot like a ball, until the count, horrified, ordered that it be taken to the entrance to the town and stuck on a pike as a warning.

Johan noticed a pouch among Medardo's clothes, and inside it, letters. He read one, then went over to the count.

"Here you have the proof. His Majesty's minister urgently requests him to make the towns of Orrun rise up and to foment disobedience toward your person."

The count read all the letters one by one, turning red with fury. It was one thing to suspect foul play in the king's entourage and a very different one to confirm it with his own eyes. No matter how much he still wanted to defend the king, it was hard to believe that the monarch was not aware of such machinations. He realized then how stupid he had been to believe in justice and in recovering what was his peacefully. The letters showed that his attack on Aiscle had been more than justified. What could they do from Castile once he had taken legal possession? Nothing. The scales had finally tipped in his favor.

He sent a soldier to ring the church bell as a signal that they were finally going to hold a General Council, and ordered everyone to stand with him. When he considered that the square was sufficiently full, he spoke:

"Today, sedition in these lands has been suffocated, and I take possession of the lands of Orrun, of the ninety leagues, the seventeen towns, the two hundred and sixteen hamlets, and the four thousand inhabitants. I am accompanied by the lords of the main towns, and I delegate civil and criminal administration to them. Pere of Aiscle will, from now on, be my deputy in the county; Johan of Tiles, the general bailiff; and young Marquo of Besalduch, the justice.

"As requested by His Majesty, you will obey me as your lord. It is my right to receive four hundred and fifty *sueldos* annually on Saint Martin's Day, with the outstanding amount from previous years, plus maintenance when I am in the town, the *maravedi* tax every seven years, five *sueldos* for grazing rights, and nothing more.

"I swear the laws, privileges, and liberties of the Kingdom of Aragon and of the county as those before me have been accustomed to swear, keep, and obey. I shall suspend the sentences of those rebels who desire peace and hold no prejudice against them. It is time to forget the past and move forward together."

The count finished his speech by putting his signature to a prepared document he had brought with him and made his new administrators sign as well. He gave each a firm handshake and bade them farewell, intending to return to Zaragoza immediately to personally inform the viceroy.

Jayme of Cuyls, hiding out in the hills near Aiscle, heard about the attack from his sister Lida. Disguised as a peasant, Jayme crept into town and learned that Medardo had been killed in cold blood. He took a small alleyway toward the square, arriving just as a soldier swung Medardo's bloody and blackened head in the air, exhibiting it like a hunting trophy.

Jayme felt like vomiting and, then, launching himself against the count and his men to erase the smug expressions from their faces. Did they really think it was over? From the count's words it seemed so. He spoke arrogantly of his rights to Orrun, how they would resume paying unjust dues to an unknown person far away. Had the revolts of the previous years served no purpose? The count was a fool. Pardon the rebels and reward his own men? Jayme himself would show him that Medardo wasn't the only one who wanted him gone. The king favored the rebellion for his own interest, of course, not for the well-being of the territory, but the king would never bother to visit such distant lands as long as they did not disturb him. With or without Medardo, the only way that Orrun would be governed by the people was by finishing off the count and his followers.

And he knew exactly where to start.

He returned to the hills and sent for Medardo's loyal men. He explained his plan and convinced them of the need to avenge Medardo's death and of the great reward they would receive from his own hands.

Drunk on victory and convinced that the land was now peaceful; nothing would be easier than finishing off Johan of Lubich in his own house.

However, Jayme would not go with them. No one must connect him to that matter, as his dream was to occupy Johan's place in his house and in the county.

Pere and Captain Agut remained in Aiscle. The former because he wanted to restore his house after so long away; the latter because his men had earned a good rest of wine and women.

After saying good-bye to Marquo, Johan first took the road to Tiles and then the fork for Lubich. He was tired and hungry, and he only wanted to get home, take a hot bath, have dinner, and ask Elvira to share his bed that night. The day had been long and intense, but there had hardly been any deaths. Medardo's death had surprised and weakened his followers and relieved not only the nobles but also the many peasants and artisans tired of the revolt, the pillaging, and the uncertainty. Like Domingo the carpenter had admitted on one occasion, it made no difference to him whether he paid dues to a count or a king; what really worried him was bringing up his family in peace and enjoying good harvests. Of course, Domingo had not been educated in the noble concepts of honor and loyalty of one lord to a higher one. It had been so since the time of Ramiro I of Aragon, five hundred years ago, as attested in the documents compiled by Pere in the marvelous archives Medardo's savages had destroyed.

He tried to put aside his mistrustful thoughts on the count's economic requests and his rapid departure, and to enjoy the grayish colors of the dusk.

Suddenly, a strong smell of burning wood came to him from Lubich. A terrible foreboding gripped him. He spurred on his horse and set off at a gallop, shouting like a man possessed for the men with him to hurry up.

Flames were coming from one of the hay barns, but no one was working to put out the fire. Johan entered the house shouting out for his wife and his daughter.

"Johan," he heard Elvira yell. "They have locked me in! They have Brianda! Run!"

"Who has her? Where did they take her?"

"To the tower!"

Johan unsheathed his sword and charged out to the patio.

"Look!" His men pointed upward in the direction of the tower.

Johan looked up and saw his daughter, gagged, dangling by one arm from the window.

"Johan of Lubich!" a voice shouted. "Come up alone or she falls!"

His men surrounded him.

"A dozen of them have occupied the tower," said one. "We could confront them, but your daughter—"

"I'll come up!" he shouted.

"Throw down your sword!"

Johan did so, and Brianda was pulled inside. Johan ran to the base of the tower. He burst through the door and some men pushed him up the narrow stone steps until he got to the landing where two men were holding Brianda. His daughter's eyes reflected terror and terrible sadness. *Why did you come?* they seemed to say. *Now both of us will die.*

"You have me now," said Johan in a firm voice. "Let her go!"

They did so and Brianda ran to his arms. Johan removed the gag and caressed her face. She did not scream or cry. She just kept her eyes fixed upon her father's in a silent dialogue. She memorized the shine of his eyes, the first white hairs in his bushy eyebrows, the fine lines around his eyes. She felt like when she was a child and he used to comfort her after a nightmare, but this time she did not think she would wake up.

"Let her go before we change our minds," said one gruffly.

Johan rested his hands on his daughter's shoulders.

"Go to your mother, Brianda." He tried to keep his voice steady but could not stop it from breaking when he pronounced her name. He took off his emerald ring and handed it to her. "Mind it. And mind yourself. No matter what happens, keep the name of Lubich alive." He kissed her tenderly and gently pushed her away. "Remember the motto of our family since the time of Prince Peter, whose father, James II of Aragon, granted him the County of Orrun in 1322." He placed his hand over his heart. "Here I take all. With me."

Brianda gave him a final embrace and barreled down the stairs, squeezing the ring so tight her palm bled, not hearing the laughs and vulgar comments of the men who ran their hands over her, not caring about bruising or scratching her skin against the stone walls. She stumbled out to the yard and grabbed a sword from one her father's soldiers with the idea of fighting herself.

"Get up there now!" she roared. "Do something!"

The man took the sword from her.

"If anything happens to you, your father's act will have served for naught. Hide yourself in a safe place, and we will do our job."

Brianda ran toward the house, but at the last second, changed her mind. She followed the narrow path behind the tower and sat down on a rock. There, where Corso had kissed her, where she had come so many times in search of peace, she now heard the shouts of the soldiers, the clash of their swords. She covered her ears with her hands, but the sound of her panicked breathing was more upsetting than the sounds of the fight. She cursed her servants, who had hidden when they saw the men. She cursed the count for having taken all his soldiers with him. And she cursed her own weakness. If only she were as strong as Corso, she alone would have defended Lubich. Tears rolled down her cheeks when she remembered Corso. Everyone she most loved was disappearing. First Nunilo, then Corso, and now her father's life hung by a thread. A few months ago, everything was happy and new for her. Now, the world seemed worse than Father Guillem's hell.

Suddenly, the noise stopped. Puzzled, she looked up just in time to see her father's body and hear his voice as he fell past her and continued to fall, smashing against the rocks of the cliff, spilling his blood at the feet of unperturbed Beles Peak, and disappearing into the abyss.

For a month, Brianda was incapable of pronouncing a word. She locked herself in her room and refused to attend the funeral of her father, Johan of Lubich, whose remains took a week to recover. She would not talk to Marquo, for whom Johan's death had increased the urgency of the wedding. She rejected condolences, even from Leonor, and even more from that shady cousin, Jayme of Cuyls, who consoled her mother too ardently while publicly proclaiming his acceptance of the count's rule. She could not stand to meet Gisabel's infant son, no matter how Cecilia insisted there was no better cure for grief than to embrace the newly born.

To Brianda, nothing mattered.

The same tears she shed for her father also served to unleash her grief over Corso's death, for which she had not been able to cry in order to keep up appearances.

The same pain that racked her heart for the loss of Johan brought back memories of her encounters with Corso, few but deep, fleeting but eternal. She would give her soul to the very devil to see his penetrating gaze, to hear his deep voice, to feel his rough skin, to taste another kiss, just one . . .

The only thing that prevented her from throwing herself into the same abyss where Johan had died was her father's last words. If nothing mattered, if she could hardly breathe, how could she keep the name of

Lubich alive? But he had not forced a promise out of her, he had simply asked. How could she ignore his request? Ending her life would mean letting her father down and dishonoring everything he had fought for, forfeiting Lubich.

Her life did not belong to her alone.

She finally swore one day that she would pull through this grief, never suspecting that what awaited her was much worse than anything her aggrieved mind could imagine.

24.

2013

A persistent, loud, and repetitive noise, as if from a strange bell, snuck into Brianda's dreams and urged her to wake up. Esteban groggily answered the telephone, and she sat up, turned on the lamp, and looked at the time: six in the morning.

When Esteban hung up, Brianda asked, "What's going on?"

"It was your mother. I don't know how to tell you this—"

"Tell me what?" The faces of her loved ones flooded her mind, and she cringed.

"Your uncle Colau died."

"But how?" Brianda blinked several times, stunned.

"She said they don't know. He went to bed before Isolina like always, and when she got upstairs he was already gone. He was a heavy smoker, right?"

Esteban took her in his arms to comfort her. She appreciated the gesture, but no tears came to her eyes. Colau had always frightened her, and on her trip to Tiles it had been clear that he did not like or trust her. She felt guilty, but her only real sadness was for her aunt Isolina.

"Did she say when the funeral is?"

"Tomorrow, in Tiles. They're getting on the road right now." Esteban rubbed his brow. "I have court all week. I can talk to my boss about some time off tomorrow, but today—"

"I can catch a ride with my parents," suggested Brianda. "You don't have to worry. Call my mother back, and let her know to pick me up in half an hour."

Brianda showered and packed quickly, remembering to include warm clothes and something dark for the funeral. She wondered whether to bring the emerald ring. Dozens of times she had thought about calling Colau and confessing, but was too ashamed. In the beginning, she could have explained that she hadn't meant to steal it, but the more time passed, the harder it got. She put the ring on now and stroked it. She felt impossibly attached to this small and valuable object. The only way to rectify the situation was to return it to its rightful place without anybody noticing, but Colau's death changed things: if he hadn't asked for it, maybe he hadn't missed it. She placed it in a cloth pouch and hid it among her clothes in the suitcase. She wondered if Isolina knew of its existence.

In the kitchen, Esteban was making coffee and she accepted a big cup. Then she said good-bye, not daring to look him in the eye so he wouldn't see her excitement at the possibility of seeing Corso again, and went downstairs to meet her parents.

During the journey, she thought of her trip to Tiles at the end of October. Then, she had been fleeing from her nightmares, from physical contact with Esteban, from herself. Absorbed in her own problems and in driving, she hadn't paid much attention to the landscape. Now, it wasn't like her problems had vanished—she was still depressed, she was unemployed, her relationship with Esteban was strained—but something was different. An inexplicable, bittersweet nostalgia began to flutter in her chest as she recognized the outskirts of Aiscle: the small clay hills, the loam gullies, the rocky course of the river, the hairpin bends before the wide valley at the feet of Beles Peak, the graveyard, the fork to Lubich, and the great linden with the fountain near Anels House.

The reason for her return was sad, yet she sensed a welcoming salute in the rustling of the leaves on the bushes, in the crunch of the pebbles under her feet after they parked the car, in the dampness of the yard in front of the old manor house, imagining a scene from centuries ago in which someone like Corso combed a magnificent black horse while a convalescing girl emerged after a long illness . . .

She shook off the vision.

Her parents hurried into the house, but Brianda lingered outside. In October, she had been greeted here by blows from a punishing wind. Now, with spring timidly showing its first growth in the fields, the breeze was strangely warm for the end of March. The wind wrapped itself around her, swirling in her hands, on her face, and in her hair, and then went away for an instant before returning to lick her again. She closed her eyes and enjoyed the sensation until a prolonged howl startled her. It seemed to be coming from the shed.

Luzer.

She crossed the garden and uncertainly rested her hand on the doorknob. A movement caught her attention, and she turned. Her uncle's enormous black dog was staring at her, chained to a post behind the shed. Safe from his reach, Brianda stared back at him. He looked like a different animal. In his eyes there was no sign of his previous ferocity. Quite the opposite. Luzer emanated sorrow, even disinterest toward her, as if, after his master's death, there was no more need to stand guard. He let out a sad, short howl and lay down.

Brianda headed inside and went to the sitting room. Several people she did not recognize filled the wooden benches in front of the cold fireplace. When Isolina saw her, she broke away from Laura's arms and walked toward her. Brianda was shocked by her appearance. Her aunt seemed to have aged years overnight, and her voice was a barely intelligible mumble.

"He knew," she said. "He had a premonition."

Brianda hugged her. The body that shook against her own seemed to belong to a very different person from the woman she knew. Aunt Isolina—chatty but cautious, smiling but restrained, attentive but never overbearing—had been consumed by death and transformed into someone strange and feeble, as if the decrepitude of the house had eaten her alive. It was hard for Brianda to understand how the death of a man like Colau could affect anyone so deeply.

Brianda wondered if Esteban's death would cause her anything like this desolation.

"The body is in the office," she heard her mother say. "Do you want to come with us?"

Brianda shook her head. It would be difficult enough to sleep in the blue bedroom just knowing there was a dead person in the house. She sought refuge in the kitchen, where she ran into Petra, who was busy preparing a huge pot of beans.

"Have you seen him?" Petra asked.

Brianda shook her head.

"Better that way," Petra said. "I've seen many dead bodies in my life, and their faces were all peaceful." She rubbed her arms. "But the look on Colau's face is horrible. I can't get it out of my head. It is the face of someone who died suffering."

The following morning, the warm breeze unexpectedly gave way to a howling north wind that made the wooden barns creak, slipped treacherously into the house, and rattled the roof tiles. As was the custom in Tiles, the priest came to Anels House to accompany Colau in his farewell to the house he had shared with Isolina for so many years. Daniel, Jonas, Bernardo, Zacarias, and two other men carried the coffin out on their shoulders and placed it in the hearse. At the church, Brianda looked for Neli but didn't see her. She really wanted to talk to her, and not solely to apologize for having left without saying good-bye.

After a simple ceremony during which Isolina's sobbing frequently broke the moments of silence, they went to the small graveyard where Brianda had left flowers back on All Saints' Day. Hunching to withstand the gusts of wind, they navigated around the iron crosses of the graves on the ground and stopped in front of the small Anels family vault. The men put Colau's coffin in one of the niches, and Jonas began to cover it with a piece of plasterboard.

Brianda watched the ritual closely. The scene was acted out with the precision of a dress rehearsal. Jonas mixed the plaster with water to close the grave as the wind made the white dust rise. Petra placed stones on the wreaths and bunches of flowers so they wouldn't blow away, and the entourage slowly filed past Isolina to offer their condolences. Everybody Brianda had met here had come to pay respects. That included Neli, who she had spotted the moment she entered the sacred site with her unruly red hair and her informal clothes, and who had hung back beside Mihaela, oddly removed from the rest of the group.

Everyone was there—except Corso.

Maybe he was away on a trip, Brianda worried. With his wife.

Standing in that tiny graveyard, Brianda thought about how death was the most definite of all good-byes. Nothing she had suffered compared to what her aunt must be going through. Isolina needed all the support and love in the world—not the self-pitying mess Brianda had been these past months. She decided it was time to focus on someone else for a change. She would look after Isolina and the house. They would go for walks and tend the garden. The best way to repay her aunt for how she had looked after her was to stay in Tiles as long as necessary for both of them to find some sort of peace.

After the funeral, the mourners went back to Anels House. So that Isolina would not have to immediately face the new and cruel loneliness, Laura and Petra had prepared food and drink for the rest of the day. And, as it had been years since her last visit to Tiles, Laura kept the conversation in the sitting room flowing, reminiscing and catching up with everyone there.

When she got the chance, Brianda went looking for Neli, who had slipped out of the sitting room. She found her alone in the kitchen, drinking a glass of water while staring out the window.

"You won't believe me, but I've thought about you a lot these past few months."

Neli gave a start and turned around.

"Why wouldn't I believe you?" she asked.

"Because of how I left. Because I haven't called all this time." Brianda hesitated, looking to make sure that nobody was coming. "Neli, I followed your advice. I bought the books you recommended and read them. Not only that. I even had some sessions of regressive hypnosis."

Neli's eyes shone.

"And?"

"I don't know where to start."

"How about the beginning?"

In a low voice, Brianda told her about the first isolated scenes she had visualized, about the longer ones that followed, and about how they all fit together to make up a strange story that seemed far-fetched.

"Far-fetched? What do you mean?" Neli asked.

"I mean, how could I actually be seeing the distant past? It seems crazy."

"And those scenes—did you experience them as real? Not like you were *remembering*, but like you were *reliving*."

"Only some of them." Brianda thought about how she had met Corso and about how she had said good-bye to him beside the river in the monastery in Besalduch, but she did not say a word about it. "The rest seemed more like a dream or a memory from a movie or a book. Why do you ask?"

Neli was silent for a few moments. Then she said, "Your mind may have processed all the information in a symbolic manner, inspired by memories and desires, but we cannot rule out the irrational. Being beyond reason does not mean being impossible. The ancients believed that from the things they saw in dreams and hallucinations it was possible to better know the essence of the soul. Maybe in these visions or reconstructions of the past, or whatever you call them, there was some clue that you can now trace—"

Brianda shook her head. She had honestly tried to believe in all that stuff, but she still suspected her imagination had just been inspired by her obsession with Corso and curiosity about Brianda of Anels. The woman's name and her execution had prompted Brianda to read stacks of books on the sixteenth century. With all that fodder, the encouragement of the hypnotist, and plenty of reason to flee the present anxieties, no wonder her mind had cooked up a good story.

"Let's suppose that there could be a grain of truth, though, OK?" Neli continued. "Think about what you learned from the visions that you didn't know before. For example, the confessional in Besalduch."

"The carpenter who made it carved into the back the symbols of the warring factions. But I could have read that somewhere."

"What about the graves? Did you see anything that would explain fainting like that?"

Brianda shook her head, and Neli's face fell.

"And the documents I found? Executions? Witches?"

"Nothing." Brianda had asked herself the same questions. She had also wondered about the document in the Besalduch archive where a husband requested the exhumation of his wife's body. But she had seen nothing during her hypnosis sessions about any of that.

"Anything else that stands out?"

Brianda squinted her eyes.

"The man who appears as my father in the past, Johan, asks me to keep the name of Lubich alive, which I don't understand. What do I have to do with that place? At the entrance to Lubich, there's a stone with Johan's name carved on it, so I probably got the idea from that."

"Colau's genealogy research could be helpful here."

Neli sighed, and Brianda wondered if Colau would have been willing to share that information with them.

"Any special objects?"

Brianda thought hard.

"A pendant, like a glass-and-silver locket, with dried flowers inside. Edelweiss."

Neli cried out triumphantly.

"Do you know what those flowers symbolize?" She did not wait for Brianda to reply. "They represent honor, the world of dreams, and eternal love that never fades."

"That's very nice, but so what?"

"Edelweiss flowers grow in remote and inaccessible places. Just as it is difficult, but not impossible, to find them, I know that, while it will be hard, you will solve this mystery."

"Of course, because you're a witch!" Brianda chuckled nervously. Neli was the only person in the world who she could talk to about this, and it was a huge relief to finally share what she'd been going through. She would never judge her or treat her as deranged. "Couldn't you be more specific?"

"Each search has its protagonist, and in this case it's you. Think about it. I'm sure you'll come up with something."

"The only thing I can think of is Colau's papers," Brianda murmured. Maybe there she would find some clue that could show her whether her elaborate regressions were grounded in any historical reality.

Laura came in with a tray of canapés, interrupting the conversation. When she left, Brianda finally decided to ask Neli something she had been wondering for hours.

"Nice turnout for the funeral, wasn't it? Although I didn't see Corso—"

She was as casual as possible, but her body gave her away. She felt her cheeks burn and her breath quicken. She prayed Neli would say she'd seen him recently and that he'd asked after her.

"He went to Italy to see his family, but he told Jonas he'll be back soon." Neli looked at her closely. "Esteban couldn't make it?"

"It was so unexpected, he wasn't able to change his work schedule."

"Is everything all right between the two of you?"

Brianda shrugged but did not answer. She had not thought about Esteban since the moment she had arrived in Tiles. Just as Beles Peak loomed over everything here, her desire to see Corso again overshadowed any other feeling in her heart.

25.

The day after the funeral, Laura convinced Isolina that the most pressing task was to sort out Colau's clothes and personal effects, donating whatever they could to charity and throwing away the rest.

"How can you ever move on if you're surrounded by his things?" she asked to her sister. "Cry all you want, but the only way to overcome fear and pain is by confronting it. Like our mother used to say, to know how to live, you have to know how to die."

Many times that day, Brianda wondered where her mother got the energy that she herself obviously hadn't inherited. Laura made them clean from the top to the bottom of her childhood home, cracking jokes about old trinkets she rediscovered, and marveling at how time had stood still. Watching carefully, Brianda saw that her mother's intensity stemmed from a desire to bottle up her own emotions in order to better help her sister. But whenever Isolina left the room, Laura raged against Colau for the visible decline in each corner of Anels.

In the middle of the afternoon, Brianda needed a rest. She felt terrible for not having told Isolina about the ring, but she couldn't find the right moment. Maybe when her parents left. She looked outside. The sky threatened rain and the air was thick. She decided to get some air before the storm came, and there, in the garden, was Luzer. He was still chained, and his water and food bowls were empty, apparently forgotten. On an impulse, Brianda reached a hand toward him. Luzer responded with a guttural growl and showed his teeth, but he did not get up nor try to attack her. Brianda pulled her hand back and retreated a few steps. Then she reached out again, with the same result. She went back to the house and looked for her aunt.

"Why is Luzer tied up?"

"I couldn't separate him from Colau," Isolina answered sadly. "If I let him loose, he would run to the grave and die there."

Brianda asked where his food was kept. She went to the kitchen, filled a bowl with water and another with kibble, went back to the animal, and left the bowls beside him. Luzer remained motionless, but Brianda saw curiosity in his eyes. An animal that missed his master that much couldn't be truly savage, she thought.

"If you do that every day," said her father behind her, "he'll end up liking you."

"I suspect that would take quite a while," she replied, thinking how much the dog's character was like his dead master's.

Daniel smiled.

"I'm finished with the paperwork for his will and the widow's pension, and I thought I'd get started on Colau's office. Isolina has agreed. Will you help me?"

Brianda jumped at the chance. Nevertheless, when she entered that guarded sanctuary, she felt apprehensive. It was difficult to get rid of the fear of being discovered at any moment, as if the door might suddenly open and reveal Colau. And not only that. Now that she was free to root around in his research, she remembered Petra's dismal observation about the body. She wondered if the man's sudden death and his horrified expression had anything to do with what was kept there, maybe something terrible he found out, maybe with the discovery that the ring was missing . . . Her heart raced and she bowed her head. What an absurd idea.

"It would take weeks to do a proper cataloging job in here," grumbled Daniel. "I don't know where to start. If it were up to your mother, she'd put it all in the recycling bin."

"That would be a sacrilege," Brianda responded. "Colau's whole life is here."

"His and many others'." Daniel picked up a pile of folders, sat in the armchair in front of the desk, and read the titles: *"Marriage Capitulations, Testaments, Chapbooks, Statutes of Indictment—"* He stopped, looking puzzled. "Um, this one says *Brianda of Anels.*"

Brianda took it out of his hands and nervously stroked the cover before opening the folder. She couldn't believe she was finally going to learn something about her ancestor.

The first paper clip grouped a copy of the documents Neli had found in the sacristy. Since she already knew about them, Brianda quickly flipped past, then suddenly remembered Colau's resistance to her knowing who had signed the executions. She stifled a yelp: Jayme of Cuyls. Like a lightning bolt, the image of a tall, good-looking man, with abundant brown hair and a cunning smile, appeared in her mind. She sat in an armchair and closed her eyes for an instant. When she saw Johan's cousin again, a shiver went down her spine. Jayme of Cuyls signed the executions. *Wait, Cuyls.* An ancestor of Colau's. Could Colau have been so ashamed that it was one of his ancestors that he'd tried to hide it? That was ridiculous. More than four hundred years had passed.

The notion made her reconsider Colau's strange temperament. Maybe she just couldn't understand because she hadn't grown up in a place like this. In villages, the collective memory was a fearsome thing and secrets were jealously guarded. Once those documents saw the light, dark rumors about the Cuylses would become implacable certainties. Even though centuries had passed.

She turned to the next page, a copy of the fragment of the request by the Master of Anels to exhume his wife's body shortly after the executions. There were some notes scribbled by Colau showing he wondered why. The third page was a copy of a will from Anels. Colau had drawn a big red exclamation mark on the page. The fourth was the beginning of incomplete transcriptions from what looked like a judicial process for the inheritance of Lubich dated at the end of the sixteenth century and discovered in the Barbastro Cathedral Archive years before.

Brianda's eyes shone. She did not know what she would learn from these papers, and she regarded the idea of finding some clue to corroborate her regressions seductive but ludicrous—and terrifying. Still, she couldn't deny that she was deeply curious and profoundly energized. It was the strongest and most positive thing she'd felt in months—other than her desire to see Corso again.

"Look at you," said Daniel. "I didn't know you shared historical interests with Colau."

Brianda smiled. "Historical research is contagious."

She recalled some of the images in her visions: a long-haired girl running in the rain, a man injured in a riverbed, the same girl shouting in the church.

"And what was Colau researching that you find so interesting?" Daniel smiled to see the change in his daughter. How long had it been since he had seen her happy?

Brianda told him about the list of twenty-four executions and that it named a Brianda of Anels.

"Isolina told me that Mom got my name from a dream. Is that true?"

"Well, she told me that when she was young, on stormy nights, she used to hear a voice from Beles Peak repeating the name."

Brianda raised her eyebrows incredulously. "Don't you find that a little hard to believe?"

Daniel shrugged. "She was young. Maybe she imagined it." He got out of the armchair and stretched. "I need to get some air. It makes me sad, thinking how a lifetime of work just ends when we die."

Daniel left and Brianda pressed the folder against her chest. Just as Brianda from the past had felt obligated to keep the name of Lubich alive, she could not leave this place until she knew what had happened to her.

"On this one, there's an exclamation mark in red—"

As she had on every night since her parents had left, Brianda sat in the sitting room and read her aunt fragments from Colau's documents. She was never sure whether Isolina was listening. Her aunt barely spoke, she often cried, and she had lost her appetite. Every day, emulating her mother, Brianda helped Isolina get dressed, brush her hair, and put on her makeup before taking her out to the garden, where Brianda continuously asked what needed to be done. Then she'd ask Isolina to make one of her favorite stews, pretending she wanted to learn the recipe. In the afternoons, they took long walks that always ended at the graveyard, where Isolina murmured to her husband through her tears. After dinner, they'd sit in front of the fire, which Brianda made sure was always stoked. She planned a shopping trip in Aiscle and a visit to Neli's house to get Isolina to socialize.

The previous autumn, Isolina had looked after her, and now it was her turn, even if their circumstances weren't comparable. And in recognizing that difference, Brianda felt forced to confront her fears, or at least to relegate them to a second plane. Esteban hadn't taken her decision well, as if he were jealous of her spending time with Isolina instead of with him, or even suspected Brianda of having ulterior motives. Maybe the moment would arrive when she could or would have to be truthful with him; meanwhile, for the first time in months, she had reason to get up in the morning.

"Let's see what earned an exclamation mark, shall we?"

Brianda began to read out loud. "'*In Dei Nomine*, Amen. Be it stated to all, that I, Nunilo, Master of Anels, being of sound mind and body, sound in memory and in word, revoking and annulling all other testaments, codicils, and other last wills, before now made, constituted, and ordained, hereby make and ordain my last testament, will, ordination, and disposition of all my possessions as well as lands had and to have wherever, in the following form and manner.

"'Firstly, I commend my soul to God Our Lord Creator, to whom I humbly beg, that as He has created it, to place it with His Saints in Glory. Amen.

"'*Item*, I wish, ordain, and command, that if God Our Lord wished me to die, my body be interred in the Church of Our Lady, in the place of Tiles, beside the altar chapel.

"'*Item*, I wish, ordain, and command, that on the day after my interment, my novena begins to be said, which are nine masses with offerings and candles, as is use and custom in said place; that funeral rites be done after my decease, and after a year; and that one hundred masses be said for my soul and that they be paid from my goods and my estate.'

"Looks like this man was serious about leaving his spiritual life in order!" Brianda joked. "He must have been rich to pay for so many masses! I hope there was something left over for his heirs."

She looked at her aunt out of the corner of her eye and was pleased to see a faint smile on her face.

"'*Item*, that all my debts found good and true and that I was obliged to pay be paid, with bills and obligations or without them, be as may, I wish them paid.

"'*Item*, done and paid and carried out all the aforementioned and by my dispositions and ordinations of all other goods and places, names, rights, instances, and actions had and to have, bonds, houses, lands, and estates, and to hereby fulfill the ordained as if by notary, I leave and institute as my heir, in agreement with my wife, Leonor, and as we have not had descendants, he whom here I consider as my son, Corso of Siena—'"

Brianda's jaw dropped. It could not be true. First a Brianda and now a Corso. She looked around to make sure she was in the sitting room of Anels beside her aunt. She was awake. She got up and handed the paper to Isolina.

"Did you hear that?" she asked. "Can you keep reading from the last line? Is there anything else?"

Isolina, more surprised by the strident tone of her niece's voice than by the discovery—just another of the many that Colau had so often shown her—skimmed the last paragraph in silence and then summarized in a weak voice: "He orders that his wife be beneficial owner of all his goods for all the days of her life. It's dated March 27, 1586."

Brianda ran to her room and came back with a pad covered in notes she'd made about wars that had ravaged the county in those years. She stopped at a date.

"Right before his military expedition serving the count," murmured Brianda. "What foresight."

"I didn't know the house had an ancestor called Nunilo. There are so many things I don't know." Isolina's eyes filled with tears. "If only I had listened more to Colau!"

Brianda, nervous, began to pace around the room. Now she understood her uncle's exclamation mark. What were the chances of there being a Brianda and an Italian named Corso in the valley more than four hundred years ago and now again? She ran to Colau's office, rummaged through his books, and found one on the chimneys census done by Count Fernando's father. The same names came up a lot, some even appearing many times, like Johan. She thought she might find another Brianda, an ancestor of the one executed, but she was sure there would be no other Corso.

She returned to the sitting room and sat down beside the fire. Nunilo had left Anels to a Corso of Siena. Another inexplicable connection, like her mother hearing the name Brianda in the wind. Suddenly, she realized the full implication of this, the rest of the reason for her uncle's red pen. Today, there was a Brianda at Anels and a Corso at Lubich—the opposite of the old papers and what she'd seen in her regressions. What the hell had happened?

"I know that expression, Brianda. What's the matter?"

"Nothing. Well, actually, I'm confused about some of Colau's notes."

"When he got deep into his research, he used to forget about time, food, distractions, even me." Isolina sighed. "I never knew anyone as stubborn as him. He wouldn't give up until he found the answers he was looking for. I think the executions had him so frustrated he couldn't even talk about it. It's nice that you want to continue his work. Can I help with anything?"

"I don't know. The whole business about the witches freaks me out."

Isolina gave her a puzzled look and opened her mouth to say something but stopped. She remained in thought for a few minutes, then said, in a flat voice, "The afternoon before he died, I peeked into his office and saw Colau sitting at his desk. He seemed so dejected that I went over to him. In his hands, he had a small box the color of blood that I'd never seen before. He placed a small folded paper in it, closed it, and put it in a drawer."

Brianda clasped her hands tightly in her lap. So, Colau had discovered that the ring was missing, and Isolina did not know it existed.

"Then," Isolina continued, "he put his arms around my waist and rested his head on my stomach. He stayed there a long time, in silence, while I ran my hands through his hair. I don't know how to explain it to you, but I think he was saying good-bye." Her chin began to tremble and she clenched her jaw. "You know I am a woman of faith, Brianda, but I find it difficult to accept my husband's death. I don't know if I can go on without him."

Brianda rushed over, took her aunt's hand, and stroked it in heartbroken silence. She wanted to help her, but didn't know what more to do. She could not understand the sort of grief that could make a person say those words. She thought of her anxiety attacks, how they could make her feel like she was dying. Isolina's words expressed a feeling diametrically opposed to the testament they had just read. What was to be feared more: one's own death or the suffering over the loss of one's beloved? Colau had died after finding out that the ring was missing. The ludicrous idea that she was responsible for Isolina's anguish rose up again, stronger this time.

Isolina went to bed, and Brianda didn't waste a second before running back to the office. She sat in front of the desk, put her hand into the first drawer, and immediately found the box. She opened it and took out the paper, which looked extremely old, and unfolded it. Some bits were missing, the words that coincided with the folds were erased, and the handwriting was strange, but with the help of a magnifying glass, she finally managed to decipher some phrases.

She did not understand their meaning, but when she read them out loud, the words came out of her throat like a long-guarded lament: "Until the day of your complete extinction . . . Your house will burn and will vanish into hell . . . And the last will know . . . that it was me . . ."

26.

"It looks like a curse," said Neli, handing back the scrap of paper. "Where did you find it?"

They were in Neli's kitchen making tea.

"Tidying up in Colau's office."

Brianda had not talked to Neli about the ring. She doubted that she'd be able to talk to anyone about it. Her life was filling up with secrets. First her infidelity with Corso, and then stealing the ring. She was plagued by guilt, but there was an air of inevitability to all of it.

Neli frowned.

"Why the face?" Brianda asked. "They're just words."

"One person's soul can affect another person's body and mind. Evil begets evil." Neli pointed to the paper. "The soul of the person who wrote this was filled with hate. The person cursed could only hope for misfortune."

"That's ridiculous." Nervous, Brianda began to set out the delicate porcelain cups with floral motifs and their saucers on the tray Neli had prepared. "Incantations, spells, curses. Who believes in that stuff anymore?"

She belatedly remembered the little pouches of good luck that Neli had prepared for her.

"Anyone who believes in the power of desire," murmured Neli. "Do not underestimate its strength." She filled the teapot with hot water, asked Brianda to carry the tray, and walked toward the sitting room, where Isolina and Mihaela were talking. "I'm so happy you all came. With so much rain, the days seem very long."

It had not stopped raining since Colau's funeral three weeks ago. The days dawned leaden and stayed that way until evening fell over the soaked fields. The seeds sown in the garden ran the risk of rotting, and the planted flowers remained huddled, waiting for the heat of the sun's rays that would make them stretch their stems.

Brianda tried to resign herself to the gloom, hoping that one day soon, something would jolt her from this monotony. Corso would come back. Or a clue would magically appear and shed light on her uncle's documents. In the meantime, the only thing to do was wait, like Persephone, until her annual period in the depths of the cold and gray underworld ended and she returned to the earth, bringing the greening of the fields, the flowering of the crops, and the fluttering of butterflies.

Since Isolina and Mihaela weren't very chatty, Brianda thought she should help Neli liven up the conversation.

"How's the restoration of the altarpiece going?" she asked. She'd seen the scaffolding on her frequent visits to the church with Isolina to pray for Colau.

"It's slow work, which means it'll take me months to finish," Neli replied. "I hope it will turn out so perfectly it doesn't add any more fuel to the madness."

Brianda was puzzled. Had the locals found out about Neli's religious beliefs? Conscious of the presence of Isolina and Mihaela, she formulated a cautious question. "Has something happened?"

"Haven't you told her?" Neli addressed Isolina.

"The truth is, I haven't felt up to anything," she answered.

"Mihaela, what aren't they telling me?" Brianda asked with an exaggerated look of intrigue.

The young woman nodded her head slightly. "Better let Neli explain it."

Neli clicked her tongue before starting, putting on an ironic, faux-cheerful voice. "Well! It turns out that there is enormous potential here that we must all exploit so as not to miss the boat!"

"Ah, is that so?" Brianda raised a cup of tea to her lips. "And what is it?"

"Witches."

"What witches?" she cried, sloshing tea on the linen tablecloth.

Neli winked at her.

"For the moment, ones in the past."

"I don't understand."

"The whole valley knows about the papers Neli found," Isolina explained. "They have become a favorite topic at the bar."

"It's all anyone will talk about," continued Neli testily. "All our so-called experts in history, anthropology, and sociology came up with a hypothesis they've now taken for reality: the Inquisition was here and twenty-four women were executed for being witches."

"But we don't know if that's what happened," Brianda objected. "The documents aren't conclusive."

"For that very reason, they can invent whatever they want!" responded Neli. "The town can build a theme park, with key rings, T-shirts, even a torture chamber—"

"Calm down, Neli." Isolina shook her head. "You are taking this matter far too personally."

Neli ignored her.

"Apparently, everyone suddenly recalls ancestors who heard wails from Beles Peak on stormy nights and sad songs in the howling wind; or who knew from the bleating of the goats when a witch was approaching; or who were terrorized by the movement of the bushes when no wind was blowing; or who felt the breath of wandering spirits asking for masses for the repose of their souls the night of All Saints . . . Somehow, this discovery gives meaning to all their inherited superstitions, mixing everything together. It's not just that they were afraid of witches here, rather that there actually *were* witches, so they think that explains why, up until recently, stone figures were put up on the chimney stacks to scare witches away, or why jarfuls of holy water were thrown in the fireplace, or why a cross was drawn in the ashes—"

"The woman from Darquas makes a cross every day on her bread before cutting it," commented Mihaela.

"They think this explains why their grandmothers nailed wolfs' and goats' feet, eagle claws and dried thistle blooms, on their doors," continued Neli, "and why they were raised setting down scissors and tongs in the shape of a cross, and throwing salt on the fire, and filling their homes with vases full of boxwood, rosemary, and olive—"

"I put out vases like that every Easter Sunday after mass," Isolina objected. "Everything you're describing is simply tradition in lots of places. It's you mixing everything together, Neli. This is really about your attitude toward the proposal put before the village meeting."

Neli turned to Brianda to explain. "I objected to Tiles being turned into a shoddy Halloween theme park for tourists, and they looked at me like I was mad. You should have been there, Brianda! They want to make maps to the circles in some of the fields where wild mushrooms grow and say the witches danced there. And put on a mock trial that ends with the accused being burned at the stake." She snorted. "And how typical that the accused were all women! I'm sure they'll say they were flying on broomsticks, killing children, and fornicating with the devil. Superstitious bullshit and historical revisionism that has nothing to do with witchcraft. Just clichés about cauldrons full of boiling toads, black cats, hooked noses, and pointy hats."

"Seriously, Neli, I think you're overstating it," said Isolina. "For a long time now, people have understood that witch hunts were really about political disagreements, and that those poor women were just scapegoats."

"For that very reason, Isolina, we cannot accept the predictable script for purely economic reasons and ignore the reality."

"And what is the reality, Neli?" Brianda now asked, looking her friend directly in the eye. Neli had asked her to believe in past-life regressions and to look for clues in her visions. Compared to that, what was a silly list of superstitions? Brianda's own mother had heard the wind whisper her name!

"The reality is that now half the village won't talk to me. Next thing you know, they'll be calling me a *witch*."

"It can't be that bad," Brianda said.

"Ask Mihaela." She turned to her. "What did your friend Zacarias say to you the other day?"

Mihaela went red. "That outsiders should not have a say in village matters," she answered.

"There you have it! My children were born here, but I'm still an outsider."

"I certainly am!" added Mihaela with irony. "When I tried to defend Neli, he told me that no one would know Romania existed if it weren't for Dracula."

Brianda turned to Isolina. "What did Colau think about the executions?"

She wondered if the neighbors had found out about Jayme of Cuyls signing the orders for them. It sounded like they had not.

Isolina took some time to answer. "The folklore part meant nothing to him," she said finally. "He was interested in the dates, historic details, and reasons behind the events."

Like me, thought Brianda.

Neli stood up and began collecting the teacups. Brianda followed her to the kitchen.

"I understand how you feel, Neli, but I also agree with Isolina that maybe your reaction was a bit over the top. Is it really so bad if they use the town's history to make money? If it helps bring more people here and this sleepy valley wakes up a bit—"

For the first time since she had met her, Brianda saw fury in Neli's dark eyes.

"Brianda, don't. Do you know actually what should be done to take advantage of the discovery and use it as a model of historic justice?"

She searched for a pen and paper and wrote down a name.

"Anna Göldi," Brianda read. "Who is she?"

"Was. It's a long story, and I don't want to be rude and leave Isolina and Mihaela alone. Look it up on the Internet, and you'll understand."

When she got back to Anels House, Brianda went to Colau's study, which had become her workspace, and found website pages that gave her some background.

Anna Göldi was known as the last witch in Switzerland. She was executed in June 1782, at the age of forty-eight, in the small Swiss canton of Glarus. A museum there was dedicated to her memory. For the last seventeen years of her life, she worked as a servant for Johann Jakob Tschudi, a physician who had political ambitions. He had accused her of having supernatural powers and of putting needles in his daughter's food. In 1782, she was arrested and tortured. She admitted to a list of crimes typical of witch trials, including entering into a pact with the devil, who had appeared to her in the shape of a black dog. She retracted her confession, but was tortured again and sentenced to death by beheading. Officially, she was accused of poisoning instead of witchcraft, although the law at that time did not impose a death sentence for attempted poisoning, and the daughter of the physician had not died. During the trial, allegations of witchcraft were avoided and, later, the judicial record was destroyed.

Brianda was not surprised by what she learned. Like so many others, Göldi had really been killed because she posed a threat to a powerful man. Apparently, Tschudi had had an affair with Göldi and then fired her. When she had threatened to reveal the matter, he had denounced her as a witch.

She continued to read until she understood Neli's point. In 2007, the Swiss parliament had declared that the execution had been a miscarriage of justice. The representative of Glarus asked for a formal pardon for her, which was granted in August 2008 with the argument that she had been the victim of an illegal trial. One of the articles described Glarus as strained by that "regression" to the past. Opinion was divided between those who wanted the stain on their history erased and those who denied responsibility for something that had happened so long ago. Finally, though, Anna Göldi was exonerated.

She heard pawing at the door and got up to open it. Luzer came in and waited for her to sit before lying down close by. After several days bringing him food and water, Brianda had decided to release him. At the beginning, he did not move from the barn, but bit by bit, he began to show interest in his surroundings until one afternoon he followed her on a walk. Since then, it seemed clear he had accepted her as his new mistress.

"I really misjudged you, didn't I, Luzer?" Brianda murmured, rubbing his back.

That night, like an intangible bridge between the material and the psychic world, the conversation with Neli and the pages about the Swiss woman stayed in bed with her until her senses gave way to sleep.

Brianda dreamt that her teenage hands held a quill that she dipped in ink and then slid along scraps of parchment beside the window in a room with bare stone walls and animal skins on the floor. On the rough paper, she poured out her desolation for the loss of Johan and Corso and her rage at new circumstances that were going to prevent her from keeping the name of Lubich alive. Like a long lament, the text flowed along the pages in the same pitiful, distraught, whiny tone. A sudden gust of swirling wind invaded her room, shuffling the pages before letting them fall softly to the floor like leaves falling from trees. Brianda gathered them up and began writing again. As if stuck in a loop, the scene tediously repeated itself waiting for a variation that never came.

It never came, but it *had* to come.

The following morning was Sunday. While she had breakfast with her aunt, Brianda thought about her dream and wondered what it meant. Isolina asked her to come to mass, and she agreed, but she asked that they leave a little early so she could talk to Neli.

Brianda drove Colau's car to the square in the lower part of Tiles. While Isolina went ahead to the church, Brianda knocked at the door of Neli's house. Jonas led her to the garden, where Neli was planting flowers with her children, taking advantage of the break in the rain.

"I read about Anna Göldi last night."

Neli took her arm and pulled her a few paces from the children.

"I suppose," continued Brianda, "that you plan to get pardons for the women. And, obviously, other folks in town will object."

"What about you?" Neli asked her. "Will you support my petitions?"

"Listen, I understand why they're anxious for any opportunity to boost the local economy."

Neli looked at her angrily. "One of your ancestors was murdered, and you don't even care!"

"It happened so long ago, I just can't imagine—"

Then she remembered Colau's need to hide the truth about Jayme of Cuyls. For him, it didn't matter that more than four hundred years had passed. Maybe it was the origin of his family's bad reputation. He had lived all his life with a permanent blot on his name. She remembered the curse that Neli had told her about: wherever a Cuyls goes, life ends.

As if she were reading Brianda's mind, Neli asked, "How will you feel when you see witch souvenirs with the name Brianda on them? You'll be Brianda the witch."

Brianda shrugged. "I don't live here."

"Right, of course, you think you can run back to Madrid and forget everything." Neli's tone turned bitter. "That's not possible now. You know it as well as I do."

"What the hell do you want me to do?"

"Come on! If there's anyone who can do something for those women, it's you. Those dreams and visions are real; it's undeniable. How else could you know all the things you do? Look inside yourself. You have to pursue this, investigate until you find the truth about what happened."

Neli went back to her gardening as the bells began to toll for mass. Brianda left through the garden gate and walked, pensively, toward the church.

Inside, she sat beside Isolina next to the chapel to the Virgin of Tiles. She could not pay attention to the mass because she kept thinking about Neli's words and remembering the portrait of Anna Göldi she'd seen online. It showed a woman with delicate features, sad brown eyes, dark hair, and rosy skin. Murdered by church and state because a powerful man wanted her out of his way. How terrible. She shivered, imagining the woman being hung by her thumbs with rocks tied to her feet. Brianda wondered how quickly she herself would confess to whatever they wanted if she were tortured. What would it feel like to kneel in the village square before they cut off her head with a sword? What would be her last thought? She tried to compare Anna's story to Brianda's. Anna was a servant who supposedly had an affair with her master. Brianda was the heir to a vast estate. Anna was illiterate.

She shivered again.

In the previous night's dream, the young Brianda wrote and wrote. If only she could read that lament! How frustrating it was to perceive an idea as true with no physical proof, and that so much information was available about Anna Göldi's case but none about what had happened in Tiles. After the executions, the members of the council had recorded a list of names and little else. Did they care so little about the deaths of so many? Or had shame and remorse left them speechless? *There are episodes in history that must not stay buried*, she thought, finally understanding Neli's anger.

She paused and glanced around the church. The same people occupied the same seats as always. The priest stood in front of the altarpiece Neli was restoring. The saints were in the chapels. The mute Virgin of Tiles had her tiny key hanging around her neck.

Brianda rested her hand on the back of the pew in front of her and examined a small slot in the wood with the tip of her index finger. Her finger fit perfectly in the small gap, which she stroked until her heart gave a start.

When had she done that very thing before?

Where had she done it?

Her breathing quickened, but instead of feeling afraid of the possibility of another vision, like the one she had suffered in that same church, she knew immediately what she had to do and where she had to go.

And she understood her dream.

As happens to the land in winter, the deepest weariness had covered her just before the blossoming of spring. Winter had taken over her mood for months, but now she felt herself crossing an invisible line that separated depression from revelation. She only had to keep her balance and not fall into the void, and any step that she took from then on, no matter how small, would lead her forward.

27.

"Do you recognize this?" Brianda opened the palm of her hand and showed Neli an old key the size of a child's thumb.

Neli nodded.

"Of course, I cleaned the rust off myself. Why did you take it?"

"Umm." Brianda smiled nervously. "I know where its lock is and I need your help?"

"This minute? I mean—" The nervous smile was contagious. "You know I want to help! But where are we going to go at nine o'clock at night?"

"To Lubich."

Neli closed the door that connected the kitchen to the sitting room, where Jonas and the children were watching television, and lowered her voice.

"Corso isn't back yet."

"Exactly. He can't find out about this, not now. I know exactly, well, I think I know exactly what I'm looking for. Is Jonas still working there?"

"Yes, and he has the keys if that's what you're asking."

Brianda sighed in relief.

"So, will you come with me? If I don't go now, I won't sleep a wink tonight, but I'm afraid to go on my own."

"Did you bring a flashlight?" Neli asked, and they grinned at each other.

Neli told Jonas that Brianda was taking her for a quick drink in the bar. She grabbed the keys to Lubich and a thick jacket and got into the car.

"I can't believe we're going to do this," Neli said when they took the fork toward Lubich, rubbing her forearms more out of nerves than cold. "Now I'm the one experiencing a regression—to my youth! Could you slow down?"

"Sorry." Brianda took her foot off the accelerator of Colau's car. "I'm just impatient. You asked me to look inside myself and, I don't know, there it was! But I'll tell you one thing: if my intuition is wrong, I'm done with all of this."

"It would be a pity," murmured Neli, "because since I met you, I've never seen you so alive." She kept quiet for a while before adding, "I'm sorry I got annoyed this morning, but all this is important to me."

Brianda nodded. "To me as well."

She stopped the car at the bottom of the gated drive and waited for Neli to find the key on the heavy bunch using the beam from the headlights.

"I should leave it open, right?" Neli asked when she got back in the car.

"Yeah. We won't be long."

How strange it was to come back to Lubich! Brianda remembered the first time she had dared cross these woods. It was a beautiful day, not a cloud or a shadow over the unfurled autumnal colors. She had been in awe on entering: the high stone wall, the wrought-iron railing, the moss on the rocks, the big patios, and the sober buildings. And after giving herself to Corso in the tower, she had left shocked by her passion and by the appearance of his wife, and worried about having betrayed

Esteban. How many times, in the solitude of her apartment in Madrid, she had remembered Corso's rough hands on her skin, the weight of his body against hers, his dark hair falling over her face. And how much she had missed him. They had been together only once, and the memory still burned as if she were branded by it.

They drove along the gravel path to the clearing in which the contour of Lubich rose in the middle of the mist. Instinctively, they shared a nervous glance. Brianda stopped the car in front of the main entrance, but did not turn off the headlights until they'd opened one of the gates. Then they used their flashlights.

In the silent night, their footsteps reverberated like gongs. Occasionally, there was also a faint noise like a clicking or a crunch. Brianda kept her eyes glued to the ground. The farther they went into the main patio, the tighter the knot in her stomach grew. She remembered a vision where Johan anxiously watched his daughter hanging from the top of the tower. She remembered the desolation in his gaze when they said good-bye, before she bumped against the stone walls of the narrow stairs coming down from the tower, before Johan's body crashed against the rocks.

She grabbed Neli's arm.

"What are you scared of?" Neli asked her. "Chain-dragging ghosts? Invisible and mischievous imps?"

Brianda did not answer, and Neli took it as a sign of assent.

"Fear is psychological. I'll show you." She turned off her flashlight and asked Brianda to do the same. "If you are open to suggestion, in that climbing vine you'll see a man's shadow. Can't you see his legs half-open to balance the shot from his arquebus?" She pointed to the carved eave of the main house. "And what about the shapes of those pipes? Don't they look like grotesque and deformed gargoyles about to jump on top of you?" She paused and lowered her voice. "And those planters at either side of the main door? They're just flowers, but they look like the teeth of the devil—" She suddenly went quiet. "Did you hear that? Is it Corso's horse in the stable or the stamping and bleating of a demonic billy goat?"

Brianda punched Neli in the arm.

"That's enough!" She didn't want to be afraid of Lubich. She wanted it to be the happy setting for her dreams of Corso.

"Suggestion is terrible, Brianda. Because of it, thousands of people have died. Imagine four hundred years ago, with no electricity. The devil was present in every shadow. As a child, did you ever see faces in the cracks on the ceiling? And always monsters, never cute boys, which shows the mind's natural inclination toward the morbid."

As if wanting to absorb its positive energy, Brianda gently placed her hands on the wooden door under the lintel where the name of Johan of Lubich was carved and the date, 1322. She remembered Corso saying he'd found the stone and placed it there, and she wondered who had removed it, when and why.

While Neli looked for the right key, Brianda closed her eyes and pictured what they would find inside. The enormous hall, the impressive staircase, the heavy doors, the excessive decoration, the small office. Her breathing quickened. She was so close to finding something.

"Hurry up!" she pleaded.

Neli finally opened the door, and, without hesitating, Brianda led her straight to their destination.

"I see that Corso made sure you knew your way around." Neli laughed. "Can you believe I've never been in here? I'd love to poke around a bit. What if we turn on a light?" She answered herself: "Better not. Someone could see it, and I don't know how we'd explain this. I have to admit, I'm afraid of getting caught."

Brianda hastened her step, not out of fear but because of the anxious knowledge that she was so close to her goal. She opened the door that led to the office where she had felt unwell, just before Corso suggested showing her the tower. She slid the beam from the flashlight around the room, left her bag and the car keys on a table in the middle of the room, and focused on the small chest on the carved-leg table that was at the back wall.

"Neli, I bet that there's a tiny carving of a boxwood sprig inside the lid."

Brianda opened it and pointed the light at the mark.

"Like on the confessional in Besalduch!" said Neli.

"It was made by the same carpenter."

Brianda slid her fingers along the minuscule pieces of bone and boxwood that decorated the drawers before stopping at the door guarded by small columns. Her hand shook opening it, and she had to take a deep breath before stroking the interior of the compartment, looking for the notch that, she was now certain, was a tiny lock.

"Here it is!" she murmured.

She took the Virgin's key from her pocket and, as carefully as she could, slipped it into the slot. It fit perfectly. She turned it to the left and heard a dead click, as if the wood was opening. She turned it to the right and the interior walls of the compartment folded to one side, as if joined by invisible hinges.

"The flashlight, Neli!"

Brianda felt the urge to cry as she took the folded sheets of paper from their secret vault. They had hidden there for centuries. Her brain refused to consider any other possibility. Another key could not exist. Nobody had read these before. Not even Corso. She was the one who had brought them to light.

As if they were the most fragile of treasures, she placed the papers on the table by her bag. Beside her, Neli held her breath, hanging back so Brianda could be the first to read them. She let several long minutes pass in silence.

"Any idea what they are?"

Brianda sighed. "It's difficult to make out the handwriting. All of Colau's documents are transcribed. With this, I can only get the odd word. We should go home and try there."

"Let me look," said Neli. "I'm used to old handwriting. A quick look and we'll go."

She took a page and pointed the flashlight at the beginning, accompanying the beam's journey with murmurs. Then she flicked through various pages, took another sheet, and repeated the action.

"Neli!" Brianda squealed, unable to wait any longer.

Her friend shook her head.

"It's not easy. They're separate notes written by the same person. I think it's something like a diary—"

Brianda shouted out in triumph. A diary! She was going to ask Neli if she could make out a name or date when the door suddenly opened, bright lights came on, and a man shouted, "What the hell?"

Brianda closed her eyes and shrank.

She had spent so long wishing to see Corso again.

And now, under the circumstances, she felt incapable of even looking at him.

28.

None of the three said a word.

Brianda fixed her eyes on Corso's leather boots, which were stationary in the doorway. Although she could not see his face, she felt him staring at her, stunned and angry. She slightly raised her gaze to the waist of his jeans and then up to his chest. As her eyes traveled up that body that she had missed so much, her shame increased. She did not dare look him in the eye.

She tried to find an excuse but couldn't think of any. In any case, not even the tangible proof that her premonition was correct could justify breaking in. Why didn't he say something? Why didn't he yell? He had all the reason in the world to do so. She remembered the last time she'd seen him, on horseback with the rain lashing against his face. She had imagined hundreds of reunions; in all of them, their eyes met, their hearts beat wildly, and they hurried into a long, warm, and silent embrace before wiping away the long separation with caresses. But reality could not be more different. She fought back her tears, not wanting to look even more stupid and infantile, and cursed her luck. Now Corso would forever remain a fantasy.

She looked at Neli, murmured, "I'm sorry," and fled. She needed to get away, not only because of cowardice or shame, as the others would probably think, but also to escape the gripping anguish in her chest. She ran by Corso, making sure not to touch him, crossed the hall, ran out to the patio, turned left, and headed toward the back of the tower. She flew down the narrow path in the dark, as if her feet had walked those rocks thousands of times and her hands had gripped those very walls.

When she heard a pebble tumbling downward, she stopped short. A hollowness in her stomach told her she stood at the edge of a precipice.

Inside the house, Neli saw that she'd have to manage the embarrassing situation on her own. Brianda's reaction had been excessive, but she could imagine the mixture of shame, frustration, and fear that she had let Corso down.

"We weren't expecting you—" she began. Depending on how Corso responded, she would give him more or less information.

"I'm so very sorry to have spoiled your plans," he replied. "You break into my house in the dark, my private writing desk is open, you are hiding something behind your back, and Brianda has fled. It's hard for me to imagine you as robbers, but you are rooting through my things without permission."

"Before you jump to the wrong conclusion," said Neli calmly, "let me explain. Following the clues we found in some old documents, we were led here to this piece of furniture."

"Clues, huh? Is this some sort of live-action role-play thing?" Corso moved closer and maintained his sarcastic tone.

Neli took a step back, intimidated by his size and the horrible scar she still wasn't used to. She thought about Brianda's regressions where she relived the life of a young girl in the sixteenth century. It wasn't a bad comparison.

"Yes. It's like a role-playing game."

"And what's Brianda's role?"

Neli smiled, realizing the only thing that interested him was Brianda.

"I'd rather she told you."

"So, did you find what you were looking for?"

"We're not sure."

"Do you mean I interrupted you?"

"More or less."

"Who planned this game for you?"

"We still don't know."

Corso laughed loudly, and Neli knew that he didn't believe a word of what she was telling him. However, for whatever reason, Corso seemed content to let the lie stand.

"Your husband's the only one with keys to this house, so it must be him, unless he gives them out all over the place—"

Neli got serious.

"I give you my word that Jonas guards Lubich very well. I stole the keys without him knowing. Please, don't say anything to him." She smiled briefly. "He thinks we're at the bar."

"I won't say a word," Corso assured her. "But are you going to tell me what those papers you're hiding behind your back are?"

"The instructions on how to continue," improvised Neli.

"Fine." Corso raised his hands in mock defeat. "I don't want you to reveal any secret that prevents your team from winning. But tell me one thing: Was Brianda acting when she ran out looking as if she had seen the devil incarnate?"

Neli thought for a few seconds.

"Go after her," Neli said. "Maybe I'm sticking my nose where I shouldn't, but with you she is incapable of acting. With you, she is always the real Brianda."

❖ ❖ ❖

The outside lights came on and Brianda heard Corso calling her from afar, but she did not answer. His voice grew louder and more insistent as he came down the narrow path at the base of the tower.

"You're always leaving me without saying good-bye," said Corso when he made out Brianda's outline in the darkness. He watched her for a few moments in silence.

Brianda felt his eyes running over her body, as if assessing her after so many months. She turned at last and looked at him, aware that her eyes betrayed that she'd been sobbing.

"I'm so very sorry about this. I can't imagine what you thought. We shouldn't have come. It was my idea." She spoke without pausing, with her jaws clenched to control the shaking in her voice.

Corso took his time before answering.

"I still don't know what to think. If you wanted to see the house again, all you had to do was ask—"

Brianda flushed. She didn't know if it was a real invitation or an allusion to their encounter in the tower.

"Neli said something about a role-playing game, but she didn't want to tell me what your role was."

Brianda arched an eyebrow. Corso's tone was no longer sarcastic, though maybe a little skeptical. She was grateful for Neli's quick thinking. It would allow her to avoid lying without having to tell the whole truth.

She straightened up and said, "I am a young woman from the end of the sixteenth century. My father has just been murdered by the enemies of the local count in revenge for the death of a rebel leader." She paused. "Now I am the master of Lubich."

Corso leaned over her.

"I like that you want to imagine yourself as the owner of this place," he whispered. "And tell me, if I wanted to play, what would my character be?"

"The foreign soldier that in the end becomes the master of Anels."

Brianda held her breath. If Corso came any closer, she would throw herself into his arms.

Corso smiled astutely.

"Interesting. And what is the reason behind this property swap? Who wrote this story?"

"I don't know yet."

"Right." Corso's tone changed. "Seriously now, you sneak into my house and you can't even tell me why?"

"I will, just not yet," Brianda insisted. "We found some papers in the writing desk that I need to look at first."

Corso frowned.

"The papers Neli was trying to hide? All the drawers in that desk are empty."

"Not all of them."

"And why are they so important to you?"

"Can I tell you once I've read them?"

Brianda wanted desperately to tell him the truth, but she didn't dare, not yet. Corso squinted his eyes.

"Very well," he agreed. "But first you have to ask me for them. What will you do to get them?"

"Anything you want!" she replied impulsively. Not for an instant had she imagined she might have to relinquish the papers.

Corso's eyes shone.

"Then I'm asking you for tonight."

Brianda blinked several times while trying to control her breathing. It could only mean he had returned alone. From the moment she had seen him in the doorway, she'd felt that, at the slightest invitation, she would let everything go, forget her conscience. She would forget Esteban and the fact that Corso was married. Yet, now that he'd spoken the words, she was filled with fear that it would be a huge mistake.

"I'll stay for a while . . . ," she said cautiously.

Corso took her hand in his, playing with her fingers, before whispering, "Good enough."

Brianda savored that moment of peace at the edge of the chasm. She had missed him so much. She did not know how this story would end, if there was any possibility of it continuing beyond tonight, or if she would ever be able to confess the whole truth about her strange visions, or if he would believe her. They barely knew each other! And he was married. It was one thing to desire someone, idealize him, and a very different one to face material reality. She did not know whether his marriage was happy. And she was still with Esteban. Maybe this was just an outlet for them in a moment of crisis. No. For her, their connection went beyond all reason. All she wanted was for Corso to remain by her side forever, taking her as she was, supporting her in her search, no matter where it led.

"I'd really appreciate it if you didn't pressure me to tell you about the papers yet," she told him. "I hope it's not too weird."

Corso squeezed her hand.

"I can't deny that you have me intrigued," he said. "But what I find really incredible is that you ran all the way out here without killing yourself. Let's get you back to the house safe. Everything else can wait."

A note on the table told her that Neli had taken the car. Brianda was grateful for her friend's intuition and discretion.

"The papers aren't here," said Corso. "Why did Neli take them?"

"She has to transcribe them for me."

Corso looked curious, but he didn't ask any more questions. He told her he was going to get a bottle of wine and left her alone for a few minutes. Brianda used the time to try and close the secret compartment of the desk. She manipulated the sides of the small compartment and repeatedly attempted to remove the key, but she failed.

"Be careful," Corso warned her from the door. "It's a fragile piece.

He put down the glasses and the bottle on a small table beside a dark red sofa and came over.

"I wanted to leave it like it was before, but I can't," explained Brianda.

Corso ran his hands along the inside of the desk. He frowned.

"I had no idea there was a secret compartment. How did you open it?"

"With this key—" Brianda guided his hand—"that doesn't want to come out."

"But where'd the key come from?"

Brianda blushed and decided to tell him the truth.

"Remember the day you showed me the house?"

Corso nodded.

"I felt a small slot inside the desk,'" she continued, "like a keyhole. The other day in the church, I noticed the key hanging around the Virgin's neck and thought it might fit. I suppose these old locks open with almost anything—"

"Maybe," Corso said. "And you found the documents . . ." Perplexed, he shook his head. "Who could have put them there?"

Brianda shrugged. What if it had been her, four centuries ago?

Corso leaned down and fiddled with the interior walls of the compartment, but they refused to return to their original position. He slid his hand along the edges.

"It seems like there's something stuck inside." He pulled and there was a faint metallic sound. "I think it's a chain." He picked up a letter opener and used it as a lever. "It's coming out!" The object lazily dragged over the wood before Corso gathered it up and announced, "It looks like a pendant."

Brianda's head swam. Corso opened his hand and there it was, the delicate glass encased in tarnished silver.

"A locket." Corso held it close to his eyes to study it. "It's beautiful, and very old. Its owner had exquisite taste! But I don't see any holy image inside. Actually, it looks like—"

"Edelweiss," mumbled Brianda.

Corso gaped at her. "How did you know?"

She did not answer. She raised her hand and tenderly took the pendant. In silent delight, she contemplated its strange and calming beauty, locked away in darkness for centuries. She closed her eyes and saw a young girl getting dressed in petticoats and a jerkin, braiding her long hair and putting on some earrings before hanging the locket around her neck.

Corso observed her. Her expression was one of calm, of contained bliss and satisfaction. He took the locket, extended the silver chain, and put it over Brianda's head.

"It's like it was made for you," he said slowly.

Brianda caressed his cheek. For the first time in a long time, she did not feel tears behind her eyes or any tightening in her chest. On the contrary, her gaze was firm and clear, her breathing calm, and her sense of self serene. She knew she would not spend that night with him, and probably not any night soon, but every moment would be for him. Now that she had found the locket, she could open up time as far as her mind and her heart wanted to take her. An undefined sensation of certainty overcame her.

"I have to go. There is something I must do."

Nothing could be more important than being with him. Yet, something told her that if they had waited so long to meet again, they could wait a little longer. Come what may, Brianda knew that Corso was the love of her life. She would live with that love for the rest of her life.

Corso understood that her mind was made up. He nodded and said, "I'll saddle Santo."

Honor. The world of dreams. Eternal love that never fades . . . the edelweiss flowers in her locket.

Brianda's hand gripped her locket as she read, with Luzer at her feet, the transcribed pages Neli brought every afternoon.

In the heat of the same sun that had ripened the fields of wheat, rye, barley, and oats for centuries, Brianda questioned her perception of time. When had her real life begun? Almost thirty-eight years ago? Perhaps the previous summer, when the first nightmares had guided her to Tiles? The watch on her wrist marked the length of all the events of her past, the changing seasons and years, her birthday on the first of May. Her heart's clock, however, whispered to her of perpetuity without beginning, middle, or end—as if her life were interminable, as if she would expand over the centuries and ages, as if she would endure beyond death.

Eternal and perpetual . . .

How many souls would sell themselves to the devil in exchange for those two words? she wondered when she had finished reading all the papers. It had been a week since she had found them.

Perhaps Isolina would have done it for just one more afternoon with Colau.

And what would she herself not do for immortality if what she'd read had really happened to her?

She didn't yet know everything; the diary ended abruptly, leaving new questions in its wake. Still, it was clear to Brianda that she would do the same as the young woman who had left brushstrokes of her fears, her doubts, her hates, and her desires on those pages.

She would think of the precise words and would utter them with the absolute conviction that, beyond the limits of reason and understanding, she would delve into the minds of others, unsettle hearts, take over healthy bodies and abandon them decomposed in an eternal recurrence, in an incessant repetition, until finally finding the one to whom she would announce, "I am returning to your skin."

29.

1587

"It's been many months, Brianda. Time to move forward."

Marquo stopped pacing the great hall of Lubich and sat in a chair beside her, opposite the stone fireplace where an enormous log burned. He stretched his hands toward the fire. The new year had started with the same winter fury that for weeks had enveloped Tiles in a persistent squall of wind and snow.

"I respect that you are grieving," he continued, "but I must insist on some confirmation of your intentions. If things were different, you and I would already be married."

Brianda righted herself in the chair without taking her eyes off the flames.

"If they were alive . . ."

Although nobody knew, "they" referred not only to her father and Nunilo but also to Corso. She had promised to wait for him, but then that letter came saying he'd been killed fighting the Moors. Each time she pictured his face, an unbearable pain gripped her heart. For months, she had refused to admit he was dead. She often dreamt of him reappearing suddenly, but each new day confirmed the absurdity of her hopes.

"It's all the count's fault. And where is he now? Their deaths were for naught."

"Don't go over it all again," said Marquo.

He knew Brianda was right. If his father or Brianda's were still alive, Count Fernando would not have dared to treat the rebels with such leniency, and Marquo, as justice of the county, would not have had to grudgingly sign pardons for so many wastrels. And to top it all, since the day they took Aiscle, the count had not so much as shown his face in the county. He'd left all responsibility in the hands of Pere of Aiscle, who only had fifty soldiers to maintain a peace that was not real. In many parts of the county, the count's insignia was still not accepted, so regular shows of force were required, fueling rumors that the count's supporters committed abuses, robbed houses, and raped women. Orrun was in disarray. People swapped the boxwood for the gorse and vice versa as they pleased and, taking advantage of the turmoil, bandits had taken over the roads, villages, and estates. There was no safe haven left.

"What's troubling you so? The rebels?" Marquo took Brianda's hand. "They will never return to Lubich, I promise you. And Count Fernando will put an end to all of this. Pere has told me that he is in France organizing a force to take control of the situation. If I were here every day, you would feel safer."

Brianda let Marquo play with her fingers. The contact was not disagreeable, but it did not make her heart leap either. She knew that, sooner or later, marriage to him was inevitable. Her unease had nothing to do with that or with the continuing attacks.

It came from the certainty that the enemy was already in Lubich.

She had been so devastated since Johan's death that her senses had been sluggish, functioning just enough to keep her alive. Now that she was beginning to pay attention to outside stimuli again, she realized she had abandoned the house.

She took her hand from Marquo's and rubbed the ring Johan had given her before he was murdered. She'd wrapped a thin strip of leather around it to make it fit on the middle finger of her right hand, and she never took it off. That small object was a daily reminder of her father's request. No matter how deep her pain, she had a responsibility to keep living. And, after all, she should be grateful Marquo had not abandoned her. He came to visit each week, waiting with laudable patience for the moment she would finally show excitement about something. She knew the young man's truest desire was in climbing socially, but he had never pretended otherwise. The same day he had kissed her for the first time in Monzon castle, he had told her the only option for a second-born son like him would be to leave Tiles, unless he found an heiress to marry. Since the count had named him justice of the county, his situation had improved, but his salary was not enough. Becoming the master of Lubich would guarantee his future. And hers.

"Stay for lunch, Marquo," she said. "And together we will talk to my mother. I've already waited too long."

"Why are you setting the table for four?" asked Brianda, puzzled by the extreme care Cecilia was taking. She had used Elvira's favorite tablecloth and laid out the best china, the silver cutlery, and the glass goblets Johan had brought from France.

"Mistress Elvira told me she was expecting a second visitor," Cecilia responded nervously, "and if I got something wrong she would lock me in the cellar."

Brianda found it strange that her mother hadn't mentioned anything. She silently straightened the forks. Elvira followed through on her threats, especially if they involved the young gypsy, whom she had never liked.

The door opened and Elvira entered, wearing her best dark skirt and accompanied by a man. Brianda felt herself go weak and leaned on the table for support. For a second, she had imagined it was her father who smiled at her mother. Something in his gestures and build had caused that fleeting sensation. But the man who was approaching was not Johan. He was tall, but not that tall. He had abundant hair, but it was brown rather than black. And he smiled too much, as if showing off his satisfaction at being there, in the great hall of Lubich, at Elvira's side.

Jayme of Cuyls. Johan had warned her about him. *"Watch out for that man,"* he had said.

Jayme approached Marquo and held out his hand, which the young man shook without much enthusiasm. His face had also darkened.

"Today is a day to celebrate," said Elvira, showing where each should sit, she and Jayme together and her daughter and Marquo opposite them.

Brianda balked. *Celebrating?* The last thing she wanted was to share a table with one of the rebels who had murdered her father. She could not understand what had gotten into her mother to smile at this man in such a forward manner. She did not know if it was just her imagination, but it seemed like Elvira was even blushing slightly. She looked to Marquo for help, but he only shrugged.

"Sit down, Brianda," Elvira ordered her. "You too, Marquo, if you are eating with us."

Both remained standing.

"I don't know what we can celebrate with a rebel," said Brianda, "if not the death of—"

"Brianda!" Elvira interrupted her. "Mind your tongue, or you'll regret it later!"

An uncomfortable silence followed, during which Jayme looked for something in his pocket. Slowly, he took out a document, unfolded it, and placed it on the table.

"Signed by Count Fernando. From now on, I am the new bailiff of Orrun, only reporting to the deputy, Pere of Aiscle, in civil and criminal matters," he addressed Marquo, "and I am your superior in matters of public order."

"But—how?" Marquo could not hide his disgust. He took the document and read it carefully. "It's true." He sat down. "How did you manage it?"

"I would ask you for the same respect that I show you, Marquo." Jayme took a long pause, as if waiting for the young man to reflect on his words. "The post became vacant after Johan's death. The count, with good and wise judgment, understood that someone like me would be useful in keeping things calm in his absence."

"Playing both sides . . . ," murmured Brianda, letting herself fall into her seat. Jayme of Cuyls now occupied her father's place at the table in Lubich and in the county.

"Was it not the count himself who asked that the past be forgotten?" Elvira began pouring the wine in the goblets and rang a bell to have the meal served. "What better way than this? Jayme only wants the best for this land."

Jayme responded with an enchanting smile, and Brianda felt like throwing one of her knives at him.

"Does Pere know?" she managed to ask.

"He'll soon be getting a letter from the count," answered Jayme. "And for his own good, he'll let it be. As I know you will, Marquo." His tone of voice became enigmatic again. "Soon, Pere will be able to retire to his house in Aiscle and stop going to those villages where they want to do nothing more than attack him."

Gisabel and Cecilia came in carrying trays of roast suckling pig. Brianda could not remember the last time they had served such a feast in Lubich, which could only mean that Elvira had planned it. Brianda could not rid herself of the sense that an axe was hanging over Lubich. She wanted lunch over with as quickly as possible. She could not eat. She could not think.

"Brianda and I also have something to tell you," she heard Marquo began to say. "Remember, Elvira, that in this very room we talked about marriage plans. We had to postpone our wedding because of the terrible events that befell this house, but it is now our wish to take up the matter again and marry as soon as possible. Your husband believed that I would make a good master of Lubich, and I hope not to disappoint either him or you."

The silence that followed Marquo's words increased Brianda's anguish. In contrast to the previous time, when Elvira immediately had begun drawing up the guest list, now her face had gone pale.

"You have nothing to say, Mother?" Brianda asked.

Elvira and Jayme exchanged glances.

Finally, Elvira spoke. "I hadn't thought of telling you yet, Brianda, but this news forces me to do so. Jayme has proposed that, when the period of mourning is over, in spring, we marry."

Brianda was dumbstruck and disgusted. The cousin her father had hated so much occupied his seat, his post in the county, and now wanted to occupy his wife's bed. And Elvira, why was she doing this? It was not out of need, so it had to be for love. She felt short of breath. How could her mother have forgotten Johan so quickly? It was not even a year since his death. The familiarity and complicity of their gestures revealed that their relationship was not new.

"I know it seems strange to you, Daughter, but I'm still too young to renounce a man's company and limit myself to being Marquo's mother-in-law and the grandmother of your children. What sort of life would that be for me? Think of all the widows you know in Tiles. Even those with children are alone."

"And you'll go with him to Cuyls."

Brianda had never imagined her mother living anywhere except Lubich. She wondered what madness had possessed her.

"What? No, Brianda. We will live in Lubich."

"Marquo and I will live in Lubich, Mother. I am the owner of this house."

Elvira lowered her voice.

"No, Brianda, you're not. Johan didn't sign over anything to you. According to our marriage agreement, I have the right to dispose of all goods as I see fit, respecting, of course, that which legally corresponds to you."

"Then it's only a question of time." Brianda pronounced the words with a rage that came from deep inside her.

"Provided we don't have a child," Jayme said, looking at her with false humility. "If God wills, it will be my firstborn who will inherit Lubich."

Brianda rose brusquely, knocking her chair to the floor. Suddenly, it was not Elvira in front of her but a stranger.

"You cannot agree to this!" she shouted, pointing her finger at her mother. "You know I am the legitimate heir to Lubich, direct descendent of the first Johan! You can't ignore my father's wishes!"

Elvira's chin began to tremble. For a second, Brianda thought her resolve would crumble, but Jayme squeezed her hand and her conviction returned.

"I'm only thirty-five, Brianda! Still, Jayme is committing himself to me without knowing if I will be able to give him a child. I know he will be a good master of this house."

"And what will happen to me?" Brianda shouted wildly. "And Marquo?"

Brianda looked at Marquo. Without saying anything, Marquo stood up, collected his sword, and left. She quickly understood, and after a few moments of shock, Brianda ran after him and caught up with him near the front door.

"Wait! This makes no sense! They won't get away with this!" She grabbed his arm in desperation. "Why won't you look at me?"

Marquo rested his hand on hers, keeping his gaze fixed on the ground.

"This changes everything, Brianda. I have nothing to offer you." He gently released himself from her fingers. "I'm so sorry."

"That's it?" Brianda let her arms fall by her sides, completely dejected. "You won't even confront him?"

"The second most powerful man in the county, supported by the count and with friends at court?"

"I'm not asking you to put yourself in danger. You are the justice here in the county. You could help me appeal to the justice of the kingdom."

"You've seen how much that has helped the count. He thinks the county is his and now he has one of the king's lackeys in control." He leaned over her, intending to kiss her on the cheek, but stopped. "This is not how it should be, but—" He shook his head, crossed the entrance hall, and went out to the patio.

Brianda's eyes filled with tears. This couldn't be happening. Marquo was a coward. Her mother had betrayed her father's and her ancestors' memory. And Jayme—her instinct had not failed her. The enemy was within.

She listened to the hooves of Marquo's horse as he rode away. She threw a glance toward the hall. She did not know what to do. If she went back to her mother, she would only shout at her. Shout at her and hit her. Her and her future husband. How she hated her! How she hated them both!

She put a shawl around her shoulders and, over her damask slippers, a pair of old leather boots that were on a wooden bench. Then she opened the door and went out. The wind lashed against her body. With no fixed destination, she crossed the patio, went through the gates of Lubich, and began to run through the fields. She heard Cecilia call, but paid no heed. The ground was wet from the rain and sleet of the previous days, and her boots sank into the mud. The damp wind clawed at her hair, turning and twisting it over her face and shoulders.

At the end of a field, she came to a stone wall and climbed it to jump onto the hidden path. The uneven pebbles nearly tripped her. Thorns cut her face, ripped her clothes, and pricked her skin. The wind seemed to strengthen by the minute and forced her to walk looking downward at the rotting red leaves covering the path. Then, the path died.

She looked up and recognized a small gully in the middle of the wood where that blond-haired man had tried to have his way with her when she was waiting for Nunilo to return from France. Only a few months more than a year had passed, but, since then, her whole world had come tumbling down. Over the gully, she spotted a narrow aqueduct she used to visit with her father to check that nothing had blocked the water. She would balance over the chasm while she waited for him. The sight of the small bridge, barely two hands wide, brought a moment of relief. She flung herself to the ground and began to crawl. She wanted to straddle the top of the narrow waterway. Her hands felt the viscous dampness of centuries-old moss. The icy raindrops slid down the orange rocks before falling into the chasm below. She felt like she had as a child, with her lower legs swinging in the air, holding the stone on either side of her thighs to prevent herself from being knocked over by the wind. She looked down, toward the immense hole that opened its jaws at her feet, and jolted at the vertigo. She lowered her head and began to sob. Everything she most loved in life was disappearing bit by bit. Nunilo, Johan, Corso, Lubich . . .

Nobody would miss her if she disappeared too.

Suddenly, she heard the drumbeat of hooves. Then, a whinny. She looked up and saw a magnificent black animal rearing at the edge of the gully and pitching its rider forward. The body hit a rock and landed facedown, too close to the freezing water. The horse began to paw nervously.

Brianda climbed carefully down the sharp rocks, her only objective to reach that body.

It was as if all the water in her clothes and the heaviness of her mood had evaporated. She knelt beside the man, moved aside the cape that had fallen over his face, and rested a hand on each shoulder to turn the heavy body around. His face was covered with blood, but she recognized him immediately.

"It's you!" she whispered.

She said his name, repeating it over and over again as she cleaned his cheeks and stroked his wet hair, trying to convince herself that Corso really was there.

30.

Corso slowly opened his eyes, certain that his mind had played tricks on him in transferring him from that hospital, where time had stood still, to this familiar wood. Blinking, he slid his gaze along the dusky sky, the trees, and the rocks, until halting at the face of the woman crying out his name. He closed his eyes again and reviewed his situation. His body hurt all over, especially his head, and a sharp pain in his side warned him that his wound had reopened. He could not understand why he saw trees from the bed he had been lying in for weeks. He did not know what type of spell could make him confuse the face of the lad who looked after him with Brianda's. He wondered why his body felt damp, why the wind was blowing so hard, and why he did not hear the sounds of the hospital.

"Corso!" Again, that voice he remembered from his dreams. "You've come back to me!"

He slowly remembered his flight, his singular goal. He had succeeded. He had found her.

"Corso?" It was Brianda. "Where have you been?"

"In hell—" he managed to say. He moistened his dry lips with the tip of his tongue and drew a weak smile. "But I promised you I would return."

Brianda leaned down and hugged him tightly.

"I thought you were dead!" She felt so happy to have him beside her that all she wanted was to keep hugging him and to tell him everything that had happened during his long absence, but she came to her senses. "I have to get you out of here."

She helped him sit up. He was thinner and his hair and beard had grown so long that he looked like a bandit. Brianda decisively got to her feet and held out her hand. With difficulty, Corso got to his knees and stood up, but his body remained bent.

"What's wrong with you?" Brianda asked, running her hands over his chest looking for a wound.

She undid the ties on his jerkin, lifted his shirt, and saw a wound half the size of her palm and open like a ripe fig. With no hesitation, she ripped some material from her underskirt, folded it, and placed it over the cut, motioning him to apply pressure. All that time, the black Friesian had waited quietly a few paces from them. Brianda approached carefully and took the reins, whispering kind words in a low voice. But without warning, the horse tensed up and opened its enormous dark eyes in fear.

"Brianda—"

Very close to Corso, a black wolf bared his sharp teeth and let out a guttural growl. Man and beast stared at each other, and Brianda's mind sprang into action. Corso was wounded and unarmed. He could not defend himself. She could not stand losing him again.

Out of the corner of her eye, she saw Corso's sword sticking out of the horse's tack. Stealthily, she tied the reins to a tree beside her and grabbed the sword. Then she let out a shout to get the wolf's attention and began to advance. The animal forgot about Corso and growled at her instead.

Brianda stopped three or four paces away but continued shouting. She made sure her legs were properly positioned to keep her balance and waited for the wolf's next move. She knew that wolves did not always attack, but it was also true that they rarely came so close to a populated area. The unusually harsh winter must have driven it down from the hills. She held the hilt with both hands and kept the sword slightly raised. Suddenly, the wolf pounced. Instinctively, Brianda raised the sword above her head and brought it down in one stroke. The sharp blade opened an easy path through the flesh of the beast. She heard a howl of pain and the wolf fell at her feet. When she realized that she had killed it, she began to tremble.

She stood there, clutching the sword, until Corso got to her and hugged her in silence. A strange sensation took hold of her. If only she had showed the same bravery in confronting that foul beast who wanted to rob her of Lubich.

It was getting dark when Brianda finally made out Anels House. She had not been back since Nunilo's death. Leonor had visited her on a couple of occasions, but her own pain had prevented her from offering solace to Brianda.

After Lubich, Anels was the best estate in the valley. All the good memories in her life away from Lubich belonged to that place.

The yard was empty. She shouted for help and waited in the saddle, still supporting Corso. Two servants came out from the stables. At the same time, the door to the house opened and Leonor appeared, protecting her head with a black cloak.

"Blessed be to God!" the woman exclaimed. "Isn't that horse—?" She brought her hand to her bosom. "It can't be!"

"Corso has returned, Leonor," said Brianda. "He is weak and badly wounded. My first thought was to bring him here."

"Where else would you go?" Leonor motioned to the men to take care of Corso, and they got him down from the horse and brought him to one of the rooms above the hall. "This is his house."

"Then, the will—" murmured Brianda.

"It was Nunilo's wish and mine too." Leonor's eyes filled with tears. "I give thanks to God for this day. The son I thought was dead has returned home."

Brianda dismounted and followed Leonor inside, limping. She raised her petticoat and found that the wolf had sunk its fangs into her. She had been so worried about Corso that she had forgotten about herself. Now she felt so exhausted she could barely stand and so stiff with cold she could not stop shivering.

Leonor promptly took charge. She ordered the servants to stoke the fire, heat water, bring clean, dry clothes to Brianda and Corso, and prepare a hot broth. She sent a lad to Lubich to let them know that Brianda would spend the night at Anels and ordered him to then go to Aiscle for the apothecary, although she feared it would be the following morning before he came, as only bandits were on the roads after sunset. She left Corso in the hands of two servants, and she herself looked after Brianda. She helped her to undress in the kitchen in front of the fire and to sit in a tub of hot water. She allowed the girl to rest a few moments and then she asked, "How did this miracle occur?"

Brianda told her everything, from the presence of the new general bailiff, Jayme of Cuyls, in Lubich to the announcement of the wedding between him and Elvira and the frustration of her own with Marquo. She related how she had felt the need to escape and how she had found Corso, whom she saved from the wolf.

"I don't know where he's been or what he's done," Brianda said. "He only told me that he was in hell." She pulled her knees up to her chest and remained in thought for a while. Her joy at finding Corso had made her forget her own situation. Her inheritance was in danger.

How could she live at Lubich now, knowing Jayme's plans? "I'm afraid my hell begins now—"

Leonor handed her a towel. "You're alive, you're young, and you're healthy. You'll be fine."

She took the containers brought by her servant, Aldonsa, a white-haired woman with an unusually thick neck. Then Leonor cleaned the wolf bite with elder, thyme, and chamomile water; then she applied a poultice of wax, hollyhock, and walnut leaves, and bandaged it.

"The man is also ready," Aldonsa told her.

Leonor waited until Brianda finished dressing. The three of them went up some wooden stairs to a large room with a view of the whole valley.

Corso lay on a high bed with his eyes closed. They had dressed him in a long linen shirt with a large opening in the chest to expose his wound. Brianda could not take her eyes off him. She had felt his arms around her, but many times she had wondered what his limbs would be like without clothes, if he would have a lot or little hair, if his skin would be white or tanned. Now she had the chance to run her eyes over his body, from the tips of his toes to the top of his head, and what she saw made her whole body flush.

"The wound has to be cleaned," Leonor said, sitting down beside him.

Brianda watched as Leonor began to wash him with the same mixture that she had used on her, but then she picked up a bowl with a different balm.

"What is it?"

"Madonna lily boiled in olive oil, field horsetail, and celandine," answered Leonor, frowning.

"What's the matter?" Brianda became alarmed.

"The bleeding won't stop."

Aldonsa came over and exchanged looks with Leonor. Leonor nodded in agreement and the servant left. She soon returned with something light in her hands. She leaned over Corso and placed a sticky white substance on his wound.

"Cobwebs!" exclaimed Brianda in amazement. "Where did you learn these remedies?"

"Observing, like you are doing now," answered Leonor. She smiled with relief when she saw the cobwebs were working. She gathered her things and stood up. "When he wakes, we'll try and get him to eat."

"I'll stay with him and let you know," said Brianda.

Once alone, Brianda sat down beside Corso and took his hand. She did not stop rubbing it until he began to regain consciousness. He stared at her with his dark eyes and smiled.

"I only saved you once and you've done it twice in one afternoon. I don't know what I've done to deserve this guardian angel."

"It was twice," she reminded him. "You got me out of trouble when they wanted to whip Cecilia. Then you stopped me from falling over the precipice when I was so sick, and brought me to this very house. We're even."

Corso looked around and recognized the place where he had lived as Nunilo's most trusted man. He felt a stab of sadness in his chest remembering Nunilo's death, his guilt in leaving him alone, and his fear of seeing Leonor again.

"We're in Anels House," he murmured.

"You're in your own house, Corso." Brianda leaned closer and squeezed his hand. "You are the new master of Anels."

She told him everything: how Aiscle was finally taken, about Medardo's death, about Johan's murder, and about new posts in the county. She repeated what she had told Leonor about the intentions of Elvira and Jayme of Cuyls, and about Marquo abandoning her.

"I will lose Lubich," she finished in a whisper. "And I won't have anything."

Corso smiled strangely.

"Didn't you promise me that you wouldn't marry Marquo? Beside the river, in the monastery in Besalduch. Then you told me to leave and pleaded with me to return. I promised you I would. Do you remember why?"

Brianda nodded. He had told her she was his Lubich. She did not understand why Corso mentioned that now. His expression had changed when she had spoken about Marquo, and she felt she had to explain.

"I waited for you day after day. A letter arrived from those who had survived. It said that the Moors had attacked you and that you fell at Surano's side. I refused to believe you were dead, but months passed and Marquo insisted. What was I to do? If I had known you were still alive, I would have kept my word. Where did you go, damn you?"

"They wounded me and left me for dead. The following day, I managed to get to Monzon. From then on, my memory is fuzzy, and I only know what happened thanks to young Azmet, who recognized my horse and connected it with you, who saved his friend Cecilia. I owe my life to Azmet. He looked after me when the monks in the hospital gave me up for dead on various occasions. Later, he warned me the king's soldiers were looking for a man who caused and was witness to the battles with the Moors, and he helped me escape. If I had known the bloodbath we would cause, I'd never have gone."

He gritted his teeth as he remembered the fierce attack launched against that town, the unnecessary cruelty in the taking of the houses, the images of men like Surano snatching children from their mothers' arms, swinging them by the feet and hitting their heads against the walls while he just fought to stay alive; the dead bodies and the blood in the streets, the square, and the church; the vengeance that befell them while they were dividing up the spoils that night, hiding in caves in the hills; the confusion and flight of some men; the look in Surano's eyes an instant before falling dead beside him.

"My only obsession was to regain the strength to get back to these mountains to find you, Brianda. I never gave up. Never."

She hung her head, ashamed that she had lost faith. Corso tried to sit up and his face twisted in pain.

"You don't know how happy it makes me to be the master of this house and not a soldier at somebody's orders, unworthy of the true heiress to Lubich, abandoned by her betrothed, who only appreciated her for her estate—"

Brianda made to move away, but he gripped her wrist firmly.

"How many times did you tell me, Brianda, that to marry well was your duty? Well, now, finally, you have no other choice but to marry me."

31.

Brianda thought that God was testing her strength, subjecting her to so many emotions in just one day.

"Marry you!" she happily repeated.

The door opened, and Leonor appeared carrying a tray with a steaming dish. Her eyes met Corso's, and she knew that Brianda had told him about his new role as master of Anels. She went to him and said, "Managing the property that was once my husband's requires a lot of strength. It will take a while to get your health back, so the sooner you start to eat the better."

"I know I'm in good hands," Corso replied, relieved she did not blame him for Nunilo's death. "And I also know that my first task as master of Anels would please Nunilo." He took Brianda's hand and announced, "I wish to marry Brianda. As soon as possible. This very day if I could. And I would like your blessing."

Leonor raised an eyebrow. So, her impression had been right.

"I'm not surprised by your desire, rather by your haste, Corso. Both of you have my approval, but you need another's—"

"I have no intention of asking my mother," said Brianda. "Did she consult me about her own plans? It will be enough that she finds out after the event."

Leonor shook her head.

"It will take days before Corso can get to the church. I don't know how to justify your absence from Lubich."

Corso smiled and said, "Call the abbot and offer him a generous donation for bringing his services here."

The following morning, Leonor sent one of her servants to Besalduch, requesting the presence of Abbot Bartholomeu in Anels House to perform the sacrament of extreme unction on a dying man.

In her room, Brianda finished getting dressed. Her wedding would not be the expected one for the daughter of Johan of Lubich. She would wear a skirt and bodice lent to her by Leonor. There would be no guests or banquet. She would not walk down the aisle on her father's arm. And yet, she could not feel luckier. In a few hours, she would be the wife of Corso of Anels. Everything had happened so fast, she felt dizzy. The abbot's blessing would join them forever. She repeated this last word several times as she fixed a small decoration of dried flowers in her hair. She missed her edelweiss pendant, but at least she had Johan's ring.

Some voices got her attention. She peeked out the window and recognized two servants from Lubich, as well as Cecilia, who was talking to Aldonsa and gesticulating nervously. Aldonsa led her inside and Brianda went down to calm her servant.

In the kitchen, Cecilia hugged her tightly.

"Mistress Elvira sent me to look for you. We were very worried until we got news you were here."

"You can see I'm fine. Go back to Lubich and tell my mother that I'll be staying here for a few days to keep Leonor company."

Cecilia fidgeted with her hands.

"Your mother has insisted that we don't come back without you. She told me to remind you that a few months remain before the mourning period for your father ends, and that you must observe honesty in your conduct and a life of retreat as corresponds to your condition."

Brianda answered with a sarcastic tone. "Tell her I am pleased she knows the obligations more befitting of a widow but not to wait for me today."

"She has threatened to remove me if I don't bring you back." Cecilia gave her a pleading look. "This very day."

"Don't worry, Cecilia, that won't happen. I can't say any more to you, but soon you will have to prepare my wardrobe and yours. Go on, be off with you."

Brianda accompanied Cecilia to the yard and waited for her to get on her mule and leave. In the distance, she saw another rider, his head covered in a hood, and her excitement increased as she recognized the abbot. She went looking for Leonor, whom she found coming down the stairs with the apothecary, and who asked her to wait in her room. There, Brianda opened the window and heard the departure of one and the arrival of the other.

"I don't think your presence is needed," she heard the apothecary grumble to the abbot, "or mine. Last night they warned me that a man was dying, but it doesn't look like it to me."

"Better to be safe than sorry," Leonor hurriedly said, handing over some coins before addressing the abbot. "And it is always better to be prepared for the Lord's final call."

Brianda waited impatiently at the door of her room. She heard voices in the hall and the door to Corso's room opening and closing. Time passed. Finally, some steps approached. She flung open the door and saw a blushing Leonor.

"At first he was reticent because of the strange situation and the rush. Corso told him that you had already lived as husband and wife and that, if the abbot denied you, the only thing he would achieve would be allowing you to continue to live in sin. But this was not what convinced him. Rather, I think he's excited to get the better of Father Guillem."

Brianda felt herself go red, but made no comment. She followed Leonor into Corso's room. She had not seen him since the previous night, and he met her with such an intense look that she trembled. He was lying on soft pillows and a thin sheet covered his legs. They had shaved his beard, gathered up his hair with a fine leather strip, and changed his shirt for a clean one, over which he wore a black jerkin. Vitality had returned to his body. Although healing would still take time, this was the Corso she had remembered during the long nights of separation.

The abbot asked her to place herself at Corso's bedside, and he began the ceremony.

"Given that the banns of marriage have not been publicly displayed on three consecutive Sundays to give members of the community the opportunity to contest this marriage, I will have to trust the word of Leonor, who will sign as witness. You have no kinship to the fourth degree, so there is no need for dispensation from the Pope or the bishop." He looked at Brianda. "You are not a victim of abduction, and you have not taken previous religious vows. Regarding the consent of the family, I will leave those consequences to yourselves. Have you got the rings?"

Brianda quickly took off her father's ring and gave it to the abbot, but realized she had none for Corso. Leonor went out and returned quickly. She placed a well-worked gold ring beside the other in Bartholomeu's hand.

"It was Nunilo's," she said, looking at Corso. "Now you must wear it."

The abbot mumbled a quick blessing over the rings and gave Corso the one he should put on Brianda's finger.

In a deep voice, and staring into her eyes, Corso repeated the abbot's words: "Brianda, with this ring, I thee wed. With this body, I thee honor and share with thee all my worldly goods."

Brianda took the other ring from the abbot, and, at the same time she said the vows, she swore to herself that her body and her soul would adore him. When she got to the last part of the vows, however, she could not prevent a shadow from clouding her gaze. For the moment, she had no goods to bring to the marriage.

Corso squeezed her hand and whispered, "You are the only riches I desire."

The abbot reminded them that they should live together in the sacred state of matrimony as ordained by God, loving each other, honoring each other, and keeping each other in sickness and in health and forsaking all others until death parted them. He raised his hands and gave them a final blessing.

"O Lord, aid Your servants who place their hope in Thee. Send them the aid of Thy sanctuary and forever help them. Be their tower of strength in the midst of their enemies. O Lord, hear our prayer and let our cry for help come unto Thee."

Corso and Brianda kept their hands joined until they had to sign the marriage contract. When she noticed Corso hesitating, Brianda realized that he did not know how to write, and she guided his hand so he could sign his name. Afterward, the abbot said his farewells. Before he left, they heard Leonor ask, "Will Father Guillem object to this marriage?"

"He will show his disgust but will maintain its validity." Bartholomeu raised his index finger to his nose. "Let him dare question my actions. My blessings are as effective as his."

Now alone, Corso put out his hand so that Brianda could lie down beside him and he embraced her.

"We can't consummate our marriage yet, but I promise I'll soon be better. Meanwhile, I don't intend to sleep a single night without your company. Tell the servants to make this room suitable for the both of us."

"The job is done." Brianda laughed. "All my clothes are in Lubich."

"We'll go for them as soon as I can ride. Then, we'll see about getting your house back."

Brianda pressed against him. "This is my house now. Yours."

"No. I know you feel the same now as you did that day under the tower, when your father was still alive and you announced your wedding to Marquo. Away from Lubich you would die, you told me. Either Lubich disappears or you get it back. There is no other way for you to be fully yourself and fully with me."

Two days later, Brianda let Leonor know that she was taking a mule to Lubich for her things. Corso had asked her to wait until he was well enough to go with her, but she was eager to have her clothes and jewels, her trousseau, and the writing desk her father had given her. She also wanted to bring Cecilia as her personal servant.

The sun blinded her as it reflected off the path that cold and sunny morning. The air was completely still. Not a sound came from the deserted fields on either side of the road. Like the lazy smoke coming from the chimneys in Tiles, she had begun her journey slowly, enjoying the memory of Corso's strong body next to hers at night, remembering the pleasure in his caresses without the hurry and fear of before. Just thinking about Corso's hands on her skin sent a tremor through her, and she hoped the day would pass quickly so she could get back to his side. All her new happiness dissolved when she thought of Lubich. Then the feeling of rage over her mother's behavior and her own desire not to give in returned. Perhaps God would punish her for her avarice, she thought. She loved Corso with all her heart, but she also had to get Lubich back for herself and her future children.

Just after she took the fork toward the forests to the northeast, she spurred on the mule to speed up. She soon spotted the stone wall and tower of Lubich and, for the first time in her life, she felt neither joy nor safety but instead alarm, like a raven announcing tragedy with its cawing.

She continued onward, wishing she'd listened to Corso and waited. How different everything would be if he rode by her side, she thought. Then, she could act with decisiveness and audacity. Maybe she could collect her things without having to see her mother. She wondered why everything had to change so quickly. What used to be her world had vanished. If only Johan were alive . . . But another thought imposed itself: if Johan were alive, she would not be Corso's wife.

The servants working in the yard recognized her immediately, and one of them came over to take charge of the mule, which he tied up beside some saddled horses. Brianda spoke to him as she always had, but the man, named Remon, replied reluctantly. Then Gisabel appeared at the door. After the death of her husband in that terrible incident that had taken Surano and his men to the lowlands in search of vengeance, the joy had disappeared from her face, but soon after giving birth to her child, she had accepted the advances of the widower Remon and regained her jovial and slightly bossy character.

"What's wrong with Remon?" Brianda asked. "He hardly said a word to me."

"With him and everybody else," Gisabel answered in a low voice. "It's difficult to get used to the master's ways."

"As far as I know, there is no master here," said Brianda, her mood stormier by the second.

"The same day you left, Jayme of Cuyls called us all together and, in your mother's presence, he declared that, as your father's only male cousin, he was now master of this estate. He comes and goes as he pleases, though he never spends the night here."

Brianda cursed. The thief couldn't even wait to marry Elvira to achieve his goal. She glanced at the tied-up horses.

"He is in the hall, with the mistress," Gisabel confirmed.

"I need Cecilia and you in my room immediately. Don't tell my mother."

"Cecilia is locked in the cellar."

Brianda felt her bad humor give way to rage. She charged into the house like a hurricane. She clambered down some narrow stone steps, seized the key from its hook, and opened the door to the cellar, a damp room with a vaulted ceiling, cobwebs, a smell of rats, moldy walls, and barrels standing on wooden beams. In a corner of the floor, lying on an old blanket, she found Cecilia, dirty and half-frozen.

"Let's get out of here," Brianda said, helping Cecilia to her feet.

Following behind, Gisabel warned her, "The master and mistress will be very angry."

Brianda did not answer. She led the servants to her room, ordered Cecilia to get cleaned up, change her clothes, and pack her things. Brianda then asked Gisabel to help her with her own. She opened the two chests where the clothes and trousseau were stored: linen sheets, blouses and chemises, headdresses, scarves and fine tablecloths. She put in her combs, flasks of perfume, a hand mirror, and her small jewelry box. She made sure that the lid of the writing desk given to her by Johan was properly closed for the journey, and her hand went to her neck to check that the small key to the secret compartment was still there. Finally, she asked a surprised Gisabel to help her strip the bed and fold her sheets, as she was intent on bringing everything.

Cecilia came back carrying her bundle and watched the flurry of activity, her eyes wide.

"Where are we going, Mistress?" she finally asked.

Then, the door burst open and Elvira appeared. When she saw her daughter and the items being packed, she looked astonished.

"Brianda!" she exclaimed. "What are you doing?" She looked at Cecilia and then at Gisabel. "You two, out now. I'll deal with you later."

Gisabel slipped out, but Brianda held Cecilia by her arm.

"You're staying with me."

Brianda stood before Elvira and looked her straight in the eyes. She had to take advantage of her rage to confront her.

"Mother, I need the servants to get some mules ready and help me with my things. I would prefer to bring everything now."

Elvira's pale skin flushed, and Brianda knew she was angry.

"And where do you think you are going?" asked Elvira, cold as ice.

"To Anels House."

"This is your house, not that one—"

"You have decided this is not my house any longer!" Brianda shouted.

"You are my daughter, no matter how much that hurts Leonor, and you'll do as I say."

"Not now that I'm a married woman!"

Elvira raised a hand to her mouth.

"What has come over you to lie to your mother like this?"

"I'm not lying. Two days ago, Abbot Bartholomeu joined me to Corso in matrimony." When she mentioned her husband's name, Brianda felt assured. She lifted her chin and continued. "He didn't die as we believed. He came back for me. Now he is the new master of Anels."

Elvira clenched her teeth, and after a few tense moments, she turned around and marched out. Brianda took a deep breath and exhaled slowly.

"You married him?" Cecilia asked. "You shouldn't have done it in January, the month of cold and scarcity. You will have dearth for the rest of your life, because as a marriage begins, so it ends."

"Be quiet!" Brianda snapped. "The last thing I need is one of your omens. Do you think my mother will call for the servants?"

They heard steps in the corridor, and Jayme of Cuyls placed himself at the entrance to the room. Behind him, Brianda saw Elvira.

"Since when can a young girl do whatever she pleases without the approval of the men of the family?" Jayme of Cuyls had menace in his eyes. He came a few steps closer, took Cecilia by the arm, and threw her out of the room. Then he turned back to Brianda. "You might disobey your mother, but I'm your guardian now."

"Actually, you should be grateful," said Brianda. "To have me out of your way. For now—" She immediately regretted being so emphatic with those last words, as Jayme raised his eyebrow in surprise.

"Is that a threat?" he asked.

"Take it as you wish. I only want you to send me some servants, so I can return to my husband."

"If what you're saying is true, Father Guillem will see to its undoing. That Corso—" He snorted in disgust, as he again walked toward the door. "Your only husband will be whoever your mother and I deem suitable."

Jayme took the door key out of the lock. When Brianda realized his intentions, it was already too late. She threw herself at him, but he pushed her away, went out, and locked the door from the outside.

"You'll stay in there until you realize your mistake and understand that your mother's decisions are the best for you and Lubich!"

For hours, Brianda shouted and pounded against the door. Hoarse and with her fists bloodied, she finally fell to the floor, and when the moon rose in the infinite space that it shared with the stars, she began to sob.

32.

Time ceased to exist in that room where she had grown up and which had now become her prison. Brianda did not know if it had been two or three times that the moon had given way to a pale sun that lit a silent and frozen world. Beside the door, there was a tray with some bread and cheese she had not touched. They had probably waited till her dejection had succumbed to drowsiness to stealthily slide it in.

She got out of bed, walked unsteadily toward the window that looked south, and observed her blurred reflection in one of the windows misted up by the cold. She was pale and red eyed, and her matted hair made her look like one of those widowed peasants to whom people gave a wide berth. She rested a cheek against the frozen pane and sighed. Happiness was a slippery state for her.

Suddenly, she heard a racket coming from the patio. She rubbed the condensation that blurred her view and saw a dozen men riding horses, from whose snouts and nostrils came a dense and intermittent mist, crossing through the entrance gates. At the front of the group, a man covered in a black cape leaned slightly over the withers of his black Friesian. Her heart jumped.

She opened the window and shouted his name. Corso looked up for a moment and motioned for her to remain calm. His attention was focused on another. Jayme of Cuyls appeared, buttoning his jerkin and cursing the servants of Lubich for having let the men enter.

"But they are the men of the deceased Nunilo!" Remon protested. "They have never been refused entry to this house!"

"I'm the one who decides who can and cannot enter!" Jayme shouted at Corso while approaching him. "Are you the leader of this group? Your face looks familiar. To what do I owe this unexpected visit at such an early hour?"

Corso looked at him. He remembered the day Surano had asked him to spy on Jayme and Medardo during the parliament in Monzon. He had noticed how Jayme did not take his eyes off Johan of Lubich. Afterward, they had met returning to Tiles, when Brianda had fallen ill. He had also seen him that morning in Aiscle before his men had caused Nunilo's death. But he had never been face-to-face with him. So, this was the man who wanted to take Lubich away from Brianda. He controlled his wish to unsheathe his sword and pierce the bastard's heart. Now that he was no longer willing to flee, murdering Jayme would lead Corso straight to the scaffold.

"I am the Master of Anels, and I have come looking for my wife," he answered with all the calmness he could muster.

Jayme took a surprised step backward. He looked at him closely and recognized him as Surano of Aiscle's companion.

"Corso—" He frowned. "We already sent a servant with word that Brianda wanted to remain at her home for a while."

"Her home is where her husband is. Perhaps she hasn't told you that we are married?"

"That marriage is not valid!" said Elvira, coming from the inside patio. "How could you think for an instant that I would permit my daughter to marry someone like you?"

Corso put his hand into his jerkin and took out a piece of paper.

"I have here a copy of the document kept by the Abbot of Besalduch with all the blessings. If you wish, you may speak with him, but I'm not leaving without Brianda."

"She doesn't want anything to do with you," said Elvira. "She returned because she saw the error of her ways. Shame prevents her from confronting you."

Corso laughed aloud.

"I would like to hear that from her lips." He raised his eyes to her window and shouted, "Brianda. Why don't you come down? Perhaps you don't want to return with me to Anels?"

"Corso!" Brianda leaned out dangerously. "I'm locked in! Help me!"

Corso's face darkened. He hung his head, gritted his teeth to control his anger, took a deep breath, and leapt off the horse while unsheathing his sword and placing its tip on Jayme's chest. Before anyone could react, his men copied him and surrounded the Lubich servants, with whom they had fought side by side in the past.

"Bring her down," Corso ordered Elvira, "if you don't want to lose this man as well." He aimed his chin at Jayme, then gestured to two of his men to go with her.

Soon afterward, Brianda came out of the house followed by her mother and ran to the Friesian, barely containing her desire to jump into Corso's arms. Before mounting, she stopped.

"Cecilia! I can't leave without her!"

She went back to the house, guessing correctly that the girl was once more in the cellar. There she freed Cecilia, asking her to quickly go and get her things. Again outside, Brianda said to Corso, "I want my chests with my belongings. Everything is prepared in my room."

Corso looked at Elvira.

"Are you going to get them or shall we come back another day?"

Elvira gestured with her head and the servants escorted by Corso's men made various trips while others prepared some mules. When everything was ready and Brianda had mounted his horse, Corso removed his sword from Jayme's chest and got up behind her. He spoke to Jayme and Elvira one last time. "Be clear about one thing. Brianda is now the wife of Corso of Anels and, as such, she has my support in all matters. Anyone who upsets her, no matter who they are, will pay for it."

He covered Brianda with his cloak, spurred the horse's sides, and left at a gallop. Brianda only just managed to exchange a brief look with her mother before Lubich disappeared in the distance. She was relieved to be with Corso again, but she felt a great sorrow that things had to be as they were. She still could not understand how Elvira could allow one of the rebels behind her father's death into Lubich and her life. It was difficult to believe that a widow's fear of loneliness was strong enough to bury Lubich's centuries of honor and glory.

They continued at a gallop until they came to the fork for Anels. There, Corso slowed down and buried his head in the nape of her neck.

"Three nights, damn it," he muttered. "I told you I would never again spend another night without you."

"So why did you take so long?" she tried to joke. She placed a hand over his wound, and he grimaced in pain. "You'll relapse because of me."

"I'd do it as many times as it takes." Corso looked into her sparkling eyes and then leaned down to hungrily kiss her, as if afraid she might disappear again.

Brianda pressed against him, but then he abruptly pulled away.

"What's the matter?" she asked.

"A group of riders."

She turned and saw a crimson-and-gold standard on a staff. The pikes and muskets glinted.

"Soldiers?"

"King's soldiers."

Brianda swallowed a moan. Her husband was still a deserter from the king's army. It was impossible that they had come up to the mountains for him, but she still worried.

"Let's go back to the others," she suggested.

Corso pulled the reins and turned back. They quickly came upon the men from Anels and the laden mules. Brianda told Corso to change horses and to pretend he was one of the men.

"I will talk to the soldiers," she said, combing her hair with her hands and gathering it up in a braid.

A few minutes later, they came up to the group of twenty-five soldiers with padded coats over their jerkins, leggings buttoned up to the knees, and faces reddened by the cold. The open-sleeved cloaks with the cross of Burgundy emblazoned on their front and rear left no doubt they were the king's soldiers. Brianda wondered what they were doing in those lands. One of them came forward. His face was long, and he had a brown goatee. He wore a thick leather garment under his armor and a helmet with a plume of red feathers. His horse was the only one covered in a rich blanket, and there was another plume of feathers on top of the armor that covered its face.

"My name is Captain Vardan."

"And I am Brianda of Lubich." She adopted a haughty pose. "Who are you looking for?"

The captain looked at her closely. By her clothes, her saddle, her manners, and the company, he deduced that the girl was of the local nobility.

"We have orders from His Majesty to guard the crossings to France."

"You are very few for so much mountain."

Vardan smiled. "There are more in Aiscle. There will soon be three thousand of us to patrol this area. I hope that will please you."

Brianda forced herself not to show any sign of alarm. Not even all the men in the county together could match a royal army of that size.

"Has the legal action been resolved over the possession of the County of Orrun?" she asked with studied indifference.

"Would you be happy if it had?" The captain squinted and Brianda suspected that he was trying to gauge which side she was on. "His Majesty has ordered that we make up for the count's incompetence in clearing this region of French and Catalan troublemakers and ending the lawless banditry."

"A task deserving of thanks," replied Brianda with all the conviction she could feign. The king had sent soldiers to put out the very fire that he himself had started. The deaths of Nunilo and Johan had served for nothing.

The captain remained silent for a few moments, looking over the group of armed men behind her.

Fearing he would notice Corso, she explained, "I am taking my belongings to my new home. As you can see by my escort, my husband, the Master of Anels, also fears the bandits."

Vardan's face showed surprise. He put his hand into his jerkin and took out a wax-sealed document.

"I bring several messages from the king to the lords of the mountains. One of them is addressed to Anels. I understood he was an elderly gentleman. I am surprised he has taken such a young wife."

"The previous master died. My husband is his son." Brianda pointed to the east. "Our house is just over there, but if you wish I can give it to him. I am honored that His Majesty remembers those he had audience with in Monzon."

The captain extended his arm and handed it over.

"I trust you to do it." He raised his right arm and signaled to his men that they were leaving. "One more thing. Is this the way to Lubich?"

Brianda nodded. "It's half a league away. You can be assured of a warm welcome there."

She could have sworn that her voice had been neutral and not biting, but the captain raised his eyebrow slightly.

"And where wouldn't I?" he asked.

Brianda shrugged. "Finding out is part of your job—"

She loosened the reins and kicked her heels into the horse's side, and it began to trot slowly. She remained perfectly erect until she passed the fountain beside the spring, where Aldonsa and other servants were filling pitchers, and reached the yard of what was now her home. There, she rested on her horse's withers and panted. Her hands were trembling.

Corso came to her side.

"You were adroit," he said. "What did he give you?"

"A letter from the king for you." She handed it to him. "He told me he had brought letters for several lords. I fear its contents."

"You'll have to tell me what it says," he said, handing it back to her. "I can't read."

Brianda broke the seal, read the document in silence, and clicked her tongue.

"The resolution of the king to incorporate the County of Orrun into the Crown is definite. They make us a generous offer to abandon the count's cause," she explained, looking him in the eye. "This was never your war, and it's possible you might find yourself on the losing side."

Corso dismounted and helped her down.

"I could even now be one of those soldiers we've just seen, with worn clothes, a vacant look, and a hunger to pillage to improve my lot. No soldier chooses his fight, but through this war I met you, and now I am who I am." He stroked her dark hair with both hands and then embraced her. "I couldn't feel any more victorious."

Brianda looked up to the sky, where the sun shone pale, almost white through the slight mist. At that moment, her only wish was to enter Anels and lock herself in with Corso, in the room from which she could see the empty fields and the smoky rooftops of Tiles, deceptively quiet before the decisions of men like the king, the count, or the master to whom they owed allegiance, content with their existence in that beautiful but remote, cold, and inhospitable place. She leaned against him to temper her trembling unease. Only by Corso's side did she feel there was nothing to fear.

He was now her future, unknown, but loved and longed for.

33.

As if the heavens had heard Brianda's wishes, it snowed that night, and continued for days. The fields and roads awoke to a thick covering of snow that made it impossible for either man or beast in the valley to move. Corso and Brianda stayed in their room as much as possible. His wound had indeed reopened on the ride to Lubich, and taking care of it was Brianda's excuse for not leaving his side.

She doubted she would ever grow tired of Corso's caresses over every inch of her skin, of his damp kisses and light bites, of his sparkling, sensual, and knowing gaze when with ardent explanations he showed her how to sit on top of him and receive him like that until he could lie on top of her. She had never imagined that contact between two people could cause such a mix of such opposing sensations, strange and pleasant. Her mind, her soul, and her body relaxed and abandoned themselves before she became excited to delirium and then afterward found a calm she had never known.

There was nothing she would not do, she thought one morning at the beginning of February, to continue like that eternally.

Someone knocked insistently. "They are asking for you," Cecilia said through the door. "Pere of Aiscle."

Brianda jumped up and began to get dressed. Corso followed suit. They went down to the hall, where they found Leonor in the company of Pere of Aiscle and a man covered in a cloak sitting beside the fire. The floor was wet from the snow that had come off their boots and clothes. Pere quickly came over to them. The position of deputy to the Count of Orrun had not sat well on him. His shoulders were hunched, and he had lost a lot of his blond hair. Looking into his eyes, Brianda could not avoid thinking of his brother, Surano. She greeted Pere warmly and asked about his wife, Maria, whom she had not seen since that day in the monastery in Besalduch, where Maria had been brought by Corso and Surano to look after her injured husband.

"How good it is to see you, Pere! I also wanted to talk to you, but the snow has delayed my visit to your house. Also, my husband has been convalescing. Do you remember Corso?" She watched Pere's face. "You are not surprised—"

"I've heard, Brianda. What the servants haven't told other servants in the tavern, at the oven, or at the washing area, Leonor has explained to me. I'm sorry about all that has happened. Before you learn about the reason I am here, tell me: Why did you want to see me? Does it have something to do with Lubich?"

"You also got a letter—?"

With a firm gesture, Pere motioned to her not to continue. He pointed to the quiet man who hid behind the cloak and said, "Pardon me, Brianda, I didn't tell you who was with me." He crossed to the fire. "Sir, Johan of Lubich's daughter and the heir of Nunilo of Anels are here."

The man took off his cloak and got to his feet. Brianda held back a gasp as she recognized the Count of Orrun. Instead of a tidy mustache, he had an unkempt beard. He was not wearing ruffs and his clothes were dirty and torn. She found him much thinner, and his poise and haughtiness had abandoned him completely. He seemed a man sunk by exhaustion and adversity.

Reading the dismay in her eyes, Count Fernando said, "You are puzzled by my appearance. I have come from France. The snows have delayed my return and made the last part of the journey difficult, but at least I didn't meet up with any soldiers."

Brianda gave a quick curtsy.

"Sir, I know from Marquo of Besalduch that you went there to organize a force with which to take control of the situation in the county. I hope your efforts have been rewarded. I cannot speak for Lubich now, but be assured that this house is still with you." She looked to Leonor and Corso, and both of them nodded.

Count Fernando gave a deep sigh and turned to the fire. Then he said, "If only there were more like you, but they get fewer with each passing day. As for the French, six hundred will come when I ask but not yet."

"Then what's next, sir?" Brianda asked, eager to know his plans. The loyalty owed to him by men like her father could not erase her worry that it would now be Corso who would have to lead the men of Anels in battle. Six hundred against three thousand were too few.

"I have accepted a truce. The king has requested me at court. The council that should have been held in Aiscle last week was postponed because of the snow and will now be held next week. I will not be there, but in any case, there won't be any confrontation because for now the same posts are being kept." He smiled bitterly. "I am counting on Jayme of Cuyls to ensure that."

Brianda's face filled with disgust when she heard the name.

"Do they know you are here?" Corso asked.

The count looked at him with curiosity. Pere had told him about the new master of the house and the circumstances behind the changes in his life.

"I see you still retain your soldier's instinct, Corso of Anels," he answered. "The king's troops didn't come only to guard the crossings to France and halt the entry of foreigners, but also to watch me, as if I were another foreigner. But you needn't fear. Your hospitality will allow my men and me to regain strength today. We will leave tomorrow. I will have an audience with the king, but on my terms. I will not go with his soldiers."

"And why does the king want you?" Brianda asked.

The sharp look Pere gave her made Brianda regret her question.

Leonor hurriedly intervened. "I will accompany you to your room, sir. You need to rest."

The count agreed and followed her.

Brianda sat beside the fire and repeated her question to Pere. "If he leaves again," she added, "it will be months before he comes back. His absence will only lose him more supporters and further weaken his cause."

Pere poured himself some wine from a jug and sat down beside her.

"If he doesn't go, he will be accused of heresy. He is now under investigation by the Inquisition. They've raised suspicions that Jewish blood might run through his veins. And not only that. There is also an order to accuse him of the murders that occurred in Aiscle when Medardo died and of allowing the entry of the French Huguenots. They know that Captain Agut helped him then and that he's asked for his help again now."

"That makes no sense, Pere!" she exclaimed.

"When the Inquisition gets involved, nothing does."

"I don't mean that. The accusations are absurd, but given the danger he faces, I don't understand why he came back. He should have stayed in France!" She frowned. "Is there anything else?"

Pere kept quiet. Corso came over to him.

"You have also been offered money to abandon the count. They want to buy everybody. And him? Have they made no offer to Count Fernando?"

Pere emptied his goblet in one gulp and rested his hands on his knees while fixing his eyes on the floor.

"His brother is in Madrid," he said at last, "negotiating the conditions of sale of the county. The count will renounce all his rights in exchange for monetary and territorial compensation—"

"And how much is that?" Brianda asked. "What is the loyalty of our ancestors and our freedom worth?"

"They are talking of fifty thousand *escudos* in one payment and twenty-five hundred *escudos* of gold in rent. The king will also give him another title in lands near the Mediterranean Sea worth eight thousand *escudos* annually."

Brianda felt her eyes fill with tears.

"Very tempting. And if he accepts, everything will have been in vain," she said. "The deaths of Nunilo, my father, your brother—why didn't he sign two years ago?"

"Precisely because he had men like them. Now he doesn't."

"Here he has only lost Lubich," Corso intervened. "He has you, me, the House of Bringuer of Besalduch—"

Pere shook his head.

"No one from Besalduch. Marquo's brother changed sides weeks ago, and Marquo has stated his wish to give up arms, as he considers them incompatible with his post as justice. Also, his future father-in-law is not one of ours."

Brianda raised her eyebrows in surprise.

"Who is he going to marry?"

"Alodia."

"He didn't waste any time," she murmured, remembering the puffy-eyed girl who had given her a dirty look in the church. "Of course, neither did I." She smiled at Corso. "And you, Pere? What do you think of all of this? What would you do if you were the count?"

Pere rubbed his temples with his hands and closed his eyes for an instant, as if freeing himself from an internal battle.

"The loyalty of my house cannot be bought—not even with a pile of gold," he answered. "I'm too old to accept these changes, Brianda.

I can understand them, but I don't respect them. There is no honor in this. The king's power over us will be much greater now. And you must fear those who have the most power, especially if they reign from afar." He took the girl's hand and looked her in the eye. "You're asking me what I would do if I were Count Fernando. His only alternative is to send us all to a certain death. What would you do?"

Pere returned to Aiscle that very day. The count and his men left the following morning. When she saw the count ride under the gate of Anels, Brianda felt certain that she would never see him again and a strange sensation overcame her. The footprints the last Count of Orrun left at his tired back would disappear quickly like Elvira's grief for Johan; like Marquo's love for her; like the memories of Bringuer and his wife and daughter, Nunilo, Gisabel's husband, Surano, Medardo, and Johan; like snow with the first temperate breeze of spring.

She wondered how much of the fault was the count's and how much was due to the times he lived in. Like her, Count Fernando had inherited a responsibility from his father, and he saw himself forced to be witness to its loss. She had grown up convinced that her father's words were sacred, unmovable, unquestionable, certain that he would defend the path set out for him from the thorns, wolves, and vermin that he encountered. That was how life had been for centuries, with no more change than that reflected in the features of the ancestors who watched over rich families from their portraits on the walls. Then, one day, the chain linking the past, present, and the future began to twist until it broke.

She did not know what was happening in other worlds beyond Tiles, Aiscle, and Monzon. She wondered if the count had fought hard enough, if he was not also at fault. She had often heard criticism from the lords of Orrun about his leniency and his long absences. She had a nagging doubt. If one day she had an heir who asked her about Lubich, how would she explain the way it was lost? Would he shrug in knowing resignation and understanding or would he look at her with reproach?

She heard footsteps and a familiar arm encircled her shoulders.

"What are you thinking about?" Corso asked.

"About Lubich. I'm going to fight to get back what's mine."

"Where do you want us to start?"

She slapped him gently on the chest.

"Weapons won't work this time, soldier. I will appeal to the courts."

"It will be a long process."

"Time doesn't frighten me."

"It does not frighten me either, as long as we are together."

Corso leaned down and kissed her.

34.

During the following years, a wintry, tenacious, and cruel climate hammered the region. Not even the oldest villagers remembered such chilling gales from the north, late spring frosts, unexpected hailstorms, intense rain that rotted the harvests, and copious snow that covered the fields below Aiscle. The harvests were insufficient and late, wine was scarce, the cows barely produced milk, children died. The faces of the peasants clouded over with a sadness and a deep fear that could not be alleviated even by Father Guillem's Sunday sermons on man's fortitude when facing the trials set by the Lord Almighty.

Sitting by the fire in Anels House on a rainy autumn day with Leonor, Brianda watched her son, Johan, playing with some ash twigs. In a few days, he would be four. He had inherited Corso's black hair and indomitable character, but the frankness in his eyes came from his grandfather. She wondered what the future held for him. There was bad news everywhere. Military disasters abroad translated into new taxes that neither the nobles nor their peasants could bear. In distant parts like the Kingdom of Castile, the harvests were also poor; the nobles complained about being undervalued, the knights about the dearth of favors received, and the clergy about the new taxes they had to pay. In nearby Catalonia, there were endless conflicts over the king's supposed violation of their laws. The peasants in some nearby baronies, taking a cue from the revolts in Orrun, were trying to free themselves from their lords. And to make matters worse, the threat of plague, the damned plague, had extended above Fonz in the south and to the borders with Catalonia in the east. The towns were closed, forbidding the entry of travelers, and all festivals had been suspended, not that the people were in any mood for celebration.

In the highlands of Orrun, it was a strange time as well, a false calm imposed by more than just scarcity. The long absence of the count and the presence of the king's soldiers had, at first, brought more pillaging by both sides. But as time passed and the number of royal soldiers increased, it seemed Captain Vardan was achieving his goal of keeping the area under control.

However, that apparent ceasefire did not mollify Brianda. Even though her childhood had been happy, she had learned that moments of peace did not last long. And since becoming a mother, her worries had become more intense. Her love for Corso grew every day, but her feelings toward her son were of a different kind. Her soul belonged to Corso, her blood to little Johan. As her father Johan had done with her, she had to inculcate in her son a sense of honor and lineage, of his ancestors and of his house.

She suddenly shivered. The answer to their suit for Lubich could not take much longer. The lawyer that she and Corso had hired had advised them to appeal directly to the parliament of the kingdom. Otherwise, the matter would have gone to the Council of Tiles—with Jayme of Cuyls as general bailiff. She was either very mistaken, or the justice, Marquo, would not have dared confront Jayme.

Johan pricked himself with a splinter and began to cry. Brianda sat him on her lap, comforting him with tender words, and sucked the drop of blood from his finger. Then, the door opened and Corso appeared. His cloak and boots were soaked. He came over and stroked

Johan's hair, but Brianda noticed he seemed lost in thought and not listening to his son's babbling explanations about his finger. He exchanged glances with Leonor and she took the child in her arms and left. Brianda got up from the floor and sat in a low chair.

"What news do you bring from Aiscle?" she asked. Pere had called a meeting of the lords of the valley.

Corso rested his arm on the stone mantelpiece.

"The Justice of Aragon has sent out a call to all corners to gather an army in Zaragoza to oppose the entry of the troops sent by the king."

"The king's troops in the capital of this kingdom?" Brianda was puzzled. "Why?"

"The king had one of his closest secretaries arrested as a traitor. The secretary fled Madrid and sought refuge in Zaragoza, exercising his Aragonese rights. The king and the Inquisition want him, but there are many who have rebelled to defend this Aragonese secretary. He has become a symbol of the people's rights."

Brianda shrugged. "No one has come up here to help us with our problems. Why would the lords of Orrun have to go?"

"Count Fernando has requested it. He believes that if the Aragonese nobles stand together against this abuse, his own cause will be better understood."

"What cause?" exclaimed Brianda. "Did Captain Vardan not take possession of the county in the king's name? Who should we believe? I presume that none of you will agree to go."

"They expect us within a week. Pere is going, and so am I."

"You—?" Brianda got up and stood in front of him. "I won't allow it! The matters of the count aren't worth your life!"

"But yours are." Corso looked at her directly.

"What does this have to do with me?"

"The justice will soon hand down a sentence on your inheritance of Lubich. If the laws are respected, you might win. Everyone knows which side Jayme of Cuyls is on. If the king takes control of the Aragonese lands, you can be sure that your stepfather will win the case in compensation for his services."

Brianda helped Corso take off his cloak and rested her hands and forehead against his chest. Corso was willing to go into battle for her, a battle that was never his.

"Lubich isn't worth your life either," said Brianda. The words sounded strange in her mouth but not in her heart. "Maybe in this we'll coincide with my stepfather. I'm sure he's refused to take up arms also."

Corso hugged her and remained quiet.

"Why don't you answer?" Brianda asked.

"Jayme didn't attend the meeting, but not because of his opposition to the justice's request. Your mother is ill."

"She has been ill since giving birth."

Jayme and Elvira had gotten married a few months after Brianda and Corso. That same year, Johan was born. The following spring, Elvira gave birth to Lorien, Brianda's half brother, after a difficult delivery that put Elvira's life at risk.

"She is dying."

Brianda closed her eyes. She had not seen her mother since moving to Anels. This made her sad, but pride had prevented her from making the journey between the two houses. On the Sundays she went to mass in Tiles instead of Besalduch, she looked for her mother in the chapel containing Johan's remains, but after Lorien's birth, Elvira had not left the house.

The sentence her father had uttered before traveling to the parliament in Monzon weighed on her like a millstone.

The people of Lubich were not easily humiliated. But on occasion, too much pride also impoverished.

The day before the men were due to join up with the Aragonese army, Cecilia informed Brianda that Gisabel was there.

"I didn't know what to do," said Gisabel, heavily pregnant with her third child, "but I came to tell you that Father Guillem has been sent for to give extreme unction to your mother—"

Brianda nodded and asked her to wait. She looked for Corso and told him that she wanted to go to Lubich.

"Fine," he agreed, "but this time I'll go with you."

They ordered the servants to prepare their horses, and at midday they crossed the gate of Anels.

Nothing had changed, Brianda thought as they took the fork. The same autumnal colors surrounded Lubich. The same damp carpet of leaves that reminded her of her childhood escapades. The sounds of the forest had yet to succumb to winter's breath. The house where she was born, the thick walls of the buildings, and the high tower were all there, indifferent to the comings and goings of the people. And it was familiar Remon, now Gisabel's husband, who took the reins of her horse. However, on approaching the main entrance to the house, a surge of anger coursed through her veins. The 1322 lintel with the name of the first Johan of Lubich had been ripped out. In its place was a stone on which the crest of Cuyls was crudely carved. She felt like screaming but held back. In that silence brought about by the proximity of death, her anger for that affront would seem incomprehensible to anyone but herself.

With Corso behind her, Brianda climbed the stairs to the bedrooms. She went without hesitation along the west passage, at the end of which were what had been her parents' bedchambers. She crossed a small room with rich furniture and fixed her eyes on the half-open door that led to the bedroom. She stopped for a moment, took a deep breath, and entered.

At one side of the large canopied bed, whose thick material had been moved aside and gathered with black bows, and with his back to her, sat Jayme, stroking Elvira's hand despondently. On hearing footsteps, he turned and quickly got to his feet. In seconds, his surprise turned to aggression.

"What are you doing here?"

"I came to see my mother," Brianda answered in a firm voice.

"You mean to say good-bye to her," he muttered.

"More reason than ever to ask you to leave us alone for a few minutes."

Jayme hesitated but left. Corso followed him to the small room.

Brianda neared the bed. She barely recognized her mother in that motionless, thin, pale figure. She took a chair and sat beside her in silence for a moment until she noticed Elvira opening her eyes.

"Mother, it's me, Brianda."

Elvira managed a weak smile.

"I've been told I have a grandchild and you have called him Johan."

"In honor of my father."

"He was a good man and husband."

"I would have said you had a different opinion."

"What do you know?" Elvira sighed. "Answer me, Brianda: Are you happy with that Corso?"

"Completely."

"More than with Marquo, who you didn't think was a bad suitor?"

Brianda nodded.

"I was barely a girl when I met Jayme," continued Elvira with difficulty. "He has always been my Corso. They separated us."

Brianda frowned.

"Then you should have understood my marriage to Corso."

"Perhaps I was wrong—"

"Yes, Mother, you were. Wrong about him and Lubich."

"Daughters do not perpetuate houses. Nobility and lineage die out with them . . ." She paused. "Have you met Lorien?"

Brianda shook her head.

"He is very like you."

"I don't want to know."

"He is not to be blamed for my actions, Brianda. Promise me that you will watch over him. Like it or not, he will always be your brother."

Brianda remembered her father's request before being murdered in the tower. *"No matter what happens, keep the name of Lubich alive."* A promise made to someone on the edge of death was sacred.

"He already has someone to mind him, Mother."

Elvira closed her tired eyes.

"Live in peace, Daughter," she murmured. "Rancor rots the soul. Forget about the suit and be content with what you have."

"I can't," said Brianda obstinately.

"You are stubborn and proud, like your father. The world he fought for had ended years ago, and he didn't want to see it—" She put out her hand to take Brianda's, which she squeezed tightly. "I have always wanted the best for you. Lubich is too heavy a burden for a woman—"

The pressure of her hand ceded, and Elvira fell asleep.

Brianda felt a knot forming in her throat. For a few moments, she sobbed in silence. Then, she leaned over her mother and placed a kiss on her cheek, conscious that it was her last good-bye. She sat up, dried the tears that scored her face, and went toward the door, where Father Guillem had just appeared. Brianda remembered the first time she had seen him, in that hospital in Monzon. She wondered if he would take the same care, would use his perfect diction, clarity, and firmness in seeing off her mother. She remembered how emphatic he had been that there was no reason to fear death if one was in a state of grace to receive God, accepting Him as the only savior of one's soul. She had often thought about those words and the effort the priest had put into helping the man have a good death. She thought about her father's murderers, about those who had killed Nunilo, about Jayme of Cuyls, about her own mother . . . May God forgive her for her thoughts, but how easy, simple, and even unjust it felt that all of them, because of their fear of death, were given the last-minute option to repent every sin they had committed.

"I have missed you lately at church, Brianda," said Father Guillem. "And your husband as well. Maybe the abbot didn't remind you of your obligations when he married you."

Brianda reddened slightly. Father Guillem, going against Elvira and Jayme's wishes and corroborating Abbot Bartholomeu's words, had not been able to question the validity of her marriage to Corso. Nevertheless, he never missed an opportunity to reproach them for preferring the services of the Besalduch monastery, where they had also baptized the baby, to his own.

"We fulfill those that correspond to us, Father, following the customs of our houses."

"Lubich is the house you were born in, and it has been able to change."

"Those who now live in it are the ones who have changed." Brianda looked back at her mother. "Its people, you, and I will die, but Lubich will continue as it has for centuries."

Father Guillem considered her words but did not reply. He bowed his head slightly and moved with a heavy step toward the bed where the lady of the house was lying. Brianda noticed that he'd lost some of his vitality. His stay in Tiles was meant to be a short one, a type of preparation in his training before continuing his journey in other climes. Every year, though, the diocese in Barbastro asked him to stay a little longer and to extend his preaching to every village and hamlet in the county. They wanted his work to make up for the local clergy's ignorance of the issues raised in the Council of Trent. Most of those priests belonged to families from the same village as their parishioners and were barely capable of religious instruction. If that was the will of God, Father Guillem's trial was long and arduous.

He missed the heat of the lowlands, inhabited by people less reserved and unbending than those from Tiles and its surroundings.

Brianda stayed and listened to the devout man's prayers for a while.

In the anteroom, after observing him in silence for a lengthy period, Jayme said to Corso, "I've been told that you are thinking of going with Pere tomorrow to fight with the Aragonese army."

Corso did not answer.

Jayme added, "You can send word now that you won't be going."

Corso gave him a puzzled look. Instinctively, his hand went for his sword. Jayme cackled.

"I have no intention of fighting you with arms. All this territory will end up belonging to the king, whether your lot like it or not. When that happens, I won't hesitate to tell them about you. Even if you cover yourself with rich clothes and call yourself Master of Anels, you are still a deserter, like Surano."

"You knew . . ."

"I have kept my contacts at court."

"You've had more than enough time to unmask me. Why do you want to do it now?"

"There is always a right moment to do things. The secretary that the king is looking for has escaped from Zaragoza to some place in these mountains with the intention of fleeing to France. You will go after him."

"You could do it yourself."

Jayme looked toward the room where Elvira was.

"I have to be here now. I need someone I can trust to ensure the success of the mission. You can take my men."

"You are more dangerous than I thought. Does this blackmail have anything to do with the matter of Lubich?"

"Don't take me for a fool. Brianda's absurd appeal follows a different route," responded Jayme, dangerously enigmatic.

The hate he had felt toward Johan had now been transferred to his daughter, but for something much more tangible than ownership of Lubich. Elvira was a strong woman, but the sorrow caused by her daughter's absence had consumed her. It seemed as if God was punishing him for having loved Elvira and for having dedicated his life to taking revenge on the person who had stolen her from him. Brianda would also suffer his punishment.

Just then Brianda came out of Elvira's room. Without speaking to or even looking at her, Jayme went past her and into his wife's room.

"What were you talking to him about, Corso?" Brianda asked.

"Nothing important."

Corso courteously allowed her to go ahead of him. He had never kept secrets from Brianda before, but for the moment he had no intention of telling her about Jayme's order. From the expression on her face, he gathered that her meeting with Elvira had been a sad one.

35.

The following morning, Corso sent a messenger to warn Pere that the men from Anels would not be going with him to Zaragoza after all. He hoped that one day he would have the chance to explain his behavior to Pere, who had become a great friend. However, he had no choice. If Jayme had him arrested for being a deserter, he would be sent to the galleys, tortured if not hanged. For this one service to the king, he would be pardoned, which in the past would have meant little to him. He could not help feeling he was betraying the House of Nunilo, but his survival and that of his family depended on this decision.

"Today brings back bad memories of that day at the monastery," Brianda said, grabbing his cloak. The men were waiting for their master in their saddles. "I asked you to return, but it took so many months that I thought you were dead. I hate that you have to go away again. I'll pray that nothing happens to either Pere or you."

In silence, Corso hugged her tightly. He then got on his horse and led the group of armed men, who, though puzzled, faithfully followed him when he signaled to take the fork for Lubich, where they were joined by Jayme's men, before heading into the mountain forests.

For days, a strong north wind cleared the snow from the fields and the roads. Then it stopped as suddenly as it had started, and December's cold, sunny days and harsh, icy nights set in. White frost shrouded the bushes.

One morning in December, a messenger brought two pieces of bad news to Anels. Elvira had died and the Aragonese army had failed in its attempt to halt the king's troops in Zaragoza.

Brianda read the document that Pere had sent to Corso. Her hands shook. Wasn't Corso with him? The letter said that, in the end, few lords and councils had answered the Justice of Aragon's call. Those that did had met up in Barbastro, where they spent days, unsure whether to intervene in a battle they saw as distant and lost. Finally, Pere had decided to continue, but when he got near Zaragoza, he learned that the king's army had entered the city on November 11, after defeating the army of the justice, who was then murdered on His Majesty's orders. The Count of Orrun had been taken prisoner.

Brianda's hand went to her mouth. She could hardly breathe. Where was Corso? The justice who was dealing with her appeal for Lubich had been murdered, and the king was in control of Aragon, which would now have to be cleared of rebels. She had grown up convinced that the rebels were those who refused fealty to their count. Now rebels were those who refused it to the king. What was her situation now? Was she suddenly in the rebel camp? Her worry turned to anguish and fury at not knowing where Corso really was. It had been weeks since she had heard from him. She could not believe he had lied to her.

◆ ◆ ◆

Two days later, Leonor, Aldonsa, and Cecilia walked with her to the church in Tiles, where Elvira's funeral was to be held. The inside of the church smelled of damp soil because they had dug a hole in the House of Lubich Manor chapel, near the altar and in front of that of House of Anels House, where they had placed the statue of the Virgin that had finally been completed by the carpenter. Carefully, several men lowered Elvira's sheet-wrapped body into the hole and, after some prayers, proceeded to cover it with earth. Jayme witnessed the whole process with the expression of a rabid dog. His lips were twisted grotesquely, showing his teeth, and his breathing was agitated. Maybe, Brianda thought, selfishness had prevented her from understanding that love and passion like she felt for Corso were not the exclusive right of a chosen few.

When the funeral was over, Father Guillem asked them to remain seated. A murmur went through the church. Everyone from Lubich, most of the people from Tiles, and some from Besalduch had attended the funeral. Marquo had sat with his wife at the back of the church, near the confessional, that curious closet Brianda had seen when her father gave her the writing desk.

Father Guillem's face expressed profound unease. Brianda could see quite a few people frowning and pursing their lips in concern.

"Many of you have shared your worries with me," said the priest, "and in these weeks I have given myself over to deep study and reflection. I fear that as we near the end of this century full of calamities, we are also approaching the final judgment I have told you so much about over the years. I hear the trumpets of angels announcing terrible cataclysms before the chosen ones can sit at the Lord's side in white clothes and the condemned are thrown into the fires of hell. I wonder if we are following Jesus's example and teachings for the eternal salvation of our souls or only for earthly happiness. And the answer is that God has given signs of His patience for a long time, but now we have provoked His ire, which wounds and punishes us like sharpened arrows in the form of wars, plague, and illnesses. We can all see that the seasons don't perform their functions as before, that the land has become exhausted, that the mountains don't offer the same abundance of pasture, that people die younger, that wolves approach our homes, and that piety and honor are in retreat."

Father Guillem took a long pause that plunged the church into a deep silence. He clasped his hands and raised them to his chest. He bowed his head, rested his chin on them, and his eyebrows wrinkled even more in painful introspection before he continued.

"I have been reviewing my books, trying to find an answer, and I have concluded that the devil is in our midst." A murmur spread and only dissipated slowly. "Yes. Virtue and goodness diminish in the presence of the malign and terrible beast of unfathomable size and cruelty that the Bible warns us about in the Book of Job. The enemy ceaselessly tries to do harm to his unsuspecting earthly victim. Nothing and nobody can escape the actions of the master of hell and of his acolytes, whose list of powers is long and worrying.

"They kill the livestock or make them sick by means of powders, fats, castings of the evil eye, words, touchings with the hand or wand. They take the form of wolves to attack the flocks and devour the animals. They burn houses, destroy crops, and make the fields as barren as the women who cannot conceive. They make attempts on our lives, create accidents and bodily harm. They kill and cause children to disappear. They create caterpillars, locusts, grasshoppers, slugs, and rats that devastate the grass and the fruit. They make the ice more abundant and the temperatures lower. Through curses, spells, and tricks they promise to release captives, fill bags with money, promote undeserving men to honors and dignities, make the old young again, and disturb our feelings and bend our will."

The door opened and, for an instant, a beam of light filled the church. Brianda looked toward the entrance and saw a shadow projected onto the floor. She had to make a tremendous effort not to cry for joy as Corso entered, looked for her, walked toward the chapel before the curious and perplexed gaze of the congregation, then sat behind her and rested his hand on her shoulder. His clothes were covered in mud, his hair was dirty, and his beard was long and unkempt. Brianda closed her eyes and inhaled the familiar odor of his sweat. She knew he had come straight to the church, unable to wait to see her. Her anger over his lie dissolved. He was alive. He was with her. Nothing else mattered. She raised her hand and rested it on Corso's.

Father Guillem took up his discourse again.

"I am telling you today about the presence of the malign being so you can unmask it. Be on your guard at night. Watch to see if the air turns sinister around you, if you sense the putrefied smell of its mouth, if you have dreams and nightmares. Be careful, the devil uses them to torment you. He will deaden your senses with his illusions. And you, men of Tiles"—he extended his arm to accompany his words—"guard your women, made by nature of a melancholic, weak, soft, and infirm disposition, inferior to you in physical and moral strength. It is not me who says this, but prestigious theologians, doctors, and jurists. Women are more fragile than men in the face of temptation and, therefore, more inclined to allow themselves to be tricked by the demons and to take the devil's suggestions as divine. They abound in harsh and vehement passions and maintain their imaginations obstinately. Their avarice is more violent than ours, their minds smaller and less prudent. Their seven essential defects drive them unwillingly toward evil, and these are their gullibility, their curiosity, their more impressionable nature, their greater wickedness, their promptness to avenge, their propensity to despair, and their charlatanism." He paused. "Let us all implore now, men and women, that God's mercy may protect us."

Once the last prayers were finished, the parishioners filed outside in stunned silence, their heads down. Corso took Brianda by the arm to lead her to his horse, but Jayme, accompanied by Marquo and his wife, blocked his path.

"Did you complete your mission?" he asked.

"We searched every village from here to the westernmost valleys, but the fugitive fled to France," Corso responded drily. "Your soldiers can tell you it was so."

"He is going to Bearn," Marquo intervened. "King Henry of Navarre's sister gives refuge to all the rebels who arrive there to organize a French incursion into Spain."

Brianda frowned. Why had Corso abandoned Pere to obey the orders of her stepfather? And why did Marquo know about it? She looked with curiosity at Marquo. It had been more than two years since she had last seen him. His hair, previously curly, was cut very short, and the sparkle in his eyes had vanished. Alodia, heavily pregnant, showed signs of impatience. She did not look well for a girl her age, thought Brianda. She was too thin, despite her swollen belly, and red marks spoiled her pale skin.

"According to my sources," Marquo continued, "they might get the support of certain lords who haven't forgotten about the murder of the Justice of Aragon by the king."

"More wars!" exclaimed Brianda despondently.

"Well, they won't get any support here," Alodia said in a slurred voice. "You heard Father Guillem. The malign one stalks us, surely disguised as a heretic. We should all unite against the invader."

"Shut up!" Marquo snapped at her. "You know nothing!"

Jayme smiled sinisterly.

"Your wife is right, Marquo. The threat hanging over us is much greater than the quarrels between the boxwood and the gorse or the skirmishes in Zaragoza. But don't you worry, Brianda—" He addressed her but did not look her in the eye. "French Bearn is far away and there are more and more king's soldiers to defend us. Our help might not be needed to achieve the peace we have also sought for so long here." He bowed slightly in farewell, but after taking a few steps, he turned and looked at Corso. "Given that you did not serve me well, you are still in my debt."

Corso muttered a curse, took Brianda's arm again, lifted her onto his horse, and got up behind her. They rode in silence for a stretch. The midday sun slowed their steps.

"Why did you lie to me, Corso?" Brianda suddenly asked. "What were you up to with the enemy?"

"In this land, it's getting more and more difficult to know who is who."

"That's not an answer."

"Jayme threatened to expose me as a deserter if I didn't do as he ordered. If I were free to escape, I'd kill him. Now my only cause is you and little Johan. I owe my loyalty to both of you. Nothing else matters."

Brianda turned and kissed him.

"I understand you, but promise that you won't lie to me again."

Corso nodded.

"Did you see the look on Jayme's face when he answered Alodia?" asked Brianda. "He spoke of peace, but his words were as dark as those of Father Guillem's sermon. There was a moment when I felt so afraid that everyone began to seem like strangers."

Corso did not answer. During his time as a soldier, he had learned to live with fear. Each day he rose not knowing whether he would lose his life, yet he had always confronted his enemies face-to-face. Father Guillem's words were much worse than any threat of war because the enemy the clergyman spoke of was not clearly identifiable. Corso did not share his thoughts with Brianda, but his chest burned with insecurity and apprehension.

Once in Anels House, he handed over the horse's reins to a servant and led Brianda by the hand to their room. In silence, he pulled off her clothes, took off his own, placed her on the bed, and began to kiss and caress her as if it would be the last time. He anxiously took possession of her mouth, impatiently imprisoned her breasts in his hands, and held her so tight she found it difficult to breathe. When he finally entered her, it was with desperation, as if the only possible peace were somewhere deep inside her.

Brianda accompanied his frenzy with tear-filled eyes. She too felt the need to love him in a way that would block out her thoughts, her worries, and her fears; to possess him so that her only perception of the world was their consuming pleasure; to honor him with the soul that gave life to this simple body that death would one day rot.

Corso suddenly stopped. Leaning on his elbows, he buried his hands in her hair and fiercely looked into her eyes.

"Let's go away, Brianda," he murmured. "Far away . . ."

36.

At the beginning of Christmastime, Brianda decorated the entrance and hall of Anels House with branches of pine and holly, and, in the hearth, Corso lit a huge ash log that burned slowly until the Feast of the Epiphany. That day, little Johan crowed with triumphant joy when he hit the traditional hollowed log, and a handful of sweets tumbled out. Like the other children in the highlands of Orrun, he was unaware of the worries of his elders, whose mood that year was ill suited to celebrating the incarnation of God in the child Jesus. Father Guillem had loaded them with fasts, litanies, and prayers of penance in atonement for all possible sins.

One morning in the middle of January 1592, the Tiles church bells began to toll insistently. Not even for the three Christmas masses and the offices of matins and lauds had such a racket been made. The pealing echoed through the fields and reverberated at the foot of Beles Peak.

"What could have happened?" Brianda wondered aloud, peering out her bedroom window. "There is no smoke to be seen, and the day is peaceful."

Corso got out of bed and began to get dressed.

"Someone is coming on horseback," Brianda announced. "He must be bringing news."

The rider was Remon, Gisabel's husband.

"I have orders from the bailiff to call and convene the council in the church in Tiles," he said, out of breath, as he drank a cup of water in the kitchen. "The masters of each house in Aiscle, Tiles, and Besalduch must attend. Men only. It will begin at midday."

"But the General Council is always held on the feast of Saint Vincent in Aiscle," Brianda replied. "Do you know what's going on?"

Remon shook his head and left.

The morning passed full of conjecture. Brianda wanted to attend the council, but Remon had been clear that only men were allowed, and Corso did not want her to relive the embarrassment she had suffered in Monzon. Finally, Corso rode alone to the church. When he arrived, the middle benches were already occupied. Jayme, Pere, and Marquo had taken their seats at a rudimentary wooden table placed before the altar. Corso went to the Anels chapel and sat down alone. He was surprised to see Alodia in the first bench.

Jayme was the first to speak. He held a wad of papers in his hands, which he flicked through every now and then.

"For a while, Father Guillem has been warning us that a terrible evil has come among us. Our prayers have not been enough, so it is now us, those responsible for civil and criminal jurisdiction, who must act immediately to root it out." He pointed to a well-dressed man of medium build, serious-looking, with bushy eyebrows. Corso recognized him as the lawyer who had initially guided them in their appeal for Lubich. "Arpayon and I have worked for several days preparing statutes of indictment as they have done in other places affected by similar misfortunes—"

Pere sat up in his seat, alarmed.

"Statutes of indictment? You intend to temporarily renounce the laws that protect the people of the Kingdom of Aragon? To what end?"

"Our situation is so delicate that we cannot wait for ordinary justice to resolve it." Jayme shot a quick look at Corso.

Corso realized Jayme was secretly thinking of their dispute over Lubich.

"May I ask what moves you with such speed?" Pere requested.

Jayme gestured to Alodia to stand up and approach the table. Marquo's wife was a pitiful spectacle; her hair gathered up in a bun highlighted the paleness of her face and her extreme thinness. With her shoulders hunched and her hands pressed against her belly, she looked old before her time.

"Our fears," said Jayme, who with a gesture included Marquo, Arpayon, and Father Guillem, "were confirmed once we heard Alodia's testimony, a testimony she will now share with you." With a look and a slight head movement, he pressed her to speak.

Alodia looked at her husband and then at the audience before she began.

"My son was born on Christmas Day. For me and those of my house, it was a gift from God that he came into the world the day we celebrated Christ's birth. The child was good and healthy until four days ago. When I woke up he was dead." She had to make a tremendous effort to speak. Visibly nervous and with a trembling voice she added, "He had the tip of his nose turned and stuck against his face, his mouth was open, and on his wrists there were marks as if he had been grabbed by someone." She began to cry. "My only consolation was that he had been baptized at birth." She cried harder. "The previous day my son was fine, and then witches killed him during the night."

"Witches!" A murmur spread through the church. Corso saw how the people whispered and nodded, as if at last naming the evil with that word made it concrete and even beatable.

Jayme patiently waited for silence to return and then asked, pronouncing each word slowly, "Would you say, Alodia, that someone gave you the evil eye and that you are a victim of it?"

The woman nodded slightly but repeatedly.

"We will not ask you to say the name publicly because as is stated in these statutes"—Jayme looked through the papers and read out loud—"against such transgressions any man or woman, even if consort, partner, or accessory to the crime, will be able to testify, given that this crime is perpetrated secretly and with demonic suggestion. The abovementioned crimes will be proceeded against—not only those that are committed from now on but also those committed before the preparation and promulgation of this order and statutes, and for which we will take oaths from all men and woman of this locality, married or widowed, so that they give testimony of all they know about any person and about those accused of profanation and witchcraft. We also order and enact a statute that those who wish to defend themselves or contract a lawyer may do so. If a copy of the process is required, it shall be given, but without the names of the witnesses to avoid scandal and enmities."

He looked up and fixed his gaze on each of them, while adding, "The crimes of witchcraft and spell-casting are so great and offensive to God Our Lord and cause such damage to people that they must be punished in the speediest possible manner. Alodia has been brave enough to inform us of what happened. I find it difficult to believe that nobody else here has been witness to the actions of witches and spells—"

Again the voices of those present rose in chorus, but this time people's conversations were frantic and overlapping. Corso heard tales about illnesses and anguish, about quarrels between neighbors, about old women walking alone at night, about some who talked ill of Lent and the clergy, about others who without working found their work done and plenty of hot bread, about songs heard during the night, about people who had woken up in the morning covered in pinches and bruises, about the increase in the number of black cats instead of the common white and gray ones, about the continuous robberies they suffered, about children who died with their bodies discolored, about people who did not smell like Christians, about some people who had refused to help others and later had miscarriages, and about others who had refused to make the sign of the cross on the ground beside the washing area . . .

"How many neighbors do we know who have died as dry as tinder or acted like rabid dogs before dying?" Jayme got to his feet and raised his voice above the tumult. "Do you not feel tired and of bad humor these days? How many of you feel a heavy hand on your hearts at night? How many of you in daytime feel agitated and bewildered because of your terrible dreams?"

"Many of us, Jayme," answered Pere, shouting to be heard. "We have had years of altercations and scarcity, but what you are suggesting goes beyond our knowledge. How are we to become our own judges?"

"We have the counsel of Father Guillem, and we put ourselves under the protection of His Royal Majesty and of the Illustrious and Reverend Bishop of Barbastro to act in the king's name." Jayme looked at Pere with a puzzled expression. "Men, children, and animals die. The crops rot, and the storms, the cold, and the hail destroy the fruit on the trees. Women are barren, and those who aren't lose their children in childbirth or soon afterward, as happened to Alodia. A terrible evil has come among us, Pere, and you suggest we shouldn't act to stop it? The guarantees offered under the Aragonese law you appeal to would convert the trials against the witches into a long process when what we need here is quick action."

Several neighbors applauded his words.

Satisfied, Jayme concluded, "Marquo will read these statutes and indictments, necessary for the imprisonment and punishment of the maleficent, useful and beneficial for the good of this jurisdiction, granted to end the damage and ruin in this district and to punish those who offend God Our Lord, in whose service we act. We will name two men among you to form part of this council, and Arpayon will sign and ratify the document."

Corso listened carefully to Marquo's reading of the document. He wanted to know with absolute precision the nature of that enemy against which he would need to protect himself and his family. He could not see it as a monster with horns and a tail, and for that reason his heart was filled with worry. He could slay any animal from the depths of hell with his sword. However, this intangible being engendered by fear, resentment, mistrust, gluttony, and envy would be difficult to face head-on. Slippery, cunning, and astute, like the worst of traitors, it would show its face when it would be already too late. The words that came out of Marquo's mouth were more dangerous than all the battles he'd ever fought.

When the justice had finished reading, Corso stood up and quickly left, unaware of the reproachful looks aimed at his back.

Once in Anels House, Corso asked Leonor and Brianda to meet him in the hall. When they came, he locked the doors and bade them sit by his side near the fire. He wanted to ensure that nobody overheard the conversation.

"They have accused spell-casters, witches, magicians, and the maleficent of all the misfortunes in the valley. To remedy this, the council has approved a statute of indictment so that anyone can be a suspect and legitimately accused of witchcraft, without need of other information. The justice can detain anyone at any time and more rapidly if there is suspicion of flight, without observing any judicial process or law of the Kingdom of Aragon."

"Marquo?" Brianda could not imagine the young man detaining anyone merely based on an accusation of witchcraft. "And he agrees to his new task?"

"The document was prepared by Jayme, the lawyer, and himself, so he must. And not only that. He will oversee the trials and interrogations of the accused and witnesses, and he will pass sentence even if it is the death penalty, as advised by the council. He will also recommend the type of torture he sees fit. They have appointed two representatives, Domingo the carpenter and Remon of Lubich, to be part of the tribunal, and neither refused." Corso sighed. "How could they? If they had refused, they would themselves have been suspect and fined."

"Heavens above!" exclaimed Leonor. "And nobody protested?"

"After Alodia spoke, there was some sort of communal recognition of what many had apparently suspected."

"Wait, what was Alodia doing there?" Brianda asked.

"They brought her so she could describe how witches killed her newborn son."

"Witches!" spat Leonor. "Aldonsa told me one of Alodia's servants told her the child had suffocated under Alodia's breast. If she didn't drink so much wine, she would be more alert. That she could make up such viciousness to disguise her own stupidity!"

"I'm afraid that no one will believe any other version," said Corso. "She has lit a dangerous flame."

"I see you're worried, Corso," Brianda said, frowning. "What have we to fear if our behavior is proper?"

Corso took her hand. "Brianda, one person's good actions and motives are questioned by another. Was I right to flee from the king's army? Yes, because that decision led me to you. But I will always be a deserter. Can you assure me that nobody has ever looked at you badly? Are you sure you have never looked at anyone with hate in your eyes? Also, per what they said this morning, it's not necessary that crimes have occurred. It's enough that the suspicion exists."

A shiver ran down her spine.

"So, what can we do about it? Lock ourselves in the house? Stop talking to our neighbors?"

"I told you a couple of weeks ago, Brianda, but you didn't take me seriously. Let's go away."

For the first time since she had met him, Brianda heard desperation in his voice.

"Go away!" Brianda got to her feet and began pacing from one end of the room to the other. "Where? This is our home!"

"Somewhere where nobody knows us." Corso turned to Leonor. "Am I the only one who senses a particular threat to this house?"

"You've just said that they'll act with more haste if they suspect flight," responded Leonor. "An escape would make you look guilty."

"When I say let's go, I am including you."

Leonor shook her head. "I'm not going anywhere. Let it be God's will. At my age, my only wish is that, when my hour comes, my remains rest beside Nunilo's."

Corso stood up. "I can't believe what I'm hearing! What has this land got that makes you stick to it with such dangerous devotion?" He went over to Brianda and rested his hands on her hips. "I have always respected your decisions and supported you, but I ask you, I plead with you, and I order you that you hurry and collect your things and those of little Johan. Tonight we will sleep in the monastery in Besalduch, and tomorrow we will travel into Catalan territory, something we have wanted to do for a long time, to see Barcelona, if anybody asks. The indictment will not last forever. We'll come back someday."

"Leave Tiles," murmured Brianda. She looked at Leonor for advice.

Leonor took a handkerchief from her sleeve as her eyes filled with tears. "Perhaps Corso is right. I will look after the house in your absence. I will miss you, especially the little lad," Leonor said, and she got to her feet. "I'll tell Cecilia to get ready as well. You must take her to look after Johan."

When the sun set in the afternoon, Corso, Brianda, Johan, and Cecilia left Anels House. To travel more quickly, they had reduced their belongings to what each of the adults could carry on their horses plus a fourth case that Corso tied to his saddle. The leather bag that hung from his belt contained enough money to cover their needs for at least a year. Young Johan, excited by the adventure, rode with Cecilia.

They did not explain the real reason for their trip to Abbot Bartholomeu, even though he had already heard about the meeting of the council from one of the monks, who had spoken with Domingo the carpenter. Without going into detail, Corso explained he had family in Barcelona that he had not seen since moving to Tiles. The abbot offered them lodging for the night in two adjoining monastic cells.

Hugging Corso in a narrow bed, Brianda prayed that everything would turn out all right. She thought of her trip to Monzon. Seven years had passed. Seven years in which everything had changed. Then, she had gone on a trip to return to a world that would never be the same again. Now she was leaving not knowing when she would return or what she would find if and when she did. If it were not for Corso, everything would look bleak. Beside him, anything seemed bearable, though in a few hours she would have to say farewell to Beles Peak.

At dawn on the following day, Abbot Bartholomeu knocked on the door.

"Get dressed and come out," he whispered. "They are looking for you."

37.

"Stay here." Corso got dressed slowly and adjusted the belt holding his sword.

As he went down the stone steps that led from the cells to the patio, Corso was worried. He stepped outside and froze. A dozen men led by Marquo stood there. Corso recognized several men of the House of Bringuer of Besalduch, and the king's captain, Vardan, with some soldiers. Abbot Bartholomeu and several monks observed the scene from a distance. Before Corso had time to react, one of the men grabbed his arms and pushed him against the wall, while another man rested the tip of his sword against Corso's stomach.

"What's all this about?" shouted Corso.

"A mere precaution so that you can listen to me calmly," Marquo answered, coming over. "We're looking for Cecilia. We've learned that you wish to take her with you."

"She looks after my son."

"Then you will share our worry if I tell you that the lad is in bad hands."

"Who says so?"

"You were at the council yesterday. The names of witnesses are secret." Marquo motioned to the two men holding Corso to release him and to go inside in search of Cecilia. "We will escort you back to your house. You've chosen a bad time to take a journey, Corso. No one should leave Tiles until we finish what we've started, and someone in your position even less so. We need good soldiers for this battle."

Corso squinted. "And which lord do I serve now?"

Marquo came closer and whispered in his ear. "Mind your tongue, Corso. I know you because I've fought with you, but things have changed. You now serve God. Repeat it until you convince yourself, and those of your house won't have any problems."

"I don't know whether to take that as a threat or to thank you," Corso snarled.

Marquo held his gaze and Corso thought he noticed a touch of confusion, as if the task he had been ordered to carry out was beyond his comprehension, as if he had to use strong words in front of his men due to his position rather than out of conviction. Corso could not help but feel sorry for him. The only thing he could imagine was that Alodia had accused Cecilia and that Marquo had been incapable of challenging his wife.

Screams interrupted their conversation, and the two men reappeared dragging Cecilia, who cried and kicked to free herself. Brianda ran behind her, with little Johan disconsolate in her arms, pleading for Cecilia's release. Once Brianda understood the situation, she faced Marquo.

"How can you do this to us?" she rebuked him. "You know us better than anybody!"

Corso put an arm around her waist and said in a low voice, "Don't say another word!"

Brianda shot him a furious look and opened her mouth to reply, but Corso hissed, "We are not in Monzon. This time I don't know how we could save her."

Brianda's eyes filled with tears. She handed Johan to Corso with the intention of going to Cecilia, whose hands were being bound, but Marquo blocked her path.

"Heed your husband, Brianda," he ordered her in a threatening tone she had never heard before.

Then, Marquo turned to Cecilia and said, "You have been accused as a witch and a poisoner. You have been heard to renounce God and take the devil as your master, adoring and honoring him. As Justice of Tiles it is my duty to present you before the tribunal to answer for your crimes."

Some of the monks blessed themselves and began to whisper.

Marquo ordered that Cecilia be put on one of the horses and they began to ride off while she screamed, her face covered in tears and her long black hair in knots. "It's a lie! I've done nothing!" She turned her head and looked at Brianda. "Mistress! Don't let them take me!"

"Where are you taking her?" Brianda demanded.

"We will lock her in Cuyls House until the trial is heard," Marquo answered. "Fetch your things. You'll be staying in Tiles."

Brianda gasped.

Cecilia's cries could be heard until she and her captors crossed the steep stone bridge. Suddenly, a whisper began to form in the surrounding woods and came to them as a wind. On the horizon, above and beyond the trees, pale clouds hovered. A cold sweat covered her body. Trembling, Brianda slid her hand to her belly. She had not said anything to Corso yet as she wanted to wait until she had missed her third period, but her second child was growing there. The day before, she had been afraid that the long journey on horseback could harm it. Now she sensed a much worse threat looming over that new life.

Corso came over and led her back into the building. They gathered their things, loaded the horse, and bade farewell to Bartholomeu.

"You have lived long," Brianda said to him sadly. "Has there ever been peace here? Can you remember any time in the past when no one came from outside to poison our blood?"

The abbot understood that she was referring to the interference of the king and to the preachings of Father Guillem. However, frowning, he replied, "Daughter, the traitor from within is worse that the traitor without—"

Brianda nodded, seeing in her mind the face of Jayme of Cuyls, now the owner of Lubich. She also thought about Cecilia's arrest by her own neighbors. The abbot's words could not have been truer.

They rode in silence and, shortly before midday, they reached Anels House. At the door, Marquo said, "Tomorrow is Sunday. Everyone is expected at the church. Everyone. You have been informed."

Brianda held his horse's mane and looked him in the eye. "I beg that you ensure they don't harm Cecilia."

Marquo pulled on the reins and left.

That night, Brianda awoke with a start. Unable to get back to sleep, she lit a candle and went to her beautiful writing desk. With the key that always hung from her neck, Brianda opened the secret compartment and took out the papers she had written over the previous years. She reread fragments about the happiest moments in her life, and she became emotional realizing that the love she felt for that soldier she had met by accident in Monzon had only increased month after month. She took a quill, dipped it in ink, and wrote:

What would I not do for you, Corso? I would kill and I would die. I would condemn my soul. All of me is with you, now and forever...

She contemplated her husband's sleeping body for a long time and then hid the pages and the edelweiss pendant in the only place where nobody, not even him, could find them. She considered hiding the Lubich ring as well, but she could not part with it.

She needed the strength of all her ancestors to help her continue without fear.

The following morning, Brianda, Corso, and Leonor went to the church accompanied by the servants from Anels House. Given that everyone had been ordered to attend, they had to bring little Johan with them. There were so many people that the meeting had to be held outside despite the chilling wind. Brianda watched anxiously for Cecilia. The door opened and she saw Jayme, Marquo, Pere, and Father Guillem, followed by Arpayon and a sixth man she did not recognize, but Cecilia was not with them.

Jayme was the first to address the crowd.

"Before the pressing danger that afflicts us, justice must be swift and severe. Yesterday we detained the first witch, who was just about to escape Tiles. Our duty is to act as required. We cannot risk this plague spreading to other areas."

Jayme asked the stranger to stand beside him. He was tall and good-looking with strong features. He had neither a mustache nor a beard and kept his chin slightly lowered, which made his gaze at people unsettling.

"Gaspar is the seventh son of a couple who produced only male children. Being a man of good standing, saintly, and a friend of God, he has been granted the extraordinary grace and the special virtue to carry out wonders. He has driven back storms, put out fires, and banished plagues of locusts wherever his services were required. He has cured many of rabies and other illnesses, but his most important faculty is another." Jayme held up a document. "These letters are a license from the Holy Office of the Inquisition of the Kingdom of Aragon recognizing his ability." He asked the stranger to raise his arms on either side of his body. "You can see the marks of Saint Catherine's wheel on one arm and a cross on the other." He paused. "I tell you this so you don't doubt for a second that he is a real witch-hunter. He can distinguish witches from those who are not."

A murmur spread among the people. Various women made to leave, but Marquo's men forced them to stay. Instinctively, Brianda pulled her cloak tighter.

Corso murmured, "The council was held the day before yesterday. Damn this Jayme of Cuyls. He's had everything planned for a while."

Gaspar ran his gaze over the crowd and, in a deep voice, said, "The woman I blow on, that woman is a witch. And I will show that she has a mark, which will corroborate my choice."

He began walking among them in silence. One by one he looked at each woman, scrutinizing them with that strange look of his. From time to time, he raised his hand to his forehead and closed his eyes, as if waiting for a revelation. Brianda gripped Corso's hand in terror. Finally, the man stopped in front of Aldonsa, Leonor's servant, and blew on her face. Two men came over and rushed her inside the church. Aldonsa did not scream. She just kept shaking her head. Brianda bit her lips to prevent herself from sobbing.

Gaspar continued. Minutes later, he blew on the face of an old woman called Antona and a middle-aged woman named Barbara. Brianda knew they both were from Besalduch. She recriminated herself for immediately noticing that the three women picked so far were old. Her fear was so great that to resist it she needed to console herself by believing the witch-hunter was ignoring the young. She then thought of Leonor, beside her, with Johan gripping her skirts, and her anguish increased. With her eyes closed, Brianda prayed that he would not pick her.

A squeeze of Corso's hand made her open her eyes.

Gaspar was at that moment in front of Leonor. He squinted his eyes and remained like that longer than he had done with the others.

Finally, he shook his head and stepped in front of Brianda, whose relief for Leonor instantly became fear for herself.

She looked into the man's eyes and saw his determination long before he blew on her face. His warm breath ran over her cheeks as softly as the blade of an accursed scythe, foretelling the death of her body and her soul.

Brianda felt herself faint. Her senses stopped working. As if in a dream, she silently watched how Corso unsheathed his sword and several men knocked him to the ground. She screamed with all her might, but she could not hear her voice. They held her by the arms, but she felt no contact. The tears poured down her cheeks, but she did not taste the salt.

They pushed her inside the cold building and slammed the door behind her. After a while, she did not know how long, the door opened again and Gisabel was thrown in, tearfully repeating the names of her children, the last one newly born. After her, Marquo, Jayme, the lawyer, the witch-hunter, and a dozen soldiers appeared.

They made the women get to their feet one beside the other and undo the stays of their bodices. The witch-hunter filed past them and stopped at Brianda.

"We'll start with this one."

He knelt down, lifted her skirt, lowered her stockings, and slowly slid his fingers and his eyes up her legs. When he got to her thighs, he stood up, took her blouse in both hands, and ripped it. Brianda began to sob. It disgusted her that his eyes and his breath set on the places that only Corso's had up until then.

She glared at Marquo, and he lowered his eyes.

"You have good reason to be ashamed," she said through clenched teeth.

"Shut up!" ordered Jayme with a glint of satisfaction in his eyes. "Don't think you'll be able to fool us any longer with your deceitful words. How did I not see it before? To think I offered to be your father!"

Brianda looked at him with hatred.

"You brought the evil to these lands," Brianda raged.

Then Gaspar made her lift her arms and stroked her armpits.

"Here is undeniable proof," he announced triumphantly. "No hair grows beneath her arms."

Jayme turned to the lawyer. "Write down everything he says, Arpayon. All just trials need proof and legal grounds to proceed."

Brianda fixed her clothes as best she could and despondently sat on a bench. While they proceeded to examine the other women, her gaze fell on a tiny object on the floor. It was the key that she always wore around her neck on a chain. It had broken when Gaspar ripped her blouse. She bent down and picked it up. She looked for the chain but did not see it. It had probably gone down one of the cracks of the worn wooden floor. She pulled a leather stay from her bodice and broke off a bit, which she put through the eye of the key and knotted.

Aldonsa was the last woman Gaspar studied before the attentive gaze of the other men. He found on her back a mark that was, as he explained, the mark left by the devil's claw when she became his acolyte. The lawyer finished taking notes, and Jayme ordered the women to remove their jewelry and put it into his leather bag. He told them he would keep it as surety for the costs of the trials and their stay in jail in case their families did not pay.

The women obeyed with sobs and whimpers, but Brianda was frozen, terrified. Jayme did not take his eyes off her father's ring. When he approached, she turned and ran to the Anels House chapel. She rested her hands on the small statue of the Virgin and dropped the leather cord around the statue's neck. Now the ring—but Jayme was upon her.

"Give me the ring, Brianda," he demanded.

Brianda refused.

Jayme raised his hand to hit her but thought better of it and called the men. They held her and forced open her fist. Jayme removed the ring, contemplated it with a cold look, and tried it on the little finger of his right hand.

"It will soon be mine," he murmured, before tossing it in the bag.

Brianda spat in his face, and he closed his eyes. He took a deep breath, opened his eyes, and punched her in the face, sending her ricocheting against the wall.

"Jayme!" shouted Marquo, quickly approaching.

"Would you defend a witch?" Jayme howled.

"She has yet to be tried!"

Jayme held his gaze, but did not reply. He walked toward the door and ordered the rest to follow him with the prisoners.

Stunned by the blow, Brianda went outside. She saw Corso tied to a tree, struggling like a savage beast. His dark hair fell over his face, which was bloody. When he at last saw her, Brianda communicated to him through her eyes, concentrating all her energy in convincing him, as she looked into his dark, rebellious eyes, not to say anything, in pleading with him to remain calm, in showing him that the battle had only just begun but that she was prepared to fight for her innocence and her life. She looked to Johan, now crying in Leonor's arms, so that Corso would understand. If she was captive, he would have to look after their son. Corso clenched his jaw so hard the muscles of his neck tensed up. With pain reflected in each inch of his face, he gave a slight nod and stopped struggling.

Jayme read aloud what Arpayon had written and informed them that the women would be transferred to Cuyls House, which they had turned into a jail, to be interrogated prior to the trial that all accused were entitled to. He also told them that the witch-hunter would remain in Tiles for a while as his work was not finished. Then, Pere interrupted him.

"Brianda of Lubich is of noble birth!" shouted Pere. "Her lineage is entitled to all the rights, privileges, and liberties of this kingdom with or without indictment!"

"If you intend to defend her, that's your own concern." Jayme shrugged.

"I will! I will prove that you are wrong! And I demand you free the master of Anels!"

Jayme agreed, and Pere himself cut the ropes.

"Father Guillem," said Jayme, "is it not true that to be obstinately of the opinion that witches do not exist is heresy?"

"It is, sir."

"Even if it is your own wife, daughter, sister, or goddaughter?"

Father Guillem nodded slightly, and Jayme turned to Pere and Corso.

"Don't forget it."

Corso ignored his words and ran to Brianda. He took her face in his hands and caressed her bruised skin where they had hit her.

"I'll kill him with my bare hands," he whispered in his wife's ear, "and I will come to save you. You know I keep my promises. I came back when you thought me dead. I'm alive to save you."

Brianda tearfully nodded. They brought over an ox-pulled cart that Jayme had kept waiting by the graveyard all that time and forced the women into it. Aldonsa looked at Leonor, who covered her mouth to keep back her sobs. Gisabel called to Remon, who hung his head. Antona and Barbara from Besalduch held on to the wooden sides of the cart with their gaze lost somewhere on Beles Peak.

Brianda rested her forehead on Corso's chest.

"Look after Johan," she begged him. "Save our son."

38.

Brianda had never been in Cuyls House. She had passed near it on rides with her father when she was a child, but they had always avoided the narrow path on the border between Tiles and Besalduch that led to a neglected copse of trees. Hidden in the undergrowth was a medium-sized house that looked abandoned. The walls surrounding the small yard were falling down; there were holes in the flagstones, and the roof was missing slates.

She was filled with a deep unease. This would be her prison.

The cart stopped in front of the main door, whose wood the sun had turned gray. The four men who had escorted them roughly forced them down from the cart, and one of them knocked on the door. Soon after, a thickset and sweaty man opened the door, let them into a dark and dirty entrance hall, and guided them to the upper floor, where a scrawny, one-eyed man was waiting for them by a door. He opened it, pushed them in, and locked the door behind them.

The room was rectangular and fairly large, but it was also dark and cold with a stone mantelpiece at the far end. Brianda presumed it was the main hall of the house, but there was no furniture or any decorations on the walls, and a moldy stain covered much of the ceiling. It was difficult for her to imagine her grandfather's brother living in such a sad place. Probably, at that time, the fire had crackled in the hearth and some thick curtains had covered the windows, but after Lida's departure for Aiscle when she married Medardo, and Jayme's for Lubich, no one had maintained Cuyls House.

A weak moan caught her attention. She exchanged glances with Aldonsa and Gisabel, and they quickly crossed to the fireplace, beside which lay a body on a pile of straw. Brianda let out a scream and knelt down.

"Cecilia! My God! What have they done to you?"

Cecilia was barely recognizable. They had cut her beautiful, long hair, and her face was bruised and swollen. Brianda wanted to hug her, but Cecilia whimpered as soon as she was touched. Aldonsa checked over her body with her hands.

"She has been whipped and has a dislocated shoulder," she said, looking around for something.

"What do you need?" Brianda asked.

"Something for her to bite on, but I don't see anything."

Brianda thought for a moment and took off one of her shoes. Aldonsa nodded in agreement.

"I have reset many sheeps' legs. I know what I have to do."

"Help us, Gisabel," Brianda asked, but the woman did not move. Fear had deranged her. She brought her hands to her face and moved away from them.

Aldonsa laid Cecilia faceup and had Brianda put the shoe in Cecilia's mouth. Then Aldonsa pulled Cecilia's arm in one sharp movement. The gypsy's eyes reflected unbearable pain and she fainted. Aldonsa tore a long strip of material from her petticoat and used it to pin the girl's arm against her body.

Brianda lay down beside Cecilia, hugged her, and cried silently until she noticed that Cecilia was waking up.

"I won't be able to resist it again," moaned Cecilia hysterically. "I won't—"

"Don't think about that now," murmured Brianda weakly, feeling her spirits and her faith abandoning her. What madness had taken over this place?

"If they come back, I'll tell them whatever they want to hear." Cecilia began to tremble and weep. "What I saw and didn't see, what I dreamt, what I did . . ." She gave a start and looked around the room, terrified. "Is it night already?"

Brianda stroked her arm.

"There's still a while to go before sunset, Cecilia." She pointed to the only window, which had all its panes missing, allowing the chill February wind to enter. "Can you see the afternoon sun?"

Cecilia sighed in relief and closed her eyes.

"I just want to die," she said before falling asleep.

"They'll kill us all!" whined Gisabel from the corner where she had hidden.

Brianda sat up and rested her back against the wall. Aldonsa paced the room several times, peeked out the window, and finally sat down also. Barbara, the widow, still had her head down, and the old and toothless Antona softly sighed, crooned, and cackled.

Nobody brought food or water for hours. Night had long since enveloped them in darkness when the door opened and the guards entered. Cecilia sat up and hugged Brianda. One of the men carried a lighted torch and the other a wooden bucket of water and some stale bread. He left the bucket on the ground and threw them the bread. The one with the torch approached and shone the light on the women one by one, showing his disgust for them. When he got to Gisabel, he hesitated.

"Why are you taking so long?" the one at the door asked.

"It's Remon's wife."

"Then leave her. She's just recently given birth."

It was Brianda's turn next.

"You must be the noble. What a pity!"

Then he turned to Cecilia, grabbed her by the arm, and lifted her without effort. "You'll do for the moment."

Cecilia began to claw at him while screaming at the top of her lungs. Brianda got up and, taking advantage of the fact that the man was holding the burning torch with his other hand, did the same. She called for the other women to help, but none of the four made a move. The guard at the door quickly threw the bucket of water over Brianda. Then the man hit her until she fell to the floor, where he continued kicking and insulting her. She rolled into a ball to protect her womb and went completely still. Finally, the blows ceased, but Cecilia's cries continued as they took her away. They locked the door and opened another close by. Voices and cries could be heard just at the other side of the wall.

Brianda thought she was going crazy. She did not dare imagine the actions that caused the metallic cracking and creaking sounds. She was unable to understand all the words they were shouting. But what made her cover her ears and begin screaming in horror was the certainty that life was ebbing out of Cecilia's body while those savages first tortured and then raped her. Her dear Cecilia. That poor girl she had once saved from a death by whipping to take her to this place where she thought she would be safe and find a man to love her, and which had now turned into a hell far worse than that described in all of Father Guillem's sermons.

She heard the men panting. First one and then the other. Then a high-pitched, heart-wrenching, crazed cry. Later, silence.

Shortly afterward, the door opened, and they dragged Cecilia's body into the room as if she were a dead animal. Brianda crawled to her and rested her hand on her head. Just that. She was incapable of saying anything to comfort her. There could be no comfort after what they had done.

The hours passed.

Brianda suddenly woke and realized that dawn was breaking. Sleepily, she looked toward the window and what she saw frightened her. Cecilia was sitting on the ledge looking back into the room. She stared at Brianda with her dark eyes, the only part of her swollen face that was recognizable, and said, "Death cannot be any worse."

She leaned back and allowed herself to fall before Brianda could do anything.

When Brianda peered out the window, Cecilia's body lay motionless in the middle of a large pool of blood.

Brianda lost all notion of time. The days passed with hysteric laughing, wailing, sorrowful moans, and pain. The guards had nailed boards to the window to prevent anyone from copying Cecilia, so Brianda only knew night was falling when the slim rays of light that filtered through those boards disappeared. With no warning, the door would open and they would take one or two women. And all who went got their hair cut. Brianda soon understood that those they tortured but who did not confess came back. She did not know what happened to those she never saw again.

Aldonsa and Gisabel were the first to leave, two or three days after Cecilia's death. Four or five days later, they took the women from Besalduch and four more arrived. From them she learned that the others had been tried and hanged immediately.

They did not touch Brianda again, but what she saw and heard was already torture. She did not feel any physical pain but an unbearable sorrow in her soul, convulsed by profound panic and dread of the nightmare her life had now become. She no longer had any tears to shed, but her heart suffered sudden palpitations, and she felt a permanent sensation of drowning and nausea. But one thought prevented her from giving in to madness, one thought nestled her on the rough, cold floor.

Corso.

She went over every one of the gestures, caresses, words, and moments she had shared with him since the day they met in Monzon. That dark, defiant shadow who had driven off the miscreants at the doors of the church; that tall, evasive soldier with long dark hair who had smitten her heart to the point of lunacy, who had become her husband and the father of her Johan and of another child growing in her womb. She recalled how the same intense shiver that she had felt when she saw his face for the first time had run down her back every time he had taken her in his arms, making her tremble with him by night and revel in his solid presence beside her by day. Such was her devotion that she was convinced the sound of hooves she heard at night came from his horse. She pictured him riding in the darkness to be as close as possible to that jail, to tell her that he would get her out of there, that he would never abandon her, and that he would seek revenge for all that horror and evil.

One morning when she was by herself, the door opened, and Pere appeared. His hair was completely gray, and he had lost a lot of weight. In less than a decade, he had become an old man. Brianda gathered all her strength to go over to him. She had spent too long surviving on scraps of bread.

Pere hugged her for a second in silence.

"I've made the council agree not to torture you because of your noble birth. I've also written to the justice of the kingdom demanding that he put a stop to this madness. I expect his answer shortly. Nevertheless, they will submit you to trial in a week, two at most. I will defend you."

Brianda squeezed his hands in thanks.

"What has brought us to this, Pere?" she moaned. "What has happened to the Tiles I grew up in? Why won't anybody stop this lunacy?"

"Everyone is afraid, Brianda. The council has approved punishments for those who aid the accused."

"Then, you are in danger as well because of me."

"For the moment, I'm still someone important. It's Corso that worries me."

Brianda became alarmed.

"Have they done anything to him?"

"He's acting like a madman. He's publicly threatened to kill anyone who lays a hand on you. His attitude doesn't help either the trial or your reputation. People are talking about your power to cloud his judgment in such a way that he dares to defy fear and common sense. I'm afraid they could accuse him. You must talk to him and calm him down."

"He's here?" Brianda shouted.

"You have an hour." Pere kissed her on the cheek, opened the door to let Corso in, and left them alone.

Brianda and Corso stared at each other for a long while, as if neither dared approach, as if both wanted to delay the moment of contact so the hour before departure would not begin. Corso looked at her like a wounded animal, with his teeth and fists clenched, controlling the rage, confusion, and pain he felt on seeing her dirty, thin, pale, weak. Brianda looked at him, holding back her desire to shout all that she had seen and heard, to tell him how Cecilia had died, to announce she was expecting another baby, to plead with him to get her out of there, to ask him to allow her to be delirious in his arms, like when he saved her from falling off her horse over the cliff.

Finally, he covered the distance that separated them and sheltered her against his chest, where she cried in silence.

"Pere has asked me to be calm, Brianda. Leonor too." Corso ran his fingers through her hair in desperation. "How can I be calm with you in here?"

"The trial will not be held for a week," she murmured, trying not to show her despondency, but conscious that another seven days would be an eternity. "You must look after Johan." She felt a sharp jab of pain when she said her son's name. She did not want to ask about him in order not to become filled with anguish.

"I can't even look at him!" Corso bellowed. "My hate is so deep that not even his company consoles me. He reminds me that you should be by my side." His voice faltered. "Those that fought together with Nunilo and your father now watch my movements. Jayme's words and threats intimidate those who could once stand against him. He makes the people afraid and then rises as the hero to save them from the evil he himself sowed. You don't know how much I regret not having killed him before, Brianda. I would prefer the galleys or the rope knowing you were alive rather than—"

"I'm still alive!" Brianda interrupted him. She ran the tips of her fingers along his lips while looking at him tenderly. "I breathe. I move. I speak to you. I feel you inside me every second I spend in this horrible place." She took a deep breath and intoned her father's words: *"The people of Lubich are not easily humiliated."*

"Damned Lubich," muttered Corso. "All this is because of that place. Those that didn't die supporting the count are now made to suffer." His tone turned contemptuous. "The count is also a prisoner. He got paid for selling his land and will now die as a traitor to the king."

Brianda bit her bottom lip to stop the sobs.

"I don't need any more bitterness, Corso," she stammered. "Where is your fortitude?"

Corso held her fragile body tightly in his arms. He lowered his head and pressed his lips against hers.

"Promise me that you'll hold out until the trial," he pleaded. "Think of nothing except me."

Brianda sealed the promise with a kiss. With each breath, she reminded him of the love she felt for him. With each nip of her teeth she revealed how much she needed him. With each press of her hands around his neck to make the kiss deeper she confirmed that nothing could break the bond that joined them, like an invisible but unbreakable chain, because they were each other's soul, beyond their mortal bodies, which would decompose sooner or later under the cold, hard land of Tiles.

39.

The afternoon of the sixth day after Corso and Pere's visit, Brianda, who had remained strong, felt her hopes disappearing as she recognized one of the two new women brought to Cuyls House. It was Maria, Pere's wife, whose pale skin looked transparent on her distraught face.

"You also, Maria!" exclaimed Brianda. "It's not possible—"

Maria wore a strange look, as if she had to try not to be disgusted by her. Brianda raised her hand to her chest, suddenly gripped by horror. The witch hunt had extended to Aiscle for one reason only: Maria had been accused to punish Pere for wanting to defend Brianda. The blackmail would force her father's friend to abandon her.

The other woman, of uncertain age, hazel eyes, and plain clothes, was going around the room sliding her hand along the wall, lost in thought.

"My childhood home is now my prison," she said before laughing.

"Your home?" Brianda asked.

"If Medardo was still alive, I would not be here."

"Lida!" Brianda recognized Jayme's sister and Medardo's widow. "I don't understand. Your own brother can't help you? He should realize the witch-hunter is a fraud!"

"The witch-hunter?" Lida let out a hysterical cackle. "He left weeks ago!"

"But who's accusing you then?"

"Anyone. Someone thinks, suspects, or suggests something, and the following day it happens. Anything will serve: a fight, a feeling, a rumor, a dream . . ." She lowered her voice. "I was foolish. I had an argument with Jayme in front of several neighbors. I asked him to stop this lunacy. I told him that Medardo fought to free us of the fear that chained us to a lord and that he would never have allowed this. I questioned Jayme's authority, and now I am here. He's the one possessed by a demon. Nobody can impede his grandiose work to clear this land of the devil, heresy, and witchcraft." She slid to the ground and burst into tears. "I've wanted to visit this house for a while, but not like this."

Brianda began pacing the room in a daze. If Jayme was capable of arresting his own sister, what could she possibly hope for? Marquo? She had long since marked him as a coward, only worried about his own survival. The only one who could speak in her favor was Pere, and now his own wife was accused. But she could not give in to despair. For Corso and for her son she would have to defend herself.

Just then, the door opened and the thin, one-eyed jailer entered. Brianda wondered how he did not tire of the routine of pain and suffering. Either his nature was rotten from birth or they were paying him so well that he could forget his scruples. Or both.

This time he came toward her and grabbed her arm.

"We don't think it's fair that you leave without a dose of what the others have had."

Brianda brusquely shook herself free.

"You know you can't touch me because of who I am."

The man grabbed her again, harder this time, twisting her arm behind her back.

"Here you women are all the same," he muttered.

He dragged her to the next room, that place she had imagined so often and now saw with her own eyes. In times past, it must have been the kitchen, as there was a large fireplace with a pot hanging from an iron chain, a stone ledge that occupied one side of the room, and wooden battens with hooks on the walls. Her stomach turned, and she had to try not to vomit. The smell was even more nauseating than in the room, where the women had to defecate in buckets; here, there were dried bloodstains on the floor. In a corner, she saw hair that had been cut off; in the fire, a pair of tongs and two red-hot irons; and hanging from the ceiling, some ropes on pulleys.

The heavy man approached her and handed her a piece of paper with some words in Latin.

"If you can read, read it. Otherwise, I'll tell you what it says."

Brianda translated aloud. "I beseech Thee, Almighty God, that as the milk of the Virgin Mary was sweet for Our Lord Jesus Christ, so will these ropes and torments be sweet to my arms and limbs. Amen." Her body shook with fear.

The one-eyed man tied her hands behind her back with twine. To this he tied a rope that went through the pulley hanging from the ceiling.

"We don't know how to make formal questions," he said. "We only ask you one thing: Are you a witch?"

Brianda said nothing. She fixed her gaze on the open window in front of her. It was night. The light of the moon drew the silhouettes of the nearby trees on the rocky mass of Beles Peak.

They pulled on the rope and began to suspend her in the air slowly, until her feet left the floor. She felt a deep, lacerating pain in her shoulders and remembered poor Cecilia. Who would help her now if her shoulder was dislocated?

But she did not scream. She looked again toward the summit of Beles Peak and distracted herself by counting the stars that crowned its top. There were dozens, hundreds. Some twinkled; others did not. She had looked at them so many times on her night rides with Corso! Did the same ones always light up and go out each night? Perhaps when they went out they died forever while others were born? She felt her body lifted a little more. The pain was so heartrending that her mind abandoned her body. She had wings to fly to those stars in that other world she only shared with Corso. Nothing they did to her mattered. They could destroy her body, rip her skin, and spill her blood, but her soul would remain always intact, immune, and inviolable for Corso.

That was her triumph over the flesh, weak and short-lived.

They pulled on the rope again. Another hand's length. Then another. She would not reveal her suffering.

"Let her down," whispered one of them, unsettled. "The devil himself must be aiding her."

She woke in the room when they came for her the following morning. Without a word, they led her to the yard and put her on the same cart that had brought her to Cuyls House the first day, escorted by two men on horseback. For much of the journey to Tiles, Brianda kept her eyes closed. The sunlight reflected off the frozen fields and hurt her eyes. Bit by bit, she got used to it and she contemplated the landscape distantly, as if the person who gazed along the fields, the walls by the roadside, the trees, and the stone houses was not Brianda of Lubich, but rather a feathery being like a butterfly fluttering here and there with innocent curiosity, waiting for the novelties of the upcoming spring.

The cart's wheels crunched along the fork toward the church in Tiles, and Brianda saw a group of riders approaching. Corso was in the middle, and she stood up and looked at him. When their eyes met, he furiously spurred on his horse, reached her, and jumped onto the cart before anyone could react. The men quickly surrounded them and halted the cart.

"There is no law to prevent me going with her!" Corso roared, wrapping Brianda in his arms.

One of the men signaled the driver to continue.

Corso silently stroked Brianda's head with the same tenderness as always, even though she no longer had her long dark hair but dirty, rough tufts. He then ran his hands along her body, as if to make sure she was missing nothing else, not even an inch of skin. He finally placed one of his large hands over her belly and frowned. He remembered perfectly how Brianda had changed, day by day, when she was pregnant with Johan. With his eyes, he asked for an explanation that she did not give and he understood that to name her present state would achieve nothing but add further cruelty to what she was already suffering.

Brianda considered his dark eyes without shedding a tear.

"You have to promise me something," she asked him. "Come what may, look after Johan. He is the fruit of the union of our blood. He will perpetuate us while he lives."

Corso nodded and his eyes shone with emotion.

"Your strength wounds me, and yet I admire it, Brianda. I've killed without remorse and have watched death with indifference, but the desperation I've seen in others now clouds my spirit as if I were a soldier in his first battle."

"The blood of my father runs in my veins. But there is something greater than that, Corso. I survive because of you. I was already dead once, when I thought I had lost you. Each day since you came back has been a gift from heaven." She lowered her gaze. "Has there been any word from the justice?"

Corso held her tighter but did not answer. Brianda understood that her battle for Lubich had been doomed from the start. Jayme's revenge was nearly complete. He had stripped her of all that was hers, and now he would attempt to take her life.

The cart went through the silent crowd that had gathered in the graveyard and stopped. Corso helped Brianda get down and went with her, his arm around her waist, into the church. In front of the altar, the members of the council waited sitting down: the lawyer, Father Guillem, Remon, and Domingo the carpenter. Pere and Marquo kept their eyes down the whole time. Jayme pointed for her to sit before the Lubich chapel so that both the attendees and the tribunal could see her face when she answered. Corso went to the Anels chapel, directly opposite. Beside him, there were two armed men.

Arpayon got to his feet and said, "Be it manifest to all that, called, convened, and gathered, the General Council shall proceed with the present criminal action against Brianda of Anels, inhabitant of Tiles, accused of numerous crimes and misdemeanors, taken for evil and a witch."

He brought over the book of the Four Gospels and asked her to place her right hand on it and to swear to tell the truth in everything she was asked.

"Like the rest of the accused and witnesses," he added, "do you swear not to speak out of hate, love, fear, blackmail, willing- or unwillingness, but only to tell the truth?"

"I swear," said Brianda, her voice trembling.

The notary sat down, and Marquo stood up. With his eyes fixed on Brianda's feet, he said woodenly, "Answer if your name is Brianda of Anels and if you are an inhabitant of Tiles."

"You know very well I am Brianda of Lubich and have lived here since I was born."

"Tell us the truth about all you have been accused of. If you do so, we will treat you with mercy. Otherwise, we will use the full rigors of the law."

"I don't know what I am accused of, and I have already been tortured so I know the rigors you are talking about." Marquo raised his gaze for the first time. He was frowning. Brianda looked at him with disdain. "Given that you are the justice, you must be aware of everything you order?"

"I didn't—" Marquo looked at Jayme, who shrugged with exaggerated innocence. Marquo coughed before continuing. "Have you had any error in faith?"

"No."

"Did you become a witch and as one attend witches' gatherings?"

"No."

"Have you killed babies or given poisons?"

"No."

"Do you know any prisoners or other women who have done so?"

"No."

"Do you think you have ever been at a large gathering?"

"Yes. And so have you."

"Have you ever had vile thoughts or imaginings?"

"Didn't you have, when you fought for the count together with men like my father?"

Jayme interrupted. "Answer yes or no."

"At this moment, yes, I do. I have vile thoughts and imaginings about you, Jayme of Cuyls. You unsettled this land, you ordered my father killed, and now you are leading this great farce."

Jayme reddened. He addressed the lawyer: "Note down this accusation as an example of the falsehoods that come from her mouth. Note that she addresses the tribunal with a defiant attitude."

Then he got up and approached her, waving Marquo away.

"We know a lot more than you suspect. Confess: Have you never been bewildered, out of yourself, not knowing what you were doing?"

Brianda remembered the previous night, when her wandering around the stars had helped her resist the pain of torture.

"You hesitate?" she heard Jayme say.

"No. I have always been aware of what I was doing."

"Your friends have told us about the witchcraft you shared with them."

"I don't know what friends you are referring to."

Jayme went to the table and gathered a bundle of papers, which he showed to the public.

"Like them, you took a toad and skinned it. You bit a hole in the skin on its head. You held the head of the creature with your hand and with your teeth you bit its skin and with one blow you left the animal alive and skinless. You kept the skin and minced the meat, which you added to a pot with brains and bones of the dead. You boiled it and then put it on some boards so the sun would dry it out. Days later, you made it into a powder and gave it to your friends, the witches of your coven." He looked at those who were sitting in the front row and added ironically, "So much detail in the recipe could not be a product of imaginings."

"I have never done what you say," said Brianda.

"You witches always deny your actions, changing your facial expressions from downcast to arrogant. This is what makes the task of unmasking you so arduous. Listen to what another of the accused said of you and your friends. One night you entered Marquo of Besalduch's house, you took Alodia's newborn child from her arms, and you brought him to the kitchen. There, you took embers from the fire and put him on top of them to burn his skin. And once he was dead, you returned him to his mother's arms without her being aware of it."

Someone in the crowd began to sob. Brianda turned and saw Alodia near the door. Beside her, several people tried to comfort her and looked disapprovingly at the accused.

"I have never done what you say!" Brianda shouted, immediately regretting her reaction. She must remain calm to ensure that the mistrust of a few did not extend like a plague over the mood of all. She looked at Corso, who kept his eyes on her. His pose was defiant and intimidating, haughty, as if he wanted to show how proud he was of her. *Look at me every time you answer,* he seemed to say. *I know you are telling the truth. Others have doubted their wives. I would never doubt you.*

"Have you perhaps seen or heard any person doing or talking about the aforementioned?" asked Jayme impatiently. He began speaking more quickly, which forced her to pay attention.

"I have not seen or heard anything, and if any have said that of me, it is a lie."

"Then neither is it true that by anointing under your armpits, your hands, your temples, your face, your breasts, your sex area, and the soles of your feet with certain ointments and poisons, you invoked the devil and on more than one night flew to the top of Beles Peak, where you gathered with your companions and the devil."

"It's not true."

"Did you see the devil in the form of a man with horns? Did you kneel in front of him? Did you kiss his left hand, his shameful parts, and the orifice under his tail, and promise fealty? Did you feel over your mouth the hedonistic smell of his wind? The devil told your companions that he would give them money and make them rich."

"No."

"Is it not true that you were with him and he told them that?"

"I have not seen the devil, I have not done what you have said, and I don't know what others have done."

Brianda was growing weary. All of this was absurd. Why was the crowd so somber? Could they really believe the things Jayme said could be true?

"Did you see his feet?"

"No."

"Would you like yours to be the same? Would you like to have the same feet?"

"No."

"Well, what were they like, if yours are not the same?"

A murmur spread through the church. In her haste to deny everything convincingly, Brianda had fallen into a ridiculous but dangerous trap.

"I did not see his feet because I never went anywhere or saw anyone."

"So, did you not dance with him or let him take you in all the orifices of your body and in the dirty parts? Did you not feel his cold, hard-as-iron member inside you? Did you not feel delight in his entry? Did you not feel his cold-as-ice humor in your sex?"

Brianda frowned, horrified that someone would dare even to put into words those sick ideas.

"No!"

Jayme also raised his voice.

"Confess, Brianda. Did you deny God, the Virgin Mary, all the saints, your baptism, your confirmation, your parents and godparents, and take Satan as your master?"

"No!"

"Is it not true that, after that encounter, you could not see the Host when it was raised in mass, or if you did, you saw it as black?"

"No!"

"Since then, have you induced others to become witches and have you taught them your tricks?"

"No!"

"You haven't done it since then—"

"I have never done it!" Brianda shouted. The interrogation was becoming a battle between idiocy and wiliness, a multitude of questions without foundation. "Where is the proof you think you have? Are the lies achieved from the confessions of tortured women your only proof? What wouldn't you say under torture?"

Jayme held silent for a while, too long. Some neighbors, uneasy, shifted in their seats.

"Do you doubt the words of those brave enough to confess the truth?" He asked the question very slowly. "Do you doubt the standing of this tribunal that only wants to cure this community of the sickness that afflicts it?"

Now it was Brianda who kept quiet. An affirmative answer fought to come out of her mouth, but prudence dictated that from then on, any wrong answer would do nothing but increase the hostility they felt toward her.

"I'm saying that you have no evidence," she said finally.

"We have and we will present it." Jayme took another paper from the table. "Was it you who brought that gypsy called Cecilia here?"

"Yes." Brianda glared at Marquo.

"Did you know that, in the lowlands, her ilk are persecuted by orders of the king and, even so, you wished to save her?"

"They were going to kill her. That is called *mercy*."

"Disobeying the king to save a witch is mercy? So confused are your principles that you see as Christian something that is not? Was it the gypsy who introduced you to witchcraft? Her guilt was demonstrated when she did not have the courage to face this tribunal."

"Have any of the accused been exonerated in these trials?" Brianda asked.

"Were any innocent?" Jayme asked the crowd. Several people shook their heads. "We will continue then. Tell us, Brianda, is it not true that Aldonsa and you saved your husband from death? The apothecary declared that Corso of Anels was cured miraculously overnight by the strange remedies that you administered to him. Did she teach you or was it the other way around?"

"There was nothing strange in any of that," answered Brianda, looking once more at Corso. "My husband is a strong man. It wasn't his time."

"It's curious. What is not strange to a witch surprises a man of science. I also find it hard to believe that a man like your husband, who had nothing, became the master of Anels. I can only think of one way for someone to rise to a position he doesn't deserve."

"It was by his own merits. I see no difference between you and him. At least he didn't steal what wasn't his—"

Jayme addressed the lawyer again.

"Be it noted that she has again accused me without proof or foundation." He turned to Pere. "Tell us, Pere. Has the justice of the kingdom decided the action brought by the accused against my person?"

Pere shook his head.

"Have I ever interfered in the decision of the said justice?"

Pere shook his head again.

"Does she have the right, therefore, to speak in such terms? My deceased wife, Elvira, and I never threw this woman out of Lubich. It was she, of unruly nature, who married in secret, against her mother's advice. And it was she who looked at her mother with such hate that she provoked her illness. Here we have more proof of her wiles, her spells." He turned toward her and shouted, "You cursed your mother and killed her by grief!"

The murmurs of the crowd increased, and Brianda felt faint. Jayme's attacks came with such speed and ferocity she had no time to think or reflect. She could never have imagined that the normal course of her life could be explained from such a perverse perspective. Jayme exploited her weakness to strike more boldly still.

"What would you expect from someone who grew up among heretics? Do you also deny that one of your father's greatest friends was a certain Agut, a Frenchman who entered these lands to fight against our king? What was Johan of Lubich's real intention: Was it to support the count or to favor the entry of the damned Huguenots?"

He now addressed Father Guillem. "In the western valleys, the king's armies are still fighting against the heretical atheists of France who extend their poison by tricking ignorant and poorly proselytized people. Here we are fighting in our own way to the same end. Is not the extermination of witches the best way of showing the definitive victory of God in the battle against evil? Our strength comes from our fear of God. Where did yours come from when you killed that wolf by yourself, Brianda?"

She opened her eyes wide, unable to hide her surprise. She wondered how he knew, even if the feat had passed by word of mouth through the servants of the houses.

"Look at her face!" shouted Jayme feverishly. "How could an apparently weak woman kill a beast with her bare hands if not aided by a greater one?" He seized Brianda by the arm and dragged her to the end of the church. "Come, Father Guillem, and hear her confession!" He forced her to kneel before the confessional. "After what we have heard and the proof we have offered, do you still dare to say you are not one of them?"

Father Guillem entered the confessional, his face crestfallen.

"I have done nothing, as you are well aware," Brianda said to the priest in a pleading whisper. "I have always acted as expected of someone in my position."

"It is often the just who most suffer and are more insistently hounded by the devil until they eventually fall. By the same token, our enemies are never easily discovered where they are welcome. Confess your sins and all this will end," said Father Guillem.

"You started this. We lived in peace before you arrived with your sermons and parchments. You dictated the questions in this interrogation."

Father Guillem shuffled in his seat.

"I warned you that you were not fulfilling your religious obligations properly."

"I take you for an intelligent man, Father Guillem. From your mouth come the words that your eyes question. We have known each other for years. This matter has gotten out of control. It is one thing to terrorize sinners and a very different one to rob us of the life given to us by Our Lord. You will pay for your cowardice."

Brianda stood up and returned, walking slowly, to her place beside the altar, opposite Corso, who was being held by two men. Jayme and Father Guillem followed her and took their places at the table.

"The interrogation has ended," said Jayme in a loud and clear voice. "Does anyone wish to say anything in the accused's defense?" A deep silence spread through the church. "Is there or has there been news of any legal impediment preventing our deliberations?" The lawyer shook his head. "Has the accused confessed, Father Guillem?"

With her head held high and her gaze melting in Corso's, Brianda answered for him. "I know that I have been condemned by you from the start, whether I confess to what you want to hear or if I tell the truth. And that certainty makes me free to speak the truth. I am innocent of all your accusations. As innocent as all the other women you have unjustly tried."

She then looked at the members of the tribunal one by one: Arpayon, Jayme, Marquo, Pere, Remon, Domingo, and Father Guillem. They were people like her, neighbors from the same valley, members of the same community, who had become vile murderers in the name of the Almighty and the king. "May God have mercy on you, even though you do not deserve it."

40.

So many people had attended the trial that the members of the council decided that no one could move from the church while they went outside to deliberate. Brianda went to Corso and sheltered in his arms under the watchful gaze of the guards and the people of Tiles, who, between whispers and silences, made the sign of the cross or shook their heads in exaggerated and false dismay.

"I know they will not be long, Corso," she whispered to him, digging her nails into his chest. "Promise me that you will take my hand and look at me when my hour comes. Promise me that you will be by my side at the final moment."

Corso's breathing became a grunt in his throat. He looked at the guards out of the corner of his eye. Brianda caressed his cheek.

"Yes, you could take his sword and easily kill them. And then what? They would kill you. You must live. For me and for Johan."

Corso pressed her hand against his cheek, partly closed his eyes, and obstinately muttered, "I've always done as you've asked. I will take your hand and I will be by your side and I will look after our child. But do not ask me to live without you, because that is impossible, Brianda. I can't. I wouldn't know how to do it." His damp eyes glistened. "What kind of life can I hope for if you—"

A stir interrupted him. The council members entered the church and walked determinedly toward the altar. Marquo took his position to announce the verdict. In a faint voice, he said, "I, Marquo of Besalduch, gentleman, citizen, county justice, and district judge of the valley of Tiles in the territory and jurisdiction of Aiscle, heard and considered the merits of the trial and the declarations made in it by Brianda of Anels, prisoner and accused, and having Our Lord as witness, from whom all just trials proceed, we declare sentence and by this, our final sentence, condemn said Brianda of Anels to bodily death, so that her natural days cease with death by hanging."

"You cannot hang her!" shouted Corso. "She is pregnant!"

His words swept through the whispering church.

"You would say and do anything to save her, wouldn't you?" said Jayme.

"It is the truth," responded Corso. "If you hang her, the child in her womb will be killed."

Jayme pointed to a balding, shrunken woman.

"You, from Darquas. Weren't you a midwife? Come and feel this woman."

The old woman approached with difficulty. She placed her bony hands over Brianda's belly and then squeezed her breasts.

"She is very thin," she said. "I can't tell."

"This is nothing more than a scheme to delay her death. We shall not continue to suffer the wiles of this witch." Jayme signaled the guards to take her outside.

"Wait!" shouted Corso. "The tribunal has not had its say! Do you all truly agree? Pere? Marquo?" One by one, they dropped their heads as he said their names. "Damn you all!"

Several voices in the crowd rebuked his curses. Jayme threw him a grim look.

"We will overlook your attitude because we know it is the evil influence of your demonic wife," Jayme said. "One day, when all this has passed, you will thank us for having saved you from her."

Brianda took Corso's hand and squeezed it hard. She began to walk outside with her eyes clouded with tears. She needed to leave that asphyxiating building, remove herself from those miserable men she now saw as deformed monsters. She wanted, no matter how briefly, to walk with Corso hand in hand for the last time in that frozen land where their hearts had burned; to slide her gaze over the valley where she had been born, raised, loved, and hated, and where she would die at the age of twenty-two, the victim of the worst of sicknesses. Not even the plague was as destructive as the vengeance, madness, and fear that had spread like a pestilence in the minds and hearts of the people of Tiles. If witchcraft really existed, she was witnessing the greatest of spells. Despite that horror, she saw before her the same fresh landscape and the same imperturbable Beles Peak that she knew from childhood, when she had lived with her father and mother in her adored Lubich.

The members of the council came out of the church and walked toward the entrance to the graveyard. The guards motioned Brianda and Corso to follow them. They went through the small gate, turned to the right, walked past the graveyard and the church along a rocky path, and came out in a small field where a simple scaffold had been built. Near it, she could see several holes in the ground and some rectangular mounds of earth. She immediately realized that the others had been buried there, including her beloved Cecilia. What terrible beings had they become in their neighbors' eyes that they could not even be buried in holy ground?

The people who had attended the trial and others who had not been able to get into the church joined the cortege and began taking up positions to watch the execution. Brianda noticed that there were many children, some as young as Johan, and she felt a stab of desperation realizing she'd never see her child again.

"It has been well worth the hangman's time to come from Jaca," she heard someone say. "This one makes fourteen!"

She went weak at the knees and held on to Corso's arm to stop herself from falling. He held her by the waist and brought her to him. He did not let go until they got to the scaffold, where the hangman, a hefty stranger with a wrinkled and expressionless face, waited with his arms crossed and his legs apart. Two beams had been thrust into the ground, and they were joined by another horizontal beam at the top. Some boards acted as improvised steps to get up on a small and rudimentary wooden platform. When it was removed, the bodies would be suspended in the air.

Father Guillem came over to Brianda carrying a small box and opened it. He took out a consecrated Host, offered it to her, and said, "May the body and blood of Christ keep you in eternal life."

She took the blessed bread on the tip of her tongue and felt it burn her. She wanted to spit it out because of the injustice committed in its name, but if she rejected the Host, her gesture would become a public confession of her guilt. She allowed it to dissolve in her mouth and swallowed. She looked at Corso and whispered, "You will keep me in eternal life . . ."

Jayme asked the hangman to proceed with the execution. Brianda looked at Jayme and saw that he was playing with something in his hands: her emerald ring. The blood boiled in her veins and hate ran like a whiplash through her body. She looked him in the eye, and, as if she had rehearsed the words beforehand, she said, "You have named me a witch, and, as such, you end my life, believing that Lubich will be yours forever as a result. Well, listen to my words, Jayme of Cuyls. What you do to me is nothing compared to what I wish for you. You will not be free of me. The Cuyls will procreate to die and only one of each generation will survive to keep your lineage until the day of your complete extinction, when the blood of your house will burn and vanish into hell. And the last will know, as certain as death does not placate the thirst for revenge, that it was me, Brianda of Lubich, who returned to recover what was mine."

The silence was deafening. Impatient, Jayme signaled to the hangman, who took Brianda's arm to lead her up to the platform. Corso pushed him away.

"I'll do it!" he howled. He took her hand, caressed it, and held it as if she were a queen ascending the throne.

The hangman put the rough rope over Brianda's head and adjusted the noose around her neck.

Brianda felt a sudden fear grip her body. In a few moments, her heart would stop beating, and the blood would stagnate in her veins. Her senses would be snuffed out in an instant, not like the languid embers of a fire, but like the flame of a candle in a gust of wind. At breathtaking speed, her mind went over the most important moments in her life, all written down and hidden away in the writing desk her father had given her, and she suddenly remembered the small key that hung on the Virgin of Tiles statue. She had forgotten to tell Corso about it.

She lowered her gaze toward him. His breathing was a convulsive pant. She knew that Corso was making a terrible effort not to break down and give in to desperation. He had promised to be with her when she made the transition from life to death, and he would keep his promise even if he were bleeding from every pore.

"When I close my eyes for eternity, I will only see you," she whispered. "I don't know how to explain it, my love, but I feel this is not our end. Don't put 'rest in peace' on my gravestone because I won't. I promise I'll defy the precepts of the hereafter to be with you. I will return to you—"

The ground opened beneath her and Brianda simultaneously felt her stomach churn, a painful snap in her neck, and a dizziness in which she still heard a deafening noise.

Like a savage and crazed giant, Corso swung at the wooden beams of the scaffold, bellowing, and began to hit them with his shoulders. At the third attempt, the top beam came loose and fell on him, slashing open his cheek, and letting Brianda's body fall to the ground. Corso knelt on the ground and took her in his arms. Her face and lips were pale.

Blood from Corso's wound dripped onto her lips, coloring them, giving them a fleeting appearance of health. Corso roared her name and Brianda's eyes fluttered. Her lips parted slightly, as if wanting to drink that liquid and quench her final thirst. She then opened her eyes, looked at him as if from afar, and allowed her last breath to leave her body, with the same gentle speed at which her eyelids sank and her head searched for its final resting place on his arm.

Corso remained mute and still, hugging her with brutal avarice, until someone came over to show him which grave she was to be put in. As if they had stuck a lance in his side, he stood up with her in his arms, walked past the members of the council, spewing saliva from his mouth like a rabid dog, and crossed through the crowd who watched with a mixture of shock and distress the aggressive grief of the master of Anels. He called his horse, climbed one of the stone walls to mount the Friesian with Brianda still in his arms, and shot off at a gallop along the roads they had traveled together over the last years.

For hours he talked to her as if she were alive, reminding her of every corner where they had loved each other, every word spoken by day and by night, every shared gesture. He went through the woods of Lubich with her to that little bridge she loved so much, where she had saved him from the wolf. As night fell, he rode up the path that took them close to the summit of Beles Peak, shining like never before in the moonlight, and he pointed to and named each house, as if nothing had happened, as if he were talking to her of a happy world, as if at any moment her eyes could begin to blink again with the vitality of one of the stars in the heavens.

He covered her with his cloak so she would not get cold. He pressed her against his chest to whisper in her ear. And he kissed her dozens of times, until her final frosty cold convinced him that she, Brianda, the reason for his existence on earth, was dead.

He returned to the rear of the church, chose the grave farthest away from the rest they had dug, jumped in, and lay Brianda down with exquisite delicacy. He sobbed over her, kissed her for the last time, placed a blue flower on her bosom, and spread his cloak over the body of his beloved so that nothing could blemish the skin that his hands had so insatiably caressed.

Finally, he began to cover her with earth, slowly, while swearing that he would wait for her with all the patience that madness would allow, that the opportune moment would come to take revenge on those who had snatched away their lives, and he would breathe only to wait for the day when she would fulfill her promise.

Until then, he would not rest either.

41.

2013

"Neli, come quickly, please!" Isolina's voice pleaded at the other end of the phone line. "Brianda! Oh my God!"

"What's the matter, Isolina? Try to calm down!"

"She's not breathing! I call her name, and she doesn't react!"

What? Neli had seen Brianda just a couple days before, and she had seemed fine, maybe a little pensive. She knew her friend had been spending hours going over that diary from the old desk in Corso's house—

Suddenly, she had a terrible realization.

"Leave her!" she shouted at Isolina. "Don't touch her! I'll be right there!"

Neli ran up to the bedroom and into the bathroom, where Jonas was taking a shower. She asked him to look after the children, quickly explaining that Isolina needed her. She snatched the car keys from the table in the hall and ran out. A racket of rain crashing against the stones greeted her. She could not remember the last time it had rained so hard, not even that day when the sudden storm had forced Isolina, Brianda, and her out of the graveyard. By the time she got into the car, she was already soaked. Even going full speed, the windshield wipers couldn't give her a clear view for more than an instant at a time, and the side windows showed a constant stream of water.

She knew the way so well that she was still able to make the drive, but she had to concentrate to prevent herself from veering off the narrow road at the fork to Anels. It was ten in the morning, but it seemed like night was approaching. Beles Peak was hidden somewhere behind the dark, low clouds. The rest of the landscape was a blur. The journey took forever.

She finally passed the old washing area and the fountain. She was almost at Anels when a figure emerged from the torrential rain and stepped in front of the car. Neli screamed and braked hard, narrowly avoiding a collision. She opened her mouth to yell, but then recognized him. Soaked to the skin, Corso leaned heavily on the hood of the car. His long dark hair fell over his shoulders in clumps, and his scarred face revealed a mixture of fear and astonishment.

"Corso!" exclaimed Neli, opening the window an inch. "What are you doing? I nearly ran you over!"

He came to her and rested his fingers in the gap in the window.

"I thought you were the doctor," he babbled, stunned. "It's too late!"

"What do you mean?"

"I just saw her! Brianda is dead!"

"Get in the car!" Neli ordered him.

Corso did not move. His gaze remained fixed on some point on the ground, letting the water from the sky lash his body, as if in punishment.

Neli rolled down the window a little more, grabbed his jacket, shook him, and repeated, "Get in the car now!"

Corso looked at her in puzzlement but obeyed.

"What do mean you saw her?" she asked, putting the car in gear.

"That night last week when I found you in my house, she said she would call me, but she didn't. I went out for a walk today, and I came here to ask about her. Her aunt brought me up to her room and—" He opened his mouth and let his head fall to his chest, as if afraid to say the words again. "I don't understand. She was so young. Why do things like this happen?"

Neli drove the last stretch in silence and parked in front of the main door. Corso's horse was wandering loose there, under close surveillance from Luzer in the shed. Neli got out of the car and ran to the front door to get out of the rain, but Corso did not follow. She ran back to the car and climbed in.

"Aren't you coming with me?"

Corso shook his head. "I can't see her like that."

"Like what? Was she stiff? Cold? Did you touch her?"

"I didn't have to. I know the look of death."

Neli turned to him.

"Come with me, Corso." She put her hand on his arm. "Do it for Brianda."

Corso frowned, confused, but something in Neli's gaze made him agree.

The front door was open. They went in and Neli called Isolina, who came running.

"What is wrong with this house?" the woman moaned. "First Colau and now her—" She burst out crying. "And no sign of the doctor. What am I going to tell my sister?"

"Take me to her room," Neli asked her. "For the moment, don't call anyone or say anything."

Isolina led them up the stairs and down the hall to Brianda's bedroom door.

Neli felt tears coming to her eyes when she saw Brianda on the bed. She was dressed in a long-sleeved white cotton nightdress. Her face was as pale and gaunt as an old wax candle, and her lips had a bluish tinge. A faint light entered through the window, and a strange quiet dominated the room, as if the crashing rain had no right to invade that place. It looked as if life had abandoned her friend's body.

She took a chair and went over to the bed. She stretched out her hand to touch Brianda's chest to check for breathing but withdrew it. She did not want any abrupt movement to upset Brianda, if that was still possible. She looked at Corso and Isolina and signaled them to remain silent and still.

"Brianda, listen to me," she began to say. "I don't know exactly where you are, but I want you to come back with me. I am going to count from ten to zero and then you will wake up."

Neli spoke the words very slowly and then counted, but nothing happened. She repeated the words and again counted, but Brianda did not move. Frustrated and confused, Neli rubbed her temples.

Corso approached.

"I told you, Neli," he said in a deep voice, resting a hand on her shoulder. "She's gone. The doctor will know what has to be done."

Isolina nodded. "That's enough, Neli," she said, letting a sob escape.

Neli frowned. She stood up and signaled to Corso to take her place. Then she leaned over Brianda.

"There is someone here who is waiting for you, Brianda," she said. "He will count from ten to zero and then you will wake up."

Corso looked at her skeptically, but Neli insisted.

"Take her hand in yours," she pleaded with him in a low voice. "Please! Speak to her!"

"Ten, nine, eight, seven, six—" he began to count, with conviction.

"Very slowly," Neli insisted.

"Six, five, four," he continued, "three, two, one, zero—"

At that moment, an explosive thunderclap shook the house, rattling the windowpanes. The weak light from outside became even weaker and the room sank into darkness.

"Corso . . ."

The three of them held their breath as a pinkish shade began to steal over Brianda's cheeks and she parted her lips.

Astonished, Corso leaned over her. "Brianda?"

Brianda heard the deep, penetrating, familiar voice interrupting her thoughts. She slowly began to become aware of her surroundings. Her body was resting on something soft. She had feeling in her toes and fingers, in her legs and in her arms, in her torso and her head. And she could hear Corso. Her neck did not hurt. She was not afraid. She was not dead.

She blinked slightly. Then, she opened her eyes, looked at him, and smiled.

"I promised you I would return," she whispered, squeezing his hand. "Separated for so long, Corso, and now it seems as if it was a dream—fleeting because it is over, but unbearably long while it lasted."

Stunned, Corso looked at Neli. She whispered some words in his ear, asking him to repeat them out loud.

"It's over, Brianda," he said in a hoarse voice. "You have returned."

Brianda's smile widened. She stretched and yawned, as if waking up from a pleasant nap.

"You are in your room in Anels House," Neli added. "Your aunt Isolina, Corso, and I, Neli, are with you."

Brianda gave her a puzzled look, as if something inside her rejected that information. She closed her eyes and, for an instant, Neli was afraid that she would return to the shadows from which she had come.

"It's raining a lot, Brianda," she said, hoping to orient her bit by bit in her new reality. "It's been drizzling all week, but today it's pouring. How about you get up, we'll have some tea and chat for a bit?"

Brianda hesitated before answering. She slid her gaze around the room and her eyes began to show some slight understanding and recognition. She closed her eyes, meditated for a moment, and opened them again.

"Neli! If you only knew what I have lived!"

"I understand." Neli patted her on the hand. "You don't know how much I want to hear about it. But promise me that you will never make another regression on your own."

"How can I explain it to you?" said Brianda, sitting up, now very excited. "It happened without me realizing it. I was rereading the diary, and I must have fallen asleep—" Her face tensed up. "Poor Brianda! It was terrible!"

"Could you please tell me what you're talking about?" interrupted Isolina. "Are you saying this isn't the first time this has happened? You scared the life out of me!"

"I don't understand," Corso murmured, getting to his feet. "I could have sworn that—"

Brianda realized what she'd said. Blushing with confusion, she bowed her head. Neli came to her rescue.

"She just went into a little hypnotic trance. That's all."

"That's all?" repeated Corso, confused.

Just then, his cell phone rang.

"Sei già qui? Non ti aspettavo prima di venerdì. Adesso arrivo."

His wife, who he wasn't expecting until Friday, had arrived early and was looking for him.

He went toward the door, where he stopped and looked first at Brianda and then at Neli. He muttered something and left.

"Corso!" Brianda called, jumping out of bed and intending to run after him.

"Let him go, Brianda," said Neli, holding on to her arm. "You will find the moment."

"But did you see his face, Neli? He looked at me with pity, like I was crazy."

Neli shook her head, though she'd also noticed Corso's dismay. Anyone would have been thrown by the scene.

"I don't think so," she said calmly.

Isolina sat on the chair beside the bed and stared at Brianda. Then, she began to cry. Brianda hugged her.

"I don't know what I have done to you, Aunt Isolina, but I'm very sorry."

Isolina let out a nervous giggle. "A trance? I came to wake you up and you were gone. I was so convinced that now it's like you came back from the dead!"

"Then stop crying, because I'm back." She dried the tears that ran down her aunt's cheeks and added happily, "How about you go make some coffee to help me wake up? Neli will stay with me while I take a shower and get dressed."

Isolina agreed and left them alone. Brianda began to tell Neli everything she had lived in her regression. Neli listened attentively, eager to fill in the gaps in the incomplete historical documents.

"So, what do I do now?" asked Brianda. "I know I have found him." She brought her hand to her chest. "I feel it in my heart." She touched her forehead. "My mind accepts it as true." She brought both hands to her cheeks. "Every cell in my body and nerve in my skin recognizes him from all those years ago—" She looked at her friend in desperation. "But Corso doesn't recognize me. He should have taken me in his arms. He should have told me he had been waiting centuries for me. But he ran away!" She burst out crying. "He must think I'm one of those crazies who gets obsessive after having sex once. If only I hadn't come to Tiles, Neli. I suffered when I didn't know my real soul, but to know it and lose him again would make me wish for eternal damnation—"

"Don't say that," Neli cried. "Give him time. You needed a lot of time to understand what was happening to you, right?"

Brianda went to the window and opened it, letting the rain splash on her face as she looked across the valley. The last time she had left this room to go to the old church of Tiles, now in ruins beside the graveyard, she had not returned for centuries. The experience was so fresh in her mind, in her heart. She needed to reconcile herself with this land that she felt more attached to every day. She turned her gaze toward the east, where the undergrowth hid the ruins of Cuyls House, and wondered if she would dare go there one day, now that she knew what atrocities had taken place behind its walls. She looked to the west and let her thoughts wander to her beloved Lubich.

What would need to happen for its current owner to once again look at her with love in his eyes?

And what if that never happened?

42.

It stopped raining two days later, but a persistent dampness continued to soak the stones and the bones.

Sitting in front of the computer in Colau's office with Luzer at her feet and a blanket on her lap, Brianda rapidly typed the last paragraphs of a document. She had decided to record everything she had learned through Brianda's diary and her regression, which remained vivid in her mind. She did not want to forget a single detail.

As if she ever could.

Now that she knew the reasons for her nightmares, her headaches, and her anxiety, she felt she would never be the same again. She was no longer the woman who had come to Tiles in October looking to calm her fragile spirits but another, much more ambitious one. The future was unthinkable without Corso. An anxiety attack was nothing in comparison to her despair at thinking that she had found him in a time when they could not be together. Her most burning desire was no longer to find peace and calm but to get used to living without them.

Her cell phone vibrated on the desk. It was Esteban. It had been several days since she had spoken to him and the previous conversations could not have been more superficial, as if any intimacy they had once shared had now completely disappeared.

She answered.

"I missed your voice," said Esteban. "How are you?"

"Fine," she answered. "You?"

"You know. Busy during the week, but Friday comes and the house seems too empty. It's been almost a month since you left. I'm taking a couple of days off to come up and see you."

"No—"

"No? No because you're coming back soon, or no because you don't want to see me?"

Brianda was quiet for too long.

"What's wrong?" Esteban asked, alarmed.

She swallowed. She knew she had to tell him the truth. Her future was clear: either Corso or nobody. It was unfair to deceive Esteban any longer.

"I've been thinking, Esteban, I just can't be with you any longer. I'm sorry. I'm so sorry."

Brianda imagined Esteban's face at the other end of the line. The long silence was charged with shock, disbelief, rejection, and fury.

"Why?" he finally asked.

If she told Esteban the real reasons, she thought, he would think she really wasn't right in the head.

"I don't love you the way I should," she answered.

"And you've come to this conclusion thanks to the solitude of the mountains or because you met someone else?" Esteban's tone was biting. "Let me guess. That devil on horseback. I could tell you were attracted to him, but I thought it was nothing. I trusted you . . ."

"He's married," said Brianda, without thinking.

"So now you just have to get him to leave his wife." In seconds, Esteban went from surprise to bitter reproach. "And you love him the way you should? That fast?"

"Yes," she answered firmly. She could not explain that she had loved Corso for centuries.

"Then there's nothing that can be done...," Esteban said in a tone halfway between a statement and a question. He remained quiet for a few moments, waiting for something from Brianda that never came, and hung up.

Brianda sat with the phone in her hand for a long while. On the one hand, it hurt terribly to see how quickly she had been able to end a relationship that had lasted years. On the other, the feeling of freedom and of having done the right thing brought her enormous relief.

Isolina peeked around the door. When she saw Brianda, she came into the study.

"I'm back," she informed her in a cheerful voice. Isolina, who bit by bit was recovering her old decisive attitude, had been down in Aiscle with Petra. She came over to the desk, but didn't sit. She didn't like to stay in the office for long, she said, as she could see her husband in every corner of that room. "What are you doing?"

"Just typing up some of Colau's notes."

"Are you OK?"

Brianda nodded. She knew Isolina's yoga experience had helped her accept Neli's explanations about the meditative state she had entered, but since that episode Isolina had kept a more vigilant eye on Brianda.

"How did the shopping go?"

"Good. We saw Corso, who was with his wife—very pretty, by the way—and he asked after you." She shook her head. "I don't know how that relationship works, coming and going from so far—"

Brianda said nothing.

Isolina added, "Ah, and tomorrow there's a village meeting in the bar. From what Petra has told me, they're going ahead with that witch tourism business. They'd like to have something ready for this summer. I don't know whether to tell Neli—"

"I'll talk to her," Brianda offered.

Isolina left and Brianda sighed, her head in her hands. Corso had not recognized her. Corso was still with his wife.

She did not know what to do. What was the use of having discovered everything if she could only share it with Neli?

She focused her attention on the screen and set about revising what she had written.

Then an idea came to her.

The following night, after dinner, Brianda drove to the bar in Tiles. She hadn't been there since November. Back then, she had been worried about running into Neli again, just after finding out she was a modern-day witch. That same night, she had seen Corso for the first time. She remembered how his face and his gaze had already seemed familiar, and how his name had risen in her mind as if it had always been there.

On this occasion, her excitement had to do with the contents of the folder she was carrying. She scanned the bar for Neli. She had called and told her about her plans, and Neli had promised she would be beside her.

Nobody was playing cards or the poker machines, and the television was switched off. Three square tables had been placed in front of rows of chairs for the meeting. Standing beside the tables, Brianda recognized the gray-haired mayor, Martin, young Zacarias, and Alberto, the owner of the bar. A couple dozen people had already taken their seats, drinks in hand. Neli was sitting in the second-to-last row with Jonas and Mihaela.

Brianda thought Neli looked very pretty. She had left her reddish hair down and was wearing a long dress adorned with several necklaces with colorful stones. Brianda laughed to herself when she noticed they'd both decided to wear something special, almost hippieish, for the occasion. She herself was wearing a thick sweater and a long skirt, with a pink shawl over her shoulders. The edelweiss pendant hung over her sweater. She wondered if Corso regretted having given it to her.

She sat beside Neli while Isolina sat in the row in front of her, beside Petra and Bernardo.

"I don't know how they'll take it," Brianda whispered.

"If you need me to step in at any point," Neli said with an excited smile, "just let me know."

The mayor and the other two men sat facing the crowd.

"It's nice to see such a great turnout," Martin began. "It seems there is great interest in the subject of witches. Well, as we've talked about the matter on other occasions, I'll get to the point. I have received suggestions from many of you. The simplest idea is to mark out a path in the woods later this spring with general information points on witchcraft and publicize it throughout the county. The torture museum is the most complicated proposal because we would need funds to prepare a room in the town hall, and making replicas for the exhibit would take time. Lastly, putting on a play would depend on the level of interest and the time people have to rehearse. Of course, first someone has to write the script! Petra, as president of the Cultural Association, has offered to take charge of coordinating it. Volunteers?"

A few laughs and comments were heard, but nobody seemed to want to raise their hand. Then, Brianda stood up.

"I'd like to say something . . ." The crowd turned to look at her, and she felt her cheeks redden. "May I come up?"

"Of course," Martin agreed, signaling her to do so.

Brianda pressed the folder against her chest and walked to the front. She reminded herself how good she used to be at public speaking. Her skin crawled, however, with memories of the hateful interrogation of the witch trial she had relived not long ago.

"You have a proposal, Brianda?" Martin asked her.

She nodded.

"You all know that my uncle, Colau, was passionate about history," she began. "When Neli found those papers in the sacristy about the witchcraft executions here, he began to research it immediately but could not finish the task before he died. So I did." She opened the folder and took out a stack of stapled batches of paper. "With all the information compiled, I have written the story of one of those women hanged as a witch."

"See, Petra?" the mayor joked. "We have part of the work done already!"

"Yes and no," said Brianda. "I ask that you read this before you go any further with plans to dramatize irrational accusations, illegal detentions, indiscriminate torture, and savage murder."

Alberto sat up in his chair.

"One minute. Are you saying you're with Neli? You want to stop us from doing anything?"

In silence, the villagers waited for her answer. Brianda stared at the designs on the marble floor while carefully choosing her next words.

"I'm not saying you shouldn't do anything, just that you respect what actually happened."

"You didn't answer my question," insisted Alberto.

Brianda looked for Neli and her eyes landed on the last person she expected to see there.

Sitting in the last row, with his arms folded, Corso had his eyes fixed on her. He did not have the placid, bored look of someone listening to a speaker. Rather, his head was tilted and his eyes were half-closed, as if he were trying to decipher a secret message behind her words, her movements, and her reactions.

Brianda wondered how long he had been there.

Then, she saw a woman lean in and whisper something to him. He nodded curtly without taking his eyes off Brianda. She recognized his wife, who had interrupted them that afternoon in the tower at Lubich. Seeing her now made Brianda suddenly and painfully jealous. She felt like shouting that Corso belonged only to her, that nobody else had any right to whisper in his ear, look at him in adoration, kiss him, and stroke his skin.

"By your silence, it's clear you must think like Neli," Alberto said. "How dare you come here from outside to tell us what we should or shouldn't do in our own affairs."

In your own affairs? Brianda thought with irritation. Did she not have a right to an opinion about Tiles? If there was anything that was completely hers in this world, it was her ties to the place for which she had suffered for centuries. Without taking her eyes off Corso, she replied in a loud, clear voice.

"I completely agree with Neli that we should use this discovery as a model of historic justice. I think we should begin by getting the case of these women recognized as a terrible miscarriage of justice and request the exoneration of all who were subjected to illegal trials. We must erase this stain from our history."

"That is ridiculous!" said Zacarias. "I don't feel responsible for something that happened centuries ago!"

The majority of those present voiced their support of Zacarias's opinion.

Brianda remembered what had happened to Anna Göldi in her Swiss village, and it brought an ironic smile to her face. The world could feel very small sometimes. Hundreds of miles away, the same words were spoken.

"I do feel responsible, because it was my ancestors, with whom we share our blood, who acted wrongly. I'm only asking you to read what I have written and judge for yourselves. If you later decide to continue with these projects, it will be your own concern, but I can personally assure you that the name of my ancestor Brianda of Lubich will be restored." She noticed that Corso frowned slightly on hearing the emphasis she'd put on the word "Lubich."

The bar filled with noisy arguments, and the mayor waited a few minutes for tempers to cool a little. He noticed that someone had raised a hand at the back and asked for silence.

Corso stood up and said, "I would like to know the story of Brianda. Maybe it's not a bad idea for us to read it and reschedule this meeting for another day."

Martin spoke quietly to the two others at the table and said, "That's what we'll do. Thank you all for coming. We'll let you know when the next meeting is to be held."

Taking advantage of the commotion and people moving toward the bar, Corso came over to Brianda.

"May I have a copy?"

Brianda handed him one with hope fluttering in her heart.

"It is also your story," she whispered.

Corso leaned closer.

"What did you say?"

"When you read it, don't be surprised to see your name. There really was another Corso. I didn't make it up."

"That foreign soldier who ended up becoming master of Anels?"

Brianda nodded, touched that he remembered the explanation about a role-playing game that she'd given him the night he discovered her and Neli taking the diary from the writing desk. Instinctively, she raised her hand to the pendant.

"It suits you," he said. "And do you know what relationship that Corso had with that Brianda?"

Brianda nodded again, absorbing his gaze anxiously, as if each second that passed was a second that could never be recovered.

"He was the master of her soul," she said. "Of her immortal soul—"

A woman's impatient voice called Corso from a few steps away. He turned and spoke to her in Italian. He then looked back to Brianda. He opened his mouth to say something, but he changed his mind and left with his wife.

The following morning, Brianda got up early. She opened the windows and saw that the new day would not be sunny either, as if the valley had permanently succumbed to gray monotony. How strange nature was, she thought. How calm it could seem, and yet hide such fury, fire, and life. Her own apparent calm hid a cauldron of emotions, from the deepest grief at having to live without Corso to a powerful drive to find a whole new life for herself.

This thought made her recognize that something had profoundly changed in her in just a couple of days. The anxiety and fear that had crippled her had disappeared. A small voice inside assured her she would survive, with the persistence of a blade of grass making its way through rugged terrain, with the courage of a soft breeze that dared to stroke the sharp needles of the firs, with the devotion of tiny raindrops dampening a seed and accompanying it in its growth. She felt her strength returning, bit by bit, and knew she could carry her centuries-old memories into the future.

She got dressed and went down for breakfast. Isolina was already in the kitchen, sitting at the table with one of the copies of the story that Brianda had handed out at the bar.

"Good morning, Brianda. I couldn't go to sleep last night until I finished reading what you had written." Her face was serene even though her eyes were tight. "I have to ask you something. Do you think Colau knew?"

Brianda had been afraid Isolina would be upset about Jayme of Cuyls. She did not know what had happened to him after Brianda's hanging, but without a doubt, Colau's ancestor was the most detestable character in the story. Because of him, his descendants had been marked by misfortune and rejected by their neighbors. In any case, in her writings she had made no mention of the curse of the Cuyls or of anything esoteric or mysterious. The story of the women condemned as witches in Tiles had to be totally believable if she wanted to get them exonerated.

"Yes. He knew that Jayme signed the executions, and I think he was ashamed of it."

Isolina stood up and poured herself more coffee.

"It wasn't Colau's fault he got so strange and untrusting over the years. He was consumed with finding out what could have happened to make his family so detested," said Isolina. "How is it possible that you were able to figure out in months what he couldn't achieve in years?"

"It was those papers Neli found; they cracked things open. It's such a shame that Colau died when he did. All I really did was put his notes in order."

Isolina sat down again. "Do you know what surprised me? That Jayme of Cuyls took revenge for love. Everything he did was for Elvira. If their parents had just accepted their marriage when they were young, maybe none of it would have happened."

Brianda's stomach turned. It was impossible for her to justify Jayme's perverse machinations, his mass murder, in the name of love. However, a sudden stab of alarm in her chest reminded her that great passions always had unsuspected consequences. Had that Brianda not condemned all the Cuyls to centuries of suffering? Had Colau's siblings not died, and many more before them? How was someone like Colau or his family responsible for what their ancestor had done?

As if reading her mind, Isolina let out a pained sigh. "Life is full of mysteries. I've been mulling over something. Remember I told you that Colau was acting stranger than usual before he died? Like he suddenly knew something was coming?"

Brianda's cheeks burned. There was something she still had to do. She thought about it every day.

"I'll be back in a second," she said.

She went up to her room, opened the wardrobe, found the emerald ring, and went back to the kitchen. She sat beside Isolina and handed it to her.

"It has the inscription of Lubich. The same as the stone in the secret graveyard."

Isolina gasped.

"Brianda's ring! To think it's been here all these years! It's gorgeous—I didn't know he had it. Did Colau give it to you?"

"I found it among his things." Brianda hoped with all her heart that Isolina wouldn't ask when she had found it. How could she explain that her attraction to it had been stronger than her common sense?

Isolina frowned and remained silent for a few moments. Then she took her niece's right hand and placed the ring on her ring finger.

"Keep it. Colau hid it because it was proof of the evil that Jayme inflicted. Maybe you can give it a new meaning."

Brianda hugged her in thanks. She wanted to tell her how important it was for her to be able to wear the ring on her finger, see it at all hours, know it was hers again. She got up to pour herself some coffee so Isolina wouldn't see the tears in her eyes.

Both remained silent until Isolina, as if she had been waiting for the right moment, said, "When Neli brought you out of that trance or whatever it was, I did a little research on the Internet. It took me a while to understand that business about karma and reincarnation, which apparently millions of people in the world believe in. You know, of course, we Catholics do believe in the resurrection of our own flesh—" She waved a hand in the air. "Anyway, it doesn't matter. The thing is that everybody, no matter their religion, needs to believe that death isn't the end. We can't just be bodies that rot in graves. We can't accept that we'll never see our loved ones again—"

Isolina laughed nervously. "Last night, before going to sleep, I had a ridiculous thought. I pictured Brianda in the story with your face, and I couldn't imagine Corso as anyone but that strange man who you look at with such devotion."

43.

Brianda went out to the yard and took a deep breath. At long last, the gray was lifting. A light mist covered Beles Peak, but a gentle breeze was blowing it away. The sun shone, not too strong, and the air was warm.

She knew exactly where to go.

She needed to go to Lubich one more time before leaving Tiles. It would not be a final good-bye now that she felt attached forever to that place, but it was time to go back to Madrid. She had to get her things from the apartment she and Esteban had shared, find another place to live, and start looking for a job for when her unemployment benefit ran out.

Although her heart was still wounded by her separation from Corso, whom she had not seen since giving him a copy of the story in the bar two weeks ago, she was physically well and mentally strong. And she had a new goal in life. She had gotten in contact with a member of parliament about starting the process of absolving the murdered women. Regardless of what tourist traps the villagers of Tiles built, she would not stop until Brianda of Lubich was exonerated.

As for Corso, Neli had strangely insisted that Brianda leave him in peace, as if her friend was aware of how hard it was for her not to go in search of him every morning. She desperately wanted to find in the gaze and gestures of her beloved some hint or sign that it was real for him too. She did not know whether Neli just wanted to save her from being disappointed, or if she needed time to prepare one of her spells to help her. Brianda smiled as she remembered the day she had discovered Neli's Wiccan altar. Back then, she had branded her as an eccentric, and yet she now had to admit that her own perception of reality had completely changed.

Immersed in these thoughts, she walked up the same path she had finally managed to follow that fateful November day. Then, dead leaves had carpeted the ground, but today, timid new buds burst forth from the branches. The freshness of the land flooded her soul like a salve.

She came to the gates of the house, where Luzer had tried to stop her back then, but this time she did not go through them. She continued walking until she reached the top of a small hill from where she could view Lubich in all its glory. She sat down on a rock and followed the lines made by the walls and roofs, stopping wherever she was hit by a memory, an image, a sensation. A plume of trembling and enigmatic smoke came from a chimney, connecting the life inside that house to the sky. She wanted to hear the voices of Johan and Elvira . . . No. She wanted to be the woman sitting in an armchair in front of the impressive fireplace, beside Corso.

A long sigh escaped her lips. Was there anything that she could or should do to convince him? An impertinent little voice inside kept accusing her of having given in too easily. But feelings could not be explained. True love did not take convincing. Corso had not reacted to her story. He had just disappeared. The message was clear.

She shook her head, got up, and continued along the edge of a big field of wheat in varying shades of green and then toward the highest woods.

She had never been there, yet she recognized the place instantly.

As she ascended, the year's first wildflowers appeared in the meadows at the edge of the forest. She bent down and stroked some of them. She envied their strength, their persistence, their tenacity to grow year after year in that cold land. She raised her eyes and looked toward Beles Peak, impassive witness to everything that lived, moved, and breathed in the valley. After endless cycles of life and death, it remained, unchanged, certain of its own infinity.

She reached an overgrown path. She had to bend down several times so that the dry branches did not scratch her face or get caught in her hair, and she twice had to stop to disentangle her long skirt from thorns. The path reached a dead end in a small clearing overlooking a gully of scarred rocks. The remnants of a small bridge jutted out at each side of the precipice. In the middle, nothing.

She climbed down, careful not to trip, and sat on a rock near the rushing stream, full from the weeks of rain. She picked up a branch and began to play with it, her mind drifting languidly with the murmur of the water.

Just then, she heard someone call her name softly, first once and then again. She turned and saw that it was not her imagination. Up in the clearing, one foot resting on a rock, was Corso. Behind him, Santo was tied to a tree.

"Is this where Brianda killed the wolf?" he asked.

Brianda nodded with a shy smile. So, he had read her story.

He came down and sat beside her. Brianda rubbed her forearms to control the slight trembling brought on by feeling him so close. Corso met her eyes; his look was intensely familiar, penetrating, inquisitive.

"I saw you in the distance and I followed."

"I'm glad you did. Now we can say good-bye. I'm going back to Madrid tomorrow."

A shadow fell over Corso's face.

"I read what you wrote, but the story isn't finished," he blurted out. "Do you know what happened afterward?"

Brianda shook her head.

"I have my own theory," he said. "Would you like to hear it?"

She nodded, intrigued.

"Corso of Anels went mad," he began. "He only lived and breathed for his son, Johan. If it were not for him, he would have ended his life and gone off in search of Brianda. He saw her in every corner of the house. He heard the wind rustling the branches of the trees and thought it was her. He cursed her for making him promise to look after Johan. Nobody spoke to him and he spoke to nobody. When he was not muttering about vengeance, his throat made not words but moans. The fields and roads felt too short because of the speed at which he galloped, the pitch-black night too bright, the wolf-plagued forest too peaceful for his rage, the silent summit of Beles Peak too loud for his shaken spirit.

"All he wanted was to die, to free himself from that punishment.

"The guilt was suffocating. He had not been able to save her. He, who had fought in dozens of battles, who had slain so many enemies, had not been able to prevent the death of his wife. Her face as the hangman put the noose around her neck, her last gaze, the touch of her hand, her vacant eyes, her cold, stiff body—the memories blazed in his mind, burning away his sanity, wilting his being, consuming his good judgment.

"After the hanging, it took him three weeks to get the lawyer to agree to be present at the exhumation of his wife's body and take note of what he saw. Corso, Marquo, and Arpayon gathered around the grave one cold evening at the beginning of April. With them was the old woman from Darquas who had not been able to tell whether Brianda was pregnant at the trial. She was there to check, in exchange for a generous sum of money, whether Brianda actually had been expecting a child.

"Corso wouldn't allow anyone to help him. He used a shovel at first, but then he knelt down and used his hands. The pain of her absence endowed his movements with an unhealthy urgency. What if he could show that she was pregnant? Would that bring her back to life? No, it would not, he thought in the midst of his madness, but at least it was making it possible to see her again.

"His fingers trembled as he lifted her body into view. There was his Brianda, her hands crossed over her bosom and holding a blue flower as soft as her skin, with a peaceful expression on her face, as if the worms had not dared sully her body, as if the earth had not managed to dampen and soften her features, so perfect, so beautiful . . .

"'In God's name, let's get on with it,' he heard Arpayon say as the man brought a handkerchief to his nose.

"Corso climbed out of the grave and helped the old woman down to take his place. With a sharp knife, she cut into the left side of Brianda's rib cage, put her hands inside, carefully felt around for a while under Corso's watchful gaze, and finally took out a small piece of flesh about three inches long and shaped like a human. She laid it on a small flagstone, which she handed to Corso.

"No one said a word while Corso wrapped the tiny body with a handkerchief, his jaws so clenched and his neck so tense that they seemed about to snap. He then helped the old woman from the hole, got in again, and kissed his wife's lips, as if saying good night, as if her sleep was not already eternal.

"When he had finished burying her for the second time, Corso took the stone with that being that could have become his child, got on his horse, and rode to Lubich, followed by Arpayon and Marquo. Night had already fallen over Tiles, filling the roads with grotesque shapes. Like a soul brought by the devil to the horrors of hell, he burst into the great patio shouting Jayme's name. It did not take long for Jayme to appear, and his initial alarm lessened when he saw the judge and the lawyer. Corso took away the handkerchief that covered what he was holding and brought it to Jayme's face.

"'You killed a pregnant woman!' he roared. 'You killed my child!'

"Jayme remained unmoved.

"'I don't feel I have committed any wrongdoing,' he said calmly. 'I am protected by the laws of indictment that we all approved.' He looked at Marquo and Arpayon.

"'You are the most hideous of murderers!' shouted Corso to his back. 'I won't wait for God to punish you!'

"'Measure your words, Corso!' Marquo said. 'Jayme is right. The law protects him. As it will if you go after him.'

"With a howl, Corso mounted his horse and disappeared into the darkness. For a time, nobody saw him. He holed up in one of the stables at Anels House, engraving a stone. With each hit of the mallet on the chisel, with each chip that came off the stone, his plans advanced in his mind, but first he had to finish that task. One day, he finally placed the stone on Brianda's grave with his own hands.

"'*Omnia mecum porto . . . ,*' he spoke to the ground. 'The motto of Lubich is false, Brianda! You did not take all with you, because you left me here, abandoned, like a sick old man, so that I may be consumed by rage. I won't have solace until you return . . .'

"New graves dotted the field, turning it into an improvised cemetery of the wretched. Every two or three weeks since the first trial, more executions had taken place in groups of two to six women, and this continued until there were a total of twenty-four victims. Pere of Aiscle could not save his wife, Maria, and Jayme of Cuyls did not wish to save his sister, Lida. Their hangings were meant to serve as proof that the work of the council was transparent before God, that no one received special treatment. However, Pere had to be replaced by another man in the council due to health problems that were blamed on the influences of his witch wife.

"The roads were never lonelier, the squares never so silent, the washing areas never as deserted. People spoke with the utmost caution. Heads stayed down in the houses, and even family members avoided speaking to one another. Children were frightened by black cats and ran away terrified if they encountered a toad. The church was often full and not only on Sundays, and the king's soldiers were extravagantly honored at Lubich.

"Spring had never bloomed with such apathy as it did that year.

"Then, one day, it all came to an end with a simple announcement from a tired Father Guillem at mass in the middle of May.

"'Blessed be this land, where the devil appeared, because it has been vanquished,' he simply said.

"'They have yet to see his face,' Corso murmured when he heard about the mass from Leonor, who had aged decades from grief and the fear that at any moment they would take her too.

"The council met and declared the matter finished. After the digression in which the will of a few superseded written law, the valley returned to the justice system in force in the rest of the kingdom, satisfied with a job well done, as if what had happened had been the only way to protect that place against diabolical threats.

"The council paid the costs of the whole affair with money from the estates of those executed and noted it down in the village accounts. The hangman left with his purse full. The jailers were handsomely paid for their work in Cuyls House, as were the carpenter and two workmen for the scaffolds, and the innkeeper for the food and drink consumed during trials and executions. Captain Vardan's soldiers returned to their task on the French border.

"Life returned to normal for everyone except Corso.

"One afternoon at the end of May, as Corso brooded in front of the fire, Leonor came into the hall of Anels House carrying a leather bag.

"'I want you to feel free to do what you must.' She handed him the bag. 'This holds my jewels, some money, and a document renouncing my beneficial interest in Anels. My sister, who inherited our parents' house in Aiscle, has also been widowed. We will live our last days together in the house where I was born.'

"'You could come with me,' Corso suggested, knowing she had already once refused to leave the place where her husband was buried.

"Leonor shook her head, saying, 'All I ask is that you tell little Johan about me.'

"Two days later, Leonor left what had been her home with Nunilo. Everything she wanted to take fit in a wooden chest that was loaded on a mule. Corso accompanied her to Aiscle. When he hugged her for the last time, he did not have to use words to show his gratitude.

"'Do as you must, Corso,' she told him. 'You have my blessing.'

"Corso went looking for Pere of Aiscle. His revenge began that very moment."

44.

"Corso found Pere at home, that place he had seen ransacked by Medardo's rebels, the same day they had hanged Nunilo. It seemed an age since then. He had gone from having nothing to having everything, then losing it all again.

"Pere did not dare look at him. Corso felt sorry for him. The tall, slim, blond-haired man who had once shared Surano's features and dashing posture was now a bald, hunched, old man. His somber good judgment had turned to nervous bewilderment.

"'I thought if I stayed quiet I would be able to save Maria,' he muttered in a dead voice. 'I first failed Brianda and then my wife. There is no punishment severe enough to ease my shame.'

"'Love makes us cowards. I did not come for your excuses but for your help,' Corso told him. 'I'm leaving Tiles, and I need you to do something for me. I want you to sell Anels and use whatever you get from the sale to buy Lubich.' He handed him a document. 'These are my instructions. You will hear from me, no matter where I am.'

"'If that is your wish, my family will buy Anels for my brother's second son,' said a puzzled Pere, 'but I don't understand why you think Jayme will sell Lubich. Or why you want it if you are leaving . . .'

"'Just do it. I trust you to do it.'

"Corso left Pere's house and went to the tavern in Aiscle, a dark, dirty dive that he left soon afterward with a couple of unkempt men who had a violent look about them.

"'You'll do as agreed'—he handed them both leather bags of money—'and when we finish you'll get the rest.'

"He went back to Anels and ordered a servant to saddle the three best horses and to prepare two bundles with the bare necessities for young Johan and himself to take on a short journey.

"When night fell, he met up at the washing area with the two men he had hired.

"'Have you brought what I asked for?'

"One of the men patted the saddlebags to signal they had.

"'All the turpentine we could find.'

"They rode to the church. When they got there, Corso ordered them to take the containers of turpentine and a rope and to follow him. He found Father Guillem on his knees in front of the altar. Corso burned as he remembered the last day he had seen Brianda alive, when she was exhibited in front of the villagers like an animal at the fair.

"'Corso,' said Father Guillem when he saw who it was. 'Mass is long over.'

"Without saying anything, Corso began to splash turpentine over the wooden pews. The two men he hired copied him. Father Guillem, alarmed, ran toward the door, but Corso was faster and grabbed him by the arm.

"'Tie him up,' he ordered the men.

"While they obeyed, he took a pair of lit candles from the Anels chapel and held them to one of the benches, the flames leaping up before Father Guillem's horrified gaze.

"'My judgment begins now,' spat Corso. 'And I find you guilty.'

"The three of them left. Corso locked the door and threw the key as far as he could, unmoved by the cries from Father Guillem pleading for help and threatening punishments that Corso thought light in comparison to the suffering that twisted and deformed his soul.

"He walked toward Brianda's grave and knelt before it.

"'Forgive me, my love,' he murmured. 'I should have done this long ago.'

"He read her inscription for the last time, went back to the men, mounted his horse, and spurred it toward Lubich. He saw nothing but darkness in front of him. He stopped before the great door and hid in the shadows while his men ran shouting into the courtyard.

"'The church is on fire!' they cried. 'For God's sake, come help! Father Guillem is inside!'

"In seconds, the yard was full of men with buckets and mules.

"'We know who did it,' said one of Corso's men to Remon. 'Where is your master?'

"'He was in the hall,' said Remon, signaling to the other servants to continue to the church. 'But he must have heard the uproar—'

"At that moment, Jayme of Cuyls sleepily came out the main door.

"'What is happening, Remon? Where has everybody gone?'

"'A fire in the church, sir! These men say they know who started it!'

"The men dismounted and came over to him. Instinctively, Jayme felt for his sword and realized he was unarmed.

"'And who was it?' he asked.

"Corso appeared before his eyes, jumped off his horse with his sword unsheathed, thrust it into Remon's stomach before he could react, and then pointed it at Jayme's chest.

"'We'll go up the tower. I want to see the fire.'

"A sob was heard, and Corso looked toward the door of the house. A terrified servant was cowering there with a child in her arms. Something in his features looked familiar, and Corso presumed it was Lorien, Brianda's half brother. He felt no compassion for the boy. Brianda had been forced to watch her father being killed; her house had been taken away from her, then she was condemned as a witch. If it was destiny that this boy witness the vengeance that had to befall his father, so be it.

"Jayme, his eyes shrouded with terror, turned to the servant and told her, 'You know where I keep my documents and valuables. Collect them and get Lorien out of here!'

"Corso ordered the men to haul Jayme into the tower.

"'You'll pay for this, Corso!' shouted Jayme over and over again. 'You'll come to the same end as your wife, the witch!'

"Corso followed in silence. When they reached the top, he placed Jayme between his sword and the abyss.

"'All of it, all of the fighting, all of the blood spilled, all because you wanted Lubich for yourself . . . So die, then, like the true master of this house did.'

"Without giving him time to answer, Corso plunged that sword, given to him by the king, into Jayme's chest. He kept his furious gaze fixed on Jayme's eyes, watching with pleasure until he heard his last breath. Then, with an inhuman shriek that terrified the two mercenaries, he threw the body into the chasm.

"In the distance, the flaming church lit up the night.

"Corso leaned his forehead against the rough stone wall for a few moments before telling the men in disgust, 'Burn it down. Burn everything.'

"The men began in the hay barns and stables. Soon, the hungry flames began to leap from one building to another. The servants fled the house, which had become an inferno where the devil, wrapped in a black cloak and with his face horribly wounded, howled, 'Leave nothing standing! Oh, Brianda! If only I had made Lubich burn sooner, you would still be with me!'

"When he had made sure that not even the most torrential downpour could save Lubich, Corso got on his horse and ordered the men to follow him. They passed a group of servants, who ran from them toward the fields. Corso saw the woman carrying Lorien in her arms.

"'Take that child to Cuyls, where his blood should never have left!' he shouted as he forced his horse to rear. 'Let him grow up and rot there! Let the wails retained in its walls drive him mad!'

"He took a final look at Lubich, a giant bonfire with its flames licking the very heavens, and let out a horrible cackle, before continuing to Anels.

"He made the men wait for him under the linden at the fountain and returned shortly afterward with two leather bags.

"'It is more than you can earn in two lifetimes. But I warn you, if you don't fulfill the last part of the bargain, I'll come back and kill you with my bare hands. Be sure I'll know.'

"'We'll do it, sir, so as never to see you again,' said one of them before leaving. 'The two jailers, the carpenter, Arpayon, and Marquo of Besalduch. This very night. They will die in pain.'

"'And we'll burn the records,' added the other.

"Corso returned to Anels and made sure that the horses were ready in the yard. He went up to his room, grabbed a blanket from the bed, and wrapped Brianda's writing desk in it. He carried it down and tied it to one of the horses. It was the only thing he wanted from that place. So many times he had seen Brianda sitting at the desk with her hair loose, writing, opening the small drawers with her delicate hands, keeping her most treasured things.

"He entered the house again, went up to Johan's room, and took the boy in his arms carefully in order not to wake up the servant. He wrapped him in a blanket and hid him against his chest with his cloak. He went outside, tied the rope joining the three horses to his own saddle, mounted the Friesian that Nunilo had given him seven years previously, and left Anels House without a second glance.

"He doubted that Tiles would ever be a place he could remember with fondness, fixed in his heart like a precious stone on a ring. The good moments he had spent there with Brianda would never eclipse the bad ones, or even hide them behind a light mist of resigned melancholy. His ire would never abate.

"Every day he would be alert to any sign that the soul of his beloved had not abandoned him completely. A gust of wind on the grass. A creak by his side. A whisper in the night. A branch tapping against the window . . .

"And he would curse every day of his life, wherever he was, because his mortal body was forced to live without her."

45.

In silence, Brianda dabbed at her ring to dry off the tears that had fallen on the emerald. They had fallen to the rhythm of her heart, with a serenity she had never felt before.

Corso took Brianda's hand and played with her fingers as if wanting to make sure she was real, that her flesh was warm.

"Is this the Lubich ring?" he asked.

She nodded. "It's beautiful, isn't it?"

It was probably the first time in centuries that the precious stone had seen sunlight, unveiling the beguiling flaw in its bluish-green depths.

He then stood up and felt for something in his pocket. A business card fell to the ground. Brianda went to pick it up and realized it was for the hypnotist in Madrid, Angel.

"Neli gave this to you!" she exclaimed, shocked by her friend's audacity. The astounding story Corso had just told her, had he relived it? She stared at him, hoping he would confirm her wish.

"She talked to me about the regressions," he said, "and she explained what happened to you when I thought you were—" He did not finish the sentence. "I hope you don't mind."

Brianda shook her head, speechless. She was so thankful to Neli, who had surely explained things in a much more relaxed way than she could have. Otherwise, Corso would not be here, looking at her as if she were the only woman in the world. He had followed her. He had sat down beside her. He had caressed her hand.

"I haven't gone to see him and, honestly, I probably won't," he said. "I don't need anyone to help me understand what I want."

"Wait, what?" she asked. "Where did you get all that information about Corso's life after Brianda's death? If you didn't see him, do you mean Corso's story isn't real?"

"Real?" repeated Corso, closing his eyes partway and smiling sardonically. "And Brianda's story is?"

He turned and contemplated the stream, his right fist still closed.

After a few moments, he said, "For me, Lubich began as a simple but suggestive sketch done by an ancestor. Nobody in my family understood, they still don't, why I'd want a pile of forgotten stones in a distant land, why I'd give up my job in the family business, why I'd put my wife in the difficult position of having to follow me on this new path." He paused. "When I began to restore Lubich, it felt like I was making my own choice for the first time. Like my previous life hadn't been real—"

He turned back toward her and a mischievous glint appeared in his eyes.

"You seem frustrated," he said.

"I—I don't know how to explain it to you. I think that—" Brianda didn't know how to say that she refused to believe it wasn't obvious to him who they really were.

Corso offered his hand and helped her to her feet.

"After I read what you had written about that woman, my heart dictated the words of the story I told you. What that Corso did after Brianda's death is nothing compared to what I would have done."

He encircled her waist and brought her toward his body.

"When I saw you that night in the bar, I couldn't shake the feeling that I knew you, deeply. And then in the tower—"

He breathed in the smell of her hair and her neck. He sought her cheeks with his half-open lips.

"Is this not enough?" Corso asked.

He found her lips and kissed her slowly, as if he never wanted to be apart, as if this soft flesh were the reason for his existence.

"I'm confused," he whispered. "All I want is to feel you close, absorb your breath, understand you. When I saw you walking with that man and he held your hand, I was furious. A voice told me that no one else had the right to touch you."

He closed his eyes and ran a hand over her back, then her arm, her thigh, and her breast, as if deciphering a secret code with his fingertips.

Brianda clung to him, burning with the same desire she had felt in the tower. But this time, the sense of need and the urgency no longer seemed mysterious. That day, she had felt she had to make up for lost time; now she understood why.

"Can you explain it to me, Brianda?" Corso stopped and waited for her to open her eyes. He kept his gaze fixed on her as if afraid that she might faint. "I feel joined to your body, your mind, your spirit, with all my strength, forever, beyond death."

"Do you honestly think my story isn't real?"

Corso put a finger to her lips. He leaned back and dropped his gaze to his closed fist.

"Maybe this will convince you that you have found me."

He opened his fingers and showed her a small object. It was a ring of worked gold.

Brianda took it in her trembling hands, and her eyes clouded with emotion.

Nunilo's ring.

"Where did you find it?"

"In a false-bottomed drawer in the writing desk. After the edelweiss pendant appeared, I took the desk apart piece by piece."

She took Corso's hand and placed the ring on his ring finger.

"A perfect fit . . . ," she said.

"You doubted it?"

Brianda threw her arms around his neck, and the surroundings became a blur.

They were not in a hidden gully in the woods but galloping on a magnificent black Friesian toward the summit of a mountain infinitely higher than Beles Peak, close to the endless clouds, their perennial souls over a perishable world.

Perhaps there was a logical explanation for all of it, Brianda thought. But logic be damned, she felt she had kept her promise.

She had defied the laws of the afterlife to be with Corso. She had returned to him.

She remembered the Jack London quote she had read on the wall of Angel's waiting room.

She also felt capable of roving the stars.

For Corso, she would be reborn incalculable times.

AUTHOR'S NOTE

In 1980, Domingo Subías, the parish priest of the small Pyrenean town of Laspaúles, in the province of Huesca, found some original documents in the church tower. The majority of these documents reference the regular running of the council—which functioned something like the offices of a present-day city hall—over more than a half century from 1576 to 1636: the leases for the butcher and the mill, the use of the mountains, neighbor's dues, common-land and grazing rights, the number of livestock heads paid by each house, and the operational costs of the district, such as those for tolling the bells, sending messengers, or buying wine for the festivals.

In these hundreds of pages (which, since they are of great sociological value, were transcribed and later published), two pages stand out for their brutality: the first is a macabre list of women hanged as witches in 1592; the second is the treasurer's accounting of the expenses for the carpenter, the hangman, and the tavern on the days of executions. Just those, as neither the accounts of the trial processes nor the trials were preserved.

The origin of this novel has to be found, therefore, in those two pages, in those names, in my innate curiosity and my relationship with

El Turbón, a mythical mountain in the county of Ribagorza in a magical area extending along the valleys of Benasque, Isábena, and Lierp. But there is something much more important and unsettling. When witch trials are mentioned, the first thing that comes to mind is the merciless actions of the Inquisition. I do not think it is too daring to suggest that many people are unaware, as I was, that the most cruel repression was carried out by the civil courts in their desire to maintain public order in the towns and villages, and that this continued long after the Inquisition itself rejected the death penalty for crimes of witchcraft in 1526. There were isolated places in the mountains where the local powers took the law into their own hands. The same questions that came to me when I began writing *Return to Your Skin* were with me for months: What could have happened in a place as small as Laspaúles for so many women to be killed over a two-month period? What sparked such a conflagration?

In all my readings, I found a common thread that can be summarized in the following manner: the persecution of witches is symptomatic of anxieties that emerge during periods of intense social change. Anxiety and fear are the two factors that precede and allow the greatest examples of evil in history.

With this in mind, I began to read about the decades before those terrible events in this Spanish Salem: a long period of civil war in the county of Ribagorza—renamed Orrun in the novel—between supporters of the feudal system and those in favor of following King Philip II. This novel is inspired by real events, and I think it reflects and explains the atmosphere immediately before the executions. Although the names of the characters in the county are fictitious, some are based on real people.

For those who would like more information, and because I think it fair to mention the work of all those who enlightened me, I suggest the following bibliography:

For a general idea about witchcraft, fear, life, and death: *El miedo en Occidente (Siglos XIV–XVIII)* by Jean Delumeau (2012), *The Spanish Inquisition: A Historical Revision* by Henry Kamen (1999), *El abogado de las brujas: Brujería vasca e Inquisición española* by Gustav Henningsen (1983); on the inquisitor Alonso de Salazar y Frías in the Zugarramurdi witches case, made into the novel *Ars Magica* by Nerea Riesco (2007), *La Inquisición española* by José Martínez Millán (2009), *Las brujas y su mundo* by Julio Caro Baroja (1966), *The Devils of Loudun* by Aldous Huxley (1952), *The Crucible* by Arthur Miller (1953), *Storia della Colonna Infame* by Alessandro Manzoni (written in 1840, with a prologue by Leonardo Sciascia in the 1982 edition), "Prácticas testamentarias en el Madrid del siglo XVI: norma y realidad" by María del Pilar Esteves Santamaría (2002), *Miedo y religiosidad popular: el mundo rural valenciano frente al desastre meteorológico en la Edad Moderna* by Armando Alberola Romá (2011), "Arte de Bien Morir/Breve Confesionario" by Rafael Herrera Guillén (2008), and *La muerte por entregas* by María Sánchez Pérez (2008). I also found the following article very revealing: "Weather, Hunger and Fear: Origins of the European Witch Hunts in Climate, Society and Mentality" by Wolfgang Behringer (1995), who analyzes the reasons for existential insecurity in the sixteenth century—climate, famine, and fear—and its terrible consequences.

For historical context, the conflicts in Aragon and Ribagorza, and the parliament held in Monzon in 1585 in the presence of King Philip II: *La rebelión aragonesa de 1591* by Jesús Gascón Pérez (2001), *Aragón en el siglo XVI: Alteraciones sociales y conflictos políticos* by Gregorio Colás Latorre and José Antonio Salas Auséns (1982), *Historia del Alto Aragón* by Domingo Buesa Conde (2000), *Historia del Condado de Ribagorza* by Manuel Iglesias Costa (2001), *Historia de Rivagorza, desde su origen hasta nuestros día* by Joaquin Manuel de Moner y de Siscar (1878), *Valle de Lierp: un bello enclave pirenaico* by José María Ariño Castel and Fernando Sahún Campo (2008), *Bardaxí: cinco siglos en la historia de una familia de la pequeña nobleza aragonesa* by Severino Pallaruelo Campo (1993), "Lupercio de Latrás, bandolero y espía" by Carlos Bravo Suárez (blog, 2008), *El Señorío de Concas* by Manuel Agud (1951), *Relación del viaje hecho por Felipe II, en 1585, á Zaragoza, Barcelona y Valencia* by Henrique Cock (1876), "Felipe II y el Monzon de su tiempo" by Amalia Poza Lanau and Joaquín Sanz Ledesma (1998, in *CEHIMO Cuadernos Número 25*), *Ribagorza a finales del siglo XVI*. *Notas sobre Antonio de Bardaxí y Rodrigo de Mur* by Pilar Sánchez Núñez (1992), *Fueros, observancias y actos de corte del Reino de Aragón* (edition of Pascual Savall y Dronda and Santiago Penén y Debesa, published in 1991 to commemorate the four hundredth anniversary of the execution of Juan de Lanuza, Justice of Aragón, in 1591), and the articles and collections of documents contributed by Manuel Gómez de Valenzuela, especially those on the statutes of indictment against witchcraft and witches.

On witchcraft in Aragon: all the writings of the expert Ángel Gari Lacruz, and the books of María Tausiet, among which I would highlight the splendid work "Ponzoña en los ojos: brujería y superstición en Aragón en el siglo XVI" (Universidad de Zaragoza website, 2004). I also would mention as useful the works of José Antonio Fernández Otal, "Guirandana de Lay, hechicera, ¿bruja? y ponzoñera de Villanúa (Alto Aragón), según un proceso criminal del año 1461" (2006), and of Manuel López Dueso, *Brujería en Sobrarbe en el siglo XVI* (1999). Carmen Espada Giner has written two novels on witch trials, published in 1997 and 1998 respectively: *Dominica la Coja: una vida maldita, un triste destino* (trial took place in 1534) and *La vieja Narbona: de las sombras del alba, al resplandor de las hogueras* (trial took place in 1498). There is also the recently published book, *La mala semilla: nuevos casos de brujas* by Carlos Garcés Manau (2013). Based on mainly unpublished documents, this book focuses on witch stories from the north of Spain between 1461 and 1662 and shows that Aragon was second only to Catalonia in the number of victims of witch hunts. Garcés

Manau includes a list of 120 women tried, the majority of whom were hanged after trials in the towns and villages. Lastly, in 1999 a reproduction of the Laspaúles manuscript was published; later, its contents were transcribed and chronologically ordered by Artur Quintana and Walter Heim, who published it in the magazine *Filología Alazet del Instituto de Estudios Altoaragoneses*.

The books that Father Guillem carried in his bundle when he traveled from the lowlands to the mountains deserve separate mention. This paragraph was originally part of the novel, but I ultimately decided to reserve it for the bibliography. Father Guillem carried a Bible encrusted with a gold fleur-de-lis given to him as a present by his mother on his ordination; the basic texts and manuals of an Inquisitor, *Malleus Malleficarum* by Heinrich Kramer and Jacob Sprenger (1971, original documents circa 1489), *Directorium inquisitorum* by Nicolás Aymerich (circa 1376), and *Formicarius* by Johannes Nider (published in 1480, written in 1435–1437), as sources to consult to understand the nature of evil, witchcraft, and Satanism; "Cuestiones Espirituales sobre los Evangelios de todo el año" by Juan de Torquemada, to facilitate teaching the Scriptures to those unfamiliar with theological speculation; "Instrucciones a los Confesores" by Carlo Borromeo, to enlighten him on the application of the precepts of the Council of Trent; several sermon tracts, including those of Saint Bernard of Siena and Saint Thomas Aquinas; some notes on the erudite Dominicans from the School of Salamanca, as he would always find time for the writings of Francisco de Victoria on the moral problems of the human condition; *De Statu et Planctu Ecclesiae* by the Franciscan Álvaro Pelayo, to be alert to the dangers of women and the sin of relaxing in his obligations as a priest; and, finally, a copy of the successful *Ars Moriendi* by an unknown Dominican, illustrated with several useful prints on a person's final moments.

Although both the research and the plot of the novel have followed more of a historic line than an anthropological one, as is reflected by the chapters set in the past, the narrative strategy of jumping centuries was something as mysterious, attractive, and controversial as hypnotic regressions.

Here readers may wish to put their credulity to the test and allow themselves to be guided by the Neli character to open their minds to the possibility of reincarnation, regression to past lives, progression to future ones, and the survival of the human soul. Some reading material to begin with, written by well-known professional psychiatrists, includes *Many Lives, Many Masters* by Brian Weiss (1988), *Twenty Cases Suggestive of Reincarnation* by Ian Stevenson (1974), *Life After Life* by Raymond Moody (1975), *Life Before Life: Children's Memories of Previous Lives* by Jim B. Tucker (2006), *Las trece vidas de Cecilia* by Ramón Esteban Jiménez (2014), and *El viaje del alma: Experiencia de la vida entre las vidas* by José Luis Cabouli (2006). And I would also recommend *The Star Rover*, the last novel written by Jack London (1915), in which the main character, a professor convicted of murder and jailed in San Quentin State Prison, wearing a straitjacket as he awaits execution, overcomes his physical torment by traveling to another plane of existence where he goes over his past lives.

That the isolated and solitary lands of the mountains were haunts for witches is something that has remained in the memory of the inhabitants of those valleys, as is well documented by Carmen Castán in her beautiful book *Cinco Rutas con los cinco sentidos por el Valle de Benasque y la Ribagorza* (2011), which, as the author says, offers us a vision not only of the tangible but also what has come to us through the oral tradition. When I was a child, in my mother's family's house, at the foot of the south face of the majestic El Turbón, my grandmother told me that some people had heard witches play the violin in the gullies, and that when the neighbors went to water their plots or pick vegetables, they brought rosary beads to protect themselves and put on the clothes that the witches, who liked to walk naked, left on the rocks.

The appearance of the Laspaúles documents showed that legends are often based in something real and concrete, then refashioned by the imagination and changed over time.

Behind the witch stories that so many of us have heard, dramatic local tragedies are hidden, some of which come to light many centuries later, as if the voices of those unjustly condemned women wanted to pass through the barriers of time and return to be heard.

ACKNOWLEDGMENTS

To Miguel Ángel Lahoz, for everything he has taught me about clothing and attire, something always useful in historical novels.

To Olga Segura, for inspiring one of the characters and reminding me that, although there is something beyond the tangible, the most important is here and vice versa.

To Antonio Merino, for always sharing his historical discoveries.

To Carlos Español, for his impeccable bibliographic recommendations. It was by chance that I had the idea for this novel when he was in the middle of in-depth research on the subject of witchcraft in our area. It is always a pleasure to listen to the hypotheses and conclusions of a good narrator, which he undoubtedly is. Everything I have learned on the subject, I owe to him.

To my friends, for being there, after so many years, and for looking after me. They know who they are.

To my family in Sopena House in Serrate, in the Valley of Lierp, for the many tasty and fruitful evenings in the shadow of El Turbón. We continue this tradition as we remember Grandmother Pilar.

To my mother, María Luz, and my sisters, Gemma and Mar, for the support they give me in my literary journey and in all the celebrations of our shared lives.

To my father, Paco, for still being there.

To my husband, José, and my children, José and Rebeca, for understanding and taking as normal my absences and difficult hours, and for being the real reason for everything.

To Cristina Pons, for always being at the other end of this invisible wire that keeps us literally connected and for turning the creation process into an absorbing pleasure.

To Puri Plaza, for her heartfelt words after reading the manuscript and her incisive comments.

To Grupo Planeta for having placed their confidence in me again, and particularly the teams I have worked with over the last three intense years of my life: to Ruth González, for her availability and friendliness; to Emilio Albi, for always being the bearer of good news and good ideas; and to Silvia Axpe, from whom I learned the inner workings of a publishing house. I owe Isabel Santos a lot; her company, her smile, her endless vitality, our mutual understanding, her decisiveness, and her unquenchable professionalism as head of communications have been fundamental on all the trips and events on what, for me, has been an extraordinary and tough adventure. And to Belén López Celada, Director of Planeta—to whom I have never had the chance to personally convey my admiration for her valor, her courage, and her drive—for being with me at unforgettable moments.

My deepest thanks, filled with warmth, to my dear editor, Raquel Gisbert, Planeta's Director of Fiction, for her correct and necessary comments and for believing in and having confidence in me and my stories. I can do nothing but learn each day from her intelligence, her perspicacity, her experience and intuition, her friendly exactitude, and her honesty.

Lastly, my special thanks to all my readers who have been and are with me, for their warm comments to me and my family.

Anciles, January 2014

ABOUT THE AUTHOR

Luz Gabás was born in 1968 in the city of Monzon, Spain. After spending a year in San Luis Obispo, California, she studied at the University of Zaragoza in Spain, where she graduated with a degree in English literature and later became a lecturer. For years she has combined her academic work with translating, writing articles, researching literature and linguistics, and participating in cultural, theatrical, and cinematic projects. She lives and writes in the beautiful village of Anciles, which neighbors the historic town of Benasque. She is the author of *Palmeras en la nieve* (*Palm Trees in the Snow*), which was a best seller upon publication in Spain and was adapted into a major motion picture, and *Como fuego en el hielo* (*Fire and Ice*).

ABOUT THE TRANSLATOR

Noel Hughes was born in 1967 in Dublin, Ireland. After earning a degree in History and Economics from University College Dublin, he spent many years in the business world before moving to Spain in 2006 and shifting his focus to English and translation projects.

Printed in Great Britain
by Amazon